# THIN RED TALES

## MILITARY ALTERNATIVE HISTORY

Edited by

## JAMES YOUNG

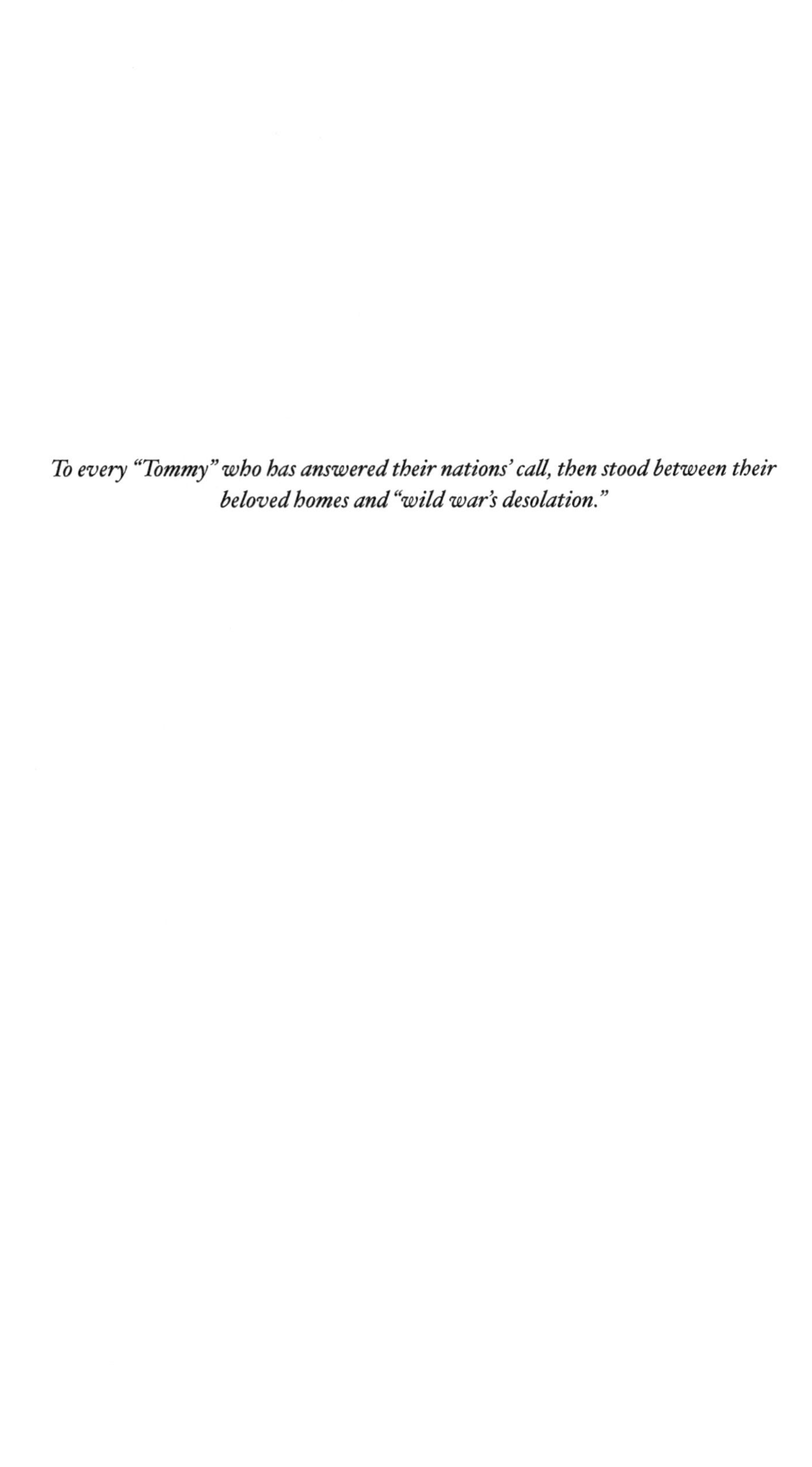


To every "Tommy" who has answered their nations' call, then stood between their
beloved homes and "wild war's desolation."

# ONCE MORE, FROM THE DESK OF ARES

## (as Relayed To Your Editor...)

Ah, ground combat. The first type of warfare. Military action in its purest, *decisive* form. Despite the claims of my sibling Athena, it is the domain Zeus granted me when you mortals graduated from mere murder to killing your fellow man more efficiently in groups. Braining your brother because he had better crops or sacrificing your child because the voices demanded is unworthy of my attention. For I am no mere Fury, but *the god of war*. Organized (even if loosely) violence is when I am moved to sway the odds, choose a path, or reward those who most tickled my funny bone, even if they weren't the best planners.

Thus in your hands, you hold fifteen tales of what *might* have been. Several of them you may recognize as being previously told by that Roman pretender to my domain. That is fine, for while Mars is but a poor imitation of my might, his recollection of my feats was acceptable. In charity, I have not only allowed these stories to be retold, but allowed his followers to tell more tales of Roman glory. From David Webb detailing a potential Carthaginian escape in "Broken Oaths and Shadowed Blades" or Philip Wohlrab exploring what would happen if Rome had survived to the era of internal combustion engines, you'll find plenty of legions in these pages.

Speaking of internal combustion engines, I must say that few things have brought me joy as Humanity finding a way to turn Prometheus's gift into yet another way to worship me. While Kevin J. Anderson, Kevin

Ikenberry, and David Weber's tales all tell you I'm a big fan of cavalry, I'm not wearing a "tanker's" helmet because it's fine leather. No, from S.M. Stirling's Black Chamber story "To the Rescue" through Jan Niemczyk's tale of an alternate World War III, I realized I am most pleased when the chariot and the funeral pyre travel as one. Doesn't mean I don't like a good infantry romp, especially when Peter Grant has it almost resulting in a thermonuclear exchange, but paeans being sung to me in the "Key of Immolation" will always have a special place in my worship.

Enough nattering from me. Behold times when Zeus did not stay my hand and Athena was nowhere to be found. Grab a beverage, seize a resting place by force, and then find comfort as this "editor" entertains you with fifteen "what ifs" or "might have beens." The Fates are fickle, and you'll see their whims turn on a sword's edge, a hoof, and a tank tread in these pages. If you like what you see here, there is also an excerpt of other works that might whet your appetite at the end. I, for one, always find that I cannot get enough of seeing alternate paths, and hopefully you feel the same.

# CONTENTS

# TO SAVE THE REPUBLIC

## Sarah A. Hoyt

Caius Terencius Varro woke up muttering obscenities undirected and unfocused. The words dropped from his lips half-growled: "Faex! Cane! Deodamnatus! Irrumator!"

Coming fully awake on the hard, uncovered couch, Caius wondered precisely about whom or to whom he was speaking. After a few moments' contemplation, he was bereft of response, unless it were "himself." Still fighting off the last vestiges of unconsciousness, he turned over and looked up at the ceilings of this provincial house which his seventy bodyguards had commandeered for him and tried to force his mind to function. That process, strangely, was easier attempted than done. Above him, there were squares of wood that someone had tried to form into a ceiling and paint into a contrivance of marble. The contrivance didn't work, and there was a corner where water had leaked in, having poured past a hole in the roof.

It was the home of some local grandee, whose name Terencius neither knew nor cared.

There was something like fear rising up in him like gorge, but more importantly, there was self-disgust and self-hatred.

*I ran*, he thought. *Like a hare, I ran from the field of battle.* Before he'd succumbed to exhaustion, there had been reports from that field, brought to him by a late-following member of his retinue. The pride of Rome lay dead by the river Aufidius. The crows and wild boars would feast well tonight on noble Roman flesh, and forty thousand Roman mothers would mourn their sons. And all of them, all of them would heap their abuse on the head of Terencius Varro, the butcher's son who had become consul.

Only a week before, he had been proud of his ascent, happy as Consul of Rome, proud of his role, standing as equal of Lucius Aemilius Paullus, man of noble blood, one of the Cornelii. And now...

Of course, Terencius had been sick of the war of harassment Fabius had led against the Carthaginian for two years, ever since cursed Hannibal had crossed to the Italian peninsula with his following of mongrels and the freakish elephants of war.

The elephants hadn't lasted long, even if long enough to cause damage to the Roman cavalry, whose horses hated the very smell of the beasts. But they had, Terencius had thought, left a stamp of fear on the psyche of Romans, perhaps on their very soul.

What else explained the attacks and retreats, the ambushes and small fights with Hannibal over these two years, the vile, petty confrontations that were as drains to Roman pride?

He and Paullus had thought so. He and Paullus, in concerted, intent talk, in the discussions prior to their standing for consul, in their decision of what to do instead.

He and Paullus. They had agreed that Rome needed to stand up, and provoke a manly battle with the Punic invader, and wipe him from Italy, remove the blot of spit from the Republic's face. Or perish of the shame.

He and Paullus.

But Paullus was dead and, at any rate, his family would never let any of the blame fall on his noble shoulders.

Which left Varro to bear the blame.

———

Rome had never raised a prouder army. And Varro was proud of it. It had been his—and Paullus's—impassioned speeches that had caused so many it enlist. It was all due to their eloquence, begging the people of Rome to have a care of their reputation, of their standing as the military power in Italy, lest they be seen as weak, their city as easily invaded and subjected to attack after attack by every passing barbarian till they collapsed.

The citizens had responded to the call. Many men had enlisted. The core of the force were blooded veterans, legionnaires remaining from the two legions Publius Scipio had salvaged from the defeat at Trebia. They'd been passed on to Germinus and then transferred to Fabius Maximus.

They had spent two years harassing and chasing—and losing—Hannibal. They'd been repeatedly ambushed by the Gauls. They'd been nearly destroyed under Minucius. And as proud fighting men, they were sick and tired of this constant retreating and fruitless chase.

Hannibal didn't fight like a man, but like a boy or a woman, playing games of deception and retreat, of ambush and then disappearing, like a creature without honor.

Which left those chasing him feeling twice as humiliated in defeat. Sure, those two legions had been augmented and rebuilt after each loss, but the core of it remembered the humiliation, and the betrayal. They knew with whom they were dealing. This force had then been augmented by the fresh recruitment of men equally tired of watching their city humiliated, even if they hadn't been on the front lines themselves.

And all of them agreed with Verro.

Verro remembered the pounding heart, the exhilaration of the moment.

For if there was no greater honor than to be born a Roman citizen, the honor must be greater still when the city elected one to defend her. When the city reposed its pride and its confidence in you.

And the confidence had been as massive as the force raised, the largest force ever raised by Rome: eighty thousand men on foot, alone.

Varro and Paullus commanded double armies each. Four legions apiece, plus equivalent allied units. In all, eight legions and eight alae. In effect, a quadruple consular army.

The night before they'd left Rome, after the festivities with which Rome had toasted its valiant defenders, a doubt had assailed Varro.

Not a strong doubt, precisely, but a slight niggling problem.

He was, after all, the son of a butcher. He'd seen his father's servants handle herds brought in from the countryside for slaughtering, and as such, he knew there was a number beyond which a group of any animal—and humans were, after all, animals, even if reasoning ones—became impossible to handle, impossible to cause to learn to act in concert.

He'd seen the handlers of large herds break them in smaller groups to bring them in safely. And a thought assailed him that perhaps this massive army they had raised—a proof that the people of Rome agreed with Varro and Paullus, that it was time to fight without subterfuge—was too large a herd, too difficult to cause to move cohesively as though controlled by a single mind. As good armies must be to prevail.

They were reclining at table at Paullus's home, and Varro—always conscious that he'd trained under Paullus and was always and always would be, in some measure, junior to this man of nobility and ancestry and education—cleared his throat and said, "Do you believe we can manage to make them fight together, as a unit?"

Paullus had grinned. "Undoubtedly. Surely, though the new recruits have only fought together for a very few months, we are all Romans. Every man has been trained in the virtues of the republic and the art of war from birth. Else, they would not be Romans but mewling barbarians. And besides, Varro, the core of our forces is experienced. And we've worked together before. We know how to coordinate our forces."

Varro had swallowed down his doubts with a handful of olives and the excellent wine that Paullus had provided.

The next morning had proved both exhilarating and terrifying. Both the doubts and the pride, the certainty and the prickling questions, had warred in his mind as they left Rome.

The dust cloud that surrounded his and the Paullus's cavalry wings was normal. The cavalry was in fact only about six thousand strong, a little light for an army of this sort.

And the dust was about normal for cavalry on the move.

But behind them came a veritable dust cloud, a lower but palpable haze thrown by the sheer massive numbers of foot soldiers on the move, and their supply transport. The supply transport, alone, must be far more than normal to feed such an army.

They'd left Rome's stores depleted, and even so, they left their mark on the countryside as they moved slowly—large forces couldn't move any other way—southeast towards the flatlands of the Adriatic coast.

Though Paullus and Varro had agreed to trade off command every other day in the traditional manner—a tradition lately violated by Fabius, not for the best as his results had proven—it did not matter. Both agreed. It was imperative that they avoid the kind of ambush that had been laid for Flaminius and his army at Lake Trasimene.

Flaminus had allowed himself to be enraged by Hannibal's destruction of the countryside. That was no surprise. Any man of honor would, since Hannibal's widespread destruction of the area that Flaminus had sworn to protect meant that he despised both Rome and, personally, Flaminus. It was like being harassed by dogs, or set about by unruly street urchins. To endure it meant that a man lost all his pride.

But he should still have been more wary. As it was, Flaminus had not thought that Hannibal, being a desert barbarian, and as such, a man without honor, would not hesitate to create an ambush.

As the Carthaginian had, near Lake Trasimene.

Hannibal had set up his troops throughout the night, carefully disposing them for battle in such a way that he would have full view of Flaminus—or anyone, really—when he and his troops entered the Northern defile. He put the Iberian and Africans that constituted his heavy infantry on a slight elevation, from which they had ample room to charge down on the head of the Roman column from the left flank. He'd put his Gallic infantry and cavalry well concealed in the hills in the depth of the wooded valley from which the Romans must enter, so they could rush down and close the entrance, blocking all retreat. Then he put his light troops on the heights at intervals, overlooking the valley, with orders to stay hidden.

The night before battle, he ordered a few of his scouts to light fires on the hills of Tuoro, some distance away, to make Flaminus think that the Carthaginians were still far away.

Knowing that Flaminus would be hot on intemperate pursuit, Hannibal camped where anyone entering the valley would see him.

As Flaminus hurried to close with Hannibal, the Carthaginian cavalry and infantry swept down from their concealed positions in the surrounding hills, and blocked the road. The Romans had no time to draw into battle array and instead fought a hand-to-hand combat with open order.

And thus at Trasimene, Hannibal ambushed Flaminus and killed fifteen thousand Romans, half the force, who had either died in battle or drowned in the lake trying to escape that way.

Flaminus himself had died, slain by Ducarius, the Gaul.

Flaminus's defeat had caused such a panic in Rome that Quintus Fabius Maximus, Verrucosus, the cautious Fabius, had been elected dictator by the Roman Assembly. And he'd initiated a year of cautious war, utterly failing to destroy Hannibal while suffering a great many defeats at the Punic invader's hands.

Oh, none as bad as the defeat at Lake Trasimene, but none of them painless, either. It was how the legions had been whittled down to a remnant.

Which was why it was imperative that they now face Hannibal as men, and put an end to his provocations. And they would.

But they were aware that while it shouldn't be possible for an entire army like Hannibal's to perform ambushes like a little force, it was obvious they would. They had at Trasimene.

Therefore, Varro and Paullus agreed.

"I have reports," Paulus said, during one of their rests in the march. "That the cursed invader's army is camped at Cannae, on the River Aufidius, waiting for us."

And Varro, who had been raised in the best traditions of Rome, but had seen his father dicker with farmers and shepherds, and had perhaps a little more insight into the mind of men for whom honor was secondary to victory, had said, "Let us not trust those reports. Remember the fires he burned on the Tuoro hills. For all we know, these troops massed by the Aufidius are some local shepherds kidnapped and dressed like his fighters. If we rush to meet them, we will doubtlessly find our rear attacked and destroyed, our camp followers and supplies annihilated, without our fighting men being able to defend them. And then we'll face having to proceed or retreat on an empty belly and with no support. I don't believe we can do that. Not while Hannibal's cursed raiders nibble at our flanks."

And so they distrusted the reports and wended slowly through, keeping their eye open for ambushes.

Their slow progress had its inconveniences, just as their size had its problems.

The slow progress also allowed for transgressions against locals. Though it was Varro's well thought-out opinion that any peasant who didn't guard his daughter—or, for that matter, his handsome son—when that mass of fighting men tore through, it was also his ultimate responsibility to at least receive the report of how the various commanders had dealt with transgressions against the local populace from theft to rape to murder.

The problem being that Italy wasn't Roman. While each of the cities and tribes had an alliance with Rome and took a subordinate role to the city, and had treatises of mutual protection and support, they weren't Rome. They had their own traditions, their own beliefs, and often their not so deeply buried hostility to the city that had defeated them or their ancestors. Any fresh violation of local rights and norms might cause a city to rebel, something perilous at this juncture.

Worse, any provocation might cause a significant number of inhabitants of a city that was still ostensibly loyal to Rome and afraid of Rome's retaliation to either carry intelligence to Hannibal or to collaborate with him in one of his cursed ambushes or deceptions. Fortunately, they had taken on in this force an unusually high number of legion commanders, and the men were usually blooded, and if not, of sufficient social influence to deal with contretemps. Why, a full third of the Senate of Rome had joined the army, and the rest of them had family in the army. That by itself provided plenty of influential people to defuse the situation.

Though the thought itself annoyed Varro, being that he was not one of the influential people, it seemed to him it was a matter of no consequence. His sons would be. And their sons after them. It was a matter of advancing the family, and himself as ancestor would reap the reward due to his sacrifices to obtain that advancement.

For him to undermine the system would mean only that there was nothing for his sons to attain.

As for their size, while it forced them to go slow, Varro knew well enough that in past engagements with the cunning Hannibal, by the time the Roman forces had broken through his center, it was too late, and their cavalry had been destroyed.

———

"Master," a voice from the door. "There is a man to see you."

Looking up, Varro saw Calvus. Calvus was one of his bodyguards, a huge man with a shaved head. He was also the son of a family who had served Varro's family since either of the two families could remember. "Master" here referred both to rank and to the relationship that had existed between the two as long as they could remember.

When Varro had been teased by older boys for his family's late arrival to wealth, Calvus had interposed his bulk and often brought the jeering to sudden silence.

"Yes?" Varro said, and sat up, rearranging his tunic. He didn't remember stripping off his armor or even his helmet, but here he was, barefoot, and in a house tunic. And remembering, as through a fog what Calvus had said, he queried, "A man?"

Calvus appeared to struggle for words. "A...foreigner."

Since to Calvus a foreigner could be anyone, from a local of this village to a Greek, Varro was not sure what that meant. He had a sudden misgiving that it was Hannibal himself, come to bid for surrender. But that was ridiculous. It wasn't to Varro that Hannibal would come for surrender or to dictate terms. And in fact, it was highly unlikely that Hannibal even knew that Varro was still alive.

Varro was unsure how many days had been since the battle. It seemed to him he'd slept a very long time, perhaps longer than a day. Or perhaps it was their journey that had taken very long.

He remembered his wing of the cavalry stampeding in a panic, carrying him with them. The shame of it burned in him. They had sworn an oath, the first time that such was done by Romans before battle. Everyone had sworn that they would not "Abandon their ranks for flight or fear, but only to take up or seek a weapon, with which to smite an enemy or save a fellow citizen."

He had broken the Oath. He was forsworn. "Bring the stranger in," he said. "But you and Servius come in with him, and keep watch, lest he strike."

Calvus left to return seconds later with the man. Varro sat up straighter. The man was—this was not even surprising—a Carthaginian. This was easy to tell at a glance, though he wore a tunic that would pass unnoticed in any peasant in this region, only his cloak giving away that he was a man of some substance. It was the sum of the parts that made it obvious. He was lighter-built and more dark-skinned than most Romans, but the most important thing about him was that he did not move like a Roman. There was something of the merchant in a foreign port to him. Sure, assured enough not to be trifled with, but glancing sidelong and an easy way of shrugging the shoulder and sidling, as though to project an impression amiability and accommodation.

The Phonecians were, after all, a merchant race, and lacked the sturdy assurance of the Roman farmer.

"Milord Varro," he said, and smiled, and nodded. And Varro, who was not a lord, nor a nobleman of any kind, hardened his heart against him. Or tried to. The thing with flattery was, of course, that it worked. It was hard not to let oneself fly into sympathy with someone who flattered one so outrageously.

"I am Abibaal," the stranger said. "And I come to you with a message from our great commander, Barca."

Varro experienced a visceral response to Hannibal's name, and started to get up from his couch and order the stranger away, before he thought better of it. He sat down again, but spoke, his voice rough and gruff but, he hoped, decisive, "I want no messages from your master. Nor do I wish to surrender. I am a Roman citizen, I. I have my pride."

"No one is asking your surrender, Consul," Abibaal said, and again, there was the sliding smile, and the bow, as though he had never thought of such a monstrosity. "Terms will be sent to Rome, but we're told that Rome will surely refuse."

The Phoenician paused for barely a second before continuing.

"It is rather that we thought, given your loss, you might not be comfortably received in Rome again."

"And what business of that is yours?" Varro snapped.

"I will be honest with you." Here, a trace of accent showed in Abibaal's excellent Latin, giving him something of a sibillant tone. "Any commander bringing such a defeat back to Phoenicia and having lost upon a single battle most of the nobility of his city would surely be crucified as an example of what happens to those who lose."

Varro narrowed his eyes at the man. Before he could shape his mouth to protest, his guest continued.

"Now, that might not happen in Rome, but surely there will be penalties for such a loss, and we're informed that you're not of such high birth that you have a large family to protect you from such penalties."

*Damn you*, Varro thought.

"More than others, we know that they are unjust. We know your entourage near-kidnapped you away from the battle front, and that if it were not for them, you'd have fought and died there, like the noble Paullus."

*This man's insolence angers me*, Varro thought, beginning to move his arm and signal the Phoenician be executed. His visitor continued as if he did not notice, shifting his eyes to meet Calvus's as he continued.

"But since you're here, and Rome might think that you turned and ran, surely Rome, who mourns their lost sons now, will soon turn to punish those responsible."

The "to include your entourage" did not need to be spoken for Varro to recognize the veiled threat. His hand fell limply to his side, the signal to slay the Phoenician ungiven.

"You must see that you are at risk, and mighty Hannibal Barca has sent me to offer you safe conduct to our ranks, where you'll be protected and a noble counselor."

*In no way will I turn traitor*, Varro thought angrily.

In his rage, Varro didn't remember what he said, precisely. He gathered later that he actually hadn't told his servants to throw the man out and whip him to death, though the image had been in his mind so strong, he would have sworn an oath that he had.

Apparently the Carthaginian smiled and left, ahead of the servants who would have thrown him out, somehow seeming to go of his own volition. This had the effect of making Varro's attendants into an escort, rather than those who expelled him. Varro was well aware of what *that* would seem like to external observers.

---

Insulted, wounded, it took Varro quite a while in solitude to contemplate the strange encounter.

When he did, he found that instead the anger he felt a strange ambivalence, as though the ground had turned slippery under his foot or as though he'd put his foot down on a stair expecting to find a step and found instead nothingness and howling wind.

Which, in a way, described the whole battle of Cannae.

---

They'd been so sure that their numbers would have them. And, in retrospect, Hannibal hadn't done any of the things he'd done before. No hiding on the hills. No lighting of false fires. Nothing fanciful or difficult. Nothing that would make it justifiable for them to be so utterly defeated.

It was only after the report of what had actually happened came to him that Varro built together, in his head, the image of the strategy the Phoenician had employed.

It had been deceptive, since that seemed to be the trend of the man's mind. It was well-known that men didn't change their mode of thinking, however much their circumstances might change. And it had been cunning, since Hannibal was in fact a shrewd general, as well as anything else. Faced with a force twice the size of his own, he had perforce to use tactics to overcome the disadvantage.

The tactics used were a thing of beauty and elegant. In the past, his center had always held, while his wings mauled at the Roman wings, until it was impossible for those to go to the rescue of the center.

But now, now that Rome had beefed up its army so they could penetrate through the well-defended center of the Hannibal's army, so they could in fact use their massive numbers as a ram and bowl over all opposition, Hannibal had made that center very weak, staffed with the poor soldiers of Iberia the Gallic Celts who would break and run at the slightest push.

His cavalry took up positions on the far left and right wings. When fully assembled, the Carthaginian line must have looked—Varro could see it in his mind—like a crescent that bulged in the middle.

Hannibal had put his stronger troops, the Libyans, at the edges of his formation. As the Roman infantry advanced into the pocket created by the retreating Gauls and Spaniards, they were enclosed by the stronger and still fresh troops at the perimeters, who then blocked all escape. With the lake blocking the only route to avoid entrapment, and the sheer number of the Roman infantry making it impossible to move, the battlefield had become a killing field, and the killing was the Carthaginians to do. For the Romans—or for most Romans—it remained only surrender or dying.

His spies had brought back the accounts of those for whom surrender was an anathema.

"They died screaming, Master," one informant had said. "Their tendons cut, they died begging that the Carthaginians cut their veins and thus end their suffering."

"Master, some say that a great many dug holes and plunged their heads into them, so as to suffocate," was the tale brought by another. "A great many more took to the lake, knowing they could never swim across, wishing for a cleaner death."

In Varro's mind, the proud army marched, all smiles, leaving Rome amid prayers and song. The fine flower of Roman nobility, many more influential than he was. Many more much better born, belonging to old clans and older families.

And then he saw it in his mind: eyes turned to a killing field, the flies buzzing in the heat of August, and landing on the unseeing eyes of the blood-and-vomit-covered corpses.

"You can smell the field from miles away, Master."

———

Varro sent Calvus to Rome and Calvus brought word back. When news of the battle had filtered back, word of the immense losses, people had taken to the streets screaming the name of kinsmen they presumed lost. Public lamentation had been violent. An envoy had been sent to the oracle at

Delphi to find out what it meant. Meanwhile, human sacrifices had been made for the protection of Rome. Human sacrifices on the mountain of Jove, something not done since remote antiquity, something they were used to considering a mark of barbarism.

Varro was thinking of this, of the hysteria that must be sweeping Rome to create so uncharacteristic a response, when Calvus came into the darkened chamber where his master had taken to sitting with a jar of wine in contemplation. Contemplating his lost honor and the fact that, as an oath breaker, he would bring not fortune and fame to his family, but a great stain. A stain which his children would have to expunge before they could attain any honors of their own. Or perhaps his grandchildren.

*My name will not be mentioned by any that come from me for a generation,* Varro thought. *Indeed, I am almost certain it will become an epithet in all of Rome.*

"What is it, Calvus?" Varro asked, his words slightly slurred.

"Master, there is a man to see you."

"If it is the Carthaginians—"

"No, Master. A Spartan."

"A Spartan, here? What does he wish?"

"To speak with you, Master."

Varro sat up straight. "Very well, same as before. Send him in, but do come you and Servius and keep me company while he is present, lest he decide to attack."

Calvus bowed and left.

Moments later, a man entered. He looked quite different from the Carthaginian. This was an older man, more experienced—it was obvious—in both life and battle. His scarred hide spoke of wounds and fights, and his dark eyes had depths that were hard to pin down exactly. If Varro had been asked, he'd have said the man looked amused.

When he opened his mouth, he spoke in clear Greek. "Consul, I come to make you an offer."

"If you've come to scare me with tales for children, of how Rome is going to crucify me—"

"No. Rome is unlikely to crucify you, Consul. We know better than that. Abibaal is young and not very experienced in the ways of Rome," the Spartan replied evenly.

Varro snorted.

"I beg you to believe that he was not saying what he said at the instigation of Hannibal Barca, who is no fool," the Spartan continued.

"Abibaal was charged with bringing you a message that you could find not only safety but honor on our side, that we understand what happened, and none of us thinks that you betrayed your men or your co-consul."

"Safety and honor from tricksters."

The man looked surprised and wounded.

"I am Spartan," he said. "We are not tricksters. If I were not here as an envoy, I might have to demand satisfaction for such an insult."

"No, not the Spartans, the Phoenicians," Varro protested.

"Ah. Their ways are not ours, Consul. That is the difference between a warrior race, or in the case of the Romans, a race of honest farmers, and merchants like the Phoenicians. They are not as blunt or honest as we are."

The Spartan's expression was briefly distasteful, as that of a man who had found a weevil in his fruit.

"Or at least that is not how they present, since they often have to wheedle, to deal, and there is some deception involved in business dealing," the battered warrior continued. "But you know, it doesn't make them necessarily fundamentally dishonest. I've been with them but not of them for over a year now. I've taught Barca his Greek, and yet, I assure you, he's fulfilled his promises to me."

Varro's eyes narrowed. He gestured for the Spartan to continue.

"What you must think of when it comes to a deal with them, is whether you're a competitor, which you are as the commander of an opposing army, or an associate, an ally," the Spartan patiently explained. "If you're the commander of an opposing army, they'll treat you as though you were a competitor in business. There is no trick they won't use to get the best of you and to win over you."

Varro's nostrils flared at that thought, his anger rising even as the Spartan sought to placate it.

"But if you're an associate, an ally, they will be true to their word and keep it as though bound by the most stringent honor. You see, it is known in business that if you don't treat your partners well, they will not trust you and will therefore then turn on you at a crucial moment."

The Spartan spread his hands plaintively.

"If the Carthaginians—if Hannibal Barca himself—gave you protection and position with him and his people, you could trust him onto death, if it came to that. He would never be forsworn."

This brought up the uncomfortable prickle of guilt again, in the back of Varro's mind, because he had in fact broken his oath. At the same time,

Varro realized he had gone down quite a wrong side spur in his protests. He'd never meant to say that he wouldn't trust Hannibal. His objection to going over to the other side was quite of a different order.

"Forget what I said," he said. "I am tired and have not slept much. I meant only to say that I'd never betray Rome. My duty, sworn, is to defend Rome from her enemies, not to make common cause with them."

"Of course," the man said. "And I understand that, but what you must ask yourself is whether it is most effective to make cause with the Carthaginians in order to defend Rome."

Varro cast a suspicious glance to the jar of wine in the corner. It wasn't particularly strong wine, and he'd added plenty of water to it, so surely he wasn't dreaming this conversation and its peculiar lack of logic, was he?

"You speak nonsense."

"Do I? As I told you, I am Spartan. My name is Sosylus. And I am fascinated with history."

Sosylus gestured at his clothing.

"I am Spartan, a warrior," he said. "As you probably know from Greek history, Spartans and Athenians have warred much. And my city started out proud and rough, a city of warriors. Each boy was brought up to be a warrior. There were no shirkers among us."

The Greek gave a smile that softened his sharp features and at the same time made Varro aware that he knew the irony of what came next.

"And no historians, either. I doubt if I'd have made it in the old days, as I was weakly when I was born, and would likely have been cast from the sacred hill by my father, to dash my brains at the bottom."

*Another barbaric process*, Varro thought.

"But still, that was what my people was, a strong and proud people, until we were invaded. You probably have heard—hasn't every educated Roman—of the three hundred who defended the mountain pass, so their very sacrifice to the gods of war, their courage, would rouse the rest of Greece to defense. And it did. It worked. Or did it? Eventually, the Persians conquered us, anyway. And changed us. And, yes, we changed them."

Sosylus paused, taking a swig from the waterskin at his waist.

"The truth is, though, that by that time we were already changing. The reason that the three hundred needed to make their final stand was that Sparta had already lost its appetite for war. It didn't rush to meet the enemy. It spoke big words, but tried to temporize."

Varro thought again of Fabius Mximus.

"And in time, it got conquered. And in time, it fell. In time, all of Greece fell. Yes, and to everyone." He paused a moment. "I bet you any of my ancestors, brought forward to see what the city has become, would be horrified and feel that the sacrifice was for naught."

"So?"

"So, what do you think of Rome? You, Varro, the butcher's son, who, through wealth and your own brains, were elevated to Consul and commanded the greatest army the city has assembled."

"Rome is the best city in the world," Varro spat angrily. "It is the only one where men are men and don't grovel at the foot of a king."

"Ah. But they do grovel at the foot of their noblemen. Their great families, their gens, all of it counts, doesn't it? How many times did people throw in your face that you were plebian-born, and not even a landowner, but the son of a butcher?"

Varro shrugged.

"It is always hard for the first one who places his foot upon the ladder of success. It can't be thought—"

"Of course. But how common is your path to success, Varro?" the Spartan interrupted. "If people are all alike, really, in Rome, and if your origin means nothing, if there are no kings, then why is it so difficult? Why aren't there more butcher's sons who ascend to commanders? Why aren't there more in the Senate? And why—and you know this is true— will you be reviled for doing the sensible thing, whether you did it on purpose or not, in escaping a killing trap?"

Varro felt the need to interrupt the man, but bit his tongue.

"Do you think if it had been the noble Paullus who had done so, anyone would have blamed him? Or do you think that anyone will believe you two were united and of a mind, both decided to attack as soon as possible; both agreed to the strategy and the place where the battle would happen?"

The Spartan gestured at Varro.

"Or will they blame you, Varro, while enshrining Paullus's memory because the Cornelians will not have it otherwise? Will they say you attacked without his agreement, perhaps even without informing him, simply so they can hold him blameless?"

"That would be difficult," Varro said. "Both of us spoke before the Senate and the people of Rome. Both of us said our strategy was the same."

"Rome is performing human sacrifices," Sosylus said. "And has sent to foreign oracles for solace. Do you believe they will remember what they do not wish to remember?"

"But why would Hannibal want me to turn? Or need me? Myself and my seventy bodyguards are as nothing before his troops and his advisors, even foreign ones such as you," Varros said.

"Ah, but you are a Consul of Rome," Sosylus replied smoothly. "You see, if Hannibal is to do more than simply harass the countryside in Italy, he must get more troops and more support from the Assembly of Carthage. And there are too many people in it who hate the Barcas, and their vendetta against Rome. Now, after Cannae, many of the local tribes have come to pledge their loyalty to Hannibal, but he doesn't know how to deal with them, and they don't seem to trust him very much. Now, if a consul of Rome itself were at her side—"

Varro wanted to Sosylus to be gone, to be thrown out, as he had told his servants that Abibaal should be thrown out—even if not whipped to death—but something stayed him. He turned to Calvus.

"See this man, Sosylus, gets a room, and bring him back when I tell you."

If Sosylus saw his position as hostage, he did not show it, nor react. He smiled and bowed, both looking odd with his craggy and scarred countenance, and he followed Calvus out of the room.

———

Varro paced. He paced the small room with the leaking ceiling and the pitted mosaics underfoot, and tried not even to think of the man to whom it belonged, and where he might be, and what he might think of the Romans who had commandeered his house.

The truth was that Rome saw itself still as a small and rural city, where her sturdy sons defended her with valor on the battlefield.

But Rome had become far more than that. Its webs of alliance and influence, of fear and trade, permeated the entire Italian peninsula. This was why Hannibal had managed to hurt her without ever coming within sight of the city.

And therein lay the problem. More and more, the lands outside Rome were not honest farms, worked by families and those connected to the family. They were vast estates, worked by slaves for the benefit of landlords who could not be called farmers.

People like the Cornelians didn't dirty their hands with any work. And they did despise those who did, no matter how far they reached from their humble origins.

Which—

Which meant Rome was changing.

Varro was not stupid—quite the opposite. He could see the time coming when Hannibal was defeated. He needed someone to convince the Assembly in Carthage to give him support. If that didn't happen, he'd run out of men and support.

And it was unlikely the revolting tribes of Italy would be able to form a cohesive bond and help the invader.

But if he had Varro...

If Varro helped, yes, Hannibal would win. But Hannibal could not run home anymore than he could manage to weld the tribes into an alliance.

He was a good general, but, ultimately, a desert raider. He wouldn't be able to think long-term.

Sooner or later, he'd die. Probably not naturally, and Varro would not need to instigate it. And then Varro would have power. Power to weld the republic back into the honest thing it was meant to be. To get rid of wealth-and-blood proud noblemen and create a strong republic where all men would be equal.

His path was now clear. He'd betray the republic, in order to save it and make it what it should be.

He walked to the door, his step firm. "Calvus, send for Sosylus, the Spartan."

Sarah A. Hoyt was born (and raised) in Portugal and now lives in Colorado with her husband, two sons, and a variable number of cats, depending on how many show up to beg on the door step. She has over 40 -- the number keeps changing -- published novels, in science fiction, fantasy, mystery, historical mystery, historical fantasy and historical biography. Her short stories have been published in Analog, Asimov's, Amazing Stories (under a previous management), Weird tales, and a number of anthologies from DAW and Baen.

To learn more about Sarah A. Hoyt and read samples of her work, visit http://sarahahoyt.com

# BROKEN OATHS AND SHADOWED BLADES

## A Story of the Unbroken Lion

### William Alan Webb

## PREFACE

Prior to the Battle of Cannae, the Roman commander for the day, Consul Gaius Terentius Varro, suffered a broken leg while mounting his horse. Co-Consul Lucius Aemilius Paullus took command of the Roman Army and avoided Carthaginian general Hannibal Barca's trap. The Romans crushed the invaders, but Hannibal slipped away and hired a merchant fleet to escape Italy. Pursued by an ad hoc Roman squadron led by Paullus, Hannibal outsmarted and outfought them to make his escape to Spain. Paullus downplayed the sea battle as a skirmish and prepared to celebrate a triumph in Rome.

Varro, meanwhile, survived. Against all odds, he began to recover. Back in Rome, he quietly seethed at being denied part of the glory for the victory at Cannae.

## 1



The last client waited in the Atrium until summoned by Zale, the trusted freedman who ran the household of Gaius Terentius Varro in the city of Rome. Thin, but with ropes of leathery muscle under taut skin, the sharp-eyed Zale lifted one eyebrow before introducing a scruffy man in dirty clothes, as if to comment the visitor needed a bath more than he needed an audience with the consul. Zale held his tongue, though, as it was not his place to screen his master's clients, no matter how disgusting or disreputable he might have found them. Nor did he need to; nobody could display disapproval using only facial gestures more than a Greek, a mannerism that endlessly amused his master.

"Titus Asisculus wishes to speak with you, Consul," he said. "He says the matter may be of great value to you."

"Does he?" Varro replied. Varro glanced at Zale, who only shook his head. Although the name rang unfamiliar to them, like any good politician, Varro masked his fatigue and tried to show genuine interest. "In such case I am intrigued to hear what tidings could be worth my time."

Seated in a sturdy chair with his injured leg propped on a low table, the Consul inspected the unknown man with an appraising eye, as if judging the value of a slave. Fatigue and hunger made him cranky, as against his physician's advice, Varro had once again greeted his clientele for the first time since nearly dying at Cannae. The shattered leg remained painful and swollen, even though healing much faster than anyone had thought possible. It now looked like he might once again be able to walk on it, perhaps before winter set in.

To Varro's right sat Quintus Caecilius Metellus, one of the Consul's closest political allies and himself the Pontifex Maximus. The two men locked eyes as Titus Asisculus doddered forward and shuffled from one foot to another. In a city of stench, Asisculus stood out as having a reek all his own.

"*Salve, Consul.* Pardon me interrupting your day like this, Consul Varro. I would never have done it had I any other choice."

"Oh? Why is that?" Metellus said, taking on the role of aide without being asked, for which Varro was grateful. The morning's strain had taken its toll on his still healing body.

"I'm owed 200 sesterce. The Consul promised! Not you, the other one."

"Paullus?"

"*Etiam, id est verum!*" *Yes, that is correct.*

"Calm yourself," Varro said. "Where are you from, Titus?"

"Herculaneum, sir. Consul Paullus promised 200 *as* to each experienced rower willing to leave immediately, in pursuit of the Carthaginian general—"

"Hannibal?"

"*Ita vero.* Or so we were told. I did not care, as 200 *as* is a great sum for me and my family. I was assigned among the lead oarsmen for the flagship *Hercules.* I risked death from the enemy fleet, but after we returned to Neapolis, we were handed ten sesterce and told to keep quiet about what had happened."

Asisculus's visage darkened as he continued.

"Many of us complained, but the Consul's legate, a man named Servilius, threatened to have us cut down by his legionaries as enemies of the state. My friends decided it was better to keep quiet, but I am a Roman citizen, Lord. It is not right for me to be treated so unjustly!"

Being younger and far less skilled as a politician that was his distinguished guest Metellus, Varro's eyebrows lifted in surprise and delight. He was savvy enough to dampen the enthusiasm in his voice, however.

"Tell me about this battle," he said.

"We caught up to the enemy south of Sardinia. I was on the starboard side of the ship, facing north, but there wasn't any land in sight. We had to be more than 20 miles from shore, although whitecaps made it hard to see much from the lower decks. What happened during the fighting, I don't know. I heard lots of yelling and swords scraping, and from other ships I heard horses..."

"Did you say horses?"

Asisculus nodded. "Yes, Consul. Mind you, I only caught glimpses through the oar windows of nearby ships, but many of the Carthaginians were on horseback when fighting. After we returned, I heard some of the legionaries mention that when they lowered the Corvus, the Carthaginian cavalry charged them before they could cross."

"Cavalry during a fight on water..." Varro muttered too low for Asisculus to hear. The thought that only Hannibal would try something so audacious fled his mind quickly, to be replaced by blame for Paullus.

*How could that idiot had not seen such a thing coming?*

"Do you know what happened to Hannibal?"

"He escaped, or so said the ship's regular crew, along with capturing two of our triremes."

"Thank you, Titus."

Varro motioned for Zale to lift his money box. Counting out three hundred sestertii, he counted them into his visitor's calloused and grimy palm.

"There is an extra hundred to pay for your troubles in coming to Rome, Titus. The Republic thanks you for your willingness to serve at a moment's notice, and let no man say that Consul Varro does not pay his debts, even if they are incurred by his fellow Consul. May I count you among my friends?"

"Why...yes, Consul. Yes, absolutely. May Jupiter himself watch over and protect you!"

The two patricians waited until Zale escorted Asisculus out before adjourning to the *triclinium* for a midday meal of pomegranates, peaches imported from Greece, salted bread, fish and cheese. Unable to properly recline with his leg still immobilized by splints, Varro sat for the meal as he had while meeting his clients.

"If what this Titus Asisculus says is true, my fellow Consul will be celebrating a triumph for a less-than-crushing victory..."

Metellus wagged his forefinger. "Be careful what you say, Gaius. I am your friend, and while I agree with your sentiment, you must be guarded in whom you confide."

"I trust you, my friend, and so I speak plainly. But yes, your words are well spoken. Rome has not heard the last of Gaius Terentius Varro."

Laughing, Metellus said, "I doubt anyone believed they had."

————

*The Emporium neighborhood, near the Tiber River waterfront, Rome, Italy*
*Prima Fax (Lighting of the Candles), 23 August, 216 B.C.*

Not even the cloth wrapped around Zale's mouth and nose kept him from gagging at the heavy stench of rancid olive oil clinging to the pile of broken amphorae off to one side. The sewer smell of the nearby Tiber River only made things worse, overlaid as it was by the usual street smells of smoke, dung, urine, fish and, occasionally, fresh bread and cooking meat. A cloak and face-wrap kept mosquitoes at bay.

Following his brutish guide through the maze of warehouses near the docks meant walking through shadows behind a single oil lamp, whose weak flame flickered in the night breezes. Dangerous shadows hid potential thieves and murderers, and with every step Zale expected to feel the sharp blade of a knife being dragged across his throat. The man he followed, a freedman named Poculus, might have been a murderer and thief, but Varro made the arrangements and Zale could only obey his master-turned-employer. If Poculus allowed Zale to be harmed, chances were good that Poculus would not survive the night...not when Zale's mission had the possibility of reversing Varro's recent misfortune.

A veneer of sticky mud from afternoon rain showers covered the paving stones near the wharves, causing Zale's feet to slide in his sandals. Because of his childhood education in Greece, once he'd been captured and sold as a slave, Zale rarely had to fend for himself on the streets. He'd always been in the master's house, rising to be a freedman and now the head of Consul Varro's household staff. It was a comfortable and honored position, one which he'd never thought would lead him into Rome's terrible underbelly.

Before his former master, an olive oil importer living on the nearby Aventine Hill, sold Zale to Varro in return for certain political favors, the Greek hoped to never again set foot in the warehouse district. Yet here he was, seeking a particular man with particular skills and no morals except those that silver could buy, a man who reveled in the deepest pits of depravity Rome had to offer. Known only as Athenos, he claimed to be a Greek like Zale, but his harsh accent marked him as Illyrian.

The narrow street they turned down ended at a building with torches and braziers lighting the only door. Zale weaved behind Athenos to avoid animal droppings and tried to recognize any of the buildings. In the darkness, though, nothing looked familiar.

"Here," Poculus said, loud enough to be heard over the clatter of a passing cart. "The *ad cucu*. Athenos comes here every night."

Smells drifting from the interior came as welcome relief from the nauseating reek of the streets. Athenos held open a heavy wooden door to allow Zale inside the crowded room. Against the far wall, a stone counter with six inset *dolia* offered a variety of fruits, nuts and dried fish, with a steaming stew on the far end. A heavyset woman cooked over small braziers, while two much younger girls attended to patrons. Tables jammed the one room where men sat and drank and threw dice, laughing and cursing at their latest turn of fortune. In the dim lighting, it took Zale a few moments to recognize the man he'd come to find.

Athenos sat across the room, his chair squared to face the doorway. Coils of black hair fell over a broad forehead but could not hide the squint as Poculus pushed through the crowd near the entrance with Zale close on his heels. No one got out of their way to let them pass...until Athenos yelled for them to do so. Grudgingly, knots of filthy gamblers moved just enough so the newcomers could push through.

The wooden chair across a scarred tabletop from Athenos wobbled as Zale sat. Poculus stood nearby, arms folded, watching for eyes that lingered a moment too long, or stared at Zale with too much suspicion. Although he'd worn a threadbare tunic, there was no hiding the freedman's soft hands or clear skin, both signs of someone eating well on a regular basis. In turn, that indicated they were probably worth robbing.

Athenos slurped wine from a wooden cup, eyes roaming over Zale with squinted appraisal, the way buyers did in the slave market. Chatter in the room that quieted when Zale and Poculus had entered now rose as dice games and drinking began again. Satisfied they could not be overheard, Zale leaned forward on his forearms and cast his voice low, speaking a western dialect of Greek.

"Do you remember me?"

Athenos grunted. "You think me addled? You worked for that oil importer."

"Yes, that is right, his name was Gaius Falcidius. You helped us collect some debts from reluctant borrowers. We paid you well."

"You paid me the going rate, but yes, I remember. Weren't you sold, though? Did Falcidius buy you back?"

"He was dying at the time, but I am free now, and here on behalf of one who would buy your services again." Zale paused to glance at the nearest patrons, to ensure nobody had become too curious about their conversation. Moving forward, his mouth was mere inches from Athenos. "The payment for this service is enough to keep you fed for the rest of your life."

The strongman had obviously heard such things before, as the skeptical tone of his response made clear. "Is that so? My weight in gold?"

"No...a half talent of silver."

One black eyebrow lifted as Athenos' demeanor changed from amusement to rapt attention. Silver was not seen very often along the Tiber waterfront, much less half a talent. Zale had known many men like Athenos: rough, dangerous and cunning, smart in their way, but not sophisticated. Of them all, though, his renegade fellow Greek had never failed to complete a job.

"Someone wants someone else dead...and I'm guessing whoever is the marked man will be noticed if he comes up floating in the Tiber."

"I'm not free to speak unless you have agreed to my terms."

"I can't agree with them unless I know them."

The moment had arrived. Zale doubted that anyone else in the crowded tavern spoke their particular dialect of Greek, but he could not be certain. If Zale was overheard, it would be terrible for his master, and fatal for him.

"If I tell you this, you will have no choice but to accept. My...the one who sent me on this errand will not allow you to live should you decline, and woe be unto you should you betray the commission."

"Threatening me is not going to work, my friend. You should know that."

"This is not a threat, Athenos. This is what will happen."

"*If* you could find me."

"Why do we argue? We both know that half a talent of silver is enough to live on for the rest of your life, and to live well, too."

Athenos finished his wine. Drumming his fingers on the table, he met Zale's stare, clearly considering how far he could push the negotiations.

"If I do this for you, I can never return to Rome, can I?"

"Never is a long time..." Seeing Athenos frown, Zale went on. "But to your point, no, Rome would not be a healthy place for you to live, not for the foreseeable future."

"Offer me half a talent of *gold* and we might reach agreement."

Zale smiled to stifle an outright laugh. "So much gold would buy an army!"

"But you're not buying an army, are you? No, you're buying *me*."

"Do not overvalue yourself, my friend. The fee stands as offered. Accept it or not. Athenos is not the only man willing to undertake dangerous tasks for such a sum."

"Dangerous, you say?"

"For half a talent of silver, did you expect to merely plant a field of grain? Now what say you, yes or no?"

"And you will tell me nothing until you have an answer?"

"Nothing."

Grubby fingers wrapped around a ceramic cup as Athenos lifted it to his mouth, an obvious ploy to stall and scrutinize Zale in the murky lighting. His intentions could not have been more obvious had he stated them: would Zale agree to increase the fee for any reason, or did Athenos need to make a decision?

"Agreed," he said a moment later. "Now who do you want killed?"

"It will not be *that* easy," Zale said. "Killing is only part of it."

**2**

Mago Barca sat in the small, lower chamber of the Carcer Tullianum. Scritching from out in the darkness meant the rats were back. While they had likely come to nibble his flesh again, if given the chance he would throttle one of the little bastards and eat them instead, alive and raw. Hunger inflamed his mind, rapidly driving him mad. As the youngest son of the mighty Hamilcar Barca, scourge of Romans during the first war with Rome, Mago had never imagined himself fantasizing about devouring raw rats. Stale bread with a crust of moldy cheese comprised the only food he'd been given since being captured weeks earlier. How many weeks, he couldn't say; time lost all meaning in the forever-night of his underground prison.

The harshness of Rome and the chill of the stone underground cell remained a constant reminder of the fate that awaited him. Each breath was a struggle, every gasp filled with the rank scent of mold and filth and death. There were others who had died here before him, waiting for the end in this tiny, cold space, their bodies left to decompose in silence, their spirits to imbue the very walls with their wailing essence.

The room was nothing more than a stone pit dug out beneath the streets in a far corner of the Forum Romanum, at the center of the known world's fastest growing cities. Mago could barely stand without scraping his head against the damp ceiling, and the air felt so thick he could chew it. Reaching out with one hand, he traced the moisture on the uneven walls, carved so roughly it seemed as if they'd been hacked from the earth by an angry child. The stone sucked the heat from his body and left his fingers numb. The floor offered little relief; it was uneven and too hard for his already weary muscles, and when he shifted, his hand brushed across loose dirt and pebbles, the remains of those who had come before him; prisoners, traitors, enemies of Rome, all those condemned to die.

*I have to get out of here.*

A thick, bitter taste fouled his tongue. With little circulation, the stench of his own excrement mixed with the moldy flavor of the underground air to assault his nose with a terrible reek. Only an unquenchable hatred of his captors prevented despair.

*No, I **will** leave this place.*

Above him, a narrow opening allowed a single shaft of light to push into the dark hole, but not enough to break the gloom. Above were only several more chambers hewn from the living rock of what the Romans called the Capotoline Hill. No, the single opening in the ceiling was more a cruel reminder of sunshine and freedom than a comfort. Through the gap, he heard the muffled voices of distant conversations, faint echoes of a world where men were still free.

Once Hannibal had destroyed Rome, which he eventually would, Mago prayed that his older brother would raze the city to its roots, leaving nothing to remind anyone it ever existed. Salt the Earth so nothing could grow, kill or enslave every man, woman and child.

In this place forgotten by man and god alike, time held no meaning. Mago measured the passage of days by the opening; during daylight it glowed as a faint gray square, while at night it vanished into the blackness of his immediate world.

The silence was absolute, broken only by the occasional drip of water from somewhere unseen, each droplet echoing through the small chamber. Sometimes, Mago thought he heard the soft steps of a Roman sentry, but they sounded like they came from a different world.

Mago shifted position, kicking the iron links of a chain that clinked against the hard walls with a metallic echo. Until that day, or maybe the previous one, he could no longer tell, the manacle had been on his wrist as a heavy, constant reminder of his captivity. The chain was short, so that he when tried to stretch out his legs, he couldn't extend them fully. Then someone dropped a ladder through the hole and unlocked him without saying a word. Shadows kept him from making out details of the man's face.

His shiver had nothing to do with the cold. Rome was a hot place to be during late summer. But underground was cool, and there could be no forgetting the purpose of his cell. The fact that someone unlocked his shackles must mean his execution drew near, for what *else* could it mean? If there was one thing the Romans were *not* known for, it was mercy, although why they would loose him before he died was something Mago could not understand.

Some said this lower cell had not merely housed captives, but had been their execution chamber, as well. Here, men had been strangled to death, their last breaths swallowed by the same stale air he now breathed. Others had been left to die of thirst, forgotten by the world above as they were swallowed by darkness and despair. Yet the more he thought about it, the less he understood why his captors would free him only to die.

In the end, it didn't matter. He was a Barca, son of Hamilcar, brother to Hannibal. Even though they had trapped him here like an animal, his spirit remained unbowed. Yet, within the confines of the Tullianum, surrounded by the unforgiving stones of Rome, it was difficult not to feel death's cold breath creeping nearer in the darkness. A clean death in battle brought honor to one's name. This foul ending would do quite the opposite.

*May the gods send me succor soon.*

Closing his eyes, he listened to the faint sounds from above, the distant voices, the muffled clanging of metal against stone. Memories took him outside once more, feeling the warmth of the sun on his skin, while the sea breezes blowing into Carthage carried the smell of the fields beyond the city walls. But in this grim and forgotten corner of Rome, those things seemed as far away as the stars.

The faint scrape of wood on rock startled him awake. Above, a flickering glow outlined the opening overhead with a yellowish light. Someone lowered the wooden ladder, prompting Mago to stand.

"Do you speak Greek?" whispered a voice.

*"Nai." Yes.*

"Good, move quickly."

"Move?"

"Yes, *move*. Climb out of there, you idiot!"

"Is it my time to die?"

"Only if you don't hurry up! I'm here to save you, not to kill you."

———

*Curia Hostilia, Forum Romanum, Rome, Italy*
*Antemeridianum tempus (forenoon), 25 August, 216 B.C.*

Throbbing pain ran up Varro's leg as he sat beside his fellow consul, Lucius Amellius Paullus. A Greek physician named Escotos warned him not to put much pressure on the leg, and to keep it elevated, but today of all days, he could show no weakness. He had to appear strong and healing well. Vengeance gave him strength.

Murmurs ran through the gathering Patricians, muted voices matched eyes cutting toward Paullus in quick, accusatory glances. News of Mago Barca's escape spread through Rome like swamp fever through a legionary camp. Overnight, the victor of Cannae's trophy prisoner went from being the focal point of a triumph to the target of the largest manhunt in Roman history. Not only was Mago Barca the brother of Hannibal Barca; he was also a talented Carthaginian general. Such a sordid affair could end Paullus's political career, not to mention draw potential charges once his term of office lapsed.

For his part, Varro had to fight the urge to smile at how well his plan had worked. A half talent of silver strained his finances, it was true, but if it meant leading a campaign against Hannibal into the Carthaginian stronghold of Spain, then the money was well spent. Conquering such a rich province could make Varro the wealthiest man in Rome and ensure his family's Patrician status in perpetuity. It would also wipe away the notion that he had displeased the gods in some way, with his broken leg being punishment for some egregious sin. Despite augurs taken by the Pontifex Maximus himself that declared Varro blameless, tongues yet wagged.

Pushing to his feet while trying not to show pain left Varro a bit lightheaded and unsteady, but he breathed deeply several times while waiting for the Senator to stop whispering. But when chatter yet echoed from the brick walls, from the seat closest to the low platform where the consuls faced the Senators, Quintus Caecilius Metellus stood and raised one arm.

"My friends, let us now calm ourselves for words from the Consul Varro."

"We have questions!" shouted someone from the rear. Varro stifled a smile; that was a comment he hadn't had to pay for. Apparently, the anger in the chamber was more than he'd dare hope for. A side glance at Paullus showed him scowling at Varro; their agreement before the meeting was for Paullus to open the session, but Varro stood first.

"Not to hear the *verba fecit* first is out of order, and would anger the gods," Metellus said in a grave voice. That shut down comments.

"Esteemed friends, I rise to defend the Victor of Cannae from scurrilous tongues that wag all too freely with slanderous accusations against my friend, Lucius Aemillius Paullus. That he is also my fellow consul only adds to my affection toward a man who won the greatest victory so far in Rome's long and glorious history."

He scanned the room, seeing that his comments did little to mollify its hostility.

"Between us, Lucius and I forged a deadly weapon to destroy the Carthaginian scum, and when I unexpectedly fell, he stepped in to crush the invaders. In the wake of that victory, this august body voted him a well-deserved triumph, something rarely done in the past. All of this is true and cannot be argued."

*Oh, but I see how many of you would argue it at this time.*

"Now, treachery has crept into our beloved city to release the captured brother of the so-called Scourge of Rome. I cannot say how or who did this vile deed, or what is being done to assuage the rage of Justitia and Mars, who must surely be angered by this event. That I will leave to the Greatest Living Roman, my co-consul, colleague, and friend, Lucius Aemillius Paullus."

Still gazing out to the lines of senators, Varro sat back in seat, ignoring Paullus's glare in his peripheral vision. Shouts immediately rose from the gallery, this time from Varro's friends, with rehearsed questions.

"Why were there only two guards watching such a valuable prisoner?"

"How did their assailants gain entrance?"

"Are the guards able to speak?"

"Who paid the guards? Did their coins come from the public treasury?"

Without waiting for answers from Paullus, others began making assumptions in their further questions.

"Why did taxes pay for a man held for *your* personal reasons, Consul?"

Paullus tried to speak, but was drowned out.

For his part Varro maintained a blank expression; it wasn't easy.

## 3



*Three miles west of Alba Longa, Italy*
*Solis Occasus, (Sunset), 24 August, 216 B.C.*

The setting sun turned the waters of Albanus Lacus a bright reddish-yellow, softened by reflections off the fading blue sky. Several miles away, the same sunlight picked out the buildings of Alba Longa, birthplace of Romulus and Remus, high atop the Alban Hills. No man of Rome could look upon such a magnificent view without feeling the inner pride that made a Roman a Roman.

None of the three horsemen in the forest were Romans. Two were Greek, one was Carthaginian.

"Let's kill him and be done with it," said the man with Athenos, speaking Greek. During the journey from Rome, they had spoken nothing but Greek, while Mago Barca did not speak at all, even when addressed in Latin. "Any closer to Alba Longa and somebody might see us. They've got to be looking for him."

Athenos answered in the same language. "Nearer the lake. I mean to sink his body."

Without preamble, their prisoner's loud voice cut the late afternoon quiet.

"That will not hide your crime, and when my brother returns, he will burn this Alba Longa to the ground," Mago Barca said. A rope tied to each ankle slipped under Mago's horse, leaving his hands free but him unable to escape.

"So you speak Greek, do you?" Athenos shrugged. "I don't give two shits what your brother does to it. I'm not a Roman."

The third man, Dymnos, lean and with wideset eyes, said, "What does he mean, Athenos? About his brother, I mean? You told me he was a Carthaginian captain being held for the triumph."

Athenos ignored the question.

"If he tries to burn Delphi, he might not like what happens," he said, trying to distract Dymnos.

"Carthage has no quarrel with the Greeks. It is Rome we will exterminate and its people we will enslave."

Athenos chuckled low in his throat. He had to give the Carthanginian credit for staying calm during their entire time together. Mago Barca hadn't flinched when, after climbing from his hole at the Carcer Tullianum, Athenos laid a knife against the Carthaginian's throat. He'd gone along with whispered instructions, even when under a covering in a cart filled with vegetables. Even when they bound him to the horse, Barca knew better than to fight back. Sure, a sword ready to split his liver provided motivation to obey, but surely Barca knew he was being taken somewhere to die...and his last words showed that he did.

"Somewhere close, yes," Athenos said. There seemed no reason to lie. "By now, word will have spread of your escape, and our orders are to make certain no one ever discovers what happened to you."

"Orders...now I understand. Someone wanted me to disappear, mostly likely to embarrass that pompous fool, Paullus. Without doubt he wanted to flay me in public, but you Romans are not so united as you would have us believe, are you? My guess would be your employer is the other consul, Varro. You must have been well paid for taking such a risk."

"*Very* well paid," Dymnos said. "But what is going on here, Athenos? I do not understand any of this."

Still holding his swordtip against Mago's side, Dymnos cut his eyes so that Athenos could meet them. A broad smile turned them into slits. Athenos nodded back. He'd hired Dymnos because he was stupid, ruthless, and would not ask questions. To men like Dymnos, five *quadrigati* was a windfall not to be turned down.

"It is not necessary that you do."

"Tell me the full truth!"

"Yes, tell him," Mago said, "since neither of you can never return to Rome."

Athenos swore under his breath. "That's enough talk, African. I'd just as soon kill you here."

Dymnos pressed in slightly with the sword. "Who *is* he, Athenos? Tell me and I will cut his guts out right there on the horse, just to shut him up."

"Whatever you're being paid is nothing compared to what my brother would give you."

"I know what he would give us," Athenos answered. "As much sharp steel as we could swallow."

It had taken a few seconds, but Dymnos finally parceled out what Mago had said previously.

"What did you mean when you said I can't go back to Rome? Who is your brother?"

Before Mago could answer, Athenos spoke first. "Don't listen to him, Dymnos. He's trying to save his neck—"

"I am Mago Barca. My brother is Hannibal."

"Kill him, Dymnos."

Once again, Dymnos turned toward Athenos, only this time with suspicion, not glee. Facial scars accented the squint in his left eye.

"Is this true? He is the Carthaginian general we've heard so much about?"

"No, fool, that is his brother. This one is nothing."

"You lied to me! You said he was a minor captain of cavalry who insulted a Senator's family. Consul Paullus plans to execute this man during a Triumph—everybody knows that. All of Rome must be hunting this Carthaginian. Why did you not tell me?"

"Because he knows you are not stupid," Mago interrupted. "He knew you would not have helped smuggle me out of the city. Whatever life you had in Rome is gone now, for it will not be difficult to parcel out who took me from my cell. He thinks you a fool."

"You are nothing!" Athenos said. His skills laid in stealth followed by direct, brutal assault. Action, not subtlety and deception. As veins pulsed in his temples, the Greek brigand could not keep desperation from his voice.

Despite his greasy clothes, filthy skin and hair, Mago Barca still commanded respect as he tilted backward, laughing.

"If it is gold you desire, then harken to my words. I am the son of Hasdrubal, who tormented Rome during our first war. I am my brother's sword and shield. Nothing, Roman? I am a demigod compared to alley trash like you."

Pausing, he looked down at Dymnos, showing contempt but no fear.

"Kill me now and be done with it, worm! My brother would pay a ransom in gold for my safe delivery to Carthaginian territory, but death if preferable to hearing your insufferable stupidity one moment longer."

Dymnos growled.

"You want to die right now?" he said. "I can make that—"

He stopped in midsentence. Instead of thrusting the swordpoint into the soft flesh under Mago's left ribcage, Dymnos stiffened. The tip of a sword glinted inside of his mouth.

Without warning, Athenos had stepped forward and plunged a finely wrought *kopis* deep into his fellow Greek's neck. Passed down from his father, the sword was the sole remaining legacy of Athenos's life in Greece.

Dark blood ran the length of the steel as spurts erupted from Dymnos's neck. Blinking, his rat-like face twisted in surprise, Dymnos cocked his head, met Athenos's eyes, and collapsed. Twitching in a spreading pool, he gurgled a few times while the thirsty dirt drank his life force.

"Tell me about this gold."

Mago grinned. "How much do you want?"

"I am a reasonable man. Considering that I will be marked for death by the Romans, and will have to massage many palms along the way...two talents of pure gold."

"We could buy the loyalty of a king for so much gold."

"Yet you could not buy your life with a thousand talents."

"First you will have to arrange passage to Spain. One talent. Such a sum will buy you a life's worth of the finest pleasures."

Athenos paused to consider whether the Carthaginian was lying to save his own life or might actually command such wealth. His experience was with men who commanded local power in one or two areas, not over whole regions and kingdoms. A talent of gold seemed unrealistically huge, and yet...what if it was real? Would such a chance ever come again?

"How do I know that I can trust you?"

"You know much about Rome, about the inside of the city. My brother could use such information. Besides, men with your experience and skill are always wanted. The question is can you get me out of Italy?"

Slowly, Athenos made his decision. "Smuggling along the docks of the Tiber is rife. I know all of the ship captains. That will be the easy part. The hard part will be getting you to Ostia without being seen."

"Can you do such a thing?" Mago said.

"For a talent of gold, I will carry you there myself."

**4**

*The Mediterranean Sea, Approaching the Coast of Spain*
*Tempus pomeridianum (afternoon) 5 September, 216 B.C.*

Unusually for that time of year, the sea was calm as the *actuaria* sailed toward the Spanish coast. Banks of oars rose and fell in rhythm with the billowing sails as a few gulls circled overhead, screeching for scraps cast overboard by the crew. The sun rode low in their faces as the sun began its journey into night, casting long shadows across the deck. It was a peaceful scene, but on the deck of the ship, two men stood staring at each other, tension hanging between them.

"You are growing bold, Athenos," Mago said, his voice soft with menace. He wore a simple tunic, his hair tied back from his face, and he looked every bit the merchant he pretended to be. Only his eyes gave him away, dark and filled with intelligence and cunning.

The Greek knew his danger too late, and knew that his safest course was to keep quiet. Yet such was not his nature.

"I tell truths," Athenos said. Used to unspoken danger and quick death, he sensed peril while considering options and contingencies. He had not planned for this moment, but now that it was here, he could see possibilities opening before him. "The Romans will likely have tracked your path by now. They will hunt you down like a dog."

"Our next port is Qart Hadasht." Mago's smile did not reach his eyes. "If they wish to follow me there, let them try."

"We are not in Spain yet. You told me that I would be paid once aboard ship... I want my gold. Do so, and I will speak for you when they find you."

"*When* they find me?" Mago chuckled, shaking his head. "You arrogant little man. You think too little of me, Athenos, or perhaps you have no knowledge how men of honor think. I am a noble son of Carthage! Do you believe I would allow myself to be captured again? No, if the Romans find me, they will regret it. And unless you mind your tongue, you will be the one with regrets."

"Me? I seek only what was promised."

"And you shall get everything you deserve. I promised to bring you to my brother, and I will."

"You promised me *gold!*"

"You will get your gold. What happens to you after that if up to Hannibal."

Athenos felt a flush of blood into his face. Fists balled involuntarily, but aside from Mago being taller and heavier than Athenos, the nearest crew members moved in close enough to intervene, if needed. They had taken the ship in Sardinia thanks to Athenos having contacts there, but loyalty among the corrupt followed power, not friendship, and Mago Barca commanded both.

"You would betray your word?"

Mago's eyes closed into slits. His voice became quiet. "Never, ever again accuse me of lying to you, *Greek*. Or you can swim to Spain. Do you understand my words?"

"I do," Athenos said, fighting down a wave of nausea. Dreams of riches faded into nightmare.

———

*Oppian Hill, spur of the Esquiline Hill, Rome, Italy*
*Intempesta Nox (Far into the Night), 7 September, 216 BC*

Unlike the city below, stifling in the stink and heat of the late summer night, cool breezes snaked through the windows of his study carrying the sweet promise of coming rain. Beyond the darkness of night, both Varro and the Pontifex Maximus, Quintus Caecilius Metellus, could see torches and braziers on the Palatine Hill nearby on the south. Smoke from oil lamps placed in wall niches lent the room a faint, fruity scent. Low flames flickered enough to shine off the intricate pattern of tiles that comprised a mosaic of Apollo and the Muses in one wall, a decoration that brought admiration from all who visited Varro's villa.

Able to walk without aid now, Varro once again plunged into politics by hosting a well-attended banquet for a few powerful Senators and their wives. Once his Consulship ended, he wanted a good province to govern, preferably Sicily.

The hour was late and his guests long gone, but Varro and Metellus sat together on cushioned seats staring out the open window. Nearly empty cups stood on a low table between them, each diluted with less and less water as the night wore on. Varro signaled to a slave in the shadow to fill his cup again.

"Now that we are alone, tell me what troubles you, Gaius," Metellus asked, swirling the wine in his own goblet. "You are unusually quiet tonight. The wine flows freely, but you seem...ill at ease."

Varro glanced at him, then set his cup aside without drinking. "You know why I am troubled, Quintus," he said, though his voice belied his words. "Although perhaps another word better suits my mood...vexed."

"Oh?" Metellus lifted an eyebrow, pretending surprise. "Surely not all of Rome is a burden to your shoulders?"

"It's our missing Carthaginian friend," Varro said. A momentary flash of suspicion toward Metellus caused him to scowl. The Pontifex Maximus knew damned good and well what troubled him, so why pretend that he did not? Yet like Varro, Metellus had many concerns for his mind, and may truly not remember. As Varro tapped his fingers against the table, their soft rhythm was the only sound in the room. "I expected to hear tidings by now. This delay is...unwelcome."

Metellus took a sip of wine, regarding Varro over the rim of his cup. "It is well that I do not know details, yet can we be certain that those who aided in the escape can be trusted?"

"Yes." Varro leaned forward, his eyes narrowing. "Athenos should have returned days ago. Mago was to vanish quietly, leaving no trace behind. It was a simple plan."

"Tell me no plans, Gaius. What I do not know cannot accidentally escape my lips."

Once again, suspicion ignited fear within Varro, but it was too late to back out now.

"I only mention possibilities, my friend, not realities."

"Ah. And this Athenos?"

"A possible Greek mercenary."

"Mercenary or murderer?"

Varro shrugged.

"In that case, if we are speaking hypothetically, then such a plan is simple, yes," Metellus agreed, though his tone suggested doubt. "But if I may surmise the background of one who would be hired for such a task, placing trust in a man like this Athenos for such a delicate task. He would be a...*complicated* tool, would you not agree? Assuming he was real."

Varro frowned, staring into his half-empty goblet. "Complicated or not, such men value silver and gold above all else. That is what I counted on, and he accepted my offer without hesitation. And yet...now..."

Varro did not finish, but the worry in his eyes made his meaning clear.

Metellus studied him a moment, deep in thought.

"Do you think...would such a man not easily be...turned?"

Varro hesitated, then shook his head even as his fingers drummed faster on the table. "I do not know. Perhaps he was delayed. Perhaps some bandits attacked him. The unknown concerns me."

Metellus leaned back and swirled the last of his wine in his cup. "Men like this imaginary Athenos can be treacherous precisely because they know the value of what they possess...and being Greek, he may feel no allegiance to Rome. Perhaps even hatred."

Varro's jaw tightened.

"If Athenos is so foolish as to attempt such a thing, he will soon discover that his life is not worth much once I learn of it."

Metellus chuckled without humor. "I do not doubt it, Gaius. But if he has betrayed you...once again, if we pretend that such a thing could be real, what then?"

Varro's eyes narrowed, and he looked past Metellus, into the shadowy corners of the room, as if seeing something hidden from his friend. "If Athenos has betrayed me, he knows too much. Enough to ruin me. He would know that I arranged Mago's escape, and that I wished Paullus's victory to be...less than complete."

Metellus's lips twitched into a knowing smile. "Paullus and his hollow victory," he said, satisfaction in his voice. "At least we have the satisfaction of having watched his embarrassment when the Carthaginian general slipped through his fingers. The people still laud him, of course, but without Mago...well, it does not have quite the same luster."

Varro leaned forward, his eyes focused. "Just so. Paullus is still lauded in the streets, but there are whispers, and his victory seems less than it was, especially now that the Senate has begun to ask how Mago disappeared."

"But Athenos could still ruin everything for you," Metellus said, his voice firm.

He refilled his cup and leaned closer before continuing.

"If he speaks, even in a quiet tavern, you could face questions in the Senate, questions I might not be able to deflect. Even if they were lies."

Varro's face grew serious, and he nodded, looking grim. All pretense vanished; Metellus already knew too much to bury him, so further dancing around the truth was pointless. "That is why I planned to deal with Athenos when he returned. His greed was useful, but now he is a liability."

Metellus nodded, intrigued.

"Yet he has *not* returned. Strange, is it not?"

Varro's fingers stilled on the table, and he looked straight at Metellus, speaking firmly.

"If he returns, Quintus, I will ensure he does not leave Rome alive. One way or another, he will be silenced."

Metellus raised his cup in a silent toast, his smile turning serious.

"Then let us drink to Athenos returning soon, so he can receive your... thanks. And if he does not, there are many ways to deal with threats."

Their cups clinked, and Metellus drank deeply, but Varro just stared at his cup, lost in thought. After a moment, he spoke again, quietly.

"Do you think, Quintus, that Paullus knows?"

Metellus shrugged, setting down his cup. "Paullus is not a fool, Gaius. He is ambitious, as much so as you and I, but not subtle. If he knows, he will likely let his jealousy and anger fester. That might serve you. Rome forgets, but Paullus cannot let an insult pass."

A small smile appeared on Varro's face. "No, he cannot, can he?" He leaned back, feeling a bit satisfied, though his mind continued to race.

"Perhaps Athenos is merely delayed. Soon, I will know. If he returns, we will reward him as promised...then ensure his silence."

"Such is the way of things," Metellus said, raising his cup one last time. "Rome demands sacrifices from all her sons, does she not?"

Varro's smile widened, sharp and calculating.

"Yes, she does, Quintus. Yes, she does."

$$\textbf{5}$$

*Steps of the Temple of Jupiter Optimus Maximus, Capitoline Hill, Rome, Italy
Mane (morning), 13 September, 216 B.C.*

Varro stood on the second-highest step of the temple, watching the grand procession of his co-consul's Triumph wind its way through the streets of Rome. The crowd roared as Paullus, resplendent in his *toga picta*, passed by in a gold-trimmed chariot pulled by four white horses. Above him waved the banners of victory and before him marched the spoils of war, captured weapons carried by slaves and gleaming in the sunlight, a testament to Rome's might and Paullus's supposed triumph over Hannibal's forces. A few haggard prisoners in tattered Carthaginian uniforms stood in for thousands more who had already been sold into slavery. Citizens of Rome jeered every one of them.

Each man among the crowd received a loaf of bread and a wedge of cheese, while children feasted on various fruits, all paid for by the man proclaimed as Jupiter for one day: Lucius Aemilius Paullus.

But to Varro, it all felt hollow, a façade to mask Paullus's failures. He allowed himself a small, hidden smile. The Triumph and honors should have been *his*. Not only that, but Paullus had already staged one victory parade...could his fellow Senators not see through the charade?

Earlier Triumphs had been somber affairs, but no more. The crowd lining the route was a sea of excitement, their cheers nearly deafening as Paullus's chariot drew near. Varro crossed his arms, his expression neutral to hide his satisfaction. While not a glaring omission, Mago's absence from the parade was noticeable, especially to those who understood the nuances of politics. Without the Carthaginian general as a trophy, Paullus' victory seemed slightly less complete, slightly less deserving of such adulation.

A gentle nudge at his elbow caused Varro to turn. Standing next to him was Quintus Caecilius Metellus, his friend's face a mixture of admiration and mild disdain as he watched the procession. Metellus raised an eyebrow, a knowing glint in his eye.

"Quite the spectacle, is it not?" he said, loud enough to be heard over the din.

"Indeed," Varro replied, his tone smooth and controlled. "A fitting tribute to Paullus, our conquering hero."

"A hero sadly missing one key piece from his collection of trophies."

"Precisely," Varro said. His eyes once again fixed on Paullus's chariot.

*One day I will be standing in the chariot, Paullus. Only I will have the Carthaginian generals in shackles.*

"Imagine if he had managed to bring Mago before the people today. They would be hailing him as the next Romulus," Metellus replied with a quiet chuckle. "But as it stands, there is a hint of incompleteness in his glory, is there not? Something subtle, but...unmistakable."

"I will not overlook such a detail," Varro said, lowering his voice to a near whisper. He had to admit: seeing Paullus accept praise for an incomplete victory gave him a rare sense of satisfaction. Here was the man who had stolen Varro's victory, now forced to celebrate a Triumph that was not quite perfect.

As Paullus drew closer, Varro noticed a brief flicker of discontent in his rival's eyes, quickly masked but not fast enough. Perhaps Paullus felt the emptiness of the spectacle himself. Varro's own smile widened. Paullus would not be able to forever ignore the whispers, the quiet comments that would follow him for years, the quiet questioning of how Mago, such an important figure, had slipped from Rome's grasp under Paullus's watch.

A senator nearby whispered something to a companion, their voices muffled but their gestures clear. Varro caught snippets of their conversation, enough to know they were discussing Mago's absence and the strange circumstances of his escape. A small surge of pride filled him; the whispers were exactly what he'd hoped for. With each murmured remark, the suspicion shifted further from him and onto Paullus. Varro knew the Senate would remember these doubts when it came time to discuss future campaigns and leadership.

Metellus leaned in close, his voice low but amused. "You will be the one Rome remembers, Gaius," he said. "The one who was there to hold things together when others let opportunities slip away."

Varro nodded and let out a slow, satisfied breath. "Let him have his triumph," he said in a calm voice. "Let him enjoy the cheers today, for tomorrow they will remember who stood by Rome when it mattered."

Paullus's chariot passed directly in front of them, and for a moment, their eyes met. In Paullus's gaze, Varro saw more than just the pride of a victor; he saw anger, barely hidden, which made Varro's satisfaction all the greater. He gave a slight nod, one that Paullus would understand as mockery but the crowd would see as a polite gesture.

Paullus's eyes narrowed before he looked away and continued with the parade, his face showing a practiced look of victory.

"It is a pity he does not see it for what it is," Metellus said. "All the glory in the world cannot hide a shadow once it has been cast."

Varro smiled, enjoying the comment. "And it cannot fill an empty vessel."

The crowd's cheering grew louder as Paullus moved down the street, but Varro did not move, unfazed by the noise. He had planted seeds of doubt, and now he could wait patiently as they took root and grew.

———

*Camp of Hannibal, overlooking Qart Hadasht, Spain*
*Meridies (mid-day), 15 September, 216 B.C.*

Disembarking took longer than expected. Once word spread that Mago Barca had returned, onlookers jammed the sea gates, crowding him to get a better glimpse of mighty Hannibal's supposedly slain brother. Calling for horses, Mago found Carthaginian troops helping him mount a feisty bay, while Athenos and as many soldiers as possible crowded a mule-drawn wagon.

Qart Hadasht was still a young city, and therefore not terribly large. To the east, a long ridgeline laid inside the protective wall, along which rested Hannibal's army. The camp occupied a large area near the base of a hill, with hundreds of tents and supply piles spread out over several acres. Riders raced ahead to spread word that Mago lived, so that crowds of men greeted him long before he neared the encampment site. Soldiers stopped their work to watch as he rode in, followed by the wagon with Athenos and several Carthaginian guards. Cheers erupted at his arrival.

"Praise Baal, General Mago has returned!"

Mago could not help but smile at the sound of it. Too long had he gone without hearing the Punic language. It felt good to be among his own people again, away from Rome and the chains they had used to try to break him. He glanced at Athenos, the mercenary who made it possible. The man's casual confidence irritated Mago. The Roman collaborator had no idea what was coming for him, or that loyalty to Carthage and the Barca family meant more than any deal made for money.

As they neared the largest tent, a tall figure with one piercing dark eye emerged. A leather eye patch covered the other.

It was Hannibal.

Mago's excitement at the sight of his brother made him want to leap from the horse and run to Hannibal, but instead Mago kept his face impassive, nodding respectfully.

Hannibal's stern countenance softened, the rare hint of joy replacing his usual grim demeanor. "Mago," he said, stepping forward. "My beloved brother. We feared you were lost. We heard you were captured by the Romans after Cannae."

Mago dismounted, handing the reins to a nearby attendant.

"They did capture me," Mago replied, a touch of gallows humor in his voice. "But Rome does not understand the loyalty and cunning of those who serve our family. Or the greed of its own citizens."

Hannibal strode with long stride to grip his brother's shoulders. "Tonight, we will celebrate your return, my brother," he said. "Your survival gives us all new strength."

Mago nodded, keeping his voice steady. "Thank you, Hannibal. But I have brought someone with me whose tale you should hear, and who has earned a reward."

Hannibal looked at Athenos, who watched the reunion with an insufferable smirk on his face, as if he deserved the gratitude of Hannibal Barca. Mago felt a surge of contempt but hid it, nodding toward Athenos.

"This man, Athenos, claims to be a friend of both Carthage *and*

Rome," Mago began, speaking loud enough for everyone nearby to hear. "He offered to kill me for the Romans...until I offered him a better deal to help me escape."

"Does he speak our language?"

"No."

Hannibal nodded, repeating the accusation for Athenos's benefit in Latin.

Athenos' smile faltered but quickly returned as he tried to deflect the accusation. "It is true," he said, giving a slight bow. "I had a deal with the Romans, but your brother showed me a better way. Honor and loyalty—"

"Honor?" Mago interrupted. "You have no honor, Athenos. Your loyalty is only to gold. Not to Rome, not to Carthage, or anyone else."

Athenos froze, sensing the change in the air. He looked at Hannibal, hoping to salvage his position.

"General Barca," he said, trying to sound humble. "I am only a man who sees opportunities. And if that opportunity is to serve you, then so much the better."

Hannibal's face was unreadable as he considered Athenos, saying nothing about the mercenary for a long, uncomfortable moment. Mago, however, knew his brother too well not to know what would happen next. He still remembered when Hannibal offered freedom to whichever prisoners killed their captured comrades in a fair duel.

"Yes," Hannibal finally said, sounding thoughtful. "It seems opportunity has indeed brought you to our camp. And if my brother made a pact with you for his salvation, then you have done your job well. What is the promised payment?"

"A talent of gold," Mago said.

Hannibal raised his eyebrows. "So much? Well, it is a paltry price for my brother's life" He nodded to one of his aides. Moments later, two men returned with a small wooden chest, each carrying one side.

"The bargain is now fulfilled, Athenos. My brother's life in return for a talent of gold, as you were promised."

Athenos again. "Let the man who questions the greatness of Hannibal not cross my path, lest he be slain by my rage. Truly you are Rome's greatest nightmare."

Hannibal gave a small smile.

"So I am. Take your gold, Athenos, and tell me the treaty is completed."

"It is."

"Good."

A short nod brought guards with stern face, who surrounded Athenos. The Greek made no sudden move, instead glancing around in confusion.

"What...what is happening?"

Mago stepped closer, speaking with disdain. "Did you really think you could just walk away?" he said. "That we would let someone who works for Rome walk away knowing our secrets?"

Hannibal spoke firmly. "Like so many Romans, you chose money over honor. You picked ease over loyalty. Such people are useless to Carthage and to me." He nodded to the guards. "Take him. Make sure he shares all he knows before he dies. Flay him, if you must."

Many hands grabbed him. Survivor of a hundred fights in the streets and backalleys of Rome's worst neighborhoods, Athenos bit and spit and kicked in his struggle to break free. This time, though, his opponents weren't soft sons of rich families come to visit the waterfront brothers; they were hardened warriors with grips of iron.

"No! General Barca, I saved your brother!"

"You did bring my brother," Hannibal said. "And I paid you for that. But Carthage has no need for men who sell their loyalty. Take him."

The guards dragged Athenos away, despite his frantic resistance. He shouted, cursed, pleaded, and bargained, his voice growing desperate as it faded under a flurry of fists.

Mago watched, taking satisfaction in each of Athenos's futile attempts. The mercenary's desperation was a fitting end for someone who chose money over honor.

Once the doomed Roman vanished into a large tent, Hannibal turned to Mago, his expression softening. Mago saw gray hairs in the older man's eyebrows and beard that had not been there four months earlier.

"It is only by the grace of the gods that you have been returned to me, Mago. Hasdrubal will never believe it."

"Is he not in the city?"

"No. It is late in the year for campaigning, but the Romans could attack us come Spring. Our brother is in the hinterlands recruiting soldiers and reluctant kings. He will be gone for several more weeks."

"Then we must be about rebuilding the army."

"As we must. And yet..." Hannibal wrapped an arm around Mago's neck. "And yet we can afford to spend *one* night celebrating your return, I think. But one night only. Then we must be about the business of destroying Rome."

The End

# HERE MUST WE HOLD

## Rob Howell

Frost filled the courtyard of Abingdon Abbey as a golden dawn promised the best of days, crisp and cool with brilliant orange, yellow, and crimson leaves on the trees.

The archivist of the abbey, cloak tightly held around himself, breath coming out in clouds, rushed across the frosted grass as quickly as his crutch would allow. He entered the scriptorium, sighing with relief when he saw his assistant had already arrived. A fire burned in the hearth and the boy was lighting the last set of candles.

"Bless you, lad." The archivist went to the fire and warmed his hands. "How much progress have you made on the copy for Peterborough?"

"All the way through Alfred's death."

"Excellent." The archivist moved to the assistant's desk and looked at the parchment. "This is well done."

"My letters are wretched, brother," protested the young man.

"You're already much better than I was at your age."

"Perhaps." The assistant glanced at the crutch and then at the scribe's gnarled fingers. "But then, I hadn't—"

"My gifts?"

"Your...gifts?" The assistant blinked. "But your hands? Your leg?"

"It is true my fingers ache more than you're ever likely to know and it would be nice to walk as I once did." He shook his head. "They are gifts nonetheless. The Lord granted them to me so I would never forget."

The assistant blinked again.

The archivist smiled. "It's of no moment now. You must continue your work. Make sure to copy that section on Aethelflaed. I'm sure the monks in Peterborough don't have it, and few enough remember her these days."

"Yes, brother."

"Good lad." The archivist limped over to the armarium set into a niche in the wall. Inside was a bound codex. He reverently lifted it out and carried it over to his table. Small pieces of parchment, dry and old, fell to the ground despite his care. He then retrieved another codex, this one much newer, and set it alongside the first one.

He stared at the older codex for a long moment before slowly turning it to a page. The old parchment cracked. The morning's gloom forced the scribe to squint at the letters. Then he opened the other codex to the corresponding page and compared his previous day's work with the words on the older pages, a difficult, tedious task even in bright light, painful at the moment.

He sighed in relief after completing the examination. He looked at the next section.

Before continuing, he bowed his head. *"Sancte Michael Archangele, defende nos in proelio; contra nequitiam et insidias diaboli esto praesidium."* He crossed himself and reached for a quill. He dipped it into the inkpot and started to move it toward the blank page. Then his hand shook, causing an ebon drop to fall to the floor.

Hastily, he pulled the pen back.

*No. Not today, of all days.*

He bowed his head again in prayer, flexing his fingers.

He tried again, but the quiver in his hand made it difficult for him to even fit the tip of the quill into the inkpot.

*I must get this right.*

He tried again, but with no better results.

*Maybe it's the cold. Yes, must be the cold.*

The scribe reached for his crutch and rose.

His assistant looked up. "Is everything well, brother?"

"It is as God would have it. My task today is one that must be done well and correctly. We all must age, though, and my eyes and hands require me to be patient on a cold, dark morning."

The assistant's eyes flicked to the codex. "You have waited years for this, if it is what I think."

"It is."

"If I may be so bold, I think God will not begrudge you performing the task after Terce."

"Nor do I, lad." He limped over to the abbey's chapel and knelt before the altar. Behind it was an icon of Mary. He bowed to her.

*Bless me in this task, Mary. Especially with* this *page.*

As had often been the case, he thought he saw her icon smile upon him. He knelt there on the relentless stone floor until Abbot Siward came in hours later to lead the abbey in their midmorning prayer.

"What is wrong, brother?" asked the abbot.

Startled, the scribe looked over. Stiffly, he pulled himself to his feet. "I apologize, my lord abbot. I needed to pray."

"The Lord will not chastise you for praying, brother," Siward said with a smile. "Nor will I. Is there anything you need?"

"No, lord abbot. I am just old, and today's task is too important for me to attempt before the sun warms the scriptorium."

The abbot considered the monk and then smiled again. "Thank you, brother."

"For what?"

"I was debating which psalm to read for Terce. Nothing seemed right. Now, it is clear that God wishes me to read Psalm 143."

The scribe bowed his head and whispered, "You needn't do that one on my account."

"No, I don't. However, I've not read it in some time, and I think it fits. Besides, I know it's special to you and I would give you all the strength I can today."

"Thank you, my lord abbot."

The other brothers of Abingdon Abbey filed in.

When they had settled, the abbot intoned, "Remember with me, brothers, the wisdom of Psalm 143. 'Blessed be the Lord my God, who teacheth my hands to fight, and my fingers to war...'"

———

Wulfstan, son of Ceola, waited for the tide to ebb so blood could flow.

Across Panta Channel, on Northey Island, Danes lined the shore waving axes, swords, and spears, yelling curses mostly carried away by the freshening breeze from the shore. At low tide, a causeway connected Northey Island with the mainland just southeast of the town of Maldon.

Northern raiders preferred such islands because a small guard would be sufficient to protect their ships.

"They say there are nearly a hundred ships," hissed Godric, Odda's son.

"So?"

"That's at least three *thousand* warriors!"

"And there's three thousand fyrd with us, not including our brother thegns and all the house-carls of Essex."

Godric looked in amazement. "They're but farmers. Hardly a byrnie amongst them, and all they bear are cheap spearheads on ash-wood poles."

"Then those of us who have taken rings from Byrhtnoth must fight all the better." Wulfstan strode forward to the edge of the causeway, leaving Godric behind.

Byrhtnoth, son of Byhrthelm, Ealdorman of Essex, already waited at the edge. Two hands and more greater than six feet, with hair white as a swan, he looked down at his newest thegn. "Do you think you can hold against them all at the water's edge, boy?"

Wulfstan considered the causeway, then shook his head. "No, lord. I'll need two others."

The ealdorman laughed. "Very well. Aelfhere and Maccus, you stand with the boy."

"As long as he does all the work," said Aelfhere. "I'm too old for this."

"As am I," said Maccus with a matching grin.

One of the Danes, shorter, broader, but with lithe, quick steps, moved forward and sent a blast from a horn across the channel. With all eyes upon him, he yelled, "You! The tall one with the white hair. Are you the Byrhtnoth we've heard of?"

The ealdorman stepped to the channel's edge. "I am. And who are you?"

"Olaf, son of Tryggvi, jarl of these men." He gestured at the host behind him. "As you can see, they thirst for the fight." He smiled. "However, if you send us rings of gold and hauberks of steel, then we'll see no need for the spear rush. Indeed, a day as beautiful as this is one for sailing. If you give us these gifts, we'll grant a truce and then enjoy the wind and spray of the sea."

"Of you I've heard and I've no doubt of your word. Here is my answer." Byrhtnoth grasped his shield and lifted his spear. "Spears of ash we shall give you, and swords of steel, as well, yet only their edges and their points. Tell your folk that here stands a good earl with loyal thegns and the fyrd about him. To our king, Aethelred, we have sworn oaths, and this land we shall defend no matter that we may fall."

"So be it. Tell your god when you see him that we gave you a fair chance."

"I shall, when my time truly comes."

The Dane laughed. He turned and said something to the men behind them. Some of them ordered their ranks and moved to their end of the causeway. Inch by inch, the causeway appeared as the tides inexorably pulled away.

Wulfstan stepped up, locking shields with Aelfhere on his left and Maccus on his right.

"This'll do." Aelfhere turned to those behind him. "The rest of you fill if we fall, but give us room."

Byhrtnoth began arranging the troops behind them. First, he called forward the few score bowmen at hand.

"Aelfnoth, you command the left. Wulfmaer, the right. Leave off until you see any bowmen on their side. We can hold this causeway easily, but not if they start killing us with arrows as we stand. Understand?"

The two thegns nodded.

"Good." The ealdorman turned to the bulk of his men. A score he had already left guarding the horses, which had allowed the English to reach Maldon in time. The others he split into three blocks, one to each side and then one, slightly larger, in the center. In the front rank of each block, he placed the house-carls, who wore steel armor and bore shields. The fyrd arrayed themselves behind that line, ready to thrust with their spears past the shields. The fyrd may have been farmers and herdsmen, but most had stood in shield walls before.

Yet never against three thousand raiders. Godric was not the only English warrior to wonder at the size of the host before them.

Byrhtnoth marched to each group in turn, giving them all the same message. "Stand firm, lads. They only want plunder and easy wealth, not your steel. They'll run once they see we're true English men." Each sent a cheer following the ealdorman. Then he and his score of personal thegns returned to the area near the causeway to stand behind Wulfstan and the two flanking him.

Byrhtnoth leaned on his spear.

The sun crept higher.

The sea crept lower.

The more impatient of the Danes started splashing over, only to have Olaf snap at them to wait.

So they taunted and insulted the English.

Who just kept waiting.

When the sun reached halfway to its peak, the tide had exposed the causeway, leaving only puddles of water here and there. Olaf motioned, and the Danes marched.

When they were three paces away from the end, the front ranks charged, hoping to overwhelm Wulfstan, Aelfhere, and Maccus.

The three defenders, however, stepped forward in unison at the last moment, and shields crashed together. The front ranks of the Danes stumbled, with those immediately behind colliding into a pile. Wulfstan stabbed down with his sword, spilling the day's first blood.

He stabbed again, this time into an exposed leg, earning a yell. Next to him, Aelfhere and Maccus bloodied their weapons, as well.

The following ranks pressed in, stepping over their fallen brothers. An axe sliced along the edge of Wulfstan's shield, cutting through the iron binding and carrying a chunk away. Wulfstan twisted back, slashing through the Dane's byrnie. He then stabbed into an exposed flank.

That exposed his own flank, but Aelfhere anticipated the youth's mistake. He stepped forward, interposing his shield and allowing Wulfstan to regain his position.

One of the pile at Wulfstan's feet apparently still lived, for a hand reached out to grasp his ankle. He tried to tug his foot away as another Danish line approached, but the hand held firmly. Desperately, Wulfstan lifted his shield high and chopped down.

A spurt of blood from the wrist rewarded his slash, but the crash on his shield drove him to a knee. He pushed himself up with a thrust at a Dane's belly. His sword slid through iron rings and the Northman stumbled back, grabbing at his entrails.

Another Dane charged in wildly, axe raised high. Maccus simply made a small step and directed him off the causeway. He splashed into the water, spluttering and struggling to gain his feet.

Yet they still came. Wulfstan's limbs tired and all three of Byrhtnoth's thegns rasped desperately for breath. Behind them, three more thegns prepared to step in, should they be needed.

By now, the dead and dying Danes provided a grisly breastwork for the defenders, but that slowed not the Northmen. They scrambled over the bodies of their brothers, slashing with axe and sword, stabbing with bright spears.

An axe chopped off most of Aelfhere's shield, but the old warrior returned the favor by breaking the axe's handle. The destruction of shield and axe gave the two warriors a moment to stare at each other, but the moment swiftly ended when another Dane pushed past.

The Northman pressed Aelfhere with his shield, trying to force him back and provide an opening for his fellows behind him. However, the dead and wounded made him place his feet awkwardly. His leg extended, and Wulfstan slashed down. The Dane stumbled, twisting away. Aelfhere finished him off. The man's shield fell to the ground and Aelfhere grabbed the Dane's in but a moment.

The attackers paused, gauging anew their options to create a breach. Meanwhile, the defenders leaned back and gasped for breath. Wulfstan heard Byrhtnoth urge the three to step back in favor of fresh replacements, but Maccus snarled back with words Wulfstan could not comprehend. They earned a laugh from Byrhtnoth.

Still gasping, they raised their shields when the Danes stepped forward. This time, a Northman bearing a shield led several clustered spearmen who, instead of charging, reached the edge of the pile and flicked their spear tips at the defenders.

Aelfhere tapped one away with his sword. Maccus tempted one spearman with a target, but slammed his shield on the top of the spear tip and chopped through the spear's shaft.

Two spear points came toward Wulfstan, one from each side. He twisted away from one while at the same time putting his shield in front of the other. However, with the bodies at his feet limiting his steps, the maneuver left him off-balance. The spearman thrust again, hitting Wulfstan's shield. His aching legs could not compensate for the lack of balance, and the thrust made Wulfstan stumble.

Maccus moved his shield to guard Wulfstan's suddenly exposed side from the following thrusts, but in so doing allowed a spear to rake along his sword arm's shoulder. He grunted in pain, but Wulfstan scrambled back into position. Maccus turned back, sword still raised, a scarlet streak running down the iron rings of his byrnie.

A horn blew from amidst the mass of Danes on the causeway. The Danes stepped back, and Olaf moved into the gap between the lines.

With a broad smile, he gestured at the pile. "You three have made the

Valkyries busy today. I've no doubt they'll lift you on their white horses when your time comes."

"Today is not that day, Dane," snarled Maccus.

"Perhaps." Olaf looked up at the sun. "But the day is not over, and we have many hours left before the tide returns."

Byhrtnoth stepped forward. "All the more time for you to sail back to your homes."

The Danish leader laughed. "I had a different thought. Your three champions here have well guarded this causeway. Some score of men and more will dine with Woden tonight. Perhaps, though, you would consider moving back and allowing my brethren to form on your side of the channel. Then we shall see what the Victory-Judge says of our worth."

"Do you doubt the worth of English men?" asked Byhrtnoth. "Are these dead here not enough of an answer?"

"I do not doubt these three men at all. Indeed, should they wish, I would accept them into my hall," Olaf replied easily. "Yet they weary, and I would allow others of my kin a chance to prove themselves."

"They do weary, but instead of allowing you to form up, I could name others to take their place. Eadric, Aelfwine, and Leofsunu are here at hand and none before have doubted their courage."

Olaf looked at the three thegns. Then he stared into Byhrtnoth's eyes. "Of *their* courage I do not doubt."

Byhrtnoth's eyebrows, as white as his hair, lifted. "But you doubt mine?"

"I didn't *say* that." Olaf gestured. "I will say that this causeway is no place for a battle. And it is truly a beautiful day to be on a ship."

The ealdorman deliberated. "There is wisdom in your words, and I will consider them. I grant you truce to carry your dead and wounded back to the island. When that task is complete, I will give you my answer."

With a grin, Olaf gestured at his men to come forward and carry the bodies away. For Byhrtnoth's part, he ordered Wulfstan and his companions to step back in favor of Eadric and the others.

Cleaning his sword, Aelfhere looked at the ealdorman. "You can't be thinking of accepting the jarl's thought."

"I am, in truth."

"Don't let your pride kill us all," snapped his old comrade. "Ofermode has oft slain many a worthy thegn."

"You think ofermode prompts me to allow them over?"

"Why else? Sure, these lads and I slew a score of theirs, but we had every advantage." He gestured to the fyrd lined up around them, eyes all turned their way. "Your fyrd are stout, it is no denying, but they are no match for the Danes."

"You may be right, but I don't know I have any other choice."

"What in God's name are you thinking?"

"You heard the jarl. They could as easily get into their ships and sail anywhere. They've already plundered Ipswich, but there are many other places they could raid. I've sworn to defend all of Essex and if I have too much pride, such great ofermode, it would be in keeping my sworn word to Aethelred, son of Edgar."

Aelfhere's eyes narrowed, and he looked back across the channel. The Danes had almost finished retrieving their dead.

Byhrtnoth put a hand on the older thegn's shoulder. "I have the Danes at hand. If I allow them over the causeway, then we'll have them penned in with the channel at their back. They'll *have* to fight through our lines. It will not be easy, but if our hearts are the bolder, then we may stand and have a chance to drive them off." He sighed. "I fear this host, if we don't stop it here, will come back time and again for our treasure. Nor will any gifts of gold and steel keep them from raiding as they please."

Aelfhere nodded. "For once you have paid the Danegeld..."

"Yes." Byrhtnoth straightened and looked about. "You take the left side."

"My place is in the front," protested Aelfhere.

"Your place *was* in the front. I would have all three of you, who held so strongly, lead the fyrd. They will be the braver for having seen your deeds, and even this respite is little enough for you after that slaughter."

Maccus joined them, arm now bandaged. He boasted, "I'm the bravest man here, but I'll admit my arms show some small signs of weariness."

Byhrtnoth laughed. "Then take the right." He gestured the two older warriors off, then leaned down to Wulfstan. "The center I give you, with but these instructions, for you well know all else you'll need."

"Yes, my lord?"

"First, send back to those we left to guard our horses. Tell them to join with the rest of your men. We'll need every spear we can muster, and I can walk back to my hall, if needed. If we live."

"And the other?"

He looked across the channel and spoke in a soft voice. "Keep your eyes on Godric and his brothers. We shall need our hearts to stay firm."

"My lord—" protested Wulfstan.

The ealdorman raised his hand. "There is no time for that. You know it as well as I."

After a long moment, the young thegn muttered, "As you command. What if they don't follow my orders?"

"The men around you all saw your deeds on the causeway. If you *lead*, all will follow."

"Except perhaps Godric."

"Yes." Byhrtnoth slipped a ring off his arm. "And if any ask, you may show them this ring of gold. You have my favor, and my thanks."

"Thank you, lord."

Byrhtnoth nodded, then yelled across the channel. "Olaf, son of Tryggvi! I grant you passage. Come quickly. I've got good English beer at my camp and fighting is dry, thirsty work."

Olaf laughed, glancing at Byrhtnoth's dispositions. "You are brave."

"God will preserve us."

"And Woden will preserve us. Perhaps today we'll find out whose god is mightier."

"When the sun sets, all will know what God alone knows now."

Olaf turned and gestured. The Danes crossed the causeway, initially with suspicion, then with confidence. They settled into a line of approximately six hundred abreast, five or six deep. The front ranks with shields and glittering swords, those behind with bright axes, and the rear ranks with spears. The line bristled with steel, lust for battle, and the promise of victory.

Ravens, hunger whetted from the fight at the causeway's edge, circled above them all.

Byrhtnoth stepped forward in the hundred paces or so that separated the lines. "Blessed be the Lord my God, who teacheth my hands to fight, and my fingers to war! For Essex and Aethelred!"

"For Essex and the king!" shouted the fyrd.

Olaf, in his sardonic way, commanded his line to advance.

Byrhtnoth shouted, "Stand firm, lads! Let them come to us." He and his thegns slid back behind the center group of men. "Wulfstan, keep them in the line and working together. They've got more armor than we do, so we have to keep the Danes as far away as possible."

Wulfstan nodded and stepped into the middle of the ranks. "Kill them as they come! They'll keep coming, climbing their dead, and then we kill more as they stumble!"

The fyrd around him raised a yell. Wulfstan noticed some of the fear in their eyes went away when they remembered his deeds from but an hour before. He glanced at Byrhtnoth, waiting stolidly to advance with his best warriors at just the right time. Wulfstan's heart soared. He yelled at Olaf, "Come, Northman! Your doom awaits!"

The jarl laughed.

Other Northmen, some fifty or sixty paces away, answered with their own war cries, but the slow, steady pace of the oncoming advance did not change. Stupid warriors charged from fifty paces.

*Pity they're not stupid*, thought Wulfstan. He paced back and forth amidst his men. "Shields! Keep yourselves locked together. Step into them at my call. That'll toss them off their feet and you can gut them on the ground!"

The shieldmen, all experienced warriors or they would have borne spears with the fyrd, nodded. His words were obvious, basic, but Wulfstan could almost hear them all say, *"Lad's young, but he knows what he's about."* They became perfectly still. Poised.

Behind him, he heard Byrhtnoth command, "Aelfnoth! Wulfmaer! Get your bowmen ready!"

The Danes were now about twenty paces away.

"Bowmen, loose!"

Above Wulfstan came a flight of arrows wobbling in the wind. The Northmen lifted their shields and scornfully blocked the meager volley. They sent their own volley. A few fyrdmen along the English side yelled in pain, but none of the shieldmen.

Fifteen paces.

Another flight of arrows from each side, with much the same result.

At ten paces, the Danes charged with a loud yell.

The fyrd around Wulfstan took a half-step back in fear, but he shouted, "Stand firm!"

For a moment, he thought the command failed, but the spearmen stepped forward just in time to support their front line.

The lines crunched together.

Shields crashed.

Swords flashed.

Flights of arrows landed among both sides.

Screams of men and metal followed.

Sprays of mud and blood came in their turn.

Ravens and Valkyries wheeled above, eyeing their harvests.

The press crushed all the warriors together. Some died simply because they couldn't move. They would go to the next world with a memory of steel approaching while they could do nothing. The press held up many who could not stand, but dead or dying, could not yet fall to the ground.

Fortunately, in the rush, Wulfstan had managed to get his shield above his head before the press would have prevented it. "Stand firm," he yelled. He struggled to get his sword above his head, as well. "English! Stand firm!" he repeated. He could strike no other blow. He finally succeeded in raising his sword just in time to block an axe from smashing into the fyrdman next to him.

Something slammed into the block of men. Warriors, English and Dane both, swayed, less in control of this sea of flesh and steel than they had been of the tide. The wave knocked some off their feet. A few of those managed to fall under their shield. After the battle, a dozen or so would manage to dig themselves out of the pile.

The rest simply died, trampled underfoot.

Wulfstan stepped on something too soft to be grass. *There's a farmer whose sowing days are done.* He almost giggled, the moment indescribably funny, but he pushed off the flesh beneath to gain an extra hand's breadth of height. That height allowed him to strike at an axe haft.

His first blow earned little but a Danish curse and an attempt to pull the axe back. The press prevented that attempt and Wulfstan swung again, this time sending splinters flying. A third time and the shaft cracked.

The Northman dropped the axe. For a moment, it sat on various shoulders, floating, then sinking beneath the surface.

An arrow thumped into Wulfstan's shield. A spear bounced off, careening past him. Warriors near him, on either side, were not so lucky. He could see more arrows rising in the distance. He managed to twist, getting his shield into a better position to ward their steel points. Crashing thumps rewarded his twist, but holding shield and sword above the fray was not without problems. The press and flow wrenched his shoulders back and forth. His muscles, not completely recovered from the fight at the causeway, made their protests known past the fear, mud, and noise.

He pushed the protests down and focused on the front line, now only two ranks away.

"Stand firm!" he yelled again.

Suddenly, the crunch of battle spat Wulfstan out of the press. In front of him a Dane, tossed out of the press in similar fashion, raised his shield and charged. Wulfstan met the charge with his own shield.

Linden wood smashed into linden wood and the two men pushed for any advantage. The Dane stabbed under their shields. Wulfstan rolled to his left and slashed at the Northman's leg, but the Dane blocked it. The pair exchanged blows crashing on each other's shield, moving around the battle as if they were the only ones on the field. The Northman got his feet under him and with a bellow of rage, pushed Wulfstan back a few paces. The Dane charged again. This time, Wulfstan did not meet him squarely but instead stepped to his left, pushing the Dane stumbling past to sprawl on the mud.

Another Dane charged Wulfstan before he could pounce on the first one. This time, the thegn stepped to the right. He smashed his pommel into the Northman's nose, splattering both with blood and knocking him back. Wulfstan followed the punch with his blade into the warrior's throat.

For a moment, no one was within five paces, and he bent forward to catch his breath. He straightened to see Godric and his brothers in line with a group of fyrdmen. Bodies, English and Dane, ringed them.

*They didn't run immediately.*

But the look in their eyes told Wulfstan their courage would not hold, especially since a line of Northmen, shields locked together, stepped toward them. The second rank of the Danes raised their axes and bellowed a war cry as they advanced.

Godric and his brothers wavered.

Wulfstan charged into the flank of the Danish line, knocking several into a pile and stumbling on top of them.

Fortunately, several of the fyrdmen stepped around Godric. They bloodied their spear on axe wielders suddenly without their shieldwall.

Godric and the two other sons of Odda simply watched, amazed.

And, in so doing, allowed Wulfstan to push himself up, stabbing blindly beneath him. An axe slashed toward his helm. He blocked it, but the blow sent him stumbling.

Again, Wyrd favored him. His stumbling brought him next to Godric and his brothers. They had their shields raised, but their eyes remained wide and terrified.

"Fyrd of Essex. Get back into your line!" Wulfstan then hissed at Godric, "Raise your shields, or I shall name you nithing and the scops will sing of your cowardice until the world ends."

Godric hesitated, eyes flicking to his brothers.

"You fight, or I will kill Odda's sons first," continued Wulfstan.

The three brothers flinched, but raised their shields. Wulfstan looked at the fyrd around him, who generally hid grins as they moved into place. He then locked his shield with the others, and they advanced into the swirling mass of steel and blood.

A few Danes, startled to see a unit in good order marching at them, backed away in search of allies.

Behind them, not ten paces away, Byrhtnoth and his thegns stood, heavily beset.

"To the ealdorman! To Byrhtnoth!" yelled Wulfstan. His line advanced, but a group of Northmen appeared out of the melee. They smashed their shields into his line, blades slithering past the iron-shod linden.

Wulfstan pushed back, struggling to keep his feet.

One of the fyrdmen supported him and Odda's sons by holding his spear in both hands along their backs, his breath coming out in harsh grunts as he pushed with all his strength. Other fyrdmen slipped their spear tips at any opening they could see.

Danish spearmen returned the favor, stabbing past their front line.

Wulfstan chopped at a spear tip aimed at his face. The Danish shieldman in front of him stuck his leg out in his effort to push through the line. Wulfstan slashed down, turning the Dane's madder-dyed pants more crimson than before.

The shieldman fell to his knee, and suddenly Wulfstan could see his face. He thrust his blade through the Dane's eye and then stepped over him to attack the second line. Inside the preferred range of their axes and spears, the blood of two more Danes reddened his steel.

The Danish line collapsed. Suddenly, Godric and his brothers had openings. They desperately slashed, driving the Northmen in front of them down. Spear tips in eyes and cheeks finished them off.

Wulfstan tried to command them to reform, but his voice caught in his suddenly desert-dry throat. After a moment, he croaked, "Back into a line."

The fyrd, also trying to recover, started to move with limbs clearly leaden. Godric shook his head, mouth open.

"Get into a line!" Wulfstan repeated with a snarl.

Odda's sons, exhausted and terrified, hesitated.

Before Wulfstan could do or say anything, a fyrdman tapped Godric's shoulder with his bloodied spear. "You heard the lad."

While they arranged themselves, Wulfstan looked for the ealdorman. He didn't see him, but then he heard his voice rising over the fray. He advanced his group around another cluster. On the other side, Byrhtnoth stood surrounded by a line of bodies. "Come, my friends! My blade still thirsts!" he yelled.

But his fight had not been completely one-sided. Blood flowed from wounds on Byrhtnoth's arms and a spearpoint had ripped along his cheek. Wulfstan also saw many friends with whom he'd never again share a meadbench in this world.

Yet he didn't stand alone. Eadric and other thegns remained at his side, despite their own wounds. More Danes pressed in. Axes flashed around the ealdorman.

Eadric stepped forward to keep them away from Byrhtnoth, but there were too many. One he warded with his shield, but the blow pushed his shield out of the way and the next blow crashed into his helm. As he fell, Eadric desperately tried to block yet another blow with what strength remained.

It wasn't enough. His blade hit the axe, but without enough power to stop it. However, the head of the axe twisted and instead of chopping through Byrhtnoth's boar-crested helm, the flat of the axe slammed into the ealdorman.

Byrhtnoth fell. The other thegns stepped over him as the Danes pushed to finish him off.

His height and flowing white hair had always proven useful in battles. He had been able to rally his warriors many times, simply by being there. Today, his easily recognizable presence meant many of the English saw him fall, despite all their prayers and blood.

"The ealdorman is down!" yelled one of Godric's brothers. Fear and panic drove him to swing wildly at all around him. Two Danes fell, but so did a fyrdman behind him. The other brother was no better, and he spilled more of both English and Danish blood onto the trampled mud.

Godric echoed the cry, "The ealdorman is down!" He, too, slashed about and warriors of both sides scattered away. He suddenly realized he had a chance to flee.

Wulfstan saw the wild look in the son of Odda's eyes. He stepped forward, punching out with his shield. Godric chopped into it. For a moment, Godric's blade stuck in the wood. Wulfstan's sword, almost before either thegn realized, chopped down, slamming into the mail just above Godric's knee.

The thegn cried and fell to his other knee.

His brothers turned their desperate focus on Wulfstan. They struck wildly with their swords.

Wulfstan released his shield and spun away from their blows. He slashed down through the neck and shoulder of one and crunched his blade into the other's helm. The last of Odda's sons fell, but whether dead or simply unconscious, Wulfstan never knew.

He looked down at Godric, sword raised.

"No!" Godric pushed himself to his feet, eyes wide in terror. Wulfstan's sword came down, but to each's surprise, Godric blocked it with his own. "No," he cried again.

"Then follow me to Byrhtnoth!" snarled Wulfstan.

Godric, eyes closed, nodded.

Wulfstan leaned in and hissed, "I'll give you leave to rest when Byrhtnoth is rescued or avenged, not before!"

The terrified thegn didn't do anything.

"Understand?" demanded Wulfstan.

Godric whispered, "Yes, Wulfstan."

"Then make ready." Wulfstan looked about and yelled at all the English in sight. "We go to Byrhtnoth," he declared. "We'll save him or leave our bodies atop his."

A ragged cheer rose, and the English formed up again, this time with Godric at the point. The fyrd followed the limping thegn and they advanced on the cluster around the ealdorman. The slow pace allowed the English line to not only stay together, but also tighten up. By the time they reached Byrhtnoth, they were as strong a line of shields and spears as ever faced the Danes.

But they also took time, time which the thegns of Byrhtnoth did not have.

Aelfwine had often boasted of his lineage in meadhalls. Many he slew with his spear on that day, but an axe ended his line.

Offa shoved his stern sword into that Dane and rushed into three others. He slew one, wounded another, and then fell as his namesake would have wished, blade to blade with the third.

Dunnere, who had chosen to stay at his farm instead of accepting Byhrtnoth's rings as a thegn, did not flinch. His spear spilled the blood of many Northmen until two northern axes rent him apart.

Above them all was Eadweard, taller even than Byrhtnoth. He broke through an advancing wall of shields. His sword flashed, but in the end the Danes surrounded and overwhelmed him.

Wulfstan cried at each death. Tears ran down his face. He opened his mouth to order the charge, but...

*No! We must get there in good order!*

So he kept pace with Godric.

Step.

Step.

And then it was time. Wulfstan charged into the Danes. Since he had no shield of his own, he simply rammed his shoulder into the middle of one of the Danish shields. He stabbed into the nose of the Northman to his right, then spun around, his back to the shield.

The eyes of the Dane suddenly next to him widened, but Wulfstan slashed across his neck.

Then the spears of the fyrd were there.

And, to Wulfstan's surprise, so was the sword of Godric. The hobbled thegn had taken advantage of the hole created by Wulfstan. With the help of the spearmen, they pressed past the line of Danish shields into the axes and spears behind.

Wulfstan fed many more ravens, as did Godric and all of the fyrd. They pushed past the Danish line and there was Byrhtnoth.

*He lives!*

The ealdorman, clearly dazed, kept trying to rise, but the press around him prevented it. Just as clearly, only the shelter of his few remaining thegns prevented the Northmen from finishing him off.

Wulfstan watched in dismay as three Danish spearmen struck at once and Leofsunu fell, his battered shield rolling away. Into the opening jumped a Dane, who slew the brothers Oswald and Eadwold with his axe. Byrhtwold, their father, avenged his sons. The axeman's head flew away.

But three more followed, axes raised high. Wulfstan rushed them, but before he could reach them, their axes felled the father upon the bodies of his sons. In his rage, Wulfstan slew not only Byrhtwold's killer, but also the other two Northmen.

Byrhtnoth tried to rise, but a new rush pushed Wulfstan back into him, knocking the ealdorman down again.

Wulfstan's blade flashed above them all, sending blood spraying about as he fed raven after raven. However, a Northman's ribs held Wulfstan's sword for just a moment. Not long, but enough to give a Danish spearman his chance. His spear slithered through the fray. Wulfstan never saw the spearpoint before it entered his side.

But Godric did, to his horror and shame.

Then the spearman stepped over Wulfstan's body and aimed at Byrhtnoth, now clear of defenders.

Godric did not hesitate.

He forgot the pain in his knee.

Moved faster than at any point in his life.

And for the first time in his life, Godric, son of Odda, charged into the fray. He gutted the spearman, slew another behind him, and then another. He dropped his shield to push bodies, shield, and broken weapons off his ealdorman.

A shadow loomed over him. Another Dane, axe raised high, stood above. He struck down and Godric raised his hands desperately.

But the fyrd had followed. A spear struck the Dane's byrnie. It did not penetrate, but it caused his blow to fall awkwardly. Instead of chopping through hands, arms, and helm, the back of the axe merely crunched onto Godric's raised hands.

Byrhtnoth, from a knee, stabbed the Dane. He pushed off Godric's shoulder and rose.

On that cloudy day, all could see his swan-white hair.

As if with one voice, all on the field, English and Dane both, cried, "He lives! Byrhtnoth lives!"

Soon after, a horn blew. The battle halted and everyone looked over. Olaf stood amidst a pile of English dead.

With a small, twisted smile, he yelled over to Byrhtnoth, "I think, perhaps, your god is mightier."

"I think He is." Byrhtnoth looked at the slaughter and the ravens already swooping down. "But there are many here that are dear to me. I would not mind if your god took them to his meadhall for a time that they can boast of their glories."

"The Valkyries bear their souls away as we speak." Olaf looked around. "Where is the one who held the center of the causeway?"

Godric knelt and cradled Wulfstan's body. "He lies here, Northman."

"I hope Woden keeps him until I get there myself. He was a good man."

The thegn nodded, washing Wulfstan's face with his tears. He ignored everything around him until Byrhtnoth came to him.

The ealdorman held out a gold ring. "Godric, your bravery has earned this."

"Mine?" Godric snorted. "I'm the least of men. Nithing, I am. The scops should write of how we forgot the oaths made on golden rings. We would have fled. Would have taken the best horses and run. Wulfstan stopped us."

"If you had fled, many of the fyrd would have followed." Byrhtnoth looked about. "And if that had happened, who knows when England could have stopped Olaf and those who followed him?"

"I know. I cared not."

Byrhtnoth sighed, running his hand over his face. "Stay here with Wulfstan. My head hurts and there is much to do."

"My sword is there." Godric nodded his chin at the blade. "Give it to someone worthy."

"You didn't flee."

"Only because of Wulfstan who would not lie dead in my arms but for my shame," Godric snarled. "And the same for the other brothers I betrayed who lie here."

Byrhtnoth said nothing more, but he picked up Godric's sword and left.

———

The sun flowed through the scriptorium now, filling it with heaven's golden light.

The scribe placed the quill down and looked at the parchment with satisfaction. His letters ran in even rows, all well-formed, and he had not needed to scratch any away to fix a mistake.

He bowed his head again. *Thank you, Mary.* His eyes focused on his fingers, which he suddenly realized ached so much he couldn't open his hands.

A familiar voice spoke in his ear. "The battle is over. You have my leave to rest."

Startled, he looked about, but there was no one in the room but his assistant. "Do you need something, brother?" he asked.

"Oh, uh—" The archivist shook his head. "I just thought I heard something. No one came in just now, did they?"

A puzzled look crossed his assistant's face. "No, brother."

"Strange. I could have sworn I heard something." His face cleared.

"But there is something you could do. Would you please go to the abbot and ask him to join us?"

"Is something wrong?"

"No, lad, but I think he needs to be here."

"As you wish." The assistant placed his quill on his blotter and left.

The archivist stared out the window and watched leaves fall off trees in the breeze, ending their lives in glorious color.

Abbot Siward walked in. "The brother said you wished to see me?"

"I did." The archivist gestured at the codex before him.

The abbot read, "CMXCI. In this year Ipswich was plundered and Siric, Bishop of Canterbury, and Aelfeah of Winchester first suggested to pay tribute to the Danish men because of the great destruction they caused on the seacoasts. And in that year, Olaf came to Maldon with XCIII ships and there the ealdorman Byrhtnoth came against him with his force; and many men were slain and drowned there on both sides. And there Eadric and Eadweard the Tall was slain and many other thegns loved by the ealdorman. Most dear to Byrhtnoth was Wulfstan, who fell defending his lord. And many ships of the Danes were captured, such that it would be years before they came again."

Siward placed a hand on the archivist's shoulders. "I am glad God chose you to copy our chronicle. It will be a glory to the abbey for many years."

"Thank you, my lord abbot." The scribe gestured at his assistant. "But it will be up to him to continue the work. I beg to be released of this burden. I am no longer capable of doing it properly."

"You have done this task since I was appointed abbot nearly eighteen years ago. Abbot Aethelwine told me you had done the same throughout his time, as well." Siward smiled. "God is well pleased with you."

The archivist stared at his hands. Tears returned, dropping onto fingers that would never untwist again.

The abbot spoke again, but this time the archivist heard a different voice—the same voice from a few moments ago. The same voice that saved him.

Wulfstan's voice.

*"Godric, ego te absolvo."*

———

## HISTORICAL NOTE

On 11 August 991, 93 ships filled with northern warriors decisively defeated the English in the real Battle of Maldon. It's possible the English slew enough Northmen they could hardly crew their ships, but no matter how many they killed, it was not enough. After the battle, Archbishop Siric and others suggested to Aethelred II Unraed to offer the Northmen ten thousand pounds to leave England alone. The king paid and the Northmen left. As Kipling would lament, though, they returned the year after with those same 93 ships. And the years following.

However, it's easy to understand why the English and others kept paying the Danegeld. The strategic mobility provided by those ships allowed them to attack where the defenses were weakest time and again. Rarely could the defenders bring any significant force to bear. The extant copies of the Anglo-Saxon Chronicle all vary slightly, but they all detail the harm this fleet brought to England for many years to follow after Maldon. The entry at the end of the story, by the way, is a cobbling together of a number of entries from the Chronicles modified to suit my purposes.

A remnant of a poem, *The Battle of Maldon*, provides our best description of the battle. I have adhered as much as possible to the poem with one major change and one significant explanation.

The explanation is a defense of Byrhtnoth. As described in the poem, Wulfstan, Maccus, and Aelfhere hold the causeway so fiercely, the Northmen ask the English to permit them to cross. Then the poem says Byrhtnoth allows this because of his "ofermode." This word is a challenging one for scholars, as it only occurs this time in extent Old English documents, but the general accepted meaning is, essentially, "over-proud." In other words, Byrhtnoth allows the Northmen to cross because of his arrogance.

While that interpretation matches the tone of the poem, some scholars have pointed out the strategic opportunity allowing the Northmen to cross provided to Byrhtnoth. J.R.R. Tolkien actually discusses the ethics of Byrhtnoth's choice in his alliterative poem *The Homecoming of Beorhtnoth Beorhthelm's Son*. It will come as no surprise that scholars continue to debate both Byrhtnoth's ethics and Tolkien's discussion.

In some ways, though, it's irrelevant why Byrhtnoth made his decision. I prefer the smart theory over the arrogant one for two reasons. The poem describes Byrhtnoth's thegns dying much as I've described them, fighting even though their lord had fallen and the battle was already lost because that's what good, honorable men did. I like the idea of Byrhtnoth being worthy of their loyalty. More importantly to the outcome of the battle, had Byrhtnoth allowed the Northmen to cross out of arrogance, I can't imagine the English would have been as eager to fight.

And that did matter. It is the cracking of their morale that probably decides the battle. In the poem, Godric and his brothers fled after Byrhtnoth fell. Godric actually rode away on Byrhtnoth's horse. Many Englishmen, seeing what they thought was their ealdorman running away, followed on Godric's heels. Obviously, my major change forces Godric to stay, and therefore all the English stand firm. The slaughter, which was already great, would thus be all the worse.

This outcome might mean the Northmen would have to leave a major portion of their ships. In that case, Aethelred would have faced a weaker fleet in years to come and he might have succeeded in creating a useful English navy using those ships as its core. He certainly tried to create such a navy, but it was never more than a nuisance to the Northmen. In fact, the Chronicle says his navy did more harm than good.

Aethelred is remembered as an ineffectual king who listened too much to bad advice (*Unraed* does not mean "unready," but instead "ill-advised"). However, given the strategic challenges facing him, it is difficult to imagine he could do much more than he did. That's a much larger discussion, though.

I'll freely admit that even with a significant victory at Maldon, the English would have still struggled to keep the Northmen at bay. However, it's a possibility, especially since Olaf Tryggvason converts to Christianity in the two or three years following the battle. I wanted my change to the outcome of the battle to matter, after all.

Finally, it's a shame that all we have is a fragment of the poem. It's powerful, evocative, and worthy of heroes. If I can hope this story will do anything, it's that it encourages you to read the poem someday, if you haven't already done so. The deeds done that day should never be forgotten in the halls of men.

# ABOUT ROB HOWELL

Rob is the publisher of New Mythology Press, creator of the Firehall Sagas, a writer and editor in Luke Gygax's World of Okkorim, a reformed medieval academic, and a retired soda jerk.

Without books, it's unlikely he or his parents would have both survived.

Find him here:

- Website: robhowell.org
- His Blog: robhowell.org/blog.
- Firehall Sagas: firehallsagas.com
- Amazon: amazon.com/-/e/B00X95LBB0
- Twitter: @Rhodri2112
- Rob's Riddles: patreon.com/rhodri2112

# SHOT HEARD ROUND THE WORLD

## Kevin J. Anderson and Kevin Ikenberry

*DUSK*
*5 DECEMBER 1812*
*NEAR SMORGON, RUSSIA*

Antoine de Montagne nestled his chin against his chest, somewhat into the fold of his officer's coat as the march stopped for the fourth time in the last hour. With his eyes closed, the din of the retreat faded to a soft roar as his desire for warmth and rest overtook his senses. A tight hand grabbed his right arm and jerked him upright.

"Captain de Montagne." The voice was low and firm. "You would do well to keep your bearing."

Montagne blinked and stared into the face of General Caulaincourt, Napoleon's second-in-command. The man's face contained a tight smile, but his eyes were chips of dull ice. "My apologies, sir."

"Sleep will come for us, Captain, but not quite yet. We have a mission to undertake," Caulaincourt said. He leaned closer. "The Emperor wishes to depart for Paris immediately; within the hour. I have arranged the Imperial Guard Horse Chasseurs to meet us at the front of the retreat. He will move along the line via sleigh and then east to Ashmiany. As a translator, you will accompany us."

Montagne brightened and felt ashamed for it. There would be warmth and sleep yet. A sleigh would speed him home, and his service could end in dignity rather than mired in the mud with dysentery or some other disease ravaging his body. In his joy, a concerned question formed. "Why not Colonel de Fleur?"

Caulaincourt flashed a thin, vindictive smile. "The Emperor is disappointed with the Russian response to his demands for surrender, and so he wishes his Translator General to suffer a bit for his failures. As you are the only other officer fluent in the Slavic and German dialects he could encounter for the first part of the journey home, he has chosen you to translate for him."

Montagne flushed with pride. "I understand, General. I shall do my best."

"I know you will, Captain de Montagne," Caulaincourt replied. "I will rejoin the Chasseurs, select a guard force for our journey, and will accompany the Emperor, as well. You wait here and join the Emperor's sleigh. Leave your horse with one of the lieutenants."

"Yes, sir," Montagne said. "I will collect my things and be ready."

Caulaincourt nodded and turned his eyes to the ragged march. "Tell no one of his plan. The *Grand Armeé* will learn tomorrow."

Montagne squinted. "Sir? The rumor is a *coup d'etat* took place in Paris. They say General de Malet has aspirations for the throne? Is it true, sir?"

Caulaincourt's thin smile broadened slightly. "Nothing travels faster amongst an army than rumor, Antoine. There is business the Emperor alone must attend to, and that is all you need to know. Our very government is at stake. Be ready to leave when the Emperor arrives. He will want to move quickly. There is peril at every turn."

*So it is true.* Montagne couldn't help but smile at the general's casual use of his first name. *And I must ride with a surly Emperor all the way to Paris.*

"Will you assume command here, sir?"

"No." A quiet storm passed over the general's face. "General Mamet will take command. I shall accompany you in the sleigh once the Chasseurs are briefed and prepared to undertake the escort mission."

Montagne said nothing. There wasn't a proper reply to the general's words any captain could utter. "I shall be ready, sir."

Caulaincourt nudged his horse and moved down the line to the east. Montagne saw him speak with several other officers as he moved forward. Caulaincourt exemplified leadership, and Montagne would have followed him anywhere. For a moment, he wondered if any of the officers whom Caulaincourt spoke to knew of Emperor Napoleon's journey home. A freshening breeze pushed cold air past his tight collar and down under his wool coat, making him shiver. Montagne's saddlebags and bedroll sat astride his horse; he would need nothing else for the journey.

Chin tucked into his collar again, he began to realize that departing with the Emperor might indeed get him home soon, perhaps even in time for Christmas. What a present that would be! Faint cheers filtered forward from the rear of the formation, and there could be no other explanation than the Emperor passing his troops in review.

Montagne patted the horse's neck and prepared to dismount. The closeness of the cheers caught his attention and he turned. The small sleigh carrying Emperor Napoleon approached and slowed to greet him as the sporadic musket-fire from the near-constantly harassing Cossacks erupted toward the rear of the march.

Montagne dismounted, collected his bags, and passed the reins to a young, shivering lieutenant before turning toward the Emperor. The twin black horses of the Emperor's team pulled a rickety wooden sleigh devoid of any of the rich trappings the great man often enjoyed during travel. The driver sat on a pedestal behind the passenger compartment under the light of a single lantern. *Necessity versus comfort.* The front rails of the sleigh came up to Montagne's chest. Above the withers of the two horses was a crook used to hold a bell. It sat curiously empty as he stepped behind the horses toward the passenger compartment.

Montagne saluted crisply and held the pose until Emperor Napoleon glanced at him and gave a half-hearted salute out of annoyance. Montagne felt his legs perceptibly shake. He'd never been in the presence of the Emperor, having only seen the great general and leader from a distance during the marches. His face was calm, almost idyllic, in the midst of the chaotic movement home. Even as the musket-fire from the French infantry roared through the approaching night, the Emperor seemed completely at ease. At his left shoulder sat another captain, wearing the shoulder brocade of a personal aide-de-camp.

Montagne boarded the sleigh and sat in a small, curved portion of the sleigh barely deep enough, or wide enough, for him. Facing the rear, he stared into the faces of Emperor Napoleon, his aide, and the driver perched above them on an elevated seat.

The aide nodded a cool welcome. "You are the translator, yes? Captain de Montagne?"

"That's correct."

Napoleon's eyes flashed to him. "You are fluent in the languages of these heathens?"

"I am, sir," Montagne swallowed. "Russian, German, and several of the Slavic dialects."

The Emperor squinted at him, and there was distrust in his voice. "How did you come to this ability?"

"My parents traveled extensively in this region, sir," Montagne replied. "My father is a professor at *École Polytechnique*. He teaches history."

Napoleon harrumphed loudly. "Perhaps I should have had you craft the surrender of Czar Nicholas. A fluent son of a historian might have done a better job. Nicholas might have capitulated instead of refusing to fight."

Montagne met the Emperor's eye, but said nothing in reply, as discretion required. Truth be told, the region surrounding them had never truly been peaceful and likely never would.

A violent flurry of rifle-fire erupted somewhere behind them—sporadic, harassing fire of the Cossacks. The brief attack ended after two methodical volleys from whichever company honored the threat and ended it, as they always did. The harassers vanished into the night.

"Damned Cossacks," Napoleon said. His face screwed up in disgust. "Men without honor never stand and fight."

"Shall I send a messenger, sir?" the aide-de-camp asked.

Napoleon shook his head. "They will fire and flee. Let them go."

With the crack of the driver's whip, the sleigh lurched forward.

The route of march for the *Grand Armeé* wound through deep forests along paths barely wide enough for the army to pass in their standard formation. As such, the Emperor and his commanders directed the artillery to move forward and set the pace, which, in the deepening snow, seemed fittingly glacial. Still, the troops cheered their Emperor, and he seemed to relish seeing them all again before leaving them in the midst of the brutal Russian winter.

There was no conversation that included Montagne. The aide and Napoleon communicated quietly, reviewing notes and dispatches. The younger captain's black hair came to a point between his eyes, and his sullen face bothered Montagne for a reason he couldn't quite identify. Every time the aide's eyes flashed to meet his own, the distrust became palpable.

Montagne turned his thoughts to his birth home in the south of France. There were no vicious winters there. He couldn't remember ever seeing his breath in the cold until they'd moved to Paris for his father to join the faculty of *École Polytechnique*. They'd spent two months of every year at their summer home in the hills above Nice. He hadn't visited there for four years or more, and the sudden longing for the warm sun and beautiful beaches on the nearby coasts threatened to bring tears to his eyes.

His reverie ended with the sudden stop of the sleigh. He rocked backward, slamming his shoulder blades into the curved railing. Napoleon and his aide pitched forward in their seats. The look on the Emperor's face changed from annoyance to rage. He stood abruptly, casting aside the blanket of furs from across his lap.

Montagne saw the Emperor's eyes flash across the formation and lock onto the nearest officers he could see.

"You! Get your men and push this sleigh. Now!"

A horde of soldiers splashed through the mud and leaned against the sleigh. Montagne stood from his seat, ready to jump out and assist them, but Napoleon barked, "Sit down!" and he sat like a scolded child.

Eventually, with numerous men grunting and pushing, the sleigh cleared the far side of the creek, but did not proceed further. The driver shouted at the soldiers, but to no avail.

Still standing, Napoleon took in the scene. He bellowed at the driver, "Move!"

The driver struggled with the reins. "Sir, we must halt the army. We cannot pass here because of the aid station. The trail is too narrow."

Napoleon surveyed their surroundings and pointed at a sparsely wooded area across the muddy stream, where fresh stumps poked through the snow. "There! Take us up that hill and we will go around."

Montagne recognized this place from their march months before. The *Grand Armeé*'s supply trains had cleared paths through the forest as they moved and sometimes paralleled the route of march. In this case, they had cut a wagon-width trail through the narrow growth of birch trees to get the supply trains to this particular ford. If memory served him correctly, there would be another cut area on the far side.

The aide turned to him in concern. "Sir, you will be away from the army. We do not know where the trail may lead."

Napoleon gave his aide a dismissive glance and looked at the driver again. "I know *precisely* where that trail leads. Go around the aid station."

The driver shouted commands to the marching army. They milled about and gradually parted to allow the sleigh through. A few soldiers stared at the sleigh with harsh glances while most gawked, wide-eyed, at their beloved leader standing in his sleigh and directing them as a conductor would an orchestra. The driver guided the sleigh into the hastily created path, through the creek bed, then successfully onto the other side.

As they climbed the small, sparsely forested hill on the narrow trail, Emperor Napoleon sat down and brought the blankets over himself again. He glanced at his aide. "Ensure the driver understands to find the first cut back to the *Grand Armeé*. We camped in this place on the march to Moscow, and I recall an access on the far side of the clearing where the wagons were able to move around the swollen creek during the summer. Now it is frozen mud. The damned thing slows me down again!"

His aide relayed the instructions to the driver and Napoleon looked across to Montagne. In the orange light of the solitary lantern above and behind them, his eyes were flinty. "General Caulaincourt informed you of my intent?"

"He did, sir."

Napoleon turned to stare forward. "I cannot fight a war in two places. Therefore, if the Russians do not wish to fight, they are not worth the efforts of our armies. In Paris, I will expunge my detractors, reconvene the government, and we will focus our affairs elsewhere. To hell with this place."

Montagne fought against asking the question on his tongue. With the advance of the *Grand Armeé*, most of Europe had fallen under French rule. Aside from Russia, which Emperor Napoleon had now apparently removed from his aspirations, his only other possible target for conquest would be England. Yet, the British were embroiled in an armed dispute with the American colonies, who were allies of the French. The Emperor said no more; instead, he closed his eyes and lowered his face into the protective warmth of his collar.

The weather changed and large flakes of snow fell in ethereal curtains. The fresh precipitation muted the sounds of the army behind them as they crested a small hill that led to a clearing. The driver turned to follow the treeline, stark white birches with naked branches. Montagne leaned over the side of the sleigh to peer into the darkness. With the nearest lantern hanging above him, Montagne could see only a few yards in front of the horses. Their steps faltered and slowed. As the crack of the driver's whip sounded, the horses reared and skidded to a halt in the snow, and Montagne saw a single bearded man dressed in heavy furs blocking their path. A Cossack.

He held a rifle in his hands.

———

*"Allez!"* the driver called to the man, and waved his whip as if to sweep the Cossack from the narrow path. Montagne spun in his seat to peer between the horses at the scene. The lone man did not move. He stood in a narrow space at the edge of a wider clearing. Two trees, barely far apart enough for the sleigh to pass, rose on either side of him.

Again, the driver called and actually cracked the whip over the horses. Unable to move, they whinnied and stamped their hooves only a few feet from the Cossack. Montagne glanced back to the Emperor, who sat with his eyes closed, as if trying to sleep. The aide looked up from his notes and met Montagne's eyes. After a moment, the aide slid the papers into a case and reached for a pistol tucked into the blankets at his feet. He nodded at Montagne. Taking his cue, Montagne stood in the sleigh and turned to face the Cossack.

"Move," he called to the man in Russian. The Cossack did not move, and he tried again in several dialects, including Latin and Greek. The fur-adorned man remained still, his rifle trained on the driver. He did not even look at Montagne, nor did he speak.

In the silence, Montagne heard approaching riders. The team of horses pulling the sleigh startled and quivered in the snow. A thunderous roar of voices screaming something unintelligible raced into the clearing from the right.

*More Cossacks!*

Montagne ducked down in the sleigh. The aide handed him a pistol and crouched, assuming a protective stance in front of the Emperor. Montagne did the same and watched the Cossacks charge out of the night, directly at them. They raised their voices in an unintelligible scream, and Montagne raised his pistol and trained it on the closest targets.

*Steady. Be steady.*

The twilight reflected off the low clouds, providing just enough light to see dozens of riders waving rifles as they rode down upon them. He whirled to his left, to the near side of the clearing at the thunderous sound of more horses approaching. Montagne saw the lone man no longer stood before the sleigh and realized what the Cossack had done.

*An ambush! Here is where we will die.*

The familiar shapes of the Imperial Guard Horse Chasseurs charged into the clearing and raced toward the galloping Cossacks. Several fired rifles from horseback, which were unlikely to hit anything. The Cossacks, however, returned the gesture both at the cavalry and at the sleigh. Rounds impacted the small sleigh near where he crouched, and Montagne dropped toward the floor next to the aide. Napoleon did not. The Emperor sat rigid in his seat, his eyes following the attack with a critical gaze.

The Chasseurs met the Cossack charge in the middle of the small clearing. Men on horseback joined in hand-to-hand combat. The guards, swords in hand, hacked and swung at the Cossacks, who defended themselves with their rifles and what appeared to be axes. Men fell from their horses. More rifle-fire filled the small clearing. Another surge of Cossacks charged into the fray, threatening to overwhelm the small detachment of cavalry; they were closer, and faster, than the first charge. The aide stood, centered his pistol and fired. One of the lead Cossacks tumbled into the snow.

Emboldened, Montagne rose from his crouch and aimed. With the barrel centered on the Cossack closest to them, he squeezed the trigger. In the burst of smoke from the barrel, Montagne expected to see a similar result, but the rider screamed and brandished an axe high above his head as he closed the distance to the sleigh.

Montagne ducked into the sleigh, and the aide handed another loaded pistol to him.

"Fire, Montagne! Keep firing!"

He took the weapon, resumed his firing position and felt a strange calm wash over him as he again centered the barrel on the target and fired. The rider tumbled into the snow not forty feet away. He felt the aide tap him on the leg with the other pistol, again loaded and ready to fire.

*So fast?*

Voices yelled from the forest to his right and snapped off his thought like a dry twig. A regiment of infantry ran up the snow-covered hill and took up firing positions at the edge of the treeline. The driver sat frozen, watching the battle before them. Napoleon's aide sat next to Montagne, his eyes on the dim battlefield.

A volley of rifle fire tore into the Cossacks. Montagne flinched at the closeness of it all, even as he raised a pistol and fired again. This time, the aide joined him. The Cossacks whirled as one and charged down on the exposed infantry, for the moment forgetting their target. A second volley was fired at almost point-blank range, and many Cossacks and their horses crashed into the snow, but not all of them. The maniacal attackers tore into the infantry. Riflemen came up with bayonets and stabbed at them, eventually knocking them from their horses, but not before there were more casualties.

The French Chasseurs circled and regrouped in the center of the clearing and charged toward the Cossacks fighting the exposed infantry. As if in a dream, the cavalry closed the distance at surreal speed. Every weapon was clearly visible, sword or rifle, as they brandished and fired. The Cossacks roared in defiance and whirled against the guards before turning back to the east and galloping for their lives. Some fired over their shoulders in a hopeful attempt to take down one of the guards, but they soon hunched forward on their mounts and ran.

———

"Driver!" Napoleon roared as he stood abruptly behind Montagne and the aide. "Move!"

Startled to action, the driver raised his reins and prepared to snap them across the backs of the team when a single rifle fired from darkness.

*BOOM!*

Montagne felt the rush of air as a musket ball rocketed through the air past them. He flinched, eyes closed, expecting to feel the impact. A heartbeat passed, then he opened his eyes and turned to the wide-eyed aide. The lone Cossack stepped out from behind a large tree, his musket barrel curling smoke into the night air. It dawned on Montagne that the weapon wasn't pointed at either himself or the aide. Nor had the Emperor been struck.

As one, they looked at the driver on the seat behind the sleigh. The top of the man's head was missing.

Montagne raised his pistol and pointed it at the Cossack as he stepped once more into the narrow path. The Cossack angrily slammed his musket into the snow. He simply stared at the sleigh for a long moment. Montagne hesitated to pull the trigger.

*He wishes to die.*

"Your army plundered our homes. They drank themselves into a stupor while they burned my family alive in my barn. Imagine losing everything to a people with whom you had no quarrel. You wanted a war, but leaders never feel the pain of the innocents who die at their hand. Now, you will understand the toll."

The hair on the back of Montagne's head stood erect as he translated. Napoleon's stern face sneered, and his teeth bared. "Get that fucking peasant out of my way! Kill him now!" Napoleon screeched, pointing at the Cossack.

*BOOM!*

Montagne flinched as the sound seemed to come from extremely close behind them. Napoleon's face grew still, and he tucked his right hand inside his jacket in a characteristic gesture. Montagne saw the Emperor look down at his hand. He removed it from the jacket and Montagne saw bright red blood. Napoleon reached for the sleigh's curved railing with suddenly trembling hands.

Beyond the sleigh, a fur-clad shadow fled into the darkness. Montagne turned the pistol on the target, centered, and fired in one smooth movement. The figure fell forward into the snow.

*BOOM!*

The aide fired his pistol seemingly next to Montagne's ear. He whipped around to see the aide had executed the Cossack, and was now lowering the pistol. There was movement between them. The aide snatched at the Emperor's shoulder, but missed. Napoleon pitched forward against the railing of the sleigh and fell forward, tumbling face-first into the snow.

"Montagne! Help me!" the aide called as he leapt from the sleigh into the snow.

Montagne knelt in the snow next to the aide. The other captain cradled the Emperor's head across his legs and peered down into his still face. Montagne stared into sightless eyes for a long moment and turned his face up to see Caulaincourt shuffling toward them.

In that moment, words failed him. His ability to translate quickly and correctly vanished. Emotions overwrote his abilities. Mouth agape, he closed it and mentally shook himself to report.

"Sir, the Emperor is dead."

Caulaincourt removed his ornate headgear and placed it over his chest. The man's eyes closed in silent prayer. Montagne tried to pray, but could not as the company of infantry swarmed protectively around the sleigh. Several of them moved into the forest and retrieved the body of the Cossack he'd killed. As they laid the body next to the man, he saw the size difference and felt tears forming in his eyes.

*My God. The Emperor is dead and France is in disarray. I failed to protect him.*
*And I have killed a child.*

*What have I done?*

Montagne closed his own eyes and tucked his chin to his chest. He knew the others would assume his grief for their Emperor, and while some of it certainly was, he felt more for those displaced and affected by war. People whom armies and generals never considered.

Teeth clenched together, Montagne fought for control and when he had it, opened his eyes to find Caulaincourt staring at him. The general's eyes were somber, but focused. He knelt next to Napoleon's body and grasped the dead man's right hand affectionately.

They sat in silence for a moment, eyes on their fallen Emperor until the infantry returned and ringed them with quiet murmurs of shock and dismay. He found his voice. "What should we do, sir?"

Caulaincourt made eye contact with Napoleon's aide-de-camp first. "Load Emperor Napoleon's body into the sleigh. You will proceed to Ashmiany for new horses and provisions. I will meet you there and escort the Emperor's body personally. We will change the horses and proceed with all possible speed to Paris."

The general cleared his throat and spoke in a louder voice.

"Lieutenant Moreau? Summon the commanders to the front of the march immediately. I will meet them there. Have General Mamet report directly to me here. For the rest of you, I am giving you an order you will follow immediately and without fail. Speak not of what has happened here under penalty of death. The army, and the world, cannot know what has taken place until we decide to tell them. Do you understand?"

Amidst the murmurs and quiet assents, the aide replied in a loud, clear voice, "Yes, sir." He got to his feet and called for the infantry to assist him. Caulaincourt stood and motioned for the translator to step to the side.

"You did well, Montagne."

He took a breath and replied slowly. "I killed a child, sir."

Caulaincourt snorted. "That child killed your Emperor. His cowardly action has taken a great man from the field. Without him, France as we know it could crumble. Our enemies could pounce upon us and wipe us from the Earth in the coming days."

The enormity of what he'd seen finally cleared in Montagne's mind. The war in Spain would certainly falter, as would the actions of the French fleet. The loss of Napoleon could embolden the British to attempt an invasion of Europe. Given the state of the *Grand Armeé*, there would not be much of a fight. With discord rampant in Paris, and the Emperor dead in the Russian snow, what might happen to the very world around them stunned Montagne to silence.

"We must keep our thoughts present." The general took a deep breath and exhaled a cloud of steam into the frigid night. His normally calm, almost placid face, appeared more troubled than when on the march. "You are fluent in English, as well?"

The question momentarily stunned Montagne. "I am, sir."

Caulaincourt took a moment to assemble his thoughts. He turned to Montagne and pulled him farther from the crowd, his voice low.

Caulaincourt sighed and looked up into the darkness. "A war on two fronts did this. We pushed too far east. Our appetites were too large. Our enemies continue to wear us down from all sides and we cannot maintain constant warfare at sea and all across Europe forever. The toll is too great."

The usually calm, composed general seemed on the edge of either anguished weeping or incalculable rage. Caulaincourt closed his eyes for a couple of seconds. When he opened them, his composure had returned, combined with a sureness, a confidence Montagne hadn't seen before. The general's eyes were clear and bright in the near darkness as he turned back to face Montagne.

"You will escort the body to Ashmiany with me and then you will acquire horses and proceed to Calais with all possible speed."

"Calais?" Montagne blurted. Caulaincourt glared at him. "My apologies, sir."

Caulaincourt continued, "You will proceed to London on my personal orders and relay a message to their monarchy directly. I will compose it and you will personally deliver it to King George III, or his Prime Minister, in London. Is that clear?"

Montagne's mind whirled. Was Caulaincourt assuming command of the *Grand Armeé*, or the entire French government? Would he plead for peace? Would he capitulate to the powers that wished the *Grand Armeé* to return to their borders?

He nodded. "Yes, sir. I will proceed directly."

"Meet me at the head of the march in an hour's time, Montagne. Do not be late. The balance of our future depends on you."

———

They arrived at Ashmiany shortly before midnight. The French encampment there was small, as most of the logistical stores to feed the approaching army pushed to the east ahead of them. The tiny, war-torn village would be glad to see the French retreat. With the army only six hours away now, the tents and wagons would be loaded and gone within a day's time. None too soon for the displaced villagers cowering in their homes.

The aide disappeared to coordinate with those in charge regarding the logistics of the return. Montagne stood by the sleigh, stamping his feet against the cold for a moment before two soldiers arrived to guard the sleigh. Each of the men glanced at the wrapped bundle on the floor of the sleigh for a moment and then took up positions on either side of it, facing away. Satisfied, Montagne moved up a slight incline and found the paddock. A lone sergeant guarded the horses. As he approached, the man stood and saluted.

"I bear a message from General Caulaincourt and require two horses on his orders," Montagne said. For the first time, he was aware of both the placement of his sword and his officer's pistol under his coat, as well as the critical nature of his mission.

"Yes, sir," the attendant said, and disappeared into the makeshift shack to gather the saddle and tack.

"Where is the quartermaster?"

The sergeant pointed down the incline to the familiar wagon trains. Two privates, likely roused by the sergeant, appeared in the doorway. One was thin and gangly with a speckled complexion, the other portly with dark eyebrows and sullen eyes.

Montagne pointed at the gangly one. "Go to the quartermaster and draw ten days rations and water."

One private disappeared, and Montagne stared at the other one. "Fetch the horses. The fastest you have."

Suddenly alone outside the paddock, Montagne turned to gaze over the small village which the logistical forces of the *Grand Armeé* called home. Though the hour was late, the village buzzed with activity. Armed men ran from point to point, as if preparing a defense. From here, he would press on to Miedniki and then to Vilna. Each had a small French logistical garrison to support the needs of the army as it retreated toward France.

Another sergeant approached and saluted. "Sir, we are preparing for an attack. Local outposts have been harassed by the Cossacks since dusk. It is best you arm yourself and report to headquarters."

Montagne bristled. "I will do no such thing. I am under orders from General Caulaincourt in command of the *Grand Armeé*. As soon as I have a proper mount, I must depart. Prepare your defense, sergeant. My mission remains unchanged."

The man uttered *"Mon dieu"* before turning back toward the village and sprinting into the night.

As Montagne stood waiting for his horses, the cold suddenly seeped far inside his coat and shoes. He grew anxious to be off on his mission, and he looked into the paddock several times, until finally the sergeant appeared with his horses. Down the hill, the gangly private and two other figures moved toward him, each carrying a sizable load. They divided the load between the two horses, and when the mounts were ready, Montagne did not hesitate. He swung into the saddle on the black gelding and did not look back as he galloped off for Miedniki.

———

Two days west of Vilna, the forests gave way to large expanses of dormant grasslands. Under their intermittent blanket of snow, the fields showed the marks of couriers and small units of the French army along the route of march as they coordinated the retreat of the main effort.

Montagne followed the trail west as fast as his horses could go. Every couple of hours, he dismounted and led them through the fields and occasional stands of forest to rest them and get his own blood flowing. Fatigue tore at him from all sides. Stopping to sleep for any length of time seemed out of the question. Every time he'd come across an encampment, he'd been too awake and refreshed to feel compelled to stop. During the long night, he'd almost fallen from his saddle twice before finding a dilapidated barn. He'd lain down in the old, musty hay for an hour at most before guilt propelled him onto the horses and moving further west.

As he rode, paying attention to the horses and his pace, Montagne's mind tried to grasp the situation. Somewhere to the south, Caulaincourt and the body of the Emperor moved at high speed to Paris. He tapped the reassuring lump under his jacket of the general's note for the British monarchy and resisted, again, the temptation to read it even under the pretense of committing it to memory.

*No.* Montagne shook off the thought and lowered himself from the saddle to walk alongside the horses for a while. *The general trusted me to deliver his message. I must trust he knows what he is doing.*

He swung his right leg up and over the horse's back as the black gelding flinched backward. Montagne ducked and reversed the movement, reaching his leg toward the ground as the whistling hum of a near-miss shot through the space where he'd been a second before. The crash of a musket firing sounded through the strand of dormant trees he'd been about to enter. His heart racing, Montagne withdrew the pistol from under his coat and visually checked its readiness. Thankful for warhorses familiar with the sound of weapons that didn't spook easily, Montagne used them for cover and looked toward the sound of the shot. In an instant, he saw a silhouetted rider on a pale horse gallop west and away from him.

He stood frozen in the snow for half a minute, trying to calm both his racing breath and his frantic mind. Had he been followed? Why would someone shoot at him? As he crossed eastern Europe, every dark corner of forest and wide-open plain had kept his eyes darting back and forth except for this one. He'd failed to stay alert and it almost cost him his life. Montagne rubbed the several days growth of beard on his chin and closed his tired eyes. He leaned his forehead against the horse's hide as he fought against the fatigue threatening to undermine his ability to focus on the work.

*The Emperor is dead. The toll has been too great.*

*You must not fail.*

He heard Caulaincourt's voice in his head. The implications of the general's unread message weren't clear to the translator, but there were two possibilities, he surmised. Surrender to the British demands and an end to the war in Spain was certainly a possibility, though Caulaincourt's own feelings about the British matched the fallen Emperor's own, and that meant surrender was out of the question. If not surrender, then was the message one of peace? Cooperation? Something else?

His eyes snapped open. "I have to ride," he said to the wind. "For France, if not for me."

Survival instincts initiated, Montagne grabbed the lead for his horse and led the pair as fast as he could run into the protection of the strand of trees his attacker had vacated. In the dark, cold forest, Montagne stamped his feet and gazed for several minutes in all directions before climbing back astride his mount and pushing west once again.

Friendly way stations grew more numerous as he rode, and he traded horses several times in the ensuing days. Yet his own fatigue wore down on him, unlike anything he'd ever experienced in his service. The forests and hills of Germany slowly became the rolling terrain of eastern France. At Roubaix, he turned northwest and made for the coast. The grasslands were brown with winter. He thought again of the sun and warmth of the family lands above Nice and he longed to turn toward Paris and ride further south without looking back.

As he rode, Montagne wondered if Caulaincourt and the other leaders shared his fatigue, and not just with the war, but with the struggle and upheaval of his country. He'd been ripped from his chosen studies and placed into the armed service of his country by a man seemingly hellbent upon destruction at all costs. Emperor Napoleon would be equally celebrated and scorned for centuries to come. The suffering of so many would be forgotten.

*Perhaps it's time I leave this all behind. For good.*

The enormity of the thought struck him as the predawn twilight spread over the sprawling coastal plain of Calais. Fishing boats crowded the harbor, afraid to move into the channel and the constant swarming presence of the English fleet. Montagne believed it would be easy to find a patriotic fisherman to risk delivering him to the British.

At the last post, just as the sun rose to the east, Montagne surrendered his horses and sought out the quartermaster for rations and additional loads for his weapons, only to be directed toward a distant, quiet tent. As he approached, Montagne listened to the whisper of caution from his mind and drew his pistol before he stepped inside. A lone dark figure sat on a stool. He looked up and raised a pistol, pointing it at Montagne's chest. Montagne's own pistol was trained on the young man's smiling face. The two stood for a moment in awkward silence.

The Emperor's aide laughed and spoke in fluent English. "Captain Montagne, I'm afraid I must relieve you of that note. His Majesty will never receive it as long as I live."

Montagne smiled at the man's audacity. "Because of your loyalty to the Emperor?"

"No, my duty to the Crown." The aide stood and stepped closer. "I give you this chance, Montagne. Where is the message?"

"Go to hell," Montagne said, and pulled the trigger. He squeezed his eyes shut, expecting the report of the aide's pistol pointed at his chest. When it didn't come, Montagne opened his eyes and saw the aide lying on his side, vainly reaching for the pistol that had fallen from his grasp. Montagne stepped forward, kicked away the pistol, and knelt.

The aide coughed, and blood sprayed from his mouth. Still, the man sneered as he struggled to speak. "France will fall, Montagne."

"Perhaps," Montagne replied. "But not today."

———

Finding a boat to traverse the channel took considerable effort. Not many sailors were willing to entertain the certainty of intercept with the British navy even while traveling under a flag of truce. War made cowards of dishonorable men. Montagne, in his addled state, wandered through the docks. Morning should have been a busy time along the docks in the wide sure harbor, but the vessels remained in their moorings as if frozen. The few fishermen at their boats watched him with uneasy eyes. Most looked away when he acknowledged them with a nod and a hopeful smile. Others turned their backs on him.

When they did, he realized how much war had changed him. As a young officer, the idea of a Frenchman turning his back on the army, and a representative of the Emperor himself, would have angered him beyond the edge of reason. But the near-constant warfare had taken too much of a toll on the populace. He understood that toll for the first time in his life. His own commitment to the mission would have waned save for his respect for Caulaincourt and his own dreams of returning home to a land at peace.

An older man with a shock of white hair under a black knit cap merely squinted at Montagne's request. He nodded and pointed at the small, single-masted boat. Before Montagne could even settle himself in the small bow, they were under sail across the placid harbor. Montagne lay in the ship's tiny bow to sleep.

Near noon, a rough hand shook him awake. Montagne sat upright at the whistle of a single cannonball arcing over their heads into the ocean. Over the stern, where the rudder sat unmanned and amidships, a warship approached. Montagne struggled to stand. He waved his arms.

"Sit down," the old man called over his shoulder. "I've hoisted the proper flag. They'll take you aboard, Captain. Just negotiate my freedom."

Montagne looked up at the simple white rectangle floating in the wind where the sails once billowed. As the warship came alongside, he looked up to see British soldiers pointing their rifles at his chest, careful sneers on their faces.

They collected him from the fisherman and roughly hauled him aboard what appeared to be a French-built *Pallas*-class frigate flagged as a British warship. His feet had barely touched the deck when the ship's captain, a pleasant-faced man with dark, windswept hair, appeared in front of him.

"You're in quite the mess, sir," he said with a grim smile.

Montagne straightened. "If you'll permit me to come aboard, Captain," he said in fluent, British-accented English. "I am carrying a message from General Armand-Augustin-Louis de Caulaincourt, the Commander of the *Grand Armeé*, for the eyes of King George III only."

The ship's captain blinked, but said nothing. "Can you elaborate further?"

"I appreciate your discretion, sir. That is a conversation best held in private. Your quarters, perhaps?" Montagne asked.

The captain nodded stiffly. "I am Captain Murray Maxwell of the *Daedalus*."

"Antoine de Montagne, senior translator for General Caulaincourt," Montagne said. He kept his gaze stern, as if asking the young captain to say nothing more. "Sir, if you would, please release the fisherman; I traveled under the flag of truce to be here. Your quarrel is not with him or his meager catch."

Captain Maxwell nodded. He turned to a burly sailor with a trimmed beard. "Master at Arms, release the fisherman. Take Captain de Montagne to my cabin. Post two guards at the door. I shall join him shortly. Mister Mowett? Make sail and continue the trials."

Montagne heard the crew spring to action as he found himself escorted belowdecks to the captain's cabin and an uncertain future. He didn't have to wait long.

The promise of delivering critical intelligence to the Admiralty, and the King himself, kept Maxwell firmly in Montagne's confidence. Upon hearing the news of Emperor Napoloeon's death in Russia, Maxwell called his sailing master. Maxwell interrupted the sea trials for the newly-commissioned *Daedalus* and reversed course for England with all possible speed, yet he told no one of Montagne's news or mission. The seas were rough during the transit, but Maxwell's treatment of Montagne never deviated from genteel and pleasant. Montagne wondered what the crew discussed in hushed tones as they glanced at him during his time on deck, but no one said anything to him save for the ship's captain.

They anchored in Portsmouth two days later, and circumventing the authority of the port commander, Maxwell arranged a coach and escort for himself and Montagne to London. Montagne had said nothing to anyone besides Maxwell about the demise of Napoleon, and it became clear Maxwell understood the information's impact on all of Europe. The young ship's captain climbed aboard the coach to complete the last leg of the journey with Montagne.

———

The coach arrived in London in the late afternoon of Christmas Eve. The slushy thoroughfares were crowded as families with children moved from place to place, enjoying the holiday cheer. Montagne thought of his own family in the south of France and his desire to join them as soon as possible. As much as he wanted to believe his time in the army was drawing to a close, and that the constant wars of the Emperor's rule of France would fade into a lasting peace, the churning in his stomach told him that unless a miracle occurred in the next few hours, he was still in the center of an enemy's country and too far from home.

Montagne watched the faces of excited children as the coach made its way to Buckingham Palace. Wearing his British naval uniform, Captain Maxwell swung out of the carriage at the palace gate and spoke to the guards, who in turn dispatched a runner to the palace. Montagne fought crippling anxiety and the fatigue of the previous fortnight as they waited for a response. At last, the *Daedalus*'s captain climbed aboard and the carriage passed through the fortified gates.

Captain Maxwell turned to him, both flushed and relieved. "His Royal Highness, the Admiral of the Fleet and Lord Liverpool, the Prime Minister, are both present, as I'd hoped." Maxwell lowered his voice, as if someone might be eavesdropping. "The Admiral of the Fleet is one of King George's sons. His Majesty has been ill for some time, and Lord Liverpool effectively runs the government and our war efforts. I said nothing of the contents of your message. I merely implied the news would be of critical importance."

"There have been rumors in France for some time regarding your king's health." Montagne smiled. "I am indebted to your trust and courtesy, Captain Maxwell."

The young officer smiled in return. "I hope the larger conflicts between our countries find a peaceful resolution. Without trying to sound naive, I believe you and I could be friends in other circumstances."

"Let us hope that peace comes swiftly."

Once the driver parked the carriage in front of the main palace entrance, they exited together. Several armed guards surrounded them with weapons at the ready. Maxwell stared at the sergeant of the guard in charge, who nodded. They were ready to proceed.

Maxwell gestured Montagne forward and fell into step at his right shoulder. "Come, Captain de Montagne." The guards pressed in, accompanying them. Montagne drew a long deep breath and tried to still his thrashing heart. Even after two years in the *Grand Armeé*, during countless actions and marches close to the front, with artillery and musket rounds passing overhead, he had never experienced such abject fear.

*They will take me and execute me without listening to a word I say. Caulaincourt's message, whatever it is, will be lost and forgotten.*

The sudden urge to laugh at the terror in his bones almost overtook his senses as they stepped inside. Entering the ornate palace, Montagne kept his head and eyes forward, refusing to be distracted by the furnishings of King George's residence. The escorts directed them into a wide corridor where two gentlemen stood waiting for them. Both were older, distinguished men wearing powdered wigs. One wore the traditional dark blue dress uniform of an admiral of the Royal Navy, and the other a dark, traditional jacket with a ruffled shirt underneath. Both were older, and Montagne noted the powdered wigs they wore likely covered hair of a similar color. The admiral was stout, if not a bit rotund, unlike the sailors of the *Daedalus* and others whom Montagne had observed along the shores of home. This man had likely never seen a posting at sea because of his lineage.

The escorts retreated to a watchful position around the four men. Captain Maxwell clicked his heels together and saluted. Unsure of the customs and courtesies, Montagne nodded and bowed very slightly at the waist to both men.

"Your Highness, Lord Liverpool. I am Captain Murray Maxwell of His Majesty's Ship *Daedalus*. Allow me to present Captain Antoine de Montagne, translator for General Armand-Augustin-Louis de Caulaincourt, Commander of the *Grand Armeé*."

His Royal Highness, the Admiral of the Fleet, frowned at Montagne. "What news do you have that is so critical to interrupt the preparations for our Christmas celebrations, Captain de Montagne?"

"You said Caulaincourt is in command of your army?" Lord Liverpool questioned immediately. His gaze intensified on Montagne. "I do not understand. Has there been a change in command of the French forces?"

Montagne nodded. "Sir, Emperor Napoleon is dead."

"What?" Lord Liverpool gasped. The men looked at each other.

Montagne met their shocked expressions. "He was killed by Cossack irregular forces outside of Smorgon, Russia, on the fifth of December as the army retreated from Moscow."

The Admiral of the Fleet harrumphed and looked at Lord Liverpool. "This is a ruse."

"Sir, with respect, I was with the Emperor as he died. There was news of a possible *coup d'etat* in Paris. As the Russian campaign stalled and the *Grand Armeé* ran low on provisions, the Emperor ordered our withdrawal. During the retreat, the Emperor told General Caulaincourt he could not govern France from the front and proceeded home. As he started his journey, Cossacks attacked. He was killed in front of his aide-de-camp, General Caulaincourt, and myself. I can personally verify that he is dead."

The Admiral of the Fleet turned to Lord Liverpool, and they stared at each other for a moment. His Royal Highness asked, "And what of the aide?"

"He died at the Emperor's side. Only General Caulaincourt and I survived the attack," Montagne lied. Their question had been far from innocuous and confirmed the true identity of the man he'd executed as a spy in Calais.

Liverpool deftly changed the subject. "What is the message General Caulaincourt asked you to deliver to His Majesty? Let us see it."

Montagne reached into his pocket and withdrew the small, wax-sealed roll of paper. "General Caulaincourt was adamant this be seen by King George III or yourself first."

"And Napoleon is really dead?" the Admiral asked again, as if he couldn't believe it.

Montagne nodded. "If all has gone well, General Caulaincourt has returned to Paris. As for the status of the French government, I cannot say."

Lord Liverpool nodded to his counterpart. "As the Prime Minister, I am charged with handling all matters of importance for the Crown while His Majesty is ill. As you are aware, His Royal Highness, the Admiral of the Fleet, is Prince William, the Duke of Clarence. While not the heir to the throne, he will review the note, as well. Is this acceptable, Captain de Montagne?"

Montagne considered the situation and knew he had no alternative. "Of course, sir."

Lord Liverpool extended a hand, palm up, to Montagne. "If you please?"

Montagne extended the rolled message to the Prime Minister. Lord Liverpool took the message, broke the wax seal, and unrolled it.

As he read, the older man's mouth fell open slightly. He laughed once, and then again, before almost clutching it to his chest. "General Caulaincourt says he is returning to Paris with the intent of dissolving Emperor Napoleon's government and establishing peace through Europe. He says the Emperor's death at the hands of Cossacks has challenged his own personal convictions for warfare," Liverpool said. "From what I know of the man, I am inclined to believe him."

The Admiral of the Fleet harrumphed again. "We must be careful in our dealings with General Caulaincourt. With the French government in disarray, anything could happen...as we've seen over the last several decades."

"Indeed. However, if this is a legitimate and honorable expression of his intent, there are great possibilities. Has our blockade been established at the American colonies?"

His Royal Highness nodded. "They should be in position. I await the confirming dispatch from Admiral Warren any day now."

Lord Liverpool's eyebrows rose, and a hint of a smile played on his lips. "How quickly can you sail a diplomatic mission to Paris?"

"Two days. The family's Christmas celebration must be preserved. I can have a ship dispatched and at the ready." His Royal Highness, the Admiral of the Fleet, nodded. Where there had been doubt in his voice before was sudden enthusiasm.

"Begging your pardon, sir," Captain Maxwell spoke. "The *Daedalus* is docked in Portsmouth now and is ready to sail. I would be honored to transport the diplomatic party."

Lord Liverpool brightened. "Done! Captain Montagne? Will you accompany the party and assist with the presentation of terms?"

"Terms?" Montagne squinted and hastily added, "Sir?"

Lord Liverpool nodded and handed the note to His Royal Highness. "General de Caulaincourt has offered, in an attempt at peace, his full cooperation and diplomatic influence. You are aware we are in armed conflict yet again with our former colonies in America?"

Montagne shook his head. "I was only aware of naval actions in the Atlantic, sir."

"Well, we have seen several engagements with the Americans on the ground, and they've held a significant advantage. That ends now. Once your navy and logistical support is withdrawn from America, we will see just how much resolve our former subjects have." He smiled again and glanced at His Royal Highness. "We shall recall Lord Wellington from Spain and instruct him to provide a thorough and complete invasion plan for the colonies. By summer, I will walk that ground myself and take their surrender personally. I've heard their capitol city is quite beautiful. Perhaps a proper flag flying over it will complete the scene?"

The Admiral of the Fleet beamed. "Quite right. His Majesty will be most pleased."

Lord Liverpool smiled at Montagne and Johnson. "You've delivered quite the Christmas present, gentlemen. Please join me for Christmas dinner tomorrow. You should have enough time to have your uniform laundered, *Colonel* de Montagne. And you, as well, Captain Maxwell."

Montagne blurted. "I'm sorry, what did you say, sir?"

His Royal Highness turned the message to Montagne, where he read Caulaincourt's flowing script promoting him officially with the duties of Translator General of *la Grand Armeé*. "I take it this is a surprise?"

"Completely, sir."

Lord Liverpool laughed. "A commanding general's staff should always carry appropriate rank for their office, especially when they've performed their duties as honorably as you have. We would never shoot the messenger, Colonel de Montagne, whether it's Christmas or not. I trust you have a family, yes? Tell me about them over a glass of wine, and we'll toast a new peace for Europe and a bright new future."

# ABOUT KEVIN J. ANDERSON

**Kevin J. Anderson** has published more than 190 books, fifty-eight of which have been national or international bestsellers. He has written numerous novels in the Star Wars, X-Files, and Dune universes, as well as the unique Clockwork Angels steampunk trilogy with legendary Rush drummer Neil Peart. His original works include the Saga of Seven Suns series, the Wake the Dragon and Terra Incognita fantasy trilogies, humorous Dan Shamble, Zombie P.I. series and The Dragon Business series.

He has edited numerous anthologies, written comics and games, and composed the lyrics to three rock albums. Anderson is the director of the graduate program in Publishing at Western Colorado University, and he and his wife Rebecca Moesta are the publishers of WordFire Press.

He worked on the recent films Dune: Part One and Part Two from Legendary Entertainment, as well as the forthcoming Dune: Prophecy TV series from MAX, and other films in development, including Persephone and Karousel.

He has 24 million copies in print in thirty-four languages. His most recent novels are Neth*er Station, Horn Dogs, Persephone,* and *Princess of Dune* (with Brian Herbert).

Kevin J. Anderson's Website: https://wordfire.com/

**Kevin Ikenberry**'s head has been in the clouds since he was old enough to read. Ask him and he'll tell you that he still wants to be an astronaut. With over twenty five years of experience in space science education, including managing the U.S. Space Camp program and serving as an executive of two Challenger Learning Centers, Kevin continues to work with space every day. A retired Army space operations officer, Kevin lives in Colorado with his family. His home is seldom a boring place.

Kevin is the international bestselling author of The Protocol War series featuring Colorado Book Award finalist *Sleeper Protocol*, which Publisher's Weekly called "an emotionally powerful debut," and the sequel *Vendetta Protocol*. Kevin is also the author (or co-author) of twelve bestselling *Peacemaker* novels in the Four Horsemen Universe as well as the military science fiction novel *Runs In The Family* and the thriller Super-Sync. Kevin has also contributed to the Nebula-award nominated Caine Riordan series by Charles E. Gannon and his alternate history novel, *The Crossing*, released in 2022. His short fiction has appeared internationally across various publications and anthologies. He regularly teaches classes for aspiring writers.

Website: https://kevinikenberry.com/

# MARCHING THROUGH

## David Weber

"I'm sorry, Cump, but it isn't possible."

There was compassion in his brother's tone, Sherman thought, looking out the hotel window at the bustling Cincinnati street, but not hope.

"John, I understand he's angry. Truly, I do. But this is more than just—"

"Not for him, Cump. And not for Tommy or Aunt Maria. And—I'm sorry—not for me, either."

Sherman turned from the window, lips tight, and his brother looked back steadily.

"You should have gone to London, Cump." John Sherman's voice was flat. "If you had, Ellen—" He broke off and shook his head sharply.

"Do you think I haven't thought the same thing?" Sherman's tone was tighter than his lips. "Do you think I don't realize everyone in the family must feel the same way? Of course I do! But I can no more undo that than I could ascend bodily into heaven, and it would seem nothing short of that will appease him."

"She was his daughter, Cump!"

"And she was my *wife*!"

"Yes," John grated. "Your *first* wife."

"Damn you, John!" His eyes flashed. "I *loved* her!"

"Then perhaps you should have remembered that before you dragged her off to that hellhole!"

"I dragged her nowhere, John! And it was scarcely a 'hellhole,' for that matter. It was certainly better than California!"

"Yes, and she hated California, too," John said coldly.

"I never asked her to come to Pineville!"

"No? Well you certainly didn't try to *dissuade* her, did you? And it took you little enough time to find solace for your loss, Cump."

Fury flashed through Sherman as that last deadly sentence struck home. Yet even as it did, the memory burned across his mind once more. The memory of Ellen, feverish, pale-faced, in the fourposter bed. The hushed voices of the doctor and Marie, murmuring in the background, while he held her hand, stroked her forehead.

"Tell Daddy I love him," she'd whispered through cracked lips.

"You can tell him yourself," he'd lied.

"Tell him!" she'd insisted.

"I will," he'd promised. "Now rest."

"I'll have time to rest soon enough."

She'd actually managed a faint smile, and her eyes had moved, seeking Marie as she stood in the doorway, listening intently to Doctor Kennebec's instructions. Then she'd looked back up at him.

"The Church says God's angels are all around us, Cump. I never expected to meet one of them *here*, though."

"I know." He'd stroked her cheek. "Rest."

"I will. I will!" Her voice had been even weaker, and her too-thin fingers had squeezed the hand holding hers. "I'm not frightened, Cump. Truly. I'm just...so tired." Her eyes had slipped shut. "Tell Daddy," she'd repeated, so faintly now he could barely hear. "Tell Daddy how much I love him."

"I will," he'd repeated. "I will."

And he had, at the funeral, while his father-in-law listened in stony-eyed silence.

It was the last time they'd spoken. He knew now that it would always be the last time they'd spoken. And now, even John...

"I thank you for coming." His voice was colder than ice, and he knew it, but there was nothing he could do about it. It was at least better than seizing his brother by the throat. "I see it was a mistake to call upon you in this matter, however. I assure you, it won't happen again, Sir. Good day!"

He turned back to the window, spine ramrod straight, arms folded across his chest, as he gazed down at the street, wondering if his brother would speak again.

Heels across the floor and a sharply closed door answered the question.

William Tecumseh Sherman's squared, proud shoulders sagged, and he closed his eyes, leaned forward to rest his forehead against the glass.

John didn't understand. He never had. And neither had Ellen. Or her father.

He *had* loved Ellen—he had! But there'd come a time when he had to stand upon his own two feet, and she'd needed to understand that. Or to support him in it, at least. Perhaps she would have, one day...if she'd lived. But she hadn't.

He opened his eyes again, his expression bleak, remembering a nine-year-old whose father had died, leaving a destitute wife and eleven children. Even at nine, he'd been hugely proud of his father—a judge on the Ohio State Supreme Court. A distinguished juror. A man with a glowing future.

Until he died and took his family's entire future with him.

Sherman knew how unspeakably fortunate he and his family had been that his father and Thomas Ewing had been such close friends, and that Ewing had been such a good man. The man who had stepped into the hole his father's death had left, taken the entire family under his protective wing.

A powerful man in Whig politics, Thomas Ewing. A profoundly respected jurist; William Henry Harrison's Secretary of the Treasury; the nation's first Secretary of the Interior under Zachary Taylor; Senator from Ohio. He'd been instrumental in securing John Sherman's election to the House of Representatives, and he was one of the men who would be sitting down shortly at what they were already calling the Peace Conference at Willard's Hotel in Washington City in an effort to stave off the Union's collapse. A man Sherman not only sincerely respected, but loved and deeply admired. His foster father, the man whose approval mattered to him more than that of anyone else in the universe.

And the man who would never forgive him for his daughter's death. Never understand—never be *willing* to understand—why his son-in-law had preferred Louisiana to London.

*I hated banking*, he thought now. *I hated it almost as much as I hated the Commissary Service. I know Henry meant it for the best when he offered me the San Francisco office, and I jumped at the chance, but I ought to have known better.*

And John was right about how much Ellen had hated California, too. She'd never wanted to leave Ohio. In fact, she'd returned to Ohio without him for seven months in the middle of his four years in San Francisco. And her parents had insisted that their daughter Lizzie remain with them in Ohio the entire time.

Even from distant California, then, Thomas Ewing's shadow had loomed over his life, and Ellen had never understood—never sympathized, at least—with his need to prove he was more than Thomas's charity ward. His admiration and love for Thomas had been boundless, yet Ellen had never understood how his sense of indebtedness had always colored them both. Never grasped what drove him to prove that he could provide his own family with the financial security of which his father's early death had deprived him as a child. To prove he could do that—could succeed where his own father, through no fault of his own, had failed *him*—without depending on anyone else's largess, however willingly that largess was offered. It was why he'd left the Army in the first place, because an Army officer's peacetime salary was too low to provide that security. It was why he'd gone into banking, despite the fact that he'd never truly had the head —or the heart—for it.

And then the bubble had burst in California. He'd closed the bank there, returned East to run another branch in New York City...only to see that go under, along with its parent bank in St. Louis, in the panic of '57. At thirty-seven, he'd found himself the unemployed father of three, with no prospects in banking in the current climate, and Ellen had been not-so-secretly pleased. Not that she'd gloated at his misfortune. She would never have done that. Indeed, the true problem was that she'd never seen it *as* misfortune. For her, it had been fate pushing them back to Lancaster and the family she loved, and she'd never truly comprehended how much he hated his dependence on her family and its wealth. She came from that world, she knew he'd been raised in it by her own father, and in her eyes, it ought to have been the natural order of things for him as it was for her.

But it hadn't been. And so even as Ellen had rejoiced at the thought of returning to Lancaster, Sherman had sought a different route. Perhaps he couldn't avoid relying upon his foster father's connections, but at least he could try to do it on his own terms. So he'd gone to Kansas, joined the real estate and law firm of his brothers-in-law, Thomas and Hugh. It was still a "family business," but he and Tommy, especially, had always been close...and Leavenworth was over six hundred miles from Lancaster.

But that hadn't worked out, either. The firm had never prospered—in no small part because Tommy had preferred to concentrate on abolitionist politics instead of business in "Bleeding Kansas"—and as it slowly sank into failure, his old debilitating friend melancholy had visited him again.

He'd grown increasingly desperate, so desperate that he'd even tried to get back into the Army, but there'd been no openings two years ago. So desperate that, despite his pride, he'd been forced back to Lancaster, forced to accept a position managing the Ewing family's coal and saltworks in nearby Chauncey. Only temporarily, of course. Only until Thomas could find something more suitable for him.

Like the position with the London bank.

Ellen had been excited about that. San Francisco was a rude, crude, raw-boned place, unable to challenge Lancaster in her eyes, but London was civilized. The largest city in the entire world. With over three million inhabitants, it was twenty times the size of Cincinnati, Ohio's largest city, and four times the size of even New York. A place with culture and wealth, the beating heart of the largest and most powerful empire in the history of the world.

And one more "new beginning" provided by her family in an occupation he'd come to loathe.

There'd been no escape. However little the opportunity excited him, it had seemed the only one available...until he'd received the letter from Louisiana, at least.

It had come to him from George Graham, a man he'd never met, and it had invited him to consider the post as the first superintendent of the newly organized Louisiana State Seminary of Learning and Military Academy. He'd never heard of the Seminary at that point, either, but he'd jumped at the chance and taken the train to Baton Rouge for a personal interview.

He'd spoken not just with Graham, but also with Paul Hébert, his old classmate from West Point and the past Governor of Louisiana, during whose governorship the Seminary had been established three years before. Graham, the Seminary's board chairman, had spent those three years acquiring funds, finding a campus, and commissioning the first buildings. Now he needed a superintendent, and since he envisioned the Seminary as following in the footsteps of the Virginia Military Institute, he'd clearly needed a military man for the post, so he'd consulted Colonel Don Carlos Buell, under whom he had served in the Mexican-American war, for possible candidates. Buell had written a glowing letter extolling Sherman's qualifications for the position, and Hébert had enthusiastically endorsed Buell's suggestion.

He and Graham had taken to one another immediately. The salary had been less than he would have been paid in London, and Rapides Parish had scarcely been a cultural mecca, but it was also a hundred and fifty miles farther from Lancaster than even Leavenworth had been. Perhaps even more importantly, the glowing terms in which Buell and Hébert had recommended him had come at a time when the black tide of his all-too-frequent bouts of depression had rolled cold and deep. They had reminded him that he *was* a capable man, a man others valued for his own achievements and ability, and the Seminary would inevitably grow. He could place his stamp upon it, build something that was the product of his hands and his heart that, in time, might deserve the respect he craved from Thomas Ewing. Besides, he'd liked Louisiana. There were things he didn't care for about Southerners, but that was true of Northerners, as well. He'd liked and respected the Louisianans, they'd respected him, and he'd accepted the offer on the spot.

Ellen had *not* been pleased when he telegraphed her that he had. She'd had her heart set on London. Besides, like the rest of her family, she had powerful Abolitionist beliefs. She despised slaveowners, and she'd refused even to visit Louisiana.

Despite that, he'd dug into his new duties, and the truth was that however disappointed Ellen might have been, *he* had never been happier, never more aware that he was building something out of his own skill and effort and determination. And his time in Louisiana had brought him back into contact with old comrades from the Army and West Point, not least Hébert, who, along with Graham, had been delighted to give him entrée into the first circles of the state. He'd spent many weekends at the Hébert sugar plantation in Iberville, and renewed his friendship with Hébert's family.

Obviously, that happiness had revealed itself in his letters to Ohio, and almost exactly a year ago today, Ellen had decided to visit Louisiana after all. Officially, she'd come to bring the children to visit him and to see with her own eyes what he was building. Actually, he had known she'd hoped to convince him to give up Louisiana and "come home," but he'd hoped he might be able to convince her to stay in Louisiana, instead.

She had stayed. But not the way he'd hoped.

He opened his eyes again, gazing bleakly down at the busy street.

Typhoid fever.

God knew there were outbreaks enough of it in Ohio, but, of course, none of the Ewings cared about that. Ellen had come to Louisiana to contract it, and that meant *Louisiana* had killed her. It meant Sherman's "stubborn" refusal to "come home" to Ohio had killed her.

It meant *he* had killed her.

Perhaps he had. He sometimes thought that, in the stillness of his own heart. And he knew her death, alone, would have driven a wedge between him and his family and his in-laws. But he hadn't left it there, had he? Oh, no.

*They hadn't been there,* he thought. Hadn't seen Ellen in that mosquito-netted bed in Iberville, while the Hébert family fought to save her. Like Ellen, the Héberts were devout Roman Catholics. Their parish priest had visited daily and Hébert's sister Marie had nursed her through every stage of her illness. Been there every single day. Slept on a cot in the same bedroom at night. Ellen's parents hadn't seen their daughter in the grip of delirium, clinging to Marie Hébert's hand as if to life itself while Marie sat with her, read to her...prayed with her. Hadn't seen Marie fighting every inch of the way, spending her own strength like fire, risking infection daily, *daring* the typhoid to take her, as well. She'd poured her *life* into the fight, refused to give up.

And in the end, she'd had to watch as Ellen slipped away from them, into the shadows.

Her parents hadn't seen *any* of that...just as they hadn't heard Marie promise Ellen, promise her through her own tears as the light faded in Ellen's eyes and that emaciated body failed her at last, that she would take care of Ellen's children as if they were her own.

For six weeks, Marie had fought that fight at Ellen's side. She'd nursed her, read to her, sat setting embroidery stitches while Ellen napped fitfully. She'd become closer to her than her own sisters in those six horrible weeks...and she'd sat on the other side of Ellen's bed when it had been his turn to hold her hand, promise her he was there. Promise her he loved her.

And it was Marie who had embraced him through her own tears as Ellen lost her final fight at last. Marie who had—

Another door opened, and his nostrils flared as he turned from the window.

"I'm so sorry, Billy," she said softly.

Ellen, like everyone else in his family, had always called him "Cump." Marie never had. Now she crossed the hotel room to lay a hand on his forearm and stand looking up at him. She wasn't a tall woman, smaller and more fine-boned than Ellen had been, and he saw the tears in her eyes.

"I should have said no," she told him in that same soft Southern voice. "It was too soon. Of course your family—Ellen's family—sees it that way."

"No." His headshake was firm. "It was what she wanted, too."

"That doesn't mean it was the right thing to do, Billy. And it's not as if Mrs. Ewing couldn't have raised the children without me. In fact, I'm sure that's what Ellen *would* have wanted, if her mind had only been clear."

*She was a stubborn woman, Marie,* Sherman thought. And she'd always defended the Ewings.

It was a pity none of them had ever so much as spoken to her.

"You may be right," he said now, "but I didn't ask for your hand only because of the children." He took that hand from his arm, raised it to his lips, and kissed it. "I asked for it because I saw you in that sickroom. Because I saw how you fought for her, exposed yourself to the same disease. Because I realized who you *are* and because I realized I loved that person. I wish, with all my heart, that Ellen were still alive, but that was in God's hands, not ours. You know that as well as I do. And I know you understand I truly loved her, and that there's a part of me that feels unspeakably guilty when I admit I love you, too. But I do, Marie. God help me, but I do."

*And so do the children*, he thought silently. The children she refused to let call her "Mother," because she would never, ever "steal" that title from Ellen. *They love you because you and your family were always there for them while their mother lay dying and I was too lost, too desperately worried about Ellen to be strong for them, too. They don't just love you—they* adore *you...and that's one more reason for Ellen's family to hate you.*

"But it's made such a mess." The tears hovered in her voice, as well, now. "What will you do now, Billy? What will become of us?"

"I don't know," he admitted. "I don't know."

He gathered her in his arms, and she laid her head upon his chest as he stood holding her and stared into the frightening void of the future. And not simply of his own future.

It seemed impossible, as they stood in this hotel room in the heart of the seventh largest city in the entire nation, yet even here, with the sounds of Cincinnati's busy streets coming to them through the closed window, the stink of distant blood was in his nostrils. He could feel it coming, and not all of Cincinnati's industry, nor all of its optimistic future, could change that.

In three weeks, Abraham Lincoln would take the oath of office as the sixteenth President of the United States, and God only knew what would happen then. But if the Peace Conference in Washington failed—and Sherman saw no way it could succeed—disaster waited for them all. South Carolina Mississippi, Florida, Alabama, Georgia, Louisiana, and now Texas had already declared their secession from the Union, and other states hovered on the brink. Volunteers were rushing to form regiments, both North and South; arms were being stockpiled; and the first wrong move on the new Lincoln Administration's part would send some, at least, of those other hovering states into secession, as well.

For decades, the Republic had sown the wind. Now harvest time had come, and all across the country, men faced the bitter decision. Did their swords belong to their nation...or to their states? Neither the doctrine of secession nor the battle cry of "states' rights" had originated in the South, but the South had embraced both of them ferociously, fanatically, taken them to the deadly height of their logical end, and Lincoln's election had ignited a fuse Sherman feared could lead to only one outcome.

Despite the Abolitionist stance of the Ewings and most of his own siblings—especially John—Sherman found much to admire in the South. And whatever the rights or wrongs of slavery, he fully understood why Southern Whites feared the Blacks who had been held in bondage for so long. The wrongs of the "peculiar institution" might be endless, yet even had the South been prepared to admit them all, it could not have magically erased that fear, and in the present, heated atmosphere—

Thirty years might have passed since Nat Turner's rebellion in Virginia, but the lunatic Brown's attempt to initiate another slave insurrection at Harpers Ferry lay barely sixteen months in the past. Its impact had loomed large on the 1860 elections, and Brown's transformation into a martyr after he'd been hanged had contributed to both Lincoln's election in the North and to the South's fury.

William Tecumseh Sherman had lived in Kansas. He knew the bloody-handed sorts of men who had flocked to both sides of the struggle there. Knew the fanatic stripe of both the pro-abolition and pro-slavery extremists, and Brown—John Brown of Potawatomie—had come from that same frothing cauldron of arson, terror tactics, and murder. If he'd been better than some, he'd been worse than many, and Sherman understood why the South saw him as the terrorist and insurrectionist he'd set out to be at Harpers Ferry. In their eyes, the abolitionists who had transformed him into a martyr and messiah had simply shown their own true colors, proclaimed precisely what they wanted to happen *throughout* the South, and that had become one more faggot to fuel the nation's blazing sectional fury.

Sherman himself believed secession was illegal, but he also doubted that it mattered very much. The American colonies' rebellion against George III had clearly been "illegal"...until it succeeded. As Sir John Harrington had said almost three centuries before, treason "never prospered," because if it did, if it succeeded, then it was no longer treason, and so *successful* secession would *become* legal after the fact. He knew too much history to think it could be any other way.

But as a soldier, William Tecumseh Sherman had sworn an oath to "support and defend the Constitution of the United States against all enemies, foreign and domestic," and as a pragmatist, he feared secession's inevitable consequences. The United States of America spanned a continent. He suspected that few in Europe realized what that meant, realized how enormous the United States actually were. Certainly few of the Europeans he'd met had seemed to truly grasp that it was twice as far from New York to San Francisco as from Paris to Saint Petersburg, or that New Orleans lay farther from Chicago than Berlin from Rome. The notion of a single nation—a republic—that size was simply something for which the history of the world offered no basis for comparison.

Ultimately, he knew, as the continent's vast, empty spaces filled, the Union would become the most powerful nation in the world. "Manifest Destiny," Mr. O'Sullivan had called it in the *Morning News* when Texas was annexed, and he'd been right. Nothing could stop that onrushing expansion. It was as inevitable as fate.

Unless...

If secession "prospered," that enormous union would crumble. It would splinter into at least two nations, and quite probably more, because once secession was validated by success, who could stop the process the next time "irreconcilable differences" flared? From one vast, growing nation, it would disintegrate into a patchwork of potentially warring states, like Europe, fighting like snarling dogs over what should have been their common birthright. But how was that to be avoided?

Sherman blamed President Buchanan, in large part, for allowing inflamed passions to drive policy to its present pitch. If he had said, bluntly, that the Federal government would use force to compel obedience to the Constitution and heeded Winfield Scott's advice to increase the strength of the Army and to garrison the Federal posts throughout the

South, then at least a line would have been drawn. The grim reality of the options would have been in the open. Instead, Buchanan had allowed partisan interests to block fresh recruitment and done nothing to deploy Federal troops. Only eighteen companies—just *eighteen*, all of them Artillery, out of an Army that numbered a bare 18,000 men—were stationed *anywhere* east of the Mississippi, and he'd done nothing to change that.

His inert response was understandable, perhaps, given his personal sympathy for the South. True, he'd used his final message to Congress, less than two months ago, to deny the legal right of states to secede. But he'd denied it only after enumerating all of the reasons that justified Southern anger...and then gone on to say that "the injured States, after having first used all peaceful and constitutional means to obtain redress," would be justified in "revolutionary resistance"—*extralegal* resistance—to the Government of the Union if that redress was not found.

A more feckless response was impossible to imagine. First, he'd infuriated the South by denying the legality of the right to secede it had championed for so long. And then he'd infuriated the *North* by asserting that the South had a *moral* right to do just that...whatever the law might say.

Looking into the future's hollow-skull eyes with bleak honesty, Sherman saw no way any successor—and certainly not one like Lincoln, elected by a simple plurality in a race where no candidate had won a majority of the vote—could recover from the position Buchanan had left him. No way anyone could avert the looming wreck. And that meant that, like all those other men, he, William Sherman, had to decide where his sword belonged.

He had decided. Not without an agonizing internal struggle, but he'd decided. That was why he'd resigned as the Seminary's superintendent last month when the state government demanded the muskets stored in the school's armory. Those muskets were the lawful property of the United States government, which had provided them to the school. He'd had no authority to hand them over to the state. And as he'd said to George Graham in his letter of resignation, "I accepted such position when Louisiana was a state in the Union, and when the motto of this Seminary was inserted in marble over the main door: 'By the liberality of the general government of the United States. The Union—*esto perptua*.'"

Graham had understood. So had Marie. Just as she'd understood why he'd felt compelled to seek an Army commission once more rather than simply stand upon the sidelines. But his efforts had been rejected in a chilly, formal letter "regretting" that "the Department can find no employment for your services at this time."

Now he knew why. His foster father, Thomas Ewing's political allies, even his own brother, had thrown their influence into denying the man they blamed for Ellen Ewing Sherman's death a commission. And there was clearly no hope of changing their minds.

"Billy?"

He looked down as Marie lifted her head from his chest.

"Yes?"

"Billy, what will you decide now?" she asked him softly. "I know you've done what you believed you had to do, and whether or not it's the choice I would prefer you make, I respect you for it. I came with you to Cincinnati, and whither you go, I will go, too, even if that's to Washington City itself. But, Billy, these people..." She shook her head. "These people are not worthy of what you've tried to give them. Of the oath you swore or the service of your sword. They aren't worthy of *you*. Perhaps, someday, they will be again. Perhaps someday they'll understand what they've thrown away. But not today, Billy. Not today. So come home. Come home, where people *do* love you, and let your heart heal."

"Marie, I can't just turn my back—" he began, but she shook her head again.

"I haven't asked you to," she said simply. "I will *never* ask you to take up arms in any cause which is not your own. I will respect your decision, whether it is to remain in Louisiana or to leave her. To serve her if it comes to war, or to give your sword to neither side. Or even to return here and once again seek to give that sword to those people in Washington City and fight *against* Louisiana, should that be what your heart demands. Whatever decision you make, I know it will be one of honor. I will be content with that, whatever it is, and wherever you may go, I will be *proud* to stand beside you. But don't break your heart beating it against the bars while the people who ought to love you lock the door against you. Give them some time to heal, to realize the truth, as well."

He gazed down at her, the sounds of the street coming through the window behind them, and realized she was right in at least one sense. He'd come here, whether he had known it or not, on a fool's errand. There was no commission for him here, no opportunity to serve. And neither was there any way to support his wife and his children when those children's grandfather would use all of his influence to ensure he couldn't.

"Very well, my love," he said finally. "Perhaps you're right. Clearly, any more time here would be wasted. And perhaps some peaceful resolution can be found, after all. But if it can't—"

"Hush, Billy." She reached up, placed her fingers across his lips. "I said I'll respect your decision, and I will. Now take me home while you make it."

———

"A courier, General."

General William Sherman looked up, then drew rein as the dust-caked courier cantered closer under the hot September sun. The youthful lieutenant reached him and saluted sharply.

"Lieutenant Stevens." Sherman returned the salute with a wry smile. "I almost didn't recognize you under all that dust. I presume you bear word from General Hampton?"

"I do, Sir." The lieutenant opened his dispatch case to extract a sealed message. "This is his formal dispatch, but I was instructed to verbally inform you that Jeffries's Brigade was attacked by enemy cavalry this morning. The attack appears to have been made by local militia, and it was repulsed with only light casualties, and several prisoners were taken. General Hampton wishes me to assure you that his column's rate of advance will not be retarded."

"I see."

Sherman called up a mental map of his columns' lines of match and nodded to himself. McPherson's defeat at Madison had smashed the last organized army in his path almost two months ago. There'd been a fair amount of skirmishing since then, more of it in Hampton's front than anywhere else, but like this affair, all of it had been fleabite bickering organized out of whatever volunteers might be to hand. Resistance might stiffen if the enemy found a way to free the troop strength to replace McPherson's shattered Army of the West, but with the intensity of the fighting in Virginia...

"Thank you, Lieutenant." He passed the dispatch to his chief of staff. "Please return to General Hampton and inform him that I would have expected no other outcome."

"Yes, Sir!" The lieutenant saluted again, wheeled his horse, and went dashing back the way he'd come.

"It must be nice to be so full of energy," his chief of staff observed, and

Sherman snorted.

"What you mean, James," he said, "is that it must be nice to be so *young*."

"I'd hardly call forty-four 'ancient,' General," Colonel Adcock replied in a dry tone.

"Then you should try experiencing it from *my* side." Sherman shifted in the saddle, and Adcock chuckled.

Sherman lifted his canteen and sipped from it as he watched the long, dusty column march past. Other columns—columns of smoke, not men and horses and guns—rose in the distance. Most came from burning fields or barns, but some streamed up from the fires heating railroad rails before his troops twisted them into "Sherman's neckties" around handy tree trunks to prevent repair crews from simply spiking them back into place. He watched that smoke and his jaw tightened as he remembered his letter to Governor Norton when he'd severed his logistics from the river and set out across Norton's state, foraging his way in a fifty-mile wide swath of destruction through the heart of its cornfields and wheat fields, its pastures and orchards, to sustain his advance.

"War is cruelty," he'd written when Norton had furiously denounced his troops' "looting" and the "savage outrages" along his scorched-earth march. "There is no use trying to reform it; the crueler it is, the sooner it will be over."

That had never meant he *enjoyed* destruction. He hated it. But so long as these people continued to support the armies in the field, they were just as much the enemy as those armies were. And those armies could not survive without the fodder they produced, the horses and mules they raised for the Army, the beeves and hogs they sent forward to feed its soldiers. The enemy's field strength had begun to dwindle as defeat followed defeat, and desertion and draft riots had become an ever-growing problem for him as war weariness cut ever deeper. Yet these rich farms continued to feed and bolster those beleaguered armies and keep them stubbornly fighting.

It was time the people of those farms learned the price of supporting a war that dragged on and on, killing men—their own fathers and brothers and sons, as well as their enemies—by the thousands, day after day. He would spare their lives, but he would also teach that lesson to them, however harshly he must. And the instant they were willing to make peace, to end the killing, he would extend a helping hand once more. He knew they would go on hating him until the day he died, whatever he did, but that mattered less than nothing beside duty and the need to *end* this before the entire continent was littered with battlefield graves.

He recapped the canteen and urged his horse back into motion.

"How much longer do you reckon this can go on, Sir?" Adcock asked, as if he'd heard his commander's thoughts, and Sherman turned to cock an eyebrow at him as they rode side by side. "It's just that it seems it's already gone on forever," the colonel continued, quietly enough no one else could hear, "and the armies are *still* deadlocked in Virginia."

"They are," Sherman replied after a moment, "and they'll stay that way. But these people have run out of armies to stop us, because they have no one to pull away from the Washington-Richmond fighting. The truth is that the war's already been won in the West, whatever happens in the East. These people may not have realized that yet, and with Washington and Richmond only a hundred miles apart, it's inevitable that all eyes are on the Army of Northern Virginia and the Army of the Potomac. But I expect it's starting to dawn on them that when they lost control of the Mississippi and the Missouri and the Tennessee, that was the beginning of the end. I knew that when we threw them out of Chattanooga. And England and France both declared *their* recognition of the truth when they established their embassies in New Orleans."

"Perhaps so, Sir." Adcock nodded, but his tone was doubtful. "It's just that *they* don't seem to realize that."

"Oh, I expect some of them did realize it even then." Sherman shook his head. "It's not something a fellow finds easy to admit, though, and there are stubborn men on both sides of this war. That's the reason we're out here burning farms and confiscating livestock, Colonel." His expression turned grim. "They won't admit it until they're so thoroughly whupped, they have no choice. And then, perhaps, we can get back to rebuilding everything we've had to destroy."

He tapped his temple with one forefinger.

"Inside here, James. Inside here. That's where we have to convince them to cave in...or they have to convince *us*. And unless I'm mistaken, we'll know in about two months which side is going to do just that."

"The election." Adcock grimaced. "You really think that will decide things?"

"I think it almost has to, after four years." Sherman's jaw tightened. "Giving in—or not giving in—always happens in the mind. And unless I miss my guess, General McClellan's already given in."

"Who do you think will win, Sir?"

"Everything indicates the vote will be a near run thing, but it's trending against the Administration, I think," Sherman replied. "And if McClellan wins—"

He shrugged, and Adcock nodded as they neared another mile marker.

"I expect all this—" the colonel waved a hand at the marching men, the columns of smoke, the creaking supply wagons of a massive army headed east, "—will have a certain influence in the final vote, Sir."

"That's why we're here, James." Sherman's eyes were bleak and dark with regret, but they were also unyielding, and his nostrils flared as he gazed at the signpost. "I never wanted to come home this way, and I'd sooner never see another farm or another town in flames. But that's why we're here. And it's why I've been pushing so hard ever since we left the river. I want this done now, while there's time for the lesson to sink in. If we can show these people—and *ours*—that we can take even their largest cities, we may just give those voters another reason to think *hard* about who's caving in to whom, come election day. So I suppose we'd best be about it."

He touched his horse with a heel, urging it to greater speed, and it sprang into a trot as they passed the signpost.

"CINCINNATI—20 MILES," it said.

# ABOUT DAVID WEBER

**David Weber** was born in Cleveland in 1952 but grew up in rural South Carolina. He was a bookworm from childhood, with an interest in history which perplexed his parents, who nonetheless encouraged and supported him in it. He was also blessed with a father from the south side of Chicago who collected autographed copies of every E. E. Smith hardcover and introduced him to Jack Williamson at the age of 10, and with a mother who taught high school and college English, ran her own advertising agency, and encouraged him to write. (And who went back to graduate school in her sixties to earn her PhD in Literature.) An avid tabletop gamer (who, alas, no longer has room in his schedule for his hobby) he's wargamed every era from ancient Rome to World War II armored conflict, and began RPG playing with Gary Gygax's *Chainmail* rules in 1972. His younger sister went on to become a hand weaver and his younger brother has been a production Potter for over thirty-five years, so it's probably not too surprising that from that start he would find his way into the world of science fiction and fantasy rather than pursue honest work. He sold his first novel to Jim Baen at Baen Books in 1989. Since then he has published 81 solo and collaborative novels. He has also edited seven anthologies and appeared in several more. He is best known for his *Honorverse*, with 34 solo and collaborative novels in print centered around his character Honor Harrington and her universe, and the Safehold series, with ten novels in print. He still lives in South Carolina with a wife, Sharon, who he is fortunate loves him enough to put up with him, their three children, three dogs, and six cats.

# TWO IF BY SEEKRIEG

## Lee Allred

*Prologue the First*
*Madrid, Spain*
*27 April 1898*

Bernhard Von Bulow, German Foreign Minister, stirred his tea with a spoon fashioned from Inca silver. The Spanish Minster of State's tea service harkened back to the glory days when an omnipotent Spain ruled an entire hemisphere. The man's office, like the Spanish nation itself, was a shrine to the past, a museum.

The young nation of Germany had no past. Germany was a nation of the future. Germany was the future.

A grandfather clock in the corner ticked off the seconds. Spain hadn't many left if she were to decide between ruin and abject ruin.

Sitting behind a desk seemingly the size of the *Nina*, the *Pinta*, and the *Santa Maria* combined, Antonio Aguilar y Correa, the Marquis of Vega de Armijo, looked ashen-faced. As well he should. Hapless Spain had been hurled into a conflict not of its making and not of its choosing with the United States. A war they were certain to lose and lose disastrously.

"What you propose—it is not that simple," complained Correa. The elderly man's long, tufted side-whiskers bobbed up and down like a plover as he spoke.

"It is that simple," Von Bulow said. "You either lose Puerto Rico and the Philippines to the Americans or you can sell them to Germany."

"For céntimos on the pesetas!"

"Better some money than none at all. The Americans not only take your colonies, but force you to pay war reparations."

"So better to lose my wallet to a friendly pickpocket than the street thug accosting me? Spare me your solicitude!" Correa spat.

Von Bulow smiled. Some Latin fire remained in the grandee's belly, at least. Fire and the willful intransigence of a penniless wastrel who won't admit dissolution.

The German diplomat set his teacup upon its saucer and dabbed his mouth with a linen napkin. The tea had proven as thin and poor as Spain itself. "You have our offer."

Von Bulow stood to leave.

The rabbity little man swallowed. He knew as did his nation that this was the only offer they would get besides one proffered by American bayonets.

"I will have to present this to my government." He spread his hands. "It will, you understand, take time—"

"I repeat: you have our offer. What you don't have is time."

———

*PROLOGUE THE SECOND*
*MADRID, SPAIN*
*2 MAY 1898*

Von Bulow realized he was near-dozing, sitting in his chair on the sun-drenched patio of the German Embassy. It wouldn't do for a minister of the Kaiser to take a siesta like a decadent Spaniard.

He bestirred himself and strolled towards to his office, his footsteps echoing in the marble halls. He supposed he'd better goose Correa again. It'd been five whole days, more than enough for even the sclerotic Spanish government to submit to the inevitable.

Five days. Long enough—just—to dash back to London, meet with the Kaiser, set certain plans in motion, then dash back to Madrid.

The embassy had provided a spacious office for his use. Elegant but sparse and simple, uncluttered by knickknacks and mementos. Yet. Young Germany's curios and mementos of global conquest were to come.

He'd just sat down at the desk when a grim-faced messenger entered and handed him a decoded cable from the *Reichssekretariate*, Germany's intelligence service.

It was Von Bulow's turn to go ashen-faced as he read.

The first part of the cable he already knew. Anticipating a speedy agreement with Spain, at Von Bulow's own promptings the Kaiser had ordered Admiral Otto von Diederichs and the East Asian Squadron, along with a transport filled with 1500 German troops out of Tsingtau, to sail for Manila Harbor. When the American fleet under Commodore Dewey arrived, the Germans would present them with a *fait accompli*.

Dewey had gotten there first.

His modern ships had smashed the relics of the Spanish squadron and were in command of both bay and the prostrate colony.

At which point Diederichs lost his head or his sanity, take your pick. He had fired upon the Americans, who promptly fired back.

A full-fledged battle ensued.

The oversized American cruiser *Olympia*—really a pocket battleship—had dealt with the hodgepodge German ships almost as easily as it had the Spanish.

The flagship *SMS Kaiserin Augusta* had gone down with all hands, including Diederichs, the cruisers *Cormoran* and *Irene* hulled, and the transport carrying 1500 German soldiers from Tsingtau—half the colony's garrison—captured.

A humiliating defeat for Germany, one the mercurial Kaiser Wilhelm II could scarcely overlook. It meant war for Germany. War with the upstart American mongrels.

And it meant disgrace and disaster for Bernhard von Bulow. The Kaiser had sent for him with arrest and no doubt worse to follow. He should have to ask that nice young man from the *Reichssekretariate* for one of his cyanide tablets.

———

*7 May 1898*
*The Presidio*
*San Francisco*

It's said you can tell a cavalryman by his face. Between sun and wind and rain, it took on the look of saddle leather. Captain Miles Stanton's face not only looked leathery, he had the etched worry lines of a man who'd spent the past ten years in the Arizona sun chasing after the Apache.

He had a cavalryman's face. What Stanton didn't have was a cavalryman's horse. His last mount had mistaken a California garter snake for an Arizona rattler and thrown its rider. Then for good measure, the big roan gelding had toppled over and fallen on the dazed Stanton.

Now, instead of preparing his calvary company for embarkation for Manila and war with Spain, he laid in the Presidio's army hospital with cracked ribs, sundry bruises, and a right arm in a plaster cast.

Staton spent his recuperation alternately cursing horse and the itch under the plaster he couldn't scratch. The ribs had mostly healed. Doctors said he'd be out in a day or two.

Out to what? His command had been given to a replacement officer. He'd probably spend the rest of the war reassigned to some training camp. Or worse, marooned behind some desk in Washington.

He made to scratch his itching arm, remembering too late it was plastered. Would that he could get plastered himself, but a phalanx of dour nurses stood between him and the officer's club.

Speaking of nurses, that new one—a pretty little thing just the right size and shape—came in insisting it was time to wheel Stanton out into the garden. He let himself be placed like an invalid in a high-backed wooden wheelchair and rolled out into the hospital garden when he could have walked, albeit gingerly, under his own power.

The mild California sun was nothing like the furnace blast of Arizona. If he hadn't been a man in a hurry with no place to go, it might have even been relaxing. It really was a lovely garden, full of fragrant flowers he didn't know the names of. The Presidio had a number of lovely gardens. It also had a magnificent view of the San Francisco harbor and all the troop ships docked that soon would be loading US troops bound for the Philippines.

"How'd you like to be on one of those?" a man's voice behind him asked.

"Who'd I have to kill—" Stanton suddenly stopped. He recognized that voice. He spun his chair around. "'Boots!'"

"Boots" Waverly, his old roommate at the Point, stood in the doorway with a gap-toothed Chesire-eating grin.

Waverly looked little older, a little paunchier, and a little pastier-faced than last time Stanton had seen him. Instead of fighting Apache, the infantryman had spent the last three years barricaded behind a desk fighting the Battle of the Potomac. It had paid off; Waverly wore full bird colonel eagles on his shoulder straps. New ones. In a get-well card signature sent just last week, Waverly signed himself a captain. Junior to Stanton, of course, by date of rank, just as Waverly had always been junior by date of rank or class in the ten years since graduation.

Waverly noticed Stanton's gaze. "Like them, 'Saddle?'" he asked, pretending to dust his shoulder tabs off. "Just on loan till they can fit me with some stars. Nothing like a splendid little war for rapid promotion."

Nothing, indeed. To fight Spain, the country had needed to balloon its standing army of twenty-eight thousand peacetime soldiers to a force a quarter-million strong. To fight Germany, it would probably need millions. They were making colonels out of captains at breakfast and generals out of majors at lunch. It wasn't just Manila that fool horse had kept Stanton from—it was mercurial wartime promotion.

"Say the word," Waverly continued. "I can get you transferred to my staff, let you wear these when I trade up for my stars."

"What, join the infantry? And give up my polo ponies?" The two of them had been trading barbs about their respective branches since they'd known each other. "You trying to corrupt me?"

"I'm trying to save your life," Waverly said. Gone was the gap-toothed smile. "The back of a horse is no place to be in modern combat. You've seen what Maxim guns do."

Stanton had, indeed. Part of his training to embark for Manila had been a hasty course at the Ft. Riley school on the new Maxim automatic machine gun the Army was slowly replacing hand-cranked Gatlings with. The instructors had simulated a calvary charge by setting up a line of watermelons impaled on wooden posts, then let loose with a one-pounder Maxim "pom-pom." The watermelons weren't just riven into gobbets of simulated man-flesh as they would have been with Gatling fire—they were obliterated. No wall of charging cavalry could approach a machine gun nest and live.

"I'll take my chances if it means getting on one of those transports," Stanton said. "Besides, Spain can't even afford rifles for its Manila garrison. I doubt they have machine guns."

"The Germans do." And the Germans had declared war two days ago. Waverly swore under his breath. "You're that determined to ship out, aren't you?"

"You that determined to stop me?"

Waverly's smile returned. "Stop you? Hang-fire, man. I came to *recruit* you. How'd you like to lead the first invasion on German soil?"

————

The nurses squawked like riled-up chickens when Stanton started hollering for his clothes, but that stopped once Waverly started waving around his magic piece of paper. Waverly had some serious clout—all the way to the Secretary of War, that's how big this thing was—and Stanton had mended enough to classify for light duty.

"Light duty my Aunt Nellie," Waverly grumbled as soon as they were out of earshot of the doctors. He climbed into the waiting buckboard, with Stanton following awkwardly. "I'm going to work you till you drop. You sure that busted wing won't get in the way of some honest sweat?"

"I'm a lefty, remember?" Stanton waggled his plastered arm in its sling. "I only use this one to salute and shake hands."

"And pat pretty little barmaids on their pretty little bottoms."

Stanton winced. "Not since that time in St. Louis." He'd ended up with a busted arm that time, too. Jealous boyfriend rather than a skittish horse, though.

A short carriage ride took them to Tent City. The illustrious General Thomas M. Anderson was gathering an entire division to send to the Philippines and wrest the islands from Spanish troops. Every flowerbed, mowed lawn, and manicured park on Presidio grounds had been given over to canvas tenting to house the gathering troops. They'd been gathering for months, and it may well be several more before the plodding general got his men aboard ships to sail.

Napoleon said an army marches on its stomach. What he didn't say was all that digested food has to go somewhere. There was nothing more constant—or fragrant—in the military than the ripe smell of flyblown johnny trenches, the open-air latrines of an Army tent city. Only the sea breeze off the Frisco harbor kept the smell on this warm summer bearable. Anderson would be lucky if half his troops weren't down with dysentery by sailing date.

"Kind of gets you right here," Waverly laughed, tapping his outsized nose. "You think this is bad, you should smell a troop ship after about a week at sea and all the johnnies are clogged up. Still sure you want to ship out?"

"I can wear a clothespin on my nose if need be."

Waverly's command sat on the edge of this miasmic canvas chaos. His oversized HQ tent stood out among the four-man tents like a pachyderm among poodles. Signage indicated it belonged to something called 3rd Composite Regiment (Provisional).

Composite was right. Stanton saw collar flashes of infantry, artillery, cavalry, even state militia.

Waverly led him to the back area reserved for planning staff, saluting a half-dozen times along the way with a look of annoyance on his face as raw-but-enthusiastic state militiamen demonstrated misplaced zeal and a tenuous grasp of military protocol.

"Gentlemen," Waverly said to his gaggle of staff officers milling around a makeshift map table, "this is the Captain Stanton I told you about. He will be leading B Company ashore for the initial landing."

Muttered greetings and awkward left-handed handshakes followed as introductions were made around the table. Stanton got the distinct impression they didn't think much of his chances. *Morituri te salutant* and flowers for the widow.

The map table they were gathered around was a sheet of wood supported on wooden sawhorses. Pinned to its surface were an oddment of papers and maps. Most prominent was a row of six painted postcards placed in a line that formed a panorama of a Chinese harbor. This was accompanied by various pages from some magazine—*Munsey's*, it looked like—that had photographs of that harbor. A hand-drawn map of dubious providence and a nautical chart almost too sea-stained to read completed the collection.

"Operation Sauerkraut," Waverly said, "so named because we're about to make some Krauts very sour, indeed." Stanton hoped Waverly's planning was better than his jokes.

The colonel nodded to a professor-looking type wearing major tabs to explain.

The port was named Tsingtau, part of the new German concession of Kiautschou. The Kiautschou Peninsula ended in a narrow finger of land jutting between Kiautschou Bay and the Yellow Sea. The finger was home to Tsingtau harbor, and the Germans had had trading stations there for decades. If the postcards and Munsey's photographs were to be believed, the harbor town looked like a miniature Berlin plopped down in the shadow of scenic Chinese mountains.

German gunboats had seized the harbor back in November right under the nose of Czarist Russia, who'd been planning to do just the same. It had been seized without the Kaiser's express authorization by a certain impetuous admiral named Otto von Diederichs. The events at Manila Bay started to make a lot more sense.

"Those mountains are where you come in, Saddle," Waverly said, pointing to the picturesque postcards. The conical Bismark Hill sat on the outskirts of the city and jutted up 400 hundred feet from the low-lying harbor. "We put your company ashore at night. The Germans wake up then with American cannon looking down from the peak. White flags and glory, Saddle. White flags and glory."

*Morituri te salutant* indeed. And this from a friend who wanted to "save" Stanton's life.

"What will the German garrison be doing while we're dragging cannon —I presume you mean disassembled mountain howitzers—up that slope?"

"Sleeping in their half-built barracks. The Germans just took over the place in November. No defenses yet, no field guns, and Dewey captured half the regular garrison aboard that troop ship. We act now, we can take Kaiser Bill's 'Asiatic Diadem' before they can dig in and reinforce."

Stanton nodded. Taking a hasty, imperfect course of action now was nearly always preferable to taking the perfect course of action later when it was too late. He'd learned that reacting to Apache raids. But this was a hasty course indeed.

"Where will the rest of the regiment be?"

Waverly's smile faded, and he sort of toed the floor. "Still aboard ship. It's like this, Saddle—"

"Better to risk losing one company than the whole regiment if it doesn't pan out?"

Waverly nodded.

Death or glory. Stunning surprise or ending up the goat in future history books, like Benedict Arnold and his hasty attempted invasion of Canada. Of course, Arnold ended up a goat for other reasons.

"Well, it beats rotting away in a hospital bed," Stanton grudged. "When do I meet my men?"

Another sheep-faced look.

"About that, Saddle—"

The Secretary of War had given Waverly his okay and a piece of paper to wave around. What he hadn't given Waverly was troops to do the job. Waverly was busy scrounging up what men he could. Dribs and drabs of unassigned regulars in transit to new commands. Hospital patients like Stanton, guardhouse malingerers, soldiers on leave, and whatever volunteers he could poach from Anderson's Manila-bound troops. Composite didn't begin to describe the 3rd Regiment.

"I seem to recall a biblical verse about making brick without straw."

"Right next to the one about making purses without pig ears," Waverly said. "Don't worry, Saddle. You've experience in your kind of combat; I've experience in mine. I know how to cut red tape and get things done while staying one step ahead of the IG—"

"—And the Provost Marshal?"

Waverly laughed. "You'll get your men, Boots. No point in us sailing if you don't."

———

Stanton glowered under the brim of his Montana Peak campaign hat. *A cavalryman like him commanding an infantry company.*

And what a company! He looked over the gaggle of ragamuffin soldiers milling about the parade field that made up his new command.

There was a leavening of army regulars Waverly had scraped up from who knows where, never mind that a glance at their cuffs and collars showed that half of them weren't infantry at all but horseless cavalrymen like himself or cannonless redlegs.

Some of those were guardhouse sweepings, some near-mended hospital cases like Stanton himself. There was even a squad from his former outfit —Buffalo Soldiers—segregated off to the side from their paler brethren.

The bulk, however, were state militiamen. Volunteers who cared more about getting into the thick of action now than waiting a month to embark for Manila with their home unit. That urge for action, to get into the fight, had even induced a few sailors fed up with scraping paint off hulls in the Navy Yard and Marines bored of lounging in barracks to volunteer for the 3rd Composite's little pleasure cruise.

No doubt the admirals and generals were yelling at each other over Waverly's creative poaching, but at least B company had bodies to fill most of its billets and every one of them a volunteer. That at least counted for something.

"Certainly a motley-looking crew," Hyram Turley, his fresh-faced second-in-command, said. The irony of Turley's own presence in the uniform of a US Navy Ensign (Reserve) was lost on the youth.

"Motley doesn't begin to describe it," Stanton muttered.

The Army was just phasing out the old Union woolen blues of the

Indian and Civil Wars to modern twill khaki, thereby stretching the term "uniform" into a rather elastic definition. Blue coats, khaki coats, sky blue pants, brown pants, khaki pants, in every conceivable combination. That wasn't even counting the smattering of sailor suits and Marine Corps fatigues.

And no two hats alike. Campaign hats, cavalry slouch hats, state militia kepis, even one or two cork pith helmets. One self-satisfied militiaman even wore a polished blue *Pickelhaube* spiked helmet that was just coming into service for Army ceremonial dress uniforms. Where he'd picked that up, only heaven knew.

Stanton muttered an old Apache curse and turned to the grizzled, white-whiskered first sergeant Waverly must have dug up from some Civil War retirement home. "Okay, Fitzgerald. Get them formed up."

The wee leprechaun of a First Sergeant, all of five-feet nothing, roared out in a ten-foot voice, "*Form it up!*" and the gaggle shuffled itself into a crude semblance of a military formation.

"*Comp'ny! 'Ten'shun!*"

Stanton let the tedious process of parade work its way through to the inevitable "B Company all present and accounted for." Stanton returned the reporting salute with his left hand.

He put on his war face and took a step forward. "Men of Company B!" he bellowed. Shouting orders to calvary troopers over the whine of Arizona winds had given him leather lungs. "While the rest of the army twiddles it thumbs waiting around for another month to go fight Spaniards, B Company will have kicked Kaiser Bill right out of the Pacific!"

The men cheered.

"We had a nice little private fight going on with Spain and the Kaiser thought to stick his nose in. Well, we're going to show him what happens when someone butts into America's business!"

Another roaring cheer.

"And it's going to be us who gets in the first licks. Not General Anderson's division—" another gesture at the nearby tents, "—not Teddy Roosevelt and his glory boys in Tampa. It won't even be the rest of Third Regiment. It's going to be us, B Company, who leads that first charge. You think Admiral Dewey's famous now? We pull this off and you won't ever have to pay for your own beer!"

This time the cheer was ear-deafeningly sincere.

"Okay, Fitz," he said. "Dismiss them, and for pity's sake, get them to a firing range. Half of them have probably never even picked up a rifle before."

"Sir, we haven't any rifles."

"Well, get them practicing on broomsticks or something." Which reminded him. "Oh, and Fitz? We have a scrounger in that lot by any chance?"

"Aye, that we do. A right and proper scrounger. When he isn't in the glasshouse."

"Let me guess. The fellow in the spiked German Easter bonnet?"

Fitzgerlad nodded. "Private Jaeger, militiaman out of Chicago, and a wee cunning sprout, he is. I'd hang on to me gold watch with both hands, if I was you, sir."

"Well, drag him over to see me in an hour. I have a little job for him."

———

A normally four-man tent served as both Stanton's quarters and office. The tent flaps were tied up to try to air out the mildew and mold.1 Aside from Stanton's sleeping cot, the tent held a map table that served as a desk, a couple folding canvas camp stools, and a discard wooden apple crate Stanton used for a filing cabinet. All the comforts of home.

Stanton watched as two Buffalo Soldiers frog-marched Illinois State Milita Private Willy Jaeger—complete with ridiculous pickle-spike headgear—to Stanton's tent.

Lamb, the senior of the two Buffaloes, let go his grip on Jaeger's forearm and saluted. "Private Jaeger as requested, Cap'n."

"Thank you, Jimmy," Stanton said, sitting at his map table. "I'll take it from here."

Lamb arched his brow, as if to say Jaeger wasn't to be trusted, but saluted and departed, taking his partner with him.

Jaeger, a smirking, weasel-faced, two-bit chiseler, made an aggrieved show of smoothing out his jacket sleeves. "Can't say I much like being dragged around by the likes of *them*. Where I come from, we call—"

"Did I give you leave to speak, *Private*?" Stanton barked. "It might interest you to know that Jimmy Lamb can sneak up on a sleeping Apache and that he has thirty-one notches cut in the handle of that Bowie knife he carries."

Jaeger paled.

Stanton tapped his fingers on the open personal file before him. "The only notches you yourself seemed to have carved are tallies on prison walls of days served."

"Judges. What do they know?"

"The Cook County judge knew enough to send you to Jolliet for life."

"Yeah, but he let me join up instead."

"And the Presidio Judge Advocate General knew enough to send you to Leavenworth."

"Yean, but he let me join your mob instead."

"Which services I can decline."

Jaeger turned an even whiter shade of pale.

"I don't like troublemakers, Private Jaeger. But I do like people who are useful."

A calculating look crept into Jaeger's eyes. "I can be useful. Very useful."

"Can you? Sit down, Private Jaeger."

Jaeger sat. unfastening the chinstrap of his German-style *Pickelhaube* as he did so. He set the headgear on the table.

Never had the Army wasted money on an object so useless. The contraption looked to be stiffened cloth over a cork frame, more akin to a British bobby's police helmet than a Prussian junker's leather war helmet. Useless in the rain, useless in the sun.

"Nice hat," Stanton said.

"Like it? I can get one for you wholesale."

"I bet you could."

The cunning look deepened. "That's what this is about? A hat?"

"In a manner of speaking. You saw the men's uniforms."

"A riotous rainbow of colors."

"I want every man in my company to have the new khaki uniform."

"The old Army requisition process proving a mite slow?" Jaeger smirked. "The quartermasters keeping all the good stuff for themselves? That's always the way with clerks. And you, thinking how I know my way around warehouses—"

"I want every man in my company to have the new khaki uniform. Full kit. Properly sized."

The scrounger grinned. "Ask any of the boys in Chicago: if it's in stock, Jaeger delivers." He paused. "Only like I tell the boys downtown when they ask, what's in it for me?"

"Besides staying out of Leavenworth?"

Jaeger laughed. "You can't lay that hoodoo on me. Job like this takes a delicate touch, and I ain't going to be at my best if I'm worrying about some rockpile. I need additional incentives to focus my mind."

"I'm a company commander. My magic wand is fairly limited."

"I figure you got enough pull for this." Jaeger leaned forward. "I've been counting sleeves, see? Lot of sleeves in this outfit and not a lot of stripes on them. I figure you'll end up making some privates sergeants and one of 'em might as well be me. Better being the sarge ordering them latrine trenches dug than to be the schlub what's digging one."

"Something might be arranged," Stanton said, suppressing a smile.

A raw militia recruit like Jaegar had no idea how much easier it was to be a private than an NCO or how crushing a weight responsibility was. The surprise might just do the Chicago tough good, might make a man out of him. Stanton had seen it happen before.

——

An army may move on its stomach, but it doesn't move at all without paperwork, even a just-formed company. Especially a just-formed company. Stanton had to establish the initial paperwork on everything.

*Need to find myself a company clerk. Wonder if Jaeger could scrounge one of those up for me, too?*

He'd smoked two pipes and made an inch-high dent in a stack of pay forms by the time an orderly from Regimental HQ presented the colonel's compliments and the accompanying summons to the presence.

"Got a couple tidbits for you, Saddle," Waverly told him when Stanton arrived at HQ. "Follow-up from yesterday." The colonel poured them both a cup of coffee from a battered tin pot he'd had back at the Academy. "First off, the *Pacific Flyer* will be ready a day early."

Waverly had rather forcibly—and probably illegally—appropriated a passenger liner docked in Frisco Bay for use as a fast troop transport. A and C Companies were even now stripping out stateroom furnishings and hanging jowl-to-jowl troop hammocks instead.

"I decided to save a little time by simply dumping the furnishings over the side of the ship rather than try to warehouse them." The owners, already hopping mad, were going to love that.

The Army could survive being yelled at; it couldn't survive delay. General Anderson's division would take over a month sailing on slow boats to the Philippines. The speedy liner would get the 3rd Composite Regiment to China in two weeks or less. Every day saved might be critical.

"Second, your boys will be getting the good stuff. I've managed to pry sixty Krags away from Anderson."

Generous. Sixty would just about equip B Company. Waverly was shorting the rest of his regiment to equip Stanton with, as he said, "the good stuff." Well, B Company was the one going into battle.

Like the new, modern khaki uniforms, the Army was just in the process of switching to a new modern rifle, replacing its single-shot trapdoor Springfield rifles with bolt-action Krag-Jorgensen repeaters. Springfields still used black powder cartridges. Krags used smokeless .30-40 rounds. Stanton preferred not giving German defenders an aiming point when firing.

"I'll have to have the men trained on them, sir."

Waverly snorted. "What's to train? You pop open the receiver gate, dump a handful of bullets in, close it back up and shoot."

"Yes, sir." The Army had gone with Krags over the German Mauser precisely because it was so easy to reload in combat. Unfortunately, some of his militiamen had an ungodly knack of fouling up even the simplest of things.

"Lastly, we've found a freighter captain who's been in Tsingtau port within the past month." He pointed across the tent where a grizzled civilian ship's captain was furiously gesticulating at one of Waverly's staff. The skipper was bellowing in accented English more *Plattdeutsch* than Noah Webster.

"He says they've begun digging gun pits in Tsingtau, but haven't received the artillery to put in them yet—"

"That's good."

"—But they've also started mining the approach to the harbor, Iltis Bay included."

"That's bad." Iltis Bay was where they'd intended to land B Company to advance on Bismark Hill.

"Change of plans. We'll land you five miles west of Iltis Bay instead. Captain Waldeck says there's a hill there twice as high, nine hundred feet. Prince-something-or-other."

"Sir, my mountain howitzers won't *reach* five miles." The little three-inch popgun was made to be taken apart and carried in five separate pieces, allowing it to be transported up rugged mountain slopes. Useful in remote areas, utterly worthless as a siege cannon.

"Won't need to. We'll use that Prinz-Heinrich-Berg peak for spotting naval covering fire while your boys descend and march overland five miles to take Bismark Hill."

And once B Company held Bismark Hill, they'd hold the city.

If they held Bismark Hill. If they could take it away from a 1500-strong garrison who'd had ample warning of attack from the Navy's guns.

"More marching than we planned, Saddle, but I'm sure your boys are up to a little hike."

"Just as long as they don't have to march in step."

———

With the flaps of his tent open at night, it wasn't quite pitch dark at four in the morning when a whisper woke Stanton up.

Jaeger was back. He'd taken the liberty of sewing sergeant stripes on his sleeves. "Got your uniforms for you, sir."

Stanton sat up and swiveled round to place his stockinged feet on the floor. "Looks like you got something else for me, too. Who's your little friend?"

A man—no, a living tower shaped like a man—stood just outside the tent. Cleopatra's Needle without Cleopatra. A corporal, from the stripe on his khaki sleeves, a corporal who stood seven feet tall if he stood an inch.

"I had to do some wheeling and dealing with the warehouse clerk. Well, this is the clerk. He wants to come, too."

The living statue snapped to attention, difficult to do with a folding Army cot in each arm. "*Sor!*" the giant rumbled in an accent even thicker than that of the freighter captain. Maybe it was a trick of the night, but he seemed to clack his heels together as he did so.

"He's Hungarian, sir. Some long impossible name. Folks just call him 'Obelisk.'"

"I can see why. Does it speak English?"

The giant grumbled something in something that sounded like Kraut-talk to Stanton. Jaeger answered back.

"He says he speaks seven different languages. English just doesn't happen to be one of his speaking languages. He can read and write it, though."

"And follow along, apparently. I take it he speaks German?"

"Like an angel, sir. Better than my folks taught me."

That might be useful. Almost as useful as taking over Stanton's paperwork.

———

*Off the China Coast*
*22 May 1898*

If there were a real-world equivalent of Dante's Inferno, sailing aboard a troopship would be it. Bad enough in officer quarters, where Stanton had to share a cubbyhole of a hammock-slung stateroom with five other officers. His seasick enlisted men were hammocked check-to-jowl in cramped unventilated hold spaces reeking of vomit and overflowing johnny buckets.

Stanton had thought the Deep South hot and humid, but the China coast in summer was hot as the hinges of Hades, with air so saturated you needed gills to breathe it.

Was it any wonder that totally against both ship regulations and Waverly's express orders that Stanton allowed his men to sleep topside on deck, "guarding" B Company's two crated Maxims and its sole mountain howitzer? Of course, the men needed supervision, so he'd started sleeping topside, too.

But first he needed to make his rounds.

He flexed his right arm as he walked. The ship's surgeon had taken off the plaster the day before. A little weak and a little stiff and sore, but at least he could scratch it now.

Except for an insomniac or two, his men were fast asleep, sawing logs under the night sky.

Given that they'd be thrown together for just short of three weeks, B Company was shaping up nicely. He'd leavened the militia platoons with Army regulars, bumping them to NCOs. The duckfeets—the Navy and Marine Corps orphans—he'd attached to the signals team. They'd stay up on Prinz-Heinrich-Berg providing security. They probably wouldn't be needed, but if they were, the Marines would serve as a stiffener.

The Buffaloes from his former calvary company Stanton had placed with him as a headquarters squad. That kept them from being mixed in with the more recalcitrant Southern boys, as well as giving him a special reconnaissance team.

Obelisk and "Sergeant" Jaeger he'd dumped in his headquarters squad, as well. Obelisk had not only shaped up as a crackerjack clerk; he'd taken it upon himself to serve as Stanton's dogsbody, bodyguard, and pack mule. It'd taken a few days' voyage, but Obelisk—ex-Count Lipot Obeliszkszky of the Sighișoara Obeliszkszkys, late of the Austrian-Hungary Empire and colonel in its army—eventually let slip he spoke English. Spoke it very well, in fact.

Asked why he kept mute, the giant said there are two types of men: those who wish nothing less than to rule other men and those who wish nothing more that to rule only themselves. He'd come to America because it was a land comprised of the latter, and he wished never to order another human being in his life. Stanton suggested perhaps the Army wasn't the place for him. The ex-count merely raised an eyebrow. How many men did a private, let alone a mute one, give orders to?

As for Jaeger, he'd put the pride of Chicago's South Side where he wouldn't get into trouble: as putative NCO over the squad. Waverly had insisted on a white NCO over the Buffaloes, and Stanton knew Jaeger wouldn't get in Jimmy Lamb's way, not wishing to be another knife-notch. Besides, it amused Stanton to watch the little street tough deal with the situation.

Jaeger sat on the deck, idly rolling dice as his Buffaloes laid sprawled asleep around him. The little chiseler's face sported fresh bandages, and one hand was bandaged up.

"Fall down a companion way?"

Jaeger looked up from his dice. "A certain individual in A Company of the sergeant persuasion objected to having to mess with my Buffaloes."

Stanton smiled at Jaeger's use of the word *my*. "You proceeded to disabuse him of said notion?"

"If you mean did I beat the ever-loving snot of the lousy mug, no I did not. He'd have gone right to Waverly, and we all know how *that* would have turned out."

Jaeger tossed his dice again. "So instead, I engaged friend sergeant in a little game of chance a little later on. Cleaned him out good." He touched his bandaged hand to his facial bruises. "These I picked up after he objected to my miraculous luck. Cleaned him pretty good that way, too, only over a reason he don't dare go to Waverly for, see?" A final toss of the dice. "Nobody messes with my Buffaloes."

"We might just make a sergeant out of you yet."

"Uh, Captain?" Jaeger said, looking up with what had to be a surprisingly earnest look on his face. "About them fancy uniforms you wanted me to get you."

The khakis were crated up with B Company's other supplies. Stanton would break them out when it came time for the company to go ashore.

"I thought you were just another iron tail on the make, wanting to have your boys look pretty for Waverly, get yourself a promotion. But I talked with the Buffaloes that served under you, and they say you're not that way at all. You're a right guy. That's why I just can't figure why—"

"Why I wanted them?" Stanton finished. "Not something that needs discussing with a private who's sewn a few stripes on his arm to get out of work details."

Jaeger gulped. "How about a sergeant trying to make a go of it, trying to learn the ropes?" Earnestness had given way to embarrassment.

"*Sergeant* Jager," Stanton said, "the two most important duties in commanding troops are the welfare of your men and getting the job done, not necessarily in that order. B Company will be going up against German regulars, the finest fighting force in the world. They think us mutts and mongrels, especially if we show up dressed the part. But if we go up that hill in modern uniforms with modern rifles, that may just give them pause, may just give us an edge. A tiny advantage, to be sure, but with fifteen hundred of them and only sixty of us, I'll take any advantage I can get to see my men make it through."

Jaeger nodded. "I see." He turned his face away. "Sir? I think there's a third duty you let out. Not letting down your men. Or your commander. I won't let you down on that hill, sir."

"I hope not, Jaeger, because you're coming with me and the Buffaloes on a very special mission."

———

*22 MAY 1898*

The *Pacific Flyer* met up with Dewey's flotilla just over the horizon from the Kiautschou Peninsula. Bobbing on the waves among the gray-hulled warships sat a dilapidated Chinese junk they'd appropriated, the vessel being key to Operation Sauerkraut. Booms on the *Pacific Flyer* were already loading B Company's guns and ammunition aboard the frail sailing vessel.

Waverly nodded at the progress from the *Flyer's* bridge wing. "You know what you have to do, Saddle. Get up that hill and take it."

"I still say I need a blocking force up that other trail."

According to Otto Waldeck, the tramp freighter captain, there were two paths leading up to the peak of Prinz-Heinrich-Berg: one going up the east slope from the main body of the peninsula, the other up the west slope from Tsingtau harbor proper.

"*Nein!* You'd haff to be *Bergziege*—mountain goat—to reach trail," Captain Waldeck spat. A quirk of geography made reaching the east slope trail from the beach a snap. Rugged cliffs blocked a path to the west slope trail.

Waldeck was coming ashore with the company to act as local guide. In the old captain's words, "I haff und wife und kinder in San Francisco und sister in Milwaukie. I come to America to get away from Kaisers und kings. I not see my boys be forced in Kaiser's Army if he win."

Stanton shrugged and saluted. No need to remind Waverly that the Buffaloes had chased Apache up and down the rugged Superstition Mountains a dozen times over. There was an old saying in the Army: better to ask forgiveness than request permission.

———

*23-24 MAY 1898*

The purloined Chinese junk, with the men of B Company safely hidden below her deck, loitered just off the shoreline the entire day. The jutted peak of Prinz-Heinrich-Berg, just a quarter mile from the water's edge, stared down at the boat from the lofty height of nine hundred feet. If there were German observers up there, one more Chinese vessel would go unnoticed if it did remain at anchor all day long for no apparent purpose. *Macht nichts!* The Eastern mind was inscrutable, *ja?*

As dusk fell, the junk weighed anchor. Just as it got too dark to see, the junk turned ponderously towards shore and ran aground on the soft sandy shore.

A frenzy of activity as B Company and ship's crew got equipment and supplies loaded ashore. The hardest part proved to be hoisting seven kicking, braying pack mules over the side—one for each of the five pieces of howitzer, one for each tripoded Maxim. Ammunition and sundries would have to be carried on the backs of the men themselves. For all of Stanton's careful planning, those new khaki uniforms were going to be sweat-stained and dirty by the time the Germans laid eyes on them.

Stanton clapped a hand on young Ensign Turley's shoulder. "You up for this, Hiram?"

"Sure, Skipper. I lead the main body up the trail, make a lot of noise. It's you who has the hard part."

Otto Waldeck spat a gob of tobacco. "Und I still say you crazy-man goink up that udder vay."

Stanton laughed. "That escarpment?" He titled his head towards a scrabbly-looking cliff. "Won't even slow my Buffaloes down." He checked his pocketwatch. "Get your boys moving. If something goes wrong and Otto's right, you'll have to take the peak yourself."

"Can do," the young ensign said, saluting with a grin on his face that shouted he still thought war a boy's game, something the Apache had knocked out of Stanton years ago.

———

The escarpment proved to be nothing. It was the steep climb up nine hundred feet of slope that had Stanton wheezing like a grampus. Jaeger looked ready to die. City types didn't go much in for nature hikes.

They crouched near a telegraph pole set in so recently the spoil dirt was still fresh. That, at least, proved the peak was manned now.

He sent Ronnie Bell up the pole where he could listen for the humming buzz of sent signals over the uninsulated line. Bell shook his head and made a cutting gesture, but Staton shook his head. If things went right, they could use the telegraph line to keep in contact with the semaphore crew left behind as the rest of them made a five-mile dash for Bismark Hill.

Jimmy Lamb he sent up the peak to count noses in the dark. "No notches unless you have to."

Lamb was gone three times as long as he should have been. Stanton had started to get almost worried. "Observation post, only," Lamb reported. "Six men, four asleep. Telegraph shack, binoculars. Gun pit dug, no guns. Rifles only." He sipped from his canteen. "I slipped down the other trail for a look-see. The boy is bringing them up slow but quiet. A half-hour to get to top, I'd say. Mules are slowing them down."

Stanton clapped his scout on the shoulder. "No reason for us to wait on mules. Boys, let's take that observation post—alive, if you can. We need information more than we need knife notches."

He gestured to Jaeger and the looming Obelisk. "Stay with me. You two would just get in the way."

At his signal, his little command moved out.

———

One of the Krauts managed to put up a fuss. His gruesome death—throat slashed ear-to-ear—served to put the frighteners on the other five, who couldn't stumble over their tongues fast enough to talk.

The hulking, stone-faced Buffaloes were frightening enough, but their Bowie knives! German dress daggers were dainty, elegant things. The size and shape of the Bowies was crude and uncivilized, as crude and uncivilized as they imagined the whole American nation of cowboys to be.

To begin with, the Tsingtau garrison wasn't German Army regulars. They were Navy sailors playing at soldiers: the III *Seebataillon*. The *Kaiserliche Marine*, the German Imperial Navy, ran both the civil and military functions of the port colony.

The harbor was indeed mined, but there were no shore batteries except a handful of land howitzers pressed into service. The colony had been expecting a freighter-load of naval guns from the Krupp works before war broke out. Dewey's patrols should soon pick them up. It had been a margin of mere days, after all.

Ensign Turley had arrived with an advance party, mostly the signals detachment. He was hastily setting things up. Three lanterns had been placed in a row facing out to sea to signal to Dewey's blacked-out ships that the peak had been taken.

"As soon as the mules make it up the hill, I'll set out for Bismark," he told Turley. "I'll leave you in command here."

The young ensign drew himself up. "Sir, if it's all the same to you, I'd just as soon come along." He pointed to a redheaded midshipman on loan from Dewey, along with the naval spotters. The midshipman was even younger than Turley, if it were possible. "If you need to leave an officer in charge, McMurray can handle things."

Only the Navy would let its men be bossed around by a seventeen-year-old boy.

Stanton nodded. He crooked a finger at the boy, who came bustling up like a tail-wagging puppy. "Midshipman, I'm leaving you in command here. Your job is simple: hold this hill. Spot for Dewey's naval fire. Prevent any breakout of German garrison troops, keep them bottled up in town. Prevent any reinforcement of Bismark Hill. Keep my force under observation. If you see anything nasty about to happen to us, pulverize it with Dewey's guns. Understand?"

The boy nodded, wide-eyed.

"Keep the telegraph line manned. Our prisoners say the line runs down the road into town, right past Bismark Hill. We'll use it to keep in contact with you and pass along any message we have for Dewey or he for us."

Another wide-eyed nod.

"Your chiefs will know what to do, son. Just sit back, relax, let them do their jobs and you'll go back to the Naval Academy next fall with a bunch of medals on your chest and commendations in your record."

The boy threw the awkwardest military salute Stanton had ever had to return.

"Good luck, sir!" McMurray squeaked.

Stanton nodded. They were going to need it.

Sixty against sixteen-hundred counting native auxiliaries. Medals and accommodations, indeed.

Or wooden crosses marked in German *Fraktur* script.

————

It was nearly daybreak before they'd reached the stepping-off point to assault Bismark Hill. The German planned to build a fortress there, three stories underground and an observation tower above. Excavation had already started and a wooden tower—a scaffold-like affair similar to those built on US Army frontier posts—thrown up.

The eastern sky began to pink with the approach of dawn. Dewey's flotilla could be plainly seen in silhouette, steaming into fire range of Tsingtau.

Signal lanterns flashed code in the diminishing dark. The Morse was in German, of course.

"What do you think they're saying, sir?" Turley asked, frustrated he couldn't read it.

"The usual Paul Revere stuff," Jaegar proffered. "The *Amis* are coming, the *Amis* are coming."

Stanton smiled at the comparison to Boston's Old North Church. "One if by land and two if by *Seekrieg*." He turned his head to where Bell waited with a tap-line tied into the telegraph wire. "Tell McMurray to tell Dewey to start laying it down. They're on to us."

————

The Germans had a field howitzer on Bismark and they had it sighted pretty good. Second Platoon was down to a couple walking wounded. Those idiot state militia had bunched up, just like Stanton had told them *not* to do.

He let out a string of Apache curses. "Signal Dewey to get his finger out *and take out that howitzer!*" Those Navy swabbies couldn't hit the broadside of a burning barn.

No, that wasn't fair. They'd done marvels keeping the bulk of the German's garrison pinned down in town. No reinforcements had reached the hill. That Kraut gun was just dug in devilishly well.

"It's not the gun keeping my men down, sir," the sergeant leading First Platoon said. He was lying prone in the same fresh artillery crater as Stanton. "The gun fires slow enough we could rush 'em. It's them two Maxims up there. Keep the barrel cooled, you can fire one of them things all the live-long day. Nine hunnerd rounds a minute. My boys can't get close." And Stanton's own Maxims couldn't get close enough to set up, either.

Interlocking field of fire and the Krauts keep shifting one, then the other to prepared firing positions so Dewey couldn't get a bead on them. Naval guns fired at a rate a tortoise would scoff at.

Jimmy Lamb cleared his throat. Stanton shook his head. "No, Jimmy. Geronimo himself couldn't sneak up on a Maxim." Not in broad daylight, not over a couple hundred yards of open ground.

Suddenly, a cheer arose behind Stanton's lines. The redlegs must have finally got their disassembled mountain cannon assembled. He'd like to get at the jackwall who designed it. Some ideas that looked good on paper were complete disasters in the field.

The redlegs didn't need to be told what their priority target was. A single inaugural shot, and a plume of dirt and smoke erupted atop Bismark Hill, accompanied by the far-flung wreckage of a carriage-mounted Maxim.

A lucky hit—they couldn't do that well again in a million years with that idiotic five-part misbegotten contraption—but Stanton would take it. There was a blind spot in the remaining Maxim's coverage now.

He called his platoon sergeants together.

"Here's what we're going to do. Instead of advancing in a loose skirmish line as per Army standing doctrine, we're going to advance by five-man squads. Ever play leapfrog as a kid? That's how we're going to do this. One squad will advance twenty yards, then hit the dirt, best cover they can find, while the rest of us provide covering fire poured on the Maxim. Then the next squad and the next and so on. Got it?"

It must've sounded cabbage-headed as all get out, but they all nodded. The looks on their faces said they thought it just might work. The Germans certainly wouldn't be expecting it, at any rate.

He waited until the sergeants had all crawled back to their platoons and explained the plan, then gave the signal to advance.

Death or glory. Victory or defeat. Medals or a wooden *Fraktur* cross.

———

*MANY DAYS LATER*

Dewey's ships laid anchored in the harbor, and an American flag flew atop Bismark Hill. Wellington would have called it a close-run thing. Stanton, in the somber of the night, remembered of it more an abattoir.

Young Hiram Turley had fallen, his innocent eyes staring questioningly up at the heavens. Otto Waldeck left behind a widow, kinder, and a sister in Milwaukee. Jimmy Lamb and Bell and all but two of his Buffaloes gone; they'd crested the lip of the Maxim machine gun nest, only to be struck down at the moment of glory.

Stanton himself laid in hospital, an arm in a sling again—his writing arm this time—from a shrapnel burst. Jaeger laid in hospital, too, a cast on his leg and a spangled blue ribbon pinned on his pajamas. He'd managed to reach the Maxim and turn it on the Germans, despite bleeding wounds taken from the same burst that took Jimmy Lamb. A sergeant to his men at last and for always.

The III *Seebataillon* barrack gymnasium survived intact, now given over as makeshift hospital for the men of B Company. Stanton, propped up in bed, dictated to the silent Obelisk. Battles ended, but the paperwork lived on.

Stanton's uniform hung in the closet. It bore the shoulder straps of a full bird colonel. Waverley had moved up, and Stanton, as promised, had moved up, as well. He was taking command of the 3rd Composite, provisional no longer, and Captain Obeliszkszky (field promotion) was taking over B Company. When the Obelisk had objected, Stanton had told him bluntly that Obelisk owed it to the men who'd made it down Bismark Hill, and that there was a difference between leading men and ruling them.

Some of the more mobile wounded had left their beds to stare out the window at the new arrival in Kiautschou Bay: a Japanese cruiser. Her red-and-white sunburst ensign snapped at her mast, whipped by the freshening winds of yet another approaching typhoon. A first one had taken down the telegraph lines to the outside world only hours after the Germans' surrender. Without news from the outside, what the Japanese ship's presence meant could only be guessed at. It wasn't firing at Dewey's ships, at least, and it had sailed into the bay in the company of a US Navy dispatch vessel, so it wasn't a threat at present.

*One war at a time*, Stanton would have thought, but they were already presently fighting two as it was.

Jaeger, unable to move from his bed, stared not at ships but at the large mural of the glories of Kaiser Wilhelm II painted on the wall opposite. The art was obscene in its fawning obsequity.

"What's *Mundus non sufficit?*" he asked of the wreathed motto.

"Bad Latin," the Obelisk answered. "It should be *Non sufficit orbis*. That's how Philip II of Spain styled his motto."

"Yes, but what's it *mean?*"

"'The world is not enough.'"

And it wasn't, not for men like Philip II or Kaiser Bill or the type of men who wished for nothing less than to rule other men.

The little sergeant rubbed his leg cast, not that it'd scratch his obvious itch. "You know, I used to think the Chicago boys were really tough. Nobody could touch 'em, not the law, not the mayor. That's why I hooked with 'em. Wanted to be on the winning side."

His bandaged fist curled and uncurled. "But this Army crowd? B Company would go through them like a knife through butter. Us banged-up guys in this *room* would go through them like butter."

The little tough squared his shoulders. "Well, forget that Chicago nonsense. Cap'n—I mean Colonel? You think I could just stay in the Army? Go whole hog, I mean? Not militia. Regular Army and everything?"

Stanton stopped his dictation midsentence. "I think we might be able to accommodate you, Sergeant." He'd already had Obelisk draw up the papers.

A single sharp rap on the open doorframe was followed by the entry of a lieutenant with corded shoulder ropes, the aiguillettes of a general's aide. "*Ten'shun!*" the aide barked, ordering a room full of wounded to their feet. Less than half were able to comply.

Waverly and a party of Japanese naval officers stood at the door. Waverly wore the twin stars of a major general.

*To the victors who stay aboard ship go the spoils.*

"Your Excellency, this is Colonel Stanton and the men who took Bismark Hill."

A diminutive Japanese admiral, portly and sporting white goatee and mustache and a cluster of starburst medals on his chest, approached Stanton's beside. He made to shake Stanton's hand.

"I am most honored," the Japanese said, blowing slightly. "I should like to discuss your exploits in detail later, Colonel, after you are recovered."

"Admiral Togo here is assuming command of Tsingtau," Waverly explained. "We're turning the Kiautschou Concession over to our new ally, Japan." Waverly's voice was pleasant enough, but his face spoke his distaste for turning over a port American blood had paid for.

"Ally?" Jaeger blurted, still not having learned a mere sergeant keeps quiet while generals and admirals speak.

'Oh, that's right. Telegraph's out. You boys wouldn't have heard yet. Bates, pass out those newspapers the dispatch boat brought in."

The general's aide rushed around the room, scattering newspapers like rose petals.

"I'll leave you fine boys to recuperate. You'll need to. The 3rd Composite will be marching all the way to Berlin!"

Waverly and the Japanese left, leaving Stanton and his men to devour the news.

They were British papers out of Hong Kong and a few days old, but they were in English and told of a world gone mad.

German regulars landing in Boston and New York. The Royal Navy firing British shells on the transports that had carried them. French armies hurling their might against the weakened German Army to reclaim their lost Alsace–Lorraine provinces. Of Russia allying itself with Germany and gathering ships and Siberian troops in Vladivostok to reclaim Tsingtau and perhaps even Alaska. Japanese fleets massing to stop them.

The Armageddon that statesmen and scribblers alike had warned against had arrived, all sparked by the insane von Diederichs at Manila. Or the explosion of the *Maine* at Havana. Or the penny-a-paper screeds of one Randolph Hearst.

Well, Hearst had the war he wanted now, and it was no longer splendid nor little.

Millions of men marching against millions of Maxims. Every hill, every slope, every rise at Bismark Hill. Every open field dotted with rows of *Fraktur* crosses.

*Non sufficit orbis.*

The world wasn't enough. Not for men like von Diederichs or Hearst or the Kaiser.

Not for Mars, the God of War.

Yet, it was the only world there was, and that world was now aflame.

Obelisk sat perched on his stool, pen in hand, the former count ready to take up more dictation. Those stacks of reports lying on Stanton's nightstand unaddressed were artifacts of a non-vanished age of Law. Chaff in the wind now. Spent brass on the floor of a machine gun nest.

A snatch of poetry came to Stanton. Ovid or Virgil or perhaps even Homer.

*No law except the Sword*
*Unsheathed and uncontrolled.*

"Put away your pen," he told Obelisk. "This isn't an age for pens."

# THE RIDE FOR THE WHITE HOUSE

## Dan Kemp

*FEBRUARY 27, 1901*

Michael Williamson eagerly strode up the sidewalk toward the National Soldiers' Home. The impressive castle-style stone building dominated the heights above the rest of Washington, DC, and had looked down on the action in 1864 when Jubal Early's force had made their try for the capital city. He dismissed that bit of history from his mind. The War Between the States wasn't either of the wars that concerned Williamson today.

The man he was looking for was where Williamson's contact on the Home's staff had told him he'd be. On the fourth bench on the right, looking southward across the city, he sat calmly, enjoying the air before lunch. The only concession to the breezy chill of February weather was an old blue wool blanket hung loosely around his shoulders.

"General Keogh, sir?"

The old man laughed. "They only gave me that star as a retirement gift. Two decades as a colonel and that was still the only way I saw the general's list. Damned tombstone promotion."

"I doubt you remember, sir, but we met in Cuba a few years ago when you were General Custer's chief of staff," Williamson said. "I was with the 1st Volunteer Cavalry then and running messages for the Colonel after his first messenger caught a Spanish Hornet. Well, then we'd heard you got hit, too."

Keogh laughed, gleeful at the memory. "Roosevelt's Rough Riders. What a bunch of men you were." He patted the bench. "Here, have a seat, young man. Keep an old man company."

Williamson did so, taking the spot at the bench's left end. "You're barely sixty, sir."

"I've been shot enough times that it ages you somewhat in advance of your actual years. Made it through '61 to '65 without a scratch, though my horse took a bad one meant for me down in Georgia. Hit twice at Little Big Horn, neither one that bad, and then of course again below San Juan Hill." Keogh winced a bit, shifting in his seat. "I won't lie, that's been a bad one to live with these last two years. The cold weather plays Hell with it. Never let anyone tell you a good shoulder hit is easy, lad. It may not look like much, but it's connected to everything."

Williamson did his best to smile. "I won't, sir. Not a lot of Spanish rifle fire on the streets of New York or Washington, though."

Keogh looked sideways at him. "What are you doing these days? Police work?"

Williamson shook his head.

"Nothing so honest, sir, and it's much more difficult. I am the Washington correspondent for the *New York Tribune*, though the business being what it is, I believe that also makes me the Washington reporter for a couple other papers elsewhere."

"Son, I haven't done anything newsworthy in years, so I can't imagine why you'd come out here on a day like this just to sit with me." Keogh chuckled, but patted at his pocket. "Damn, I'm out of cigars."

"Well, you have been present for large number of actions, many of which were truly pivotal. Just between us two cavalrymen, you rode with a lot of names that now figure prominently in the history books. And one of those is on the front page of the newspapers even now."

Williamson watched the old man's face closely, looking to gauge his reaction.

"Since almost all the others are dead now, I assume you mean my old friend from down South who has a Presidential inauguration on Monday?" Keogh sighed and leaned back on the bench.

"Yes, sir, 'Fighting Joe' Wheeler himself, being a general of two armies and now about to become President of the United States. What's it like seeing an officer you served so closely alongside now entering the White House?"

That elicited a chuckle from the older man. "It's not as if General

Wheeler is at all unfamiliar with the Capitol, from his many years in Congress before he returned to service. And I suppose he is more familiar with the way things are usually done than General Custer would have been."

Both men laughed at that, but Williamson then pressed into the gap. "What if he'd lived? Do you think General Custer might have been President?"

Keogh shook his head. "That's a hard and difficult question, son. I'll start with one thing by way of an answer. General Custer's many great gifts did not include an appreciation for established procedure. His West Point years alone proved that." While a cadet, Custer had racked up 726 demerits, perhaps the most of anyone in the Academy's history who had actually graduated.

"Is that how he survived the great battle at Little Big Horn?"

Keogh slid a small silver flask from his pocket, took a sip, and laughed. "Ah, lad, now that's a tale that's been told before." Wordlessly, he offered it to Williamson. "Scotch, I'm afraid. The Irish sort is hard to come by in these parts."

Williamson accepted and took a sip of his own before returning the flask. "But not told by you, sir," Williamson smiled. "And with General Custer dead and everyone still living being out of uniform now, maybe some unanswered questions can be probed."

Keogh sighed, looking out over the capital city. He was lost in thought for a long few moments, mentally traveling back decades. When he finally spoke, it had a dreamy and distant tone that hadn't been there before. "The first thing to remember is while George Custer had made a lot of seemingly reckless moves in his career, very few people said he was stupid, and even fewer people said it twice."

"And once he was a dead hero in Cuba, no one could speak ill of him at all," Williamson observed.

"You sergeants are all cynics, but still, that's true enough—" Keogh was interrupted by the distant ringing of Washington's various church bells marking the noon hour. He *harrumph*ed a bit. "Lunchtime. Stay for the meal? It's Wednesday, so it's beef stew today, and it's usually quite good. We'll keep talking as we go."

Williamson bowed his head in acceptance. "I gratefully accept." He stood and offered his hand to the old officer to help him up, but Keogh waved it off with a smile.

"I'm not feeling so poorly today." He rolled his blanket over his arm, and led the younger man back up the sidewalk. Williamson fell in on his left. "So where shall I begin?"

Slightly wrong-footed by the question, Williamson had to think quickly. "How about we start with the campaign into the Little Big Horn?"

Keogh shook his head. "Obviously, but the important thing there is why that campaign was fought in the first place. That battle did not occur in isolation, lad. It only felt like it did out under that vast sky. But we'd been scrapping with the Lakota for years, and no one then or since ever gets into the why."

Williamson looked at the old man with sudden curiosity. "I was barely born yet, sir, and while I did read a lot of books, not a lot of them were exactly serious scholarship."

"Fair enough," Keogh nodded. "Really, it starts with the Treaty of Fort Laramie in '68 and its eventual breakdown after the Black Hills gold rush of '74."

"As I understand it, the short version of that is we promised the Indians a whole lot of land and then let them keep a good bit less of it."

"And the only real law out there before statehood had been the Army and a few small-town sheriffs. Then the Army had been preoccupied with the War of the Rebellion, Civil War, War Between The States, whatever you wish to call it, between 1861 and 1865, and only a token force had been left out West when the real war was seen as being back east of the Mississippi River. Really, the politicians focused on Virginia. Nobody gave a damn what Grant was doing out West up until after he took Vicksburg. They only cared about the Eastern Theater."

"A theater in which then-Lieutenant Custer had shone brightly," Williamson noted.

"Yes, well, the Congress didn't want old Bobby Lee's army marching up its marble stairs, so that kept their attention. Still, all that is well-traveled ground."

"Including your heroism with General Buford on the first day at Gettysburg."

Keogh smiled slyly. "I played a very small part in that, but it was an experience that shaped the advice I gave Custer later."

The two men handed off their coats and Keogh's blanket to the even older fellow working the cloakroom desk, tipping him a nickel each. They then filed into the enormous high-ceilinged dining room, where hundreds of voices murmured and silverware clinked on plates. Only once they had their meals and sat down did the real conversation resume.

Keogh chewed a bit. "The stew's not bad today, as I said. The cooks must be in a good mood. Yes, that first day's experience at Gettysburg shaped my advice to Custer as we headed westward out of Fort Lincoln in '76, bound for the Dakota territory and eventually into what's now Montana."

Williamson leaned forward intently. "See, General, this is the part of the story that's gone untold for the most part."

"That's because most of those who knew it to tell it are dead now."

Williamson felt a spark of enthusiasm, that moment writers knew when an article revealed the potential to be a book instead. "All the more reason to write it down now, never mind the newspapers. There's a whole generation of cavalrymen who are going to need to know the whos and whats and whys as they study at West Point or Fort Riley or wherever."

Keogh laughed. "Son, the West is won, Cuba is free, and even the Philippines have gone quiet now. Where shall we send the next generation to win their spurs?"

Williamson laughed. "Ask General...well, about-to-be President Wheeler. But we aren't to that part of the tale yet, are we, sir?"

Keogh sat back, considering his words as he mopped his plate with a bit of bread. "Since you frame it in those terms, I suppose the story begins with 1876. As you know, General Crook was tasked by the War Department to herd the Indians back to their reservations."

"A sizeable task," Williamson observed.

Keough snorted derisively. "Then the damn fool wanted to start it in the winter rather than waiting, and that even bigger damned fool Joseph Reynolds picked a fight with the Cheyenne at Powder River and lost. No relation to John Reynolds who we lost that first day at Gettysburg. If only he'd lived... Anyway, the Cheyenne had been on our side until that blunder. Instead of letting it go, Crook gets orders to try again instead of letting the tribes spend the summer chasing the buffalo herds as they always had and using the coming of winter to herd them home."

"That brought them into conflict with the white settlers?"

Keogh nodded. "It also annoyed Washington. They had signed treaties that obligated the tribes to stay inside certain lines on the map, but as they were following migrating game, the buffalo didn't know they were supposed to stop at this particular point or another, so the Indians didn't stop, either." Keogh looked around thoughtfully. "Someone may need these seats while they're still serving lunch, so we'll get out of their way. Follow me, lad."

Williamson followed Keogh off to one of the Home's several sitting rooms, where they settled. "Then there were the Black Hills."

That elicited a nod from Keogh. "No white man gave a damn about those hills until they found gold in them in '74, only the Indians refused to give them up."

"And at this point, Custer was running the regiment and not Colonel Sturgis?"

"Sam Sturgis. God above, everyone forgets about him. Long detached and completely overlooked." Keogh paused, and Williamson could see the wheels of memory turning in his head. "He'd been captured by Mexicans in the '46 war as a lieutenant, I think, and then he spent most of the next war doing nothing of note save being whipped by the late and fearsome Nathan Bedford Forrest out west."

Keogh shook his head. "But he was a Regular cavalry officer, which by those ironclad rules of seniority, guaranteed him his spot in the post-war Army as most of the temporary help was sent home. Since no one at the War Department really wanted a mediocrity like him commanding the 7th, either, he had been detached from the regiment for quite some time, despite being the colonel commanding on paper. He was running the cavalry resupply depot in St. Louis and supervising the recruiters."

"And having to do another man's job didn't bother Lieutenant Colonel Custer?"

That pulled a laugh out of the old general. "God in heaven, no. In practice, it was Custer's regiment in all but name. And for all that we had Generals Terry and Miles or Sheridan sending us orders at different times, that still didn't mean we didn't do what the hell we wanted out there."

Williamson nodded, then laid down his first big question. "Which brings us to when you and the 7th were ordered out west into the summer of '76."

Keogh nodded. "Oh, I'll start at the beginning of that. Think of your own Cuba experience. Your first war, my...fifth, maybe, depending how you count the various Indian campaigns," Keogh said, leaning forward towards Williamson. "When you are going out far from home into a wild and barren land, supplies are everything, and if you don't have the right ones, you're done for before you begin."

"Understood, sir."

"First thing to be seen to were the carbines," Keogh said, holding up a finger. "You can't fight a war without guns, and we had new ones. The Trapdoor Springfield, they called it. It was Army Ordnance's way of being cheap and using as many old musket parts as they could while still fielding a 'modern' breechloader."

Keogh shook his head with a rueful expression. "Put politely, the first ones were shit," the old officer spat. "Copper made a very poor cartridge casing, but that was what the Armory tried at first since it was cheaper than brass."

The former sergeant chuckled. "How did you get around that, sir?"

"Well, we'd had a perfectly acceptable repeater in the cavalry already back during the war, so the first thing we did was go get the old guns back. The other Custer handled most of that."

"Ah, Tom Custer. Why him?" Williamson wondered aloud.

"He had the Medal of Honor twice," Keogh replied. "That made him important in our little caper. See, if you believe the folklore, if we'd been caught he would be the least likely of us to be court-martialed." The old man chuckled. "You should have seen the look on George Custer's face..."

———

*FORT ABRAHAM LINCOLN*
*PRESENT-DAY NORTH DAKOTA*
*APRIL 13, 1876*

Brevet-Major Tom Custer walked alongside his older brother on the parade ground's edge. The companies were pulling short rifles out of crates and the instructional drilling with them had already begun.

The elder Custer took a moment to notice what had been old was now new again. "Spencer carbines? Where in the name of Hell did you find these?"

"A surplus dealer in New York was acquiring a large number of them to sell to the French," Tom replied. "These were already crated up at the St. Louis Depot to be turned in now that those wretched Springfield breechloaders are being fielded, so some of the crates...fell off the train car."

Suddenly suspicious, George pointed and counted, doing a bit of mental arithmetic. "That's nearly a hundred crates of guns at ten each, making about a thousand, plus the ammunition and other bits. That's a lot of crates to merely fall off a train."

"All right, all right, so we made the whole car fall off of the train," Tom snapped after making sure no one was nearby. "Stop asking questions you don't want official answers to, George."

"And we're doing this why, Tom? This looks like courts-martial for several of us."

"Because the Trapdoor Springfields are garbage," Tom stated emphatically. "The Indians have better guns than we do, and if this regiment rides out with the Trapdoors against hostiles armed with lever-action Winchesters and other modern arms, one of them will be wearing your pretty blond scalp as a headdress."

Tom gave his brother an earnest gaze. "Certainly a few of us officers have already bought better, you with your Remington and me with the Winchester and that Sharps, as well," Tom said, gesturing at his brother's rifle. "For what's being asked of us as a unit, we owe the troopers better."

"Who was that fellow in the Western Theater whose whole unit went out and bought better rifles for their advance on Chattanooga?"

"Wilder. Had a whole brigade with Spencers, the long rifle version. But we don't have the time to get other guns or a friendly bank to underwrite the deal like he had."

The planning continued, with Majors Reno and Custer coming and going. But the hour was getting late and the elder Custer was getting petulant. At the end, it was down to Captain Keogh and the elder Custer, and the subject had departed horse forage and carbines for even heavier guns.

"I don't want to take the Gatlings," George snapped. "They'll slow us down."

"We'll still be faster than a traveling Indian village," Keogh observed.

Custer shook his head, not yet having cut his famous blond locks. "I don't like it a bit. We'll need the speed."

Keogh sighed. Advising his notoriously mercurial commander was rarely easy. "This isn't about dash and flair—this is about a slow methodical advance and the strong possibility that we end up over our heads," Keogh said. "Even with the Spencers, we'll need the additional throw of lead with help so far off."

"Cavalry has a few advantages. Mobility and firepower are most of them. But when the tribes have those, as well, that makes it too much of an even match for my liking." Custer slouched in his desk chair. "You may be right."

Keogh nodded, as would a fellow conspirator. "So we'd better be sure we have the firepower to carry with us, and bigger guns to fall back to. Think of Gettysburg, sir."

Custer smiled. "You mean a wild charge of horsemen against other horsemen at the field behind the main battle?"

"No, sir, not your action behind the main lines. I mean what the late General Buford did on the first day," Keogh said. "It's the seizure of key terrain. We get on that high ground and use those Gatlings to hold off the attack to follow."

Custer nodded at the insight as Keogh continued. "At first, it's a matter of intelligence gathering and accurate reconnaissance. Pickets forward, pick the high ground to be held, rally, then push forward again."

Keogh gestured with his hands in a leapfrogging motion.

"Eventually, you move that base of fire up to the next piece of key terrain, and repeat the process," Keogh continued. "That's why I found a pair of three-inch ordnance rifles the artillery had abandoned here and found some men with experience to crew them."

"It will be slow," Custer said with a sigh. "I don't want to be slow."

"Speed doesn't matter so much as correctly knowing what's around us," Keogh retorted. "When Harry Heth of Buford's Division nosed in against us at Gettysburg, he thought it was just a few hundred of the Pennsylvania militia. Even with the Arikara and Crow scouts, expect we'll only find a good-sized band Lakota or Cheyenne if they want to be found."

"And if they want to be found, it's because they think they can win." Custer frowned, swearing under his breath.

"And no one wants their name associated with a disaster, sir, no matter how heroic," Keogh pressed. "Remember Honsiger Bluff?"

Custer's force of two companies had been encircled by a much larger Indian force, but had held on and broken out. The battle had cost the 7th its veterinary surgeon, the Dr. Honsiger for whom the site was later named.

Custer nodded, the lesson sinking in.

"Or like at Trevilian Station," Custer replied with a shudder. Keogh knew the man was remembering getting his cavalry brigade pinned in between two Confederate infantry divisions, then barely getting out, even with a lot of help from the rest of the division. Custer shook his head to throw off the old memories.

"Myles, I think you're right. While I've been lucky thus far, I do think you're right. We'll emulate Buford and not Jeb Stuart."

———

Keogh shrugged off the days gone by, ending his retelling and returning to the sitting-room present. "It was a slow march, but a deliberate one. We knew what was around us and wouldn't be surprised. Finally, we found that village at the Little Big Horn and probed toward it."

"Kicked a hornet nest, by all accounts."

"But we'd planned for it, and the Gatlings and the three-inchers were set on the ridge above the river along with half the regiment. That gave the lead element something to fall back to and covering fire while they did so."

Williamson looked wistful. "I think every schoolboy in America studied that fight. That scrap back across the river ford was an ugly one."

"Well, half of what you studied was probably wrong. Sorting it out accurately took a while, and at that point nobody except a few of us who'd been there cared that much for the details. We lost Tom Custer at the river crossing. He probably should have had a third Medal of Honor for that fight. He and Rain-In-The-Face killed each other as they'd long promised, and with that duel, he personally created a gap and bought the time for the last of the skirmishing force to get back up Medicine Tail to the main position on the ridge.

"Then the gap slammed shut and the rest came at us. It was hard and ugly work, but we bled the first two waves of attackers badly enough that the Indians actually called for a truce to fetch their wounded and dead. Custer gave it to them, but he somehow kept them talking. That opened up negotiations for what became the Treaty of the Little Big Horn."

"That was where Custer pledged the US Army to the defense of the Lakota's territorial claims?" Williamson asked.

"Not just the Lakota. Remember the Crow and Arikara were already government allies, and there were other players on the field, so to speak. That damned fool Reynolds had already alienated the Cheyenne, so bringing them to listen took some effort. But with the breakdown of the Fort Laramie boundaries, new ones were needed, and Custer had credibility with the Indians. He'd counted coup when it mattered, and while he'd brought the white men to their sacred Black Hills, they in turn trusted him to hold a line as he'd held what they call Custer Ridge now."

"That must have made a lot of enemies back East."

"God, did that raise hackles in Washington, but it really was an elegant solution to Custer's mission. He and the other columns had been sent out there to get the tribes back on their reservation and head off a war, and he did it. He pinned the Army in the middle as the honest broker. Had the Army undercut him, it would have made an even bigger war, or more properly, a series of wars."

"A series of wars?" Williamson looked confused.

"Think it through, my lad. How many treaties were there? It would have raged from Arizona and Texas all the way to the Canadian border once the other tribes realized that it meant all the agreements were fraudulent. Yes, too many treaties had been broken already, but Custer had the warrior prestige with the tribes to start anew. With the news quickly getting out over the telegraph and into the papers, Custer was recast as the peacemaker where he'd been the Indian-fighter."

Williamson nodded. "And this was where the Presidential rumors started."

"Well, yes, and at that point, Custer had some awkward decisions to make. He wasn't quite at twenty years of service yet, and wouldn't be until 1881, so a full retirement was out of the question for five more years, but there was still talk of him resigning his commission and entering politics instead."

"And yet he didn't."

Keough let out a little post-meal burp before continuing. "1876 was the Centennial, and a Presidential election year. Grant, whom he'd bedeviled for years, was not seeking a third term, following the precedent going back to General Washington's time in office. But Fortune had turned her smile on him too late for George's own good."

"How so?"

Keogh shook his head ruefully. "Timing. In politics as in war, timing is everything, lad. The Republican convention had happened two weeks before the Little Big Horn fight. Even if his name could have been forced upon the ballot, it would be unlikely that Custer could have wrapped up affairs with the Seventh and headed back East in time to campaign before Election Day in November. Why ride away from a fight you've won to start another fight you'll lose?"

"So despite being the sensation of the moment, he really had no chance."

"No, he didn't, and I don't think he wanted it as much as some later writers speculated that he did."

"What makes you say that?"

Keogh took a deep breath, and leaned back in his chair. "I'll tell you plainly: I don't think he liked his odds of getting the high office he wanted. Electoral politics is an uncertain business, and too many people want to be President for whatever reason. The competition for one office makes a logjam rather than a horse race."

"And instead he chose to remain in uniform?"

"I suspect that was General Sherman's doing and the War Department at large. A promotion for his heroism was certainly fair, but in so doing, I feel they definitely lured him to stay out West. Being promoted to full colonel and upstaging Sam Sturgis as the commander of the 7th stroked his not-inconsiderable ego and put him a big step closer to his real heart's desire."

"Which was?" Williamson was already thinking about the book this would become.

"George really wanted to be General Custer again. Not merely a second lieutenant appointed an acting brigadier general of volunteers, or a brevetted major general while being a permanent captain, but legitimately on the Regular Army list as General Custer. Brigadier would do—he wasn't that worked up about it, but being referred to as 'General' for old times' sake when there were silver oak leaves on his shoulders rather than stars... that did make him feel awkward."

"I never had thought about it that way," Williamson admitted.

"And I'd be lying if I said there wasn't anything in it for me. With both his brother Tom and Major Reno dead, he needed a proper second-in-command, and he tapped me for it. I stayed a captain on the Regular list for a while longer, but was brevetted to lieutenant colonel and was usually in daily command of the 7th as we rebuilt and Custer was off playing diplomat amongst the tribes."

"You didn't go with him for those?"

"Not often. There was too much to be done, and one of us needed to mind the store and keep the regiment functioning if we were going to maintain the fragile peace that he'd crafted."

"Then what?"

Keogh shrugged. "Twelve years of nothing much out West. Custer went on to a higher headquarters or two. The Army was basically marking time. That was fine. We were perfectly happy to have nothing much happening, but then the *Maine* blew up in Havana harbor."

"There had to have been a couple surprises. Several of the tribes voting to apply for statehood to guarantee their borders be enshrined by Congress was a clever bit of work."

"Yes, but those were political surprises, not military ones. The political sort weren't our problem. Then all Hell broke loose in Cuba, which meant it broke loose in Washington. Finally, our telegraph lit up."

"How did you make the command structure for that?"

The old man chuckled. "Well, first Custer had to get the command. See, at a time of emergency call-up when the Army is expanding, first the War Department has to figure out who's senior. That takes a few days. They also hope the senior man knows what he's doing. That's not always the same thing. When you're trying to mobilize a division or a corps, you want someone who's had a large command before, but time worked against us in our case."

"Thirty-three years since Appomattox Court House," Williamson mused. "At the time, I personally didn't think higher than troop, or maybe regiment on a good day. It never dawned on me until I was running messages for the Colonel, meaning Colonel Roosevelt, how...*old* all of you were."

Keogh laughed until he coughed. "I should be offended, but you're right. There weren't just that many of us left. In a perfect world, Sherman, maybe Sheridan, would have commanded, but they were both recently dead. George Thomas of Chickamauga fame would have been a strong choice, but he'd been dead for thirty years. John Schofield was terminally disloyal to his superiors, but Grant and Sherman had both liked him, anyway. Mandatory age-retirement had caught up to him."

"And finally someone thought of Custer the Peacemaker."

"The personalities involved made it worse. Russell Alger was the Secretary of War, which made things awkward, as he'd been one of George's regimental commanders back in that Michigan cavalry brigade he'd commanded. Did well at Gettysburg and Trevellian Station, then he made a fortune in timber and railroads after he'd gotten out in '65. The money got him politically connected, which is how he ended up in the War Department as Secretary. But that lack of ongoing military experience after the four years of the big war made George even less likely to listen to a former underling."

———

*The White House*
*Washington, DC*
*April 12, 1898*

The Oval Office was crowded, with Secretary of War Alger looking toward President McKinley. The President had asked Congress for a declaration of war, something for which the Army was wholly unready, and Alger was flat-footed. "By seniority, the field command should go to General Shafter."

"The man is at least three hundred pounds and dying of gout," President McKinley snapped. "He makes Winfield Scott look healthy, and Scott's dead. You want to send Shafter into a tropical hellhole where he can get malaria or yellow fever to go with it?"

Alger shrugged. "I suppose it has to be Custer, then. The problem is if Custer wins, he's going to want to be President."

"Lots of people want to be President—usually fools who haven't tried the job and don't know any damned better," McKinley grumbled.

"Yes, but having known George nearly four decades now, the man can be remarkably persistent once he has an idea in his mind."

McKinley was not the least bit pacified. "If he can win us this war, he can have this damned office when I'm done with it and if the voters agree. But do we want to send a cavalry general to go fight in a jungle?"

"Do we have anyone of any branch who knows anything about fighting in jungles?" Alger threw up his hands in frustration. "It might as well be Custer. Love him or hate him, the man has been a national hero for thirty years, so there's bound to be a stink in the press if he's kept out of it."

———

Keogh continued his storytelling. "Then once Custer had the command, it was a matter of staffing the headquarters and building an expeditionary force. We were told, yes, told, that Congressman Wheeler from Alabama would be joining us as the Cavalry Division's commander. President McKinley made that call for political reasons, but Wheeler was actually quite welcome."

"He was?"

"We needed the help, lad. I was outside in the hallway for that meeting, but you know how voices carry in these stonework buildings."

———

*The War Department*
*Washington, DC*

*April 17, 1898*

Custer looked across the table in his commandeered office at Wheeler. "They called you the War Child. Here I am even younger than you, and still in command."

Wheeler eyed his new superior officer coldly. "Yeah, well, that's what you get for being on the winning side last time. Just remember that I didn't take Nathan Forrest's shit, so don't think I'm going to take yours, George. I've known you since you walked up the hill from the ferry dock at West Point, remember?"

Custer nodded. "Oh, I haven't forgotten. That's why when the President floated your name to me, I didn't take it as a public relations stunt like the New York papers did. You're good, Joe. Damned good. We could have used you out West if you hadn't been in Congress."

"Not many of us made it back into the blue uniform, even the few who wanted it."

"That was a different war. This one worries me. We haven't fought a European army since 1814, and we didn't do so well in that one."

Wheeler shrugged. "We've learned a lot about the profession since."

Custer looked unusually pensive. "We hope we have." He shrugged off his momentary doubt. "Well, Joe, you now command the Cavalry Division. That will be two brigades made of three regiments per. Who do you want to command them?"

Wheeler shook his head. "First things first. What regiments?"

"Five regular, two of those colored, and one made of volunteers."

"Oh, no. You mean Roosevelt's crew of millionaires, madmen, cowboys, and criminals?" The unit, dubbed "Roosevelt's Rough Riders" in the press and rallying in Texas, were symptomatic of America's sudden enthusiasm for war with Spain.

Custer looked somewhat contrite. "Well, Leonard Wood is the one in command."

Wheeler kicked one booted leg up on a stool and bit the end off a cigar. "Wood's serving at the former Assistant Navy Secretary's convenience since Roosevelt isn't remotely qualified to command a regiment, despite the whole unit being his idea. In time, he may be qualified to command it, but he's not ready, not yet. And let's not forget that Wood may be a colonel, but he's a surgeon by trade, not a cavalry officer."

Custer sighed. "Noted, repeatedly noted, though to be honest, I had quite forgotten that part about Wood. He's far, far down my list of headaches. Enough about Roosevelt's men for now. What about the others? Who are we taking?"

Seemingly focused on lighting his cigar, Wheeler was completely concentrating on his new division. "Ideally, nothing but combat experienced officers. Even the Indian Wars fizzled out over years ago, partly thanks to you, so none of the company-level officers or first-enlistment men will have seen action. Someone needs to have heard enough shots fired in anger that they won't lose their mind the first time bullets come our way."

Custer nodded in agreement. "They call them troops now, not companies, the same way artillery comes in batteries. Happened fifteen years ago and I still get confused. Old habits and suchlike, you know."

Wheeler waved dismissively. "Painting a pig brown doesn't make it a cow. Call it what you like." He puffed his smoke and smiled. "Regardless, we will need a few more ex-Confederate officers besides me if we're going to sell this as a 'reconciled America against the world' thing. God, I can't believe I'm saying this, but as much as I often hated Nathan, we could truly use that mad bastard right about now."

"Forrest? You'd really bring Forrest along?" Custer slid back in his chair with a grin.

Wheeler threw up his hands, waving his cigar and sighing in frustration. "We need the quality, but it doesn't matter because Forrest's been dead for twenty years. That's our biggest problem. Everyone still on this side of the grass with the experience we really need is just too old or too sick to do us any good now. Even Pete Longstreet wanted in in this war, but he's 77 so he got told no."

"Not everyone's dead. You remember Tom Rosser?"

"Don't think I've seen him since we were still cadets, but he was your friend from Texas. Rode with Stuart in the East, as I recall."

"Yes, and we scrapped frequently through the war. Kept it lighthearted, I suppose," Custer said, a slight smile crossing his face. "We had the occasional prank like stealing each other's luggage or chasing each other up and down the Shenandoah. The Woodstock Races, the newspapers called it. Not making it a matter of personal hatred gave the soul a break from the grimness of the whole thing as it neared the bloody finish."

Wheeler sighed, laden with his own memories, then dragged on his cigar. "I feel that at a deep level myself."

Custer met Wheeler's gaze, each man trying to judge the other's thoughts. "But he's still alive and relatively healthy. Been out building railroads and such, but he's still commanded a cavalry brigade in combat before. We're short on that experience."

"You sold me. Find him and get him on a train here. I'll let him have a brigade until he proves to me he shouldn't. Who else have we got?"

"There's old 'Bull' Sumner's son," Custer said after a moment. Sam spent most of the war on his father's staff, but he was a Regular cavalry officer with the 5th when he wasn't. Afterward, he went out to Colorado with the 8th and then finally the 6th Cavalry against the Indians. Solid Regular officer, nothing spectacular, but then I suppose the burden of providing spectacle falls on me."

Interest kindled in Wheeler's eyes. "So he's seen a big headquarters command up close before. Good. What's he doing now?"

"Still commanding the 6th, and they're already assigned to the force so he's coming."

Wheeler leaned back, pensively contemplating the ceiling. "Part of me wants at least one intact Regular regiment under a Regular commander I can use as my ace in the hole."

"Remember, you have not one but five Regular regiments with their usual commanders. And we fought the War with volunteers." There was no question in either man's mind which war he meant. To those who'd served in it, it would be the only real one.

"And we were fighting against other volunteers," Wheeler countered. "I was an acting brigadier general before I would have ever made captain under other circumstances, and I only succeeded as often as I did because the other side, yours, wasn't that much better than we were even on a good day."

Custer nodded thoughtfully, his expression pained.

"The same could be said of me, of course," Custer replied. "As for Sumner, I can use someone with senior staff experience near me besides Myles. I have come to rely on him so much over the decades that I do need to pack a spare."

Wheeler shook his head.

"Sumner gets the other brigade, then. He'll be at all the commanders' calls and planning meetings as he should, so we can both exploit him properly. Now, not that it's strictly my problem, but who's commanding our infantry?"

Custer consulted the list. "Three brigades of three regiments each, all under Brigadier General Jacob Kent. There's a name I haven't heard in years. He was in my class at West Point and I last saw him in Montana a decade ago running border patrols between the settlers and the reservations."

Wheeler grunted in thought. "What the hell's he doing in this now?"

"Same damned thing we are. He's got the seniority to be here without having died yet."

Blowing a cloud of cigar smoke, Wheeler grumbled. "We need to get us some younger officers in this business, George. We're too old for this."

———

Back in the present, Williamson sighed. "Again, it's amazing how old so many of you senior commanders were."

"That we were, Sergeant. We most certainly were. Strict seniority will do that to an officer corps. But now that we had a skeletal speartip of an army," his expression conveying just what he thought of their force, "we had to get it all in one place and then sustain it."

"That didn't seem to go so badly," Williamson mused. "We ate a lot of barbecued pork down there in Georgia. Food was nearly as good as the 1st's original assembly area in Texas where beef was plentiful."

"The only reason you and the rest were in Georgia at all was because Custer threw the original plan out the window," Keogh said with a laugh. He turned to watch as a young nurse walked by, giving the equally young Williamson an appraising glance she thought neither man would notice.

*You're a fine fair woman,* Williamson thought, *but I have just as fair at home,* giving her what he hoped was a merely friendly smile as Keogh continued.

"Supplying an expeditionary Army across the water was a wholly new matter, you'll understand," Keogh stated, his tone pained. "We didn't know what we were doing. Logistics for us for decades had merely been running a train from an Army depot and meeting it with wagons wherever the tracks ended."

The older gentleman ruefully shook his head as he remembered the chaos of mobilization.

"No one knew how to put that same force on a ship and deal with it when it got there. We'd never done it before. Then the War Department wanted us to stage in Tampa Bay to acclimate to the tropics. Terrible idea."

"How so?"

"Custer sent me down to look at the site," Keogh replied. "The supply situation there was miserable and it was mostly a fever swamp. Most of us would have been sick even before we left. As you said, we camped up in Georgia instead, on fine dry land a few miles inshore with a good wind, and sailed from Savannah."

"And that caused a lot of delays, as the papers said at the time," Williamson recalled. "I don't see how we could have done it any faster, though."

"Of course there were delays," Keogh snapped, then looked apologetic for his outburst. Reining in his tone, he continued.

"Sorry. I just remember the complaining from the War Department and I am still somewhat sensitive to the subject. We were supposed to launch in the second week of June. As it was, it was mid-July before we boarded the ships in Savannah. Custer didn't care."

Once more, Keogh paused before meeting Williamson's gaze. "See, Custer knew he had one chance to do this right, and dash and flair wouldn't get it done. Like Grant's slow-rolling drive on Richmond, better to go well than go quickly."

Williamson made a note. "How do *you* think that worked out for him?" Williamson asked. "As I know what the conventional wisdom says."

"Custer ignored the demands from Washington to ship out," Keogh replied. "He'd balked Presidents before. We all remember his standoff with Grant over the Indian agents' trading post scandals, and he certainly wasn't going to take too much hectoring from McKinley, who, despite being President, was of far lesser rank and experience."

"And what of the rumor that went through the camp that we were going to be dismounted to walk with the infantry? That seemed to circulate right until we sailed."

Keogh took another sip off his flask, and wordlessly offered it to Williamson, who waved it off. "The War Department did suggest that, saying there would be insufficient shipping for the horses and their supplies."

"Seemed like a way to make it an all-infantry war using the cavalry to supply more men."

"And you wouldn't be wrong," Keogh agreed. "The War Department was making numerous suggestions because they didn't know what the hell they were doing, but in fairness, almost no one else did, either."

"At our level, we had no idea."

Keogh shrugged. "Would it have done you any good to have known all of our problems above you? No. You men needed to form in your troops and be solid in your duties. That went as much for the Regulars. Some of them had been spread over hundreds of miles and a dozen sub-posts for twenty years and hadn't operated as intact regiments since Appomattox. But first, we knew we needed those mules to carry everything from the shore to wherever the fighting was. It was either carry the mules to Cuba to carry supplies or carry them ourselves when we got there."

"Logical."

"And, to be cold, we needed the mules more than we needed cavalry horses," Keogh continued. "Until more ships were finally arranged, there was a plan to leave one of the two cavalry brigades behind while stealing one of its regiments."

"Really?" Williamson hadn't heard that rumor before.

Keogh waved it off. "And what a stink that would have made. Couldn't leave your outfit, the 1st Volunteer, for political reasons. You were mostly wealthy and connected. He would have wanted his old friend Rosser commanding whichever brigade did go. We definitely would have taken the 6th, since Custer wanted Sumner on hand as a spare asset. Just as well it still worked out the way it did."

"So once we had the movement of supplies ironed out, what of the supplies?"

"You're a reporter now," Keogh said. "I doubt I have to explain what became enshrined in history as 'the Army beef scandal.'"

Williamson merely winced and nodded. "We heard about the problems with the canned rations, but we never actually saw any until much later."

Keogh smiled proudly. "That was all on George. One of his better moments, really. When the first bad batches of canned beef showed up, he took an overnight express train north to Washington and dumped two cans of that formaldehyde-smelling offal on Secretary Alger's desk at the War Department. The fact he now worked for Alger never crossed his mind—to his way of thinking, it was thirty years ago and Alger was still a subordinate to be corrected when needed and bullied when necessary."

"How did that end?"

"At that moment, President McKinley was in the building and heard the noise of the arguing. You may remember he'd been his regiment's commissary sergeant at Antietam, and made a reputation for courage for feeding his men under direct fire. He came in, saw what the War Department was calling food, and then fired Alger on the spot."

Williamson chuckled, motioning for the flask. "So that story's true?"

Keogh grinned at the memory. "That it was. So we took ship, and landed in Cuba a mere five weeks late. We'd considered waiting for the dry season in a few more months, but we needed those afternoon downpours to keep the horses watered."

"Kept the voting public from losing interest in the war, either."

"A valid consideration, though you're still a cynic. Still, the wet season did us few favors past that. Soon General Wheeler was down with the fever, as were many of the men. It would have been far worse without the mules. Moving supplies in so the men could eat was the highest priority if we were going to get the army into Santiago. Tired men who haven't eaten are guaranteed to get sicker faster, as you saw, and what was there to eat in that part of the country?"

Williamson smiled ruefully. "There wasn't much. The Cubans ate out the countryside before we'd even landed."

"As you remember, we still had both brigades of cavalry. 1st Volunteer, 1st Regular and the 10th—you were screening and probing in front of the infantry with Tom Rosser in command. The 3rd, 6th and 10th were clustered together behind them under Sumner. In the event of a weak spot, they would be the breakthrough and exploitation force. With Wheeler down, Rosser took the Cavalry Division, with Wood moved up to Second Brigade while keeping a close eye on the very green Colonel Roosevelt."

Williamson took another pull on the flask before passing it back.

"Then we reached the foot of the San Juan heights," Keogh continued. "Though we didn't want to launch any significant frontal assaults against fortifications with only one small corps on hand, we needed those hills if we were to take Santiago."

"We tried pushing two of the troops uphill on foot in the dark as skirmishers, but we scattered and nearly mistook each other for Spaniards with fatal results." Williamson shuddered a bit at the memory.

Keogh nodded. "We had to wait for daylight. And then those damn Spanish sharpshooters went to work at the first glint of sunup and we lost Tom Rosser, among others."

———

To his right, Rosser jerked from the saddle and collapsed. Custer quickly dismounted and ran to his old friend's side. "Tex, dear Tex, just hold still. The medical orderlies are coming."

Rosser clutched his side, spitting blood and gasping for breath. "Won't do much, Fanny. No Woodstock Races for us this time. Least the goddamn Spanish won't steal my—" He shuddered. Silently, he raised his hand, and Custer gripped it. Their hands locked for a long moment, and then Rosser went limp.

Custer stood and swore, shoving his emotions deep. Wheeler was in the hospital and he'd now lost his second cavalry commander. "Damn it all. I'm running out of officers," he muttered. He turned to the pack of messengers and started pointing.

"You," pointing at a corporal in Regular blue, "head back to the hospital and inform General Wheeler that General Rosser is dead. Not much he can do, but he still needs to know." Custer pointed next at a rider in the 1st Volunteers' khaki. "Go find Colonel Wood at Second Brigade and inform him General Rosser is dead but that he is to carry on with the plan. In a pinch, I'll take the Cavalry Division myself." Both men saluted and galloped off.

Another rider in blue galloped into the small clearing. "General, sir, message from 1st Brigade!"

Custer fairly snarled. "It better be good news!"

"No, sir! Colonel Sumner is wounded, but expected to survive. Lieutenant Colonel Carroll from the 6th Cavalry has assumed command for now."

"Wonderful. You get back there and tell Carroll that Rosser is dead and I've got the Cavalry Division personally." He snatched his canteen from where it dangled, rinsed his mouth, and spat before drinking deep while the messenger rode away. "How is this morning going to get worse?' he asked aloud.

Looking back to the north, Custer's headquarters reconnaissance party was coming back under his longtime right hand when the lead rider slumped in the saddle. The horses didn't miss a step as they broke into the treeline where the remainder of the general's party gathered.

"Myles, my God! Not you, too!" Custer cried out as Keogh rode up.

Keogh waved at his general with calculated disdain, clutching his shoulder. "I've been shot before, damn it. I'll be all right. Get the men up that hill, sir, and I'll be along once I'm sewn up."

———

The old man rubbed his shoulder absentmindedly, lost in thought. "I actually rode back to the hospital by myself. I didn't want to take anyone else from what headquarters we had left, and if I stayed, I'd be distracting George when he really needed to be concentrating on the task at hand. So I was getting patched up and wasn't there when he finally entered the closest thing America has to immortality."

"Those damned Mausers," Williamson sighed. "That was a hell of a rifle. Better than the Krag, I think. I picked one up, but it was out of ammunition, so I gave it to one of our local guides. I think he kept it more as a badge of rank than anything until he found some bullets. Did you see General Wheeler leave the hospital?"

"I think he was gone before I left. He would have had to in order to make it to San Juan Hill in time. He probably stole that horse—"

"Borrowed, sir, borrowed. Bad luck to say the next President of the United States is a horse thief. Our division commander merely commandeered a mount to reenter the fray, as was his prerogative of rank."

Keogh chuckled. "Well phrased, Williamson. I'll have to hunt all this down after you write it."

———

George Custer was back in his true element. It had been too long.

Over thirty years now. Over thirty years since that first fight, back at what the ex-Confederates still called First Manassas. The Eastern Theater. The Dakotas, Montana. Now here in this hot, humid jungle. *God, did I miss this, the sound of guns fired in anger.*

Victory Junior might not have been quite the horse his namesake had been, since that spectacular Kentucky thoroughbred he'd ridden in Montana twenty years ago had been the mount of a lifetime. Regardless, the big roan didn't miss a step going up the hillside at the trot, enthusiastically weaving back and forth picking his way. Off to the left with the Second Brigade, he saw Roosevelt out in front of his 1st Volunteers on his Little Texas. What a sad excuse it would be for a cavalry charge if they hadn't had their mounts with them...

Roosevelt's men were just reaching the blockhouses atop the hill, distinctive in their purchased khaki. The 10th Cavalry was just past their flank, recognizable by the black skin and blue uniforms. The 1st Cav, the real Regular one, was past them out of sight. He'd be there in a moment himself to decide the next move. He wished Myles was there to see it. Then—

———

"The attack was straightforward. You know it as well as I do, since you were actually there. Unfortunately, that was it for George. He'd just made the summit behind Roosevelt and your regiment, and was moving to give him further orders when he caught that round to the chest."

"I didn't see it happen, either, General, as I was on our other flank, but I did see Remington's sketch of it. Eventually, he painted the whole scene."

A distant sadness took Keogh's face again, and the flask came back out. "Roosevelt told me he'd dismounted when he saw Custer unhorsed. He was still breathing, or trying to, but died in Roosevelt's arms."

Williamson took the offered flask and sipped. "And somehow Wheeler got there a few moments later, feverish but lucid. A friend of mine in A Troop was close by. He told me the general emptied his Colt pistol at the distant Spanish lines, screaming in rage. When he ran out of ammunition, he took Custer's pistol and emptied that, as well."

"At least he remembered which army he was in and wasn't cussing the Yankees like he did earlier in the week." Keogh took the last swig from the flask. "If we need more, I have a whole bottle and a half upstairs in my rooms. Anyway, though he was still quite sick, Wheeler assumed command of the expeditionary force. He had a lot of help, but he felt one of us needed to stay out of the hospital to be in charge. The Spanish surrendered days later, and we all got out of there before the weather and the diseases killed us all."

"Then what?"

"We sailed to New York and were ashore by the first of October. Roosevelt mustered out, and soon after he was elected governor. The rest of the force, the Regulars, all dispersed back to what we'd been doing, mostly out west. The War Department then sent Wheeler off to the Philippines for another tour of duty. He returned the next year as a hero again, this time of his third war, and the Democrats, not being fools, didn't let Bryan take a second swing at the ball in the 1900 election. Wheeler was nominated *in absentia* at their convention before he was even formally retired from the Army."

"I wonder how he took that?"

:"He doesn't live far from here. Go ask him," Keogh snorted.

Williamson sighed again. "I am a rather junior reporter to claim a moment of the President-elect's time. Perhaps someday I shall have the chance."

Keogh paused, pondering his words. "I know some of what happened. Truth be told, Wheeler was rather embarrassed. President McKinley had returned his military career to him, and had given the South some of its lost dignity back in the doing. Wheeler took that quite seriously."

"So he didn't want to be President?"

That pulled a laugh out of the older man. "Son, no man who sat in Congress as long as Joe Wheeler did doesn't think of moving up the ladder sooner or later. I just don't think he wanted it the way it happened. He actually went to the White House and met with McKinley after he was nominated and well before the election just because he didn't want any hard feelings."

Williamson sighed. "Oh, to have been a fly on the wall for that one."

Keogh smiled. "Oh, I had dinner with General Wheeler not long afterward. I know what happened, more or less."

"Could you—"

"No. And I wouldn't tell it to you exactly, anyway, as it was told in private. It's enough for you to know there was no bad blood between the two. McKinley understood that Wheeler was being used by the party of which he'd so long been a member, and at the same time he was enough of a politician that he relished a little friendly competition."

"Which he never got," Williamson observed.

The week before the 1900 election, McKinley was shot by a disgruntled office-seeker and died two days prior to the polls opening. "That put the vice president at the head of the ticket even if the ballots were already printed. What was his name...had heart trouble. Began with an H."

"Hobart, sir. Garrett Hobart."

Keogh snapped his fingers. "That's it, him. Railroad lawyer from New Jersey, and again, he had that heart trouble. Anyway, as you saw, with McKinley dead and nobody trusting Hobart's health, even much of the Republican Party broke for Wheeler. And that was a pretty fair call, considering Hobart had the heart attack he was going to have anyway on Election Night and didn't even live until dawn to see the full shellacking he took."

"Didn't seem to affect the down-ballot races much," Williamson cynically observed.

"Oh, why would it? Except for McKinley being dead and Hobart a weak reed physically, there was no ill will toward the Republican Party at large. Wheeler had bipartisan appeal since he was seen as the senior surviving hero of the martyred McKinley's 'splendid little war,' never mind being seen as the right hand of the equally martyred Custer."

"And Custer's death was seen as a fitting and glorious end for a three-war hero."

Keogh shrugged. "He was doing a fine job of running the war, but I wouldn't call his end especially fitting. No real dash or heroism. There's just a lot of junk flying around in the air on a battlefield and George happened to be standing in front of some of it. That bullet just had his name on it, that's all."

"The details don't matter. It's the myth. Imagine if things had gone differently out west in '76 and you'd been run over in the Montana country by the Lakota. Would Custer be a hero or a villain in that tale? How would the story shape over time? Legend always wins out over the facts, General."

"I told you, son. Call me Myles. Let's go find a glass or two of that whiskey and drink to our absent companions."

"Who knows? General Wheeler may still be spry enough to stand for reelection in 1904. Colonel...well, *Governor* Roosevelt will no doubt be sick of Albany by then and his thoughts will turn to the national stage. Maybe they can race each other up San Juan Hill again?"

Dan Kemp is a former member of the Army's 101$^{st}$ Airborne Division who partly reinvented himself as an author of military thrillers, military science fiction, and alternative history. His primary body of work is the *Athenaeum Inc.* military thriller series at Cannon Publishing, which began as "a thinly veiled *Kelly's Heroes* ripoff." Thus far, Dan's short stories have appeared in anthologies at Raconteur Press, Bayonet Press, and in two military alt-history collections for James Young. He sincerely promises the rest of the Norwich Mafia he will properly use that expensive master's degree and write that urban warfare book someday, just as soon as people stop yelling at him for more *Athenaeum* sequels.

LinkTree (i.e., one stop for everything): linktr.ee/daniel.g.kemp

# TO THE RESCUE

## S.M. Stirling

"I can see why December isn't prime tourist season in France," Colonel Theodore Roosevelt—junior, and usually known as "Ted" to his friends—said.

"Yeah, I was expecting beaches and bathing beauties and casinos, sir," McGregor said in his Missouri rasp from the gunner's position below and behind the commander's cupola.

He could see out, too, though more narrowly through the telescopic sight of the cannon.

There certainly weren't many girls not over-encumbered with clothing and morals visible on December fifth in this year of not-much-grace nineteen sixteen. Not in this up-country north-central part of France near Nevers, at least. It had been snowing off and on for days, and the temperature was in the twenties in this early morning hour. Surprisingly, that was low enough to be a little chilly even in the usually stuffy engine-heated interior of an armored fighting vehicle, with its stinks of exhaust, hot lubricating oil, sweat and nitro powder. Weather and politics were synchronized this year all over the northern hemisphere, as a wretched autumn that had ruined crops from Kansas to China shaded into record cold, so that the countless refugees trudging the roads and sleeping in ditches could freeze as well as starve.

"And I think there are people here who don't like us, sir," McGregor added.

Roosevelt grinned to himself as something clanged off the turret of his Lobo Mk. I. It was probably shrapnel or a shell fragment, but might be a rock the shelling had kicked up. He pitied the infantry out there. Anything on a battlefield could kill them. There were only a few weapons that could kill a tank, and there weren't very many of them at any one spot. That was the whole point.

The vision blocks of the tank were an improvement on the ones in the Lynx Mk. V armored car he'd been using until recently—tanks were a novelty this year, whereas he'd ridden across the border into Mexico in one of the first experimental armored cars with Pershing in '13—but the view was still limited. Right now, it mostly involved the rest of the 2nd Cavalry (mechanized) HQ company's vehicles spread out over the white-and-black winter fields, and the night-colored poplar shapes of dirt thrown up by German whizbangs—shells from 77mm field guns.

Each had a bright momentary red spark at its heart, like a malignant evil eye winking at you as the slab-sided mass of riveted armor lurched forward at about twice the walking pace. He barred his teeth as one close round made the tank rock as it crested a slight ridge. That jarred his left arm, currently in a sling due to a round even closer than that; the medics had tried to make him head for the rear right away, but there was work to do first.

*Time for morphine and convalescence later. That's a keep-their-heads-down barrage. German doctrine tells their infantry to hug the bombardment. They're coming.*

The 27th Division had gone into line against the Germans right off the boats and trains. It was an illustration of the difference between even well-equipped and trained green troops and real combat veterans, though they were learning fast—the survivors were, at least, right now learning how to do a fighting retreat. Time to knock the pursuers back on their heels...

The bombardment moved further south.

*Aimed at the 27th...or what's left of it, not us,* he thought. *They haven't realized what's coming up on them. The enemy infantry should be in sight soon.*

He could see bodies in the infinitely drab grey-brown-green of modern American field uniforms, and a Lewis-gun team in a crater waiting for the boys in equally inconspicuous *feldgrau*; the colors weren't that different, so the quickest visual recognition signal was the shapes of the helmet, the flared turtle dome of the American model and the coal-scuttle German. The Americans were trying to help the French to dig in and establish their new Loire Front solidly. The storming advance of the Kaiser's legions *had* slowed, at least. The new duo of Generals Foch and Lyautey, who were as much government as France had these days, claimed it was because they were getting a grip on things.

Roosevelt's own opinion was that the Germans were slowing down mainly because they were outrunning their supplies, not because of French resistance; bringing anything across the wreckage of the old Western Front and its poisoned remnants had to be a nightmare. And he thought Foch and Lyautey knew it, which was why they were shoveling every French civilian into anything that could cross the Mediterranean and dumping them in French North Africa—newly christened as the National Redoubt.

*When the Huns get the railways working again over the old front line, it's kitty bar the door,* he thought grimly. *Our logistics stink even worse, and we can't improve them by making prisoners repair a rail line and die.*

They'd hit the 27th and its neighbors an almighty knock with their *stosstruppen* and infiltration tactics, which were just as nasty as the reports said, or more so. The only good thing was that they weren't using V-gas anymore, and hadn't since the sixth of October.

*That's because they know we captured hundreds of tons of V-gas when we took the U-boats they sent to destroy our east coast cities. They don't want it shot back at them.*

V-gas stood for *Vernichtungsgas,* Annihilation Gas. Some were calling it horror-gas; it was fantastically more lethal than chlorine or phosgene or even nitrogen-mustard, some sort of nerve agent so deadly that a tiny dot the size of a period at the end of a sentence on your skin would kill. The Zeppelins had unloaded hundreds of tons of it on the Entente's capital cities, and shells had rained down as much more on trenches, artillery parks and railway junctions from the North Sea to the Swiss frontier. A million troops and three times that number of civilians had died in the course of one day. Indirectly, it had killed as many again since then, and the toll wasn't complete. Reports said even Hindenburg and Ludendorff had been surprised—and the Kaiser fainted dead away, not having been told about it before the massacre of his British royal relatives and legions of their subjects.

*But they* don't *know we* don't *have much horror-gas ready to deploy yet because it's so hard to get it out of the rocket-mortar shells without killing everyone concerned.*

Fortunately, the American tanks showed two could play at the game of deadly surprises. There was more ringing hail on the armored hull of his beast—the men were calling it the *Lobo*, the wolf, as well as the codename that had stuck as a descriptor for the type of machine in general. After the Intervention, modern American military jargon was chock-full of bits of Spanish.

The clanging on the hull went on and on, a Maxim gun's distinctive stutter, and 7.92 rounds went peening off the steel in trails of sparks he could see through the vision blocs, enough to mow down a company's worth of men caught in the open. Machine-guns had ruled the Great War's battlefields...until this year.

A ruined stone farmhouse lay ahead, blackened by fire and with its roof caved in, smoke-marks up from all of the windows...but ruins made good strongpoints, and he caught muzzle flashes from a basement window. They might not know what a tank was or what it could do, but they did know it was American—the white star was a giveaway.

"Driver, tank halt. Loader, HE," he said into the speaking-tube.

There were three men in a Lobo Mk. I's turret, and together with the gear, they filled the squarish shape—that was one more crewman that his old Lynx armored car had needed in Mexico. A Lynx used a pom-pom firing little shells from a belt as its main armament.

The loader was a weasel-quick, wiry-strong young man named Martinez who swore he was from Laredo, Texas and probably actually hailed from well south of there. Regardless of nationality, Martinez was snake-quick as he plucked a 57mm shell out of the rack at the rear of the turret and slammed it into the breech of the six-pounder cannon. One of the privileges of command was picking the best from the replacement pool as the Great War and conscription continued the yearly doubling or tripling the Army had undergone since the plunge into Mexico in 1913. And the—unwritten—policy was to accept Mexican volunteers and provide identity papers to regularize them. He'd noticed Martinez that spring when the first tanks reached them, and he needed to expand the three-man crew of his personal Lynx to five.

Desmond up in the bow geared down and then put the tank into neutral, and Roosevelt jammed his good hand against the front of the cupola as the massive weight surged forward and back and then settled still on its treads. The sheer inertia of these beasts required care.

The British had been working on tanks, too, when London was destroyed on October 6th, though they'd gotten no further than prototypes. Their *landships* had been pushed by the head of the Navy, of all things, a man called Churchill who'd fallen from office, gone out as a battalion commander and met a shell almost immediately, which had taken the steam out of it. The two projects even had the same cover story as armored water-tanks, hence the name.

Roosevelt had seen the plans for theirs. There were advantages to the fact that his father was President, and that General Wood, the Chief of the General Staff, was a longstanding friend of the family and honorary uncle. Helped along by the fact that Roosevelt Jr. had won the Medal of Honor during the Mexican Intervention in a way even his father's enemies admitted was fully justified, though they tended to attribute it to both father and son being bloodthirsty maniacs.

*Which is just what you'd expect of hysterical poltroons like William Jennings Bryan and Woodrow Wilson.*

The British experimental vehicles were huge rhomboidal monsters with the guns in sponsoons on the side of an absurdly high hull rather than a turret, and no suspension between track and hull at all—possibly because their top speed was about four miles an hour, as opposed to twenty for the Lobo. The American version had tracks running on three two-wheel bogies on each side, cushioned by massive springs. It wasn't a soft ride, but it was much better than nothing at keeping you from being battered to death.

"Up! Up!" Martinez shouted as the breechblock clanged shut, which meant *loaded and ready*.

"Target machine gun: ten o'clock, range six hundred, McGregor," Roosevelt said to the gunner. "In that basement window."

"Got it, Colonel," the gunner said, spinning the traversing wheel. They'd been together since '13.

*Including that monumental screwup in Durango. By God, just* surviving *that was worth a medal! Turning it around... I should have gotten promoted to God, j.g., not just handed the Medal of Honor and a Major's bars!*

The turret moved with a whir and clack of manually-driven gears meshing—there was talk of an electric or hydraulic motor, but everything was short, time most of all. McGregor's foot flicked up the guard-bar with a clang and touched the firing pedal.

"On target!"

"Fire!" Roosevelt barked.

*One of the things I like about armored cars...and tanks...is that you get to fight personally even if you're a commander...and you're* not *being irresponsible.*

*Crack* on the last syllable of the order, and the six-pounder cannon recoiled like the piston in an engine, just missing the loader as he bent and ducked in drilled reflex.

*"Hit! Hit!"* McGregor said.

The twenty-six tons of the tank rocked back on its suspension slightly—that was pure Newton, since the shell moved at eighteen hundred feet per second. There was a backflash from the basement window as it exploded within...then a bigger one, with sparks flying out at high speed and a crackling like fireworks on the Fourth of July. The noise of the secondary explosions was audible even through the armor and engine-growl. Someone had left a can of belted machine-gun ammunition where they shouldn't, or maybe a crate of grenades.

*Or both. Probably both.*

Seconds later, smoke began drifting up—evidently, there was something in there still ready to burn, too.

Then figures in *feldgrau* and coal-scuttle helmets broke free of the re-burning ruined farmhouse. One had a Lewis gun in his arms, and several of the others had Thompsons, unmistakable with the drum magazine; all of them had stick-grenades thrust through loops on their webbing, and they were moving in a quick zigzagging sprint towards a location picked in advance.

*Those boys have been to school.*

Roosevelt didn't need to say anything; his crew had been ready for survivors to break cover rather than choke or fry.

McGregor cut loose with the coaxial machine-gun, a .50 Browning, and the bow-gunner—an Oklahoman named Albert Drowning Bear—was an artist with the .30 in a ball-mount in front of him. He claimed his name also meant "Chief," which was what everyone called him. He was also a wireless radio enthusiast, which helped, since unlike most, this commander's vehicle had a two-way set as of June 15th, and he doubled as its operator.

Tracers stabbed at the Germans and dirt spurted up all around them. Several fell, limp or thrashing. Roosevelt felt a cold satisfaction. Germany had attacked America first, and without warning, back at the beginning of October.

*Though granted, we were obviously getting* ready *to intervene*, Theodore thought. With the Mexican Intervention's demands winding down as the Protectorate turned peaceful, the Army and Navy had both been newly enormous and thoroughly prepared. Even more ominous from the

German perspective, the Army had begun to add multiple divisions per month as universal service took hold.

Only inspired work by the US secret services had kept the V-gas strike from killing millions of Americans, too. Despite warning and frantic evacuation, over a thousand military and civilians *had* died in Savannah, which was the only port where the U-boat had survived long enough to surface and launch.

So Germans, in general, had it coming...

The survivors went to ground in an outbuilding and shot back, showing more balls than brains—or just less experience with tanks. A Lewis gun was nearly as portable as a rifle; both sides built their squads around them now.

*Dad made our Army adopt the Lewis back in '13,* he thought.

The innovative, scientifically-inclined President had had to fire the chief of the Ordnance Department, a reactionary fossil named Crozier, to do it.

*Then the Kaiser made the German Army adopt it when he saw that newsreel film of Dad shooting a Lewis from the hip in '13...which was just so absolutely like him, and the Kaiser. Then in '14, they thought up the quick-change barrel, and we adopted that. Then Thompson came up with his gun, and God, wasn't that useful in Mexico...so the Germans copied that in 9mm last year, and found it was even more useful for trench fighting. Everyone copies everything these days. Isn't Progress grand?*

"Driver, forward to that stone wall two hundred yards northwest. Loader, HE."

*Clang* again, as the loader worked the lever of the breech and the shell sprang out to clatter with others at the bottom of the turret basket. A fresh wave of sharp-smelling gasses from nitro powder joined the staler previous residues, to a chorus of coughs; that was why you delayed opening the breech after a shot, if you could.

Roosevelt kept a mental list of suggestions and wrote it down most evenings unless he was fighting for his life; *some way of keeping fumes out of the turret* went on it now. It had been bad enough with the breeches of a machine-gun and a pom-pom in with you. A real cannon bid fair to choke the crew like poison gas, especially when artillery fire made you keep the hatches closed—that hadn't been a problem in Mexico, where the enemy started with a few guns and kept none after a couple of months.

They halted again by the stone wall, but before he could give the order to fire, heavy Stokes mortar rounds began smacking into the place he'd marked as where the German Lewis-gun team had set up, though they were bobbing and weaving between one firing position and another. The finned bombs—those were an American innovation, though Stokes was British—were nearly silent until they arrived; he couldn't hear them at all inside the turret or even the *bampf* of firing.

Then they exploded with a fast *crump-crump-crump*, as fast as the gunner could drop them down the tube, throwing dirt and dirty snow and rock...and probably parts of bodies and weapons...into the air.

He looked back, and saw that another tank—this one a turretless model functioning as a mortar carrier—had come up a few hundred yards back and opened fire, showing commendable initiative. The American army thought highly of that; unfortunately, so did the other side. Two more of the same type accelerated forward as it did; those would each have a squad of dragoon infantry with Thompsons and grenades, ready to hop out over the side and mop up.

He grinned again, the distinctive tooth-baring expression he shared with his father: it was with pride this time. The 2nd Cavalry's motto was *Toujours Prêt*—Always Ready—and they were living up to it. He'd been in the 2nd since 1913, when the Mexican Intervention started, beginning as a captain and moving up to command the regiment as of this spring—and helped them live up to it.

The radio had been clicking for a minute. As they halted, Drowning Bear spoke:

"Sir. Orders from Division."

There was a rustle as the loader leaned forward; glancing down, Roosevelt could just see a big brown hand—Chief was a big man, and about two-thirds Cherokee—extending backward with a page torn off his message pad. His father's famous Rough Rider regiment had included a lot of men of Indian or part-Indian or Mexican blood. The vast volunteer influx in '13 had imitated that, along with much else, and Chief had been among the rush to the colors.

Martinez handed it up to McGregor, who passed it to the commander.

"It's a pretty odd message, sir," he added as the colonel read.

It started: *Orders from GHQ follow—*

Roosevelt's eyebrows went up; that meant Expeditionary Force HQ just outside Marseilles. Regimental commanders didn't usually get directives from that level. From the date-stamp, they'd come in during the last half-hour, which meant minimal time taken on coding, something only done for urgent matters that would be over too quickly to make the enemy listening in relevant.

"What the hell?" Roosevelt said as he took in the brief directive. "Chief, you sure of this?"

The 1st Mechanized Division was the point of the spear, though— they'd been brought over despite the logistical problems of feeding their thousand-odd vehicles with gasoline because they could really *move*, four or five times the speed of a conventional infantry outfit even without counting their ability to punch through opposition. The 2nd Cavalry were the very *tip* of the point of the spear, and probably the only coherent American unit close enough to what seemed to be a sudden emergency to have any hope of getting there in time.

*American agents with crucial repeat crucial secret enemy device have crashed in captured German airship at your square G-7.*

He glanced at his current tactical map; Square G-7 was about six miles away, across territory under Entente control until last Monday and which nobody really controlled at present... According to the French ordnance survey this map was based on, there was absolutely nothing there except a large farmhouse or small manor, some outbuildings, a road and woods and fields, the woods thickening towards the north and west.

"All right, this is like something out of *Argosy All-Story*," he muttered.

That was the magazine that published the likes of Edgar Rice Burroughs and A.A. Merritt; at nearly thirty, Roosevelt considered himself beyond his youthful consumption of that sort of thing. Though he had a good friend with a first-class mind only a few years younger who devoured them, interplanetary travel, lost cities, lost races, evil occult masterminds and mad scientists with secret weapons and all.

"On the other hand, God knows this war has been full of nasty technical surprises," he went on.

"Damn right, sir," McGregor said.

"October 6th, for starters, Colonel," Drowning Bear added.

Roosevelt read on: *German air and ground forces moving to recapture material. Maximum repeat maximum priority that agents and material be recovered regardless of cost. Proceed with all speed. Air units also moving to support; recognition code in force. Impossible to overstate importance of mission.*

"Well, that's unambiguous, at least," he muttered.

*Do it or die trying* was about what it amounted to. Experienced soldiers rarely jumped for joy when they got that sort of order from on high.

Then he went on aloud: "Chief, acknowledge, say *will carry out*, then a message to the battalion commanders."

He looked at the map again, thinking rapidly. At least all the battalion and squadron commanders' vehicles had wireless—much more than would be present in an ordinary infantry unit. And they would need some extra transport for whatever-it-was that had the General Staff's knickers in such a painful twist.

"Dispositions as follows—"

———

"Well, that's spectacular," Roosevelt said, lowering his binoculars.

The gunner and loader were head-and-shoulders out of their hatches, too—the cold damp air was paradise after the choking stinks inside—and were looking up, as well.

"It's fucking awesome, sir," McGregor said.

Martinez whistled softly. *"¡Híjole!"* he said.

Which meant roughly the same thing—everyone in this crew could speak fair Spanish, and Roosevelt was quite fluent. He didn't swear much himself, but it didn't disturb him the way it did his father, who would walk out of a room if someone started a mildly smutty story.

Then the loader went on in English:

"Many brave men will die very soon now."

There must've been eighty or a hundred German airplanes diving from the north, dots swelling into shapes and the insect buzz of their engines growing towards a roar—sleek molded-plywood Albatross V fighting-scouts, the latest German model with twin Maxims. From the south came a similar sound, and an equal number of French Spads and Curtis Pumas— these climbing slightly, since the high overcast was lower there. They must've been closing on each other at two hundred and fifty miles an hour, combined speed...or better.

"We're not here to watch a football game," he said, as the *tacka-tacka-tacka* of machine-gun fire punctuated the engine-growl. "Here come the scouts."

A guvvie was coming down the frozen ruts of the muddy, tree-lined country road from the north—a little four-wheel-drive Model T in Army colors. It was crowded, with Captain Sanders of the regimental reconnaissance company, one of his men at a pintle-mounted Browning .30, and a scout-sniper team, one man with a scope-sighted variety of the old bolt-action Springfield called a Sharpshooter, and his spotter-partner cradling a Thompson. They wore white-and-brown covers over their winter parkas and helmets, and the rifle was decked out in strips of burlap to break the telltale outlines.

"Report, Corporal," Roosevelt called.

The spotter with the Thompson unwound his lanky height from the Guvvie, hopped down, sprang lithely onto the bow of the commander's Lobo and up to the turret. Close-to, his face had a narrow knobby angular look that his hillbilly twang confirmed. Many of the best scouts and snipers came from the southern hill country, and an old Regular Army outfit like the 2nd recruited from all over the country, not just from a single military conscription district.

"Well, we-uns went up the road a ways, Colonel," he said with respect but no particular formality, tracing the north-trending road on the map with a gloved fingertip. "Them lumps unner the snow, they wuz bodies, like you figured."

Roosevelt's eyes went northward for a moment; that was about a thousand yards north and east, not far from the roadside.

"Whose?" he said.

"Frenchies, sir—civilians, a lot of 'em women and kids."

The Tennessean spat over the side of the tank into the snow, which might be an expression of opinion, or just a result of the chaw of tobacco that bulged one lean cheek and had stained his teeth brown, or both.

"Massacred?"

The Intervention in Mexico had been merciless enough, especially in the three years of putting down guerilla-bandit resistance by the likes of Villa and Zapata after the first stand-up battles, but what had happened in France over the last few weeks had set whole new standards in butchery. Equaled only by the Turkish destruction of the Armenians, but in the heart of what had called itself the civilized world and on an immense scale, as the whole population of France seemed on the move.

"No, sir. Just...daid. Yes, that's dialect. From the looks of 'em, they ran as far an' as fast as they could after what the Boche did to Paris, then just laid down hungry and died in their sleep," the observer continued. "Them hard freezes we been gettin' the last week would do it, with them havin' no food to speak of and bein' city-folk not used to movin' cross-country and not dressed for it, neither. There were some fires, burned out. All right pitiful to see, let me tell you."

His finger moved across the printed silk, up the road to the northeast until after it straightened and turned due north.

"Then just like the map says, there's a farmhouse—big place before it burnt, sorta like the one a planter would have down to Nashville way. There's outbuildings west of it, barns and stables 'fore they wuz wrecked up. Now *here*—"

His finger tapped a spot north of the buildings, about a thousand yards.

"Was where that there airboat came down. Crashed, but not too hard an' not burned. Not one of them big 'uns with a frame inside, looks like. Gondola 'bout, oh, fifty, sixty feet long, envelope about five, six times that afore the gas got out and it came down like an ol' wet sock."

Roosevelt nodded. "Semirigid, Naval type. We use similar ones."

*Which is because there was mutual copying again.*

"We didn't get close 'cause I could see movement east of the house, thousand, two thousand yards out and they'd see *us* if we broke cover, but I'm pretty sure whoever came down in that airboat lived through it an' made tracks for the farmhouse. And there's folks there—I could smell their smoke, cookin' smells like."

Roosevelt looked over his shoulder to the southwest. He could hear the thudding of artillery back there: German whizbangs, something louder that was probably howitzers, and the distinctive sounds of American field artillery, too. The 1st Mechanized was mixing it in with whatever the Germans were sending forward, while he'd pushed northeastward at a slant right across the front of the German force with nothing more than some light skirmishing, with men shocked and terrified at the unexpected impact of the tanks. They'd moved fast, too; he glanced at his wristwatch, a new fashion for men that the Great War had brought in, and it was still a little shy of 1030.

*Such a temptation to hook northwest and take them in the flank,* he thought. *But this up ahead must be exactly what the orders from GHQ were talking about. And orders are orders...*

"Chief," he said to the radio operator. "On the regimental push: we're going to rush them, in column up the road, and don't deploy until we're under fire. Captain Johnson—" who commanded the reinforced company of dragoon infantry and their mortars, "—is to swing west and take the outbuildings when we're in sight of the objective. Dismounted action and be cautious about fire support; there are friendlies in the farmhouse. Detach one platoon of dragoons to follow the HQ company. Lieutenant

Kovacs—" which was a Magyar name, and meant...*smith*; some things were apparently universal, "—is to have his engineers ready for a hasty salvage mission on the crashed airship. Get me confirmations."

Chief did. A year or two ago, Roosevelt would have had to take time to get his commanders together and give his orders face-to-face, or risk one-way communication by runner if he was in a real hurry...which was generally the case. Sending things in code made the process far quicker and smoother.

The drawback, of course, was that this still wasn't like being able to talk to someone. Pretty soon, wireless radio-telephones would be small and rugged enough to be used for jobs like this, but that day wasn't here yet.

He cocked an eye upward at the melee in the sky. His youngest brother Quentin—at nineteen, just barely old enough for field service and with a teenager's conviction of his own immortality—was a fighting-scout pilot. When you combined that natural recklessness with the burden that being called Roosevelt put on a young man...not only from their father and the memory of San Juan Hill, but now from Ted's own Medal of Honor, too... that was a dangerous combination. Quentin might be up above his head right now.

A burning fighting-scout falling in a corkscrew nose-down spin plowed into the ground not two hundred yards to the north and exploded in a ball of flame, throwing bits and pieces all around. The tank commander shook his head; nothing to be done about that. Soldiering wasn't a safe profession.

"Let's go!" he said, and waved a hand around his head and chopped it forward.

*Before someone can strafe us from the air,* he added to himself. *And our flanks are as exposed as a cootch-dancer's, too.*

———

A green flare went up from behind the ruined manor; that was Captain Johnson going in, and automatic weapons fire chattered: the typewriter clatter of Thompsons, and something sharper and faster that he didn't realize.

*Goddammit, the Germans are inside there, too!* Roosevelt thought.

Tanks had any amount of punch, but they were an invitation to friendly fire losses if you tried to shoot into a hand-to-hand melee. His height gave him a good view of a fight he couldn't intervene in until his infantry came up—they'd dismounted and were running forward, but seconds counted.

"Get those!" he barked to McGregor.

The gunner was already turning the turret, and his first burst walked towards half a dozen Germans running towards the farmhouse, all of them carrying some sort of stubby automatic rifle with a curved high-capacity magazine, one he didn't recognize at all. They very sensibly pivoted in place and started running the other way, towards a creek running northwest-southeast about four hundred yards away.

"Load HE!" Roosevelt barked. "McGregor, let them have it as soon as they're far enough away!"

Behind the waist-high remains of the manor-house wall, a deadly drama was unfolding. A big blond man, helmetless but in a German officer's uniform, smashed an American away, blood flying as the butt of the German's weapon cracked across his face.

A wounded man lying on the floor—also, oddly enough, in German uniform—was trying to shoot him with a Thompson, but it clicked empty.

Behind them in what had probably been a rear room, maybe a kitchen, a short figure in a leather flightsuit struggled to raise a Lewis as a German came at her in a limping but snake-fast rush, with a sharpened entrenching tool raised, his hideously scarred face contorted and pale blue eyes staring. Another American in flight gear fired a Sharpshooter sniper rifle from the hip.

*Crack!*

The little German's body snapped sideways as the bullet hit the blade of his entrenching shovel, punching through it and at a slant into his belly, the distorted shape of the bullet pinwheeling like a tiny buzzsaw. He screamed and staggered right into a burst from the Lewis gun that sent him flopping backward, with most of his torso smashed into fragments of meat and bone. The gunner froze; nobody else was on their feet there, but two women in tattered civilian clothes were bandaging a wounded man in a French uniform that was almost as ravaged.

And out in the burned remnants of barn behind the house, a brief savage firefight was raging, American Thompsons against the German whatever-they-were, a couple of grenades, and then a shout in an unmistakable hillbilly rasp:

"All daid, Loo-tenant! Ever'thang clar here!"

*CRACK!*

The tank rocked, oddly since the turret was turned to one side; Roosevelt darted a quick glance that way and saw most of the fleeing Germans fall, though one man managed to dive into cover. Inside the front room—what had once been an elegant country living room, with the smashed remnants of a piano still lying in one corner—the flight-suited American dropped the sniper rifle. A knife came up in his—

*No, that's* her *hand—I recognize that knife!* Roosevelt thought, as whispers of blasphemous amazement dropped from his lips.

—Her hand, but her left was pressed to her side and face twisted in a rictus of effort.

The big blond German pulled his rifle free; the point of the bayonet had struck in the boards of the floor. He saw the knife-wielder.

*"¡Híjole!"* she blurted, confirming his guess.

He'd known that voice since they were both children; Luz O'Malley— Luz O'Malley Aróstegui, daughter of one of the Rough Rider officers who'd gone to Cuba with his father, and childhood friend.

*And Black Chamber agent since 1912. No wonder there's a secret weapon stolen from the Germans! She's the one who handed us Villa!*

The German screamed, an endless racking snarl, weapon leveled as he charged in a blur of motion. She left it until the last second, and twisted to her right, sweeping the knife at the rifle. Steel clanged on steel and the German went past her, dodging her backhand cut at his face by going under it with cat-quick grace. Roosevelt's breath caught.

*Crack!*

The German jerked and fell. The wounded American on the ground in German uniform started to laugh, looking at another ragged woman where she laid flat two paces away with a Luger in a clumsy two-handed grip. A woman...girl, he realized...half- dropped, half-flung a head-sized chunk of rock she was carrying down on the German's wound and slumped backward herself, collapsed against a snag of wall.

And Luz hobbled over and kicked the fallen German in the head, hard enough to make him go limp—but carefully, Roosevelt noted, not hard enough to kill him.

*"¡Ay!* But I bet that hurt you worse than it did me," she panted.

The one with the Lewis gun came up, sans machine-gun, and Luz leaned a hand on her shoulder—it was yet another woman—as she hobbled to the doorway.

Luz started to smile. The woman she was leaning on buried her head in

Luz's neck and sighed, sliding an arm around her waist, and they helped each other out into the open.

"Hola," Luz said, as she closed her navaja and slipped it into the pocket of the flightsuit.

Then: "Ted? *Ted?*"

Roosevelt pushed his goggles up onto the leather helmet he wore. He spoke into the cone of the speaking-tube in front of him, and the engine noise dropped to a ratcheting idle amid a cloud of blackish acrid-smelling exhaust fumes.

"Luz?" he said.

Almost as incredulously, now that he was really sure, looking past the flightsuit, and the scrapes and dirt and blood. The sharp, comely dark features were unmistakable, full-lipped and high in the cheekbones, despite the way she wore a bandana over a head that seemed to lack her usual raven-black bobcut.

"What the hell are *you* doing here?" he said.

"Spy work," she replied.

*Yup, I guessed right,* Roosevelt thought.

She pointed to the wreck of the airship to the northwest.

"Secure that, would you? Important ultra-secret German machinery in there. We need to get it back to our lines, pronto, and shipped home."

He called and waved and sent a squad of the dragoons to guard it: the engineers followed, moving their Model T truck—the new model, with four rear wheels—carefully.

"And what are *you* doing here, Ted? Not that I'm not grateful, but..."

He looked around at the wreckage of the farmhouse, and signaled several men with Red Cross armbands forward.

Then he slapped the side of the turret, where the 2nd Cavalry's palmetto leaf and eight-pointed shield were painted in white.

"I'm doing what the cavalry always does, Luz—ride to the rescue!" he said. That was what happened in those lurid tales in *Argosy All-Story* magazine she liked so much.

She laughed, though from the look of it, that hurt. Ted Roosevelt joined in, though it jarred his arm and *that* hurt.

"Old times," he said. They'd been wounded in the same actions before, too. "Old times, Luz."

———

# ABOUT S.M. STIRLING

**S.M. Stirling** is a writer by trade, born in France but Canadian by origin and American by naturalization. He currently resides in New Mexico. His hobbies are mostly related to the craft -- a love of history, anthropology and archaeology, and an avid interest in the sciences. The martial arts are his main physical hobby.

His works include the Draka alternate history trilogy (currently issued in a combined volume under the title *The Domination*), the *Nantucket* series, and the New York Times Bestselling *The Emberverse* series.

To learn more about S.M. Stirling, visit https://smstirling.com/ .

# THE BLUBBER BATTLE

## The First Falklands Campaign

## Joelle Presby and Patrick Doyle

*APRIL 1916*

"Finally! Let's get off this rust bucket and go blow some shit up!" Lieutenant Marshall said.

The officer's pale skin and dark hair combined with his infectious grin had a recruiting poster polish to it, which was ironic since Navy staffers and political handlers alike had learned to avoid letting him anywhere near officer candidates or voters. His resemblance to his important uncle only intensified the effect.

Lieutenant Marshall threw a grease-stained set of coveralls at me underhand, and a grin lit up his face like I hadn't seen on him since we left the Port of Hamburg.

*This man will be the death of me.* I struggled into the rough cloth, pulling it on over my pressed uniform. I hoped we'd be on land only for a night or two, but this entire plan was short on details. Petty Officer Wicklow'd suggested we double the layers in this backwards southern hemisphere weather, and I agreed we'd be grateful for them during the chill nights.

*And I'd not mentioned that it'd decrease our chances of being hung as spies if it all went wrong.*

The USS *Denver* (CL-14) was a U.S. Navy protected cruiser in fine repair with a history of transporting lots of raiding parties small and large. It almost certainly did not qualify as a rust bucket. I checked the ship's deck for senior officers who might take offense and found none.

Nearly two dozen of the toughest sailors I could find assembled on deck in uniforms stained by years of coal dust shoveling. This lot would fade into the darkness quite as well as our brave rowers back in Port Doula had. Petty Officer Wicklow, with his telltale Boston Irish red hair, had the seventeen others lined up smartly and walked between them, checking their packs and their boots. At least our petty officer had served on several raids in the past, even if the lieutenant and I were new to this business. Belatedly, I thought about just what the boss had said.

"We're only to take out the wireless station, sir. Then right back to the ship," I whispered at the lieutenant's ear. It wouldn't do to undermine him in front of the crew. He'd gotten used to some unorthodox ways of doing things in our time abroad.

There'd been that attack on Port Doula, where we'd been rather more active as military observers than one would generally expect. And then he'd been sent to Germany with me tagging along, to see if the goodwill from the role he'd had in Afrika might allow him a close view of military aeroplane developments.

It had.

He, and then I, had learned to fly the damned things and then shoot from the damned things. It had gotten bloodier and bloodier from there.

I stood at attention in my very best formal imitation of a solid U.S. Navy chief who hadn't gone tearing after Lieutenant Marshall on all those escapades. He gave me a bearhug and spun me around by one shoulder to leave both of us facing the team.

*So much for military discipline.*

The seventeen sailors looked on with mixed interest and amusement. Petty Officer Wicklow's eyes twinkled, and our boss gave him a slight nod of acknowledgement before raising his voice to be easily heard by all.

"The chief's doing a chief's job reminding me of our narrow orders. But what do you think, boys?" The delight in Lieutenant Marshall's eyes promised nothing the political campaign managers back home were going to like.

*Damn it, so what if he's "unmanageable" and "a blight on the vice president's political prospects"? Why did they have to tell him that right before shipping us off to be quietly useful?*

"Ah, no, I'm to say, 'Gentlemen.' And pretend to be one myself." He gave me an exaggerated wink.

*Sir, please don't embarrass yourself. These are regular American servicemen, not sons of the rich playing at aeroplane flying or foreigners accepting of odd ways from strangers.*

Lieutenant Marshall executed a disaster of a German court bow, making fun of himself. It was much worse than the much practiced one he'd used when presented to the Kaiser back when he'd thought being amenable was the quickest way to be allowed back into an aeroplane.

"I'm not so good at talking." He shrugged.

*Not quite a lie,* I agreed with his self-assessment. *If he could talk just a little bit less about the nasty parts of war, he'd be excellent at talking. Instead, his talking got us all here.*

"And yeah," my lieutenant continued, "you've probably heard it all already. Yes, the Vice President is my uncle. Yes, President Wilson has still not recovered, and my uncle intends to seek the nomination and ask the country to let him run things officially. But that other stuff in the papers isn't quite right: I only shot down a couple of British warplanes dropping bombs on my friends..."

*And learned how to fly* Eindeckers *and flew one of those first dozen aeroplanes to have Fokker's machine gun on it when, actually, he was only ordered to tour German bases and learn what he could about military uses of the aeroplane.*

It was only my long years of service that allowed me to keep a poker face while several months of memories, more bad than good, flashed through my head.

*But sure, boss, we can pretend it was all exactly what Rear Admiral Fiske expected.*

"And then," he said, "I got recalled home to write stacks of reports about how to make aeroplanes with guns on them."

"And to make speeches," Petty Officer Wicklow added. "I was at the one in Virginia where you answered that reporter asking after Lieutenant Thompson and how that crash looked and the trouble it was to get the body parts together for the burial."

"Glad we aren't getting into any aeroplanes," Davis, a young sailor in the back, muttered, to the general agreement of the group.

*Never mind that bullets are quite good enough at making people dead,* I added to myself. *Never mind what you're carrying.*

Davis's pack included most of our explosives, and he'd actually volunteered to carry it. He was plenty brave enough walking around on the ground.

"Like I said, I'm not so great at talking," Lieutenant Marshall acknowledged. "They didn't much want me speaking up once they realized

I was going to answer the questions about what it was like over there. People die when folks start fighting, and I figure it's only worth doing if there's something important to be fighting each other about.

"So let's be clear on what we're doing now. On the other side of that..." He pointed at the horizon, a dark blue line of South Atlantic Ocean meeting a pale sky of fading light. "Is a collection of little islands filled mostly with sheep and rotting whale carcasses. The Malvinas, or Falklands, if you'd rather. A couple decades now, they've been claimed as a British Overseas Territory. Not so polite of them to be taking American lands, and we're going to do something about it."

"Um, we are going to take down their wireless station, that's it," I said, with what I hoped was an agreeing sort of expression on my face. I did *not* look like a recruiting poster.

"So we will." Marshall gave me a jovial shoulder punch. "Tell the fine gents what we know about the locations."

"Um. Right, sir." I hadn't expected to have a speaking role. I hastily pulled from my pack a copy of the coastal chart I'd nabbed from naval records back when I'd first heard whispers of this plan while we were in Virginia. "Uh, this island is the one with most of the people living on it, unfortunately, but it's, of course, where the wireless antenna is, too. Plenty tall and easy to see in daylight, but we're going over in the dark on account of wanting to not get seen ourselves. They've got it high enough and high-powered enough to signal Montevideo in Uruguay and Buenos Aires in Argentina. Both those mainland countries are neutral in the European war just like us, um, of course," I added.

"For however long that lasts," one of the sailors snarked. That was Allen, a sandy-haired, broad-shouldered recruit who idolized the lieutenant and spoke out of turn too often, but if even he was paying attention, then everyone in the bunch was listening close.

I ignored the comment, but couldn't suppress my own thoughts: *Attacking a Brit territory isn't the way to stay neutral, if anyone ever learns who did it.*

"The wireless is here." I tapped a spot on a peninsula where the tower itself was marked as an aid to navigation. Not far to the south of it was a small ridge labeled Sapper Hill that might be useful if it were tall enough. We'd have to scout it, so I moved on rather than mention it now.

"That tower is about two miles away from the town proper. It's a village, really, and the British call it Port Stanley."

Lieutenant Marshall gave me an encouraging nod and beckoned the group to huddle around me.

"So, uh, Stanley is there." I pointed at a couple other aid-to-navigation marks for a church steeple and a building described in the mariner's notes as "Governor's House."

"And maybe we don't even meet up with anybody but a night operator or two, if they bother to have one." A note of hopefulness crept into my voice, so I did my level best to add in what cautious information I'd been able to glean from buying rounds for that one merchant sailor I'd found in a Norfolk dock bar who'd worked a whaler down this way.

*Best money I've ever spent, honestly.*

"There's some sort of town watch. Could be a tough group with all the ship repair shops closed. Or, um, nearly so. That is, now that Panama's canal is open and the merchant ships don't make the trip around the Horn anymore."

I gave a pleading look to the lieutenant. I'd never been part of a raiding party before and really wasn't sure what I was supposed to be saying.

Petty Officer Wicklow noticed and stepped up.

"Hundreds of muscle-bound out-of-work dock workers too buzzed to feel any pain, but lacking sufficient funds to be truly drunk, and with nothing better to do of a night than wander the beaches looking for a fight, then," Wicklow summarized, most unhelpfully. The man had a thick Boston accent, but the group had been together too long for me to hope nobody understood him. "And they'll be locals, too, more's the pity. Not really Brits."

I remembered then that his family had lost all they'd had in Ireland before coming over, and he was very much looking forward to getting some licks in against the British. Lots of Americans still liked the idea of letting the continentals have their Great War alone, but not all. Some couldn't wait to join Germany, Austria-Hungary, and Italy in the fight against the Entente powers.

The lieutenant took one look at the mixed expressions of eagerness and fear on the assembled faces and let out a genuine belly laugh.

"Ha! As if they could take you boys!" Marshall's confidence spread through the men and banished the uneasy expressions, as even Brown, our smallest sailor, stood taller.

"We will," Marshall admitted, "go in quiet-like to avoid waking His Governorship, but don't think it's because we're afraid of some minor militia. My aunt met the governor's wife at an event once when both were in Nova Scotia, and it'd be awkward if we had to shoot her husband." He gave the group a wink.

*Quiet?* I carefully did not look at the spools of wire and explosive charges we had already loaded onto our small boats.

"Right, then." I clapped my hands together. "Everyone check their packs are secure. As soon as dusk falls, the *Denver* will steam in to drop us off. Then we'll have some hard rowing to do, a quick scramble over the beach, watch things for just a bit to get the lay of the island, then we do some good old-fashioned destruction."

*So, so neutral.*

"After that, we scramble back to the *Denny* again."

Allen blinked at me. "Scramble back? But won't the ship just steam into the harbor to pick us up?"

"Did you hear anything Chief said?" Williams, our radio expert, rolled his eyes. "We go in. We take the island's communication rig out, and we come back. Might be a lot of rowing after, depending on how far out the *Denver* is and if we miss the tide."

"What if we just took the whole place over, though?" Petty Officer Wicklow mused. "That'd sure put paid to these British Overseas Territories, wouldn't it, sir?"

"That it most certainly would," Lieutenant Marshall agreed.

*No, sir, don't go thinking like that,* I pleaded. *Because that'd put us in the war, for certain.*

I looked around the ship's deck to see if the cruiser's captain or any other officer of rank might come over to say a few words and just maybe straighten things all out. The decks were conspicuously empty besides our almost two-dozen-man landing party.

"Uh, what do you think, Chief?" the radioman asked.

*The lieutenant's political handlers were idiots if they expected someone who routinely went off-script on the campaign trail would make a good choice as the leader for a politically delicate raid,* I thought. *And a vice president's nephew was a long way from being a deniable link if they wanted to pretend this was an unauthorized attack, in the event we all ended up captured or dead. Unless...*

*Oh, shit. Maybe they did want into the war and needed a good reason. Like a dead hero. God help us.*

"I think our lieutenant will lead us right in and right out," I lied.

"So we should leave American soil under British control?" Marshall asked the men.

*Hell yes!*

"This is South America, sir. Not any sort of part of the United States," I protested.

"Still America," Davis pointed out. The others looked at him and nodded, giving me sidelong looks, as if I needed to go back and study my geography a bit more.

*As if I didn't know more about British Overseas Territories than any self-respecting American ought to.*

"Should we leave a place for hostile ships to coal up and restock on ammunition so that they can take their embargoes over to our side of the ocean?" Marshall shook his head. "I'd rather not. But, Chief Hays, if you really think it's in the interest of the people of the United States of America..."

I sighed. The lieutenant had an irritating tendency to be right.

"What the hell, sir. Why not? It's not like these Falkland Islands could have any real strategic importance to the Great War over in Europe. But your uncle might have you write an apology note to King George V or something after."

*Or go ahead and declare war like it seems the political handlers have wanted all along.*

"They can trade notes, then," Lieutenant Marshall agreed. "It'll make him feel better about all the apologies the British have been making about taking our merchant cargoes.

"This is the first step, boys," Marshall said. "We may only knock over a wireless tower and destroy a few war supplies this time in, but America is done letting the Brits build forts on our shores. Let's go take back America!"

*Argentina might have a few things to say about that.* I kept my grumbling thoughts off my face while everyone from Seaman Brown to Petty Officer Wicklow cheered.

———

Our rowboats scraped onto the sand in the dim moonlight. Bleached whale bones, stripped of their lucrative blubber and everything else of any remote value, gleamed in white shards scattered over the sand.

"Whales," Marshall said with a speculative tone in that single word.

The rest of us kept strict silence in case our voices carried across the cove to some garrison or troop manning the port guns.

Petty Officer Wicklow and three others crunched up the sand to near the peak of a seagrass and scrub-covered rise. Continuing up on their bellies, Wicklow lifted a glass, ducked down again, and peered at his wrinkled map and repeated the process several more times.

With quick hand gestures, he sent the sailors scrambling over the rise and off in three directions to scout and return.

On a tip from that Norfolk merchant seaman, we'd avoided any coves likely to hold carcasses still being processed. The governor had strict limits on the number of whales allowed to be taken in each season, but the blubber's value kept going up, especially as it proved more and more useful to His Majesty's war effort.

*Logistics,* I was coming to suspect, *might win wars more than aeroplanes or even battleships. Though in this case, maybe logistics could end a war... But probably not.* I paused to kick a whale bone and pulled my boot back in disgust to find it hadn't been picked as clean as it should have been. *We could maybe strangle the supply lines?* I wondered if it'd be possible.

Whale oil typically made soap. But it also produced glycerin as a by-product, which was converted in turn to nitroglycerine, a component of cordite, the oh so useful standard propellant for artillery shells and small arms ammunition.

Norwegian captains and Norwegian shipping companies owned most of the whaling fleets, and Norway was neutral in the war. But they used British Overseas Territories as supply ports and sold primarily to the Entente side of the war. When we'd been in Germany, they were so short on glycerin supplies that there were posters in all the portside bars begging fishermen to kill anything at all with blubber, even little seals and dolphins. The United States might need to have something to say about those "Overseas Territories" that happened to be located in the Americas.

"Not just coal at issue here, huh, sir?" I pointed out, keeping my voice as soft as I could manage.

Lieutenant Marshall nodded quiet agreement.

"Several senior officers pulled me aside before we left. They'll all have to deny everything if we don't pull this off. But quite a few men will also be patting themselves on the back for their insight and strategic brilliance, as well, if we win."

"When, sir," I corrected.

He smiled wanly. "If we get separated, get as many of the boys off the island as you can. The *Denny's* captain assured me he'll try a pickup no matter what happens."

*Oh, hell no. Don't imply the ship might abandon us all here if it gets too risky!*

"They've only got two shore guns!" I protested. *A ship's a fool to fight a fort,* my mind reminded me. *Even a wimpy fort.* "But sir—"

"And they have a quite reasonably sized militia if they ring up the bells hard enough before we get into position."

"We hold the governor hostage, then?" Petty Officer Wicklow suggested. I started. He'd ambled up to us without me hearing him and had both Williams and Allen with him.

"Might work," Williams replied.

"Nah." Lieutenant Marshall shook his head. "My aunt says he's not so popular around here. Keeps limiting the increases on the whaling and elephant sealing."

"But they'll have no work for their sons if they don't cap it down now?" Allen whispered with a note of protest raising his voice enough for Wicklow to shush him.

"Didn't say the governor was wrong to do it," Marshall acknowledged with a softer tone. "Just folks don't necessarily appreciate being stopped from killing their golden geese."

Seaman Davis, lying flat up on the rise, signaled warning, and we all went silent and unholstered our rifles.

The sound of feet on sand crunched way too nearby. Then the brush rustled on both our left and right, and I just about had a heart attack until a sheep lifted its head high to blink at me before leaning back down to gnaw on some tender green shoots.

Laughter spread through the group, and I was grateful nobody had shot at any of the sheep now wandering across our beach.

The three scouts returned with nothing useful to share other than the belated information that sheep were wandering freely all around our position.

We divided ourselves into two groups, and in minutes we, too, were crunching along on seagrass-covered sand away from our hidden boats to circle wide of the herd in case a shepherd came looking to pen them up for the night.

Sweaty and tired, with our packs of explosives grown far heavier with the night march, we reached Sapper Hill a few hours before dawn. Petty Officer Wicklow repeated his work with the scouts and then turned the glass over to the boss.

Lieutenant Marshall looked at our target, and with careful thoroughness, scanned right all the way to the lighthouse at the point and left to Port Stanley himself. Sliding back down to the indent where I waited, he handed the glass back to Wicklow.

"Chief, I have an idea," he said.

*Uh oh.*

The most fleeting grin passed over his face, despite being quickly suppressed. It was nothing more than a twitch at the corner of his mouth, but I knew the Lieutenant.

*Not good. Very, very not good. Whatever this is, he thinks it's a good idea. No, a* really *good idea. Oh, hell. If we survive this, he better be buying my drinks for years.*

"Get up there and take a look," he said.

I did.

Looking down the shallow slope, we were a mile or two from the port area on the western edge of Port Stanley, where the wealth of the former shipyard stood tall next to empty piers. The line of the inlet's shore curved towards us with a whale carcass and a dotting of storage buildings along the coast. Directly ahead, the radio tower rose high into the sky ahead of us, with a small almost shed-like building at its base. Off to the right, more scrub grass and rocks meandered along the shoreline all the way to the lighthouse at Cape Pembroke.

The cold ground seeped the warmth out of me and replaced it with damp. With no trees, the ever-present wind howled unabated over the barren landscape of the island. The thick grey clouds raced eastward across the sky above us while intermittently releasing a fine mist to ensure we stayed wet and cold.

I gave Wicklow back the glass. He collapsed it and returned it to a brown leather case as we scooted backwards below the crest of Sapper Hill. Wicklow had three sailors positioned and watching our flanks to ensure we weren't surprised by a wandering islander. Those scouts were far enough away that we could speak without being overheard. The rest of our group huddled back in an upcropping of rocks to stay out of sight while we decided where to lay our explosives.

Lieutenant Marshall huddled over a sketch in the dirt. He'd made a map of the area with a groove in the sand to mark the shoreline, another thin line for the path running from the lighthouse to Port Stanley, and a third for the crest line of Sapper Hill. Rocks marked the lighthouse, the town, and the whale carcass.

"Did you see all those barrels down at the coast?" He pointed at the whale rock.

*Uh, those dark splotches behind the rotting bones?* I wondered.

"Of course, sir." Wicklow said, "The whalers won't fill their holds with the oil barrels when they're doing the flensing on land and sending the boat right out again to get another one before the season ends."

"Worth a lot, do you think?" Lieutenant Marshall said.

"Yes, sir," Petty Office Wicklow said. "The whale oil's good for lots of things. Soap and lamp oil, it used to be. But these days, mostly cordite and whatnot."

*Where are you going with this, boss? We need to have that wireless tower down or a nice thick haze of black smoke around it soon so the* Denny *gets the signal to come get us.*

"Exactly. Far too much whatnot, we can't just leave those barrels."

*No time for that, sir!* I protested mentally. Petty Officer Wicklow leaned in, delighted. "You want we change the objectives, boss?"

"I'm thinking so." He pointed up at the radio tower. "If we take that down, how long do you suppose it'd take them to get the wireless back up and running?"

"At least a couple months," I said, determined to be the voice of reason. "The papers said it was a Marconi crew brought in special that installed it a few years ago, back in 1911. They'd need another one down to repair or rebuild it."

"But they would repair it, or maybe even decide they didn't need a wireless station here, after all." Marshall held up a hand to delay more objections from me. "But any whale oil we destroy stays gone."

Stabbing a finger at the map, he said, "There is the port and here nearer to us are the barrels." He pointed to another location slightly south of the piers. "If we trot along here and come up from the south, we can get a good look and make sure they aren't just empty and waiting for the next whale or something."

"Won't be empty," Wicklow said with confidence. "The empties will be back with the barrel wright waiting for a ship's purser to buy them."

"Um, sir, we need to signal the *Denny*. The lookouts will be watching the radio tower. We didn't pack enough explosives to take it down and blow up some rotting whale bits."

Wicklow pressed his lips together.

Lieutenant Marshall grinned. "Good thing oil burns on its own, then, isn't it, Chief?"

"Ah. Yes, sir," I acknowledged.

We made quick arrangements for Wicklow to take a team in to secure the radio communications shed and wire our explosives to bring it down while the lieutenant and I did our own scouting of the new secondary objective with a couple of the sailors sent along with us to carry a spare detonator, some wire, and a bit of coal to get a nice big fire going.

We jogged along a footpath in the direction of Port Stanley, making good time on the relatively flat path, with clear moonlight to guide us. We'd be running back this way after to rejoin Wicklow and the rest of the men, so I kept a keen eye out for anything that might trip us up on the way back.

Two scouts waited for us at a bend in the path, with one flat on his belly watching the way to Port Stanley, and another downslope and signaling us to keep coming while he watched the other man for any sign to tell us to scamper off the path and take cover on the other side of Sapper Hill.

We reached the beached whale carcass, and Lieutenant Marshall gathered us round. I had to stop myself from doing a circuit of the neatly lined barrels myself. The scouts had already checked for guards and found not a soul left behind.

*Where the hell is everyone?* I wondered.

"Okay, boys," Lieutenant Marshall said. "We need to get one of these cracked open and slopped around on the others to be good and sure they all burn. Once the fire gets going here, it'll draw attention, and we don't have time to stay and mind the fires." He scratched a quick map of the island in the dirt and pointed out where to go if anything went wrong. "Any questions?"

There were none, but Lieutenant Marshall made eye contact with every man and got a nod of acknowledgment from each, anyway. Allen and a couple other sailors produced marlinspikes from their packs and punched holes in the closest barrel. I splayed out the detonator wire to full length and was getting ready to position a secondary charge in an oil-wetted cranny between four barrels, when *CRACK!*

I leapt back and spun in a circle, looking for attackers.

A couple more spurts of rifle fire rang out and Seaman Allen pointed behind us at the radio tower.

*Oh no.* "Petty Officer Wicklow's team found trouble," I said.

"We'll show them trouble," said the lieutenant.

He whistled sharply, making no effort to be quiet any longer, and we all pulled back from the shoreline. With no time for anything else, I tossed the secondary charge into the middle of the barrels and hoped for the best.

At a nod from the lieutenant, Allen plunged down the detonator, and we ran for the wireless station.

A *whoomph* went up behind us, and the fire lit our way through the first bend in the path.

A look over my shoulder showed little flames racing over the tracings of spilled oil and quickly turning back to blackness without the dark red char of the barrels themselves catching fire.

*Too late now.*

We sprinted and waited in a maddeningly slow leapfrog. The lieutenant and two sailors ran to the next bend and stopped to peer ahead, while Allen and I watched our rear, and then charged on past Lieutenant Marshall's group to the next point while they took our role.

We were almost on top of the disturbingly not-burning radio shed when more shots rang out.

I dove to the ground immediately as the gunfire reverberated over the sound of the wind. At least one of those bullets ricocheted uncomfortably close. I pulled my rifle close to my chest and rolled to the right to get behind some rocks.

A figure stood up from the other side of the rock and bellowed: "Ceasefire! You idiots, ceasefire!"

Petty Officer Wicklow pulled me to my feet and dusted me off. "Sorry, Chief," he whispered. "Everyone's nervous."

Davis peered, white-faced, from the side of the radio shed. "Oh! It's you, Lieutenant!" he called out with obvious relief.

"Anyone hit?" Marshall asked in an urgent undertone.

A grumbled murmur of responses came back with a negative.

"Guess it's a good thing the lieutenant didn't ask for any Marines to come along," Seaman Allen said to Wicklow. "Marines probably wouldn't have missed."

The petty officer shrugged.

"Yeah," Seaman Davis said. "But Marines wouldn't've gotten spooked by rats and sheep! I figured they must have had some reasons for not bringing 'em."

Lieutenant Marshall and I exchanged a look.

*I had no idea we could've asked for Marines.*

His raised eyebrows back seemed to say, *Me, either, but I'm glad we aren't dead.*

The sailors with us advanced on Seaman Davis with hands starting to ball into fists.

I cleared my throat, and they paused.

"I, I, I'm...sss..." Seaman Davis stammered nervously, looking from his fellow sailor's grim faces to mine and Lieutenant Marshall's.

*A little late for apologies.*

"Forget it," the lieutenant snapped. "We don't have time for a court-martial right now." Turning to me, he said, "Someone may have heard that shot." And then looking at Petty Officer Wicklow, "Or all those other shots."

"Ah. Sir." The petty officer turned a shade of red visible even in the predawn light. "We, um, secured the radio tower and took a prisoner."

"There were guards?" I asked.

"Yes." He shifted back and forth. "We took him prisoner."

"One guard," Lieutenant Marshall noted. "And all those shots were at sheep?" Lieutenant Marshall exchanged another look with me.

*What is going on?*

"And then some rats came out," Davis volunteered. "Spooked Petty Officer Wicklow something fierce, so he shot at them, and then we all thought we must be under attack, so we shot at things, too. Harry freaked out and dropped down onto the floor with his hands over his head and jus' said, 'Don't kill me, don't kill me' over and over, like."

Davis shook his head, as if this were a completely unreasonable response. Then he brightened after a moment, remembering one success worth noting.

"And we killed a sheep!" He nodded with pride at a small mound of dirty fleece I'd not noticed earlier.

"Seaman Williams shot the sheep," Wicklow corrected. "You missed."

Lieutenant Marshall scrubbed his face with his hand.

"Okay," I said. "We've got a tower to bring down."

"But who is Harry?" Marshall said.

"Our prisoner," Petty Officer Wicklow answered, as if that were perfectly obvious. "He's been extremely compliant. Seems to think we're likely to shoot him if he even looks at us sideways."

"Can't imagine where he'd get that idea," Lieutenant Marshall said.

*Me neither, sir*, I thought, not even bothering to hide my annoyance. *Me neither.*

"Right. Petty Officer, let's get everything wired and see to moving the prisoner to somewhere he doesn't get roasted alive, all right?"

Wicklow seized the opportunity to redeem himself, and set the sailors to completing our demolition project. The shed itself at the base of the tower was a simple wood thing, but a steady damp rain had started to fall and thoroughly soaked the timbers. I wished for a couple barrels of whale oil to get the fire good and smoky in case the tower survived the blast, but I couldn't even see a glow over the rise for the oil barrels anymore. Full dawn had broken, and sunlight burned brighter than any flickering flames that might have remained from our attempt at adding a secondary target.

We'd packed charges specifically for this task and wasted some of it, but hopefully we still had enough. Wicklow had three different detonator lines running from charges around the communications shed and at the base of the tower. The wires snaked along the ground over a slight rise up to that very rock outcropping where I'd ducked our welcome bullet volley.

Williams unspooled the third and final wire. Using his knife, he scrapped the insulation off and wrapped the bare metal onto a knob on the detonator box.

The lieutenant watched as some of the men made the final preparations, while Petty Officer Wicklow checked to make sure Harry stayed back over the next rise a little further down the path, with about half of our sailors set to guard him. Mostly, I wanted them there to keep any curious sailors from wandering back into the radio shed to check the charges one last time and getting themselves blown up. But I could only use so many for scouts without them getting in each other's way. We had a full circle of lookouts now, with everyone being very, very clear on not shooting at our own people, ensuring no more nasty surprises.

"Sir, the charges are all ready to blow," Williams reported to the lieutenant.

I peered back at Wicklow's group. He lifted his head just over the rise and gave me a thumbs up. My lookouts crouched and laid on rises and behind outcroppings all around us in pairs, with one looking out and one signaling back to me. Each pair gave me the "everything fine" sign.

"If you'd like to do the honors, Lieutenant?" Williams finished and gestured to the detonator box with the handle fully extended upward.

Kneeling next to the detonator box, Lieutenant Marshall put both hands on the handle. Looking around at all of us, he said, "Everyone down." Williams and I ducked down and covered our ears. When he was satisfied that everyone was behind some cover, Marshall slammed down the handle.

A boom flattened the shed into kindling. The tower still stood.

Williams mouthed something that seemed apologetic. He looked at the two remaining wires, and seemingly at random selected another to attach next.

The western sky flared suddenly bright as a million oil lamps. Then a fraction of a second later, the deep roar of the explosion swept over us, and everyone instinctively winced at the deep, reverberating sound. Williams stared in slack-jawed awe at the billowing smoke.

I stayed down and twisted back and forth to check on each of my lookout teams. They caught my glares and turned back to their work.

A steady ringing of church bells echoed over the bay. Port Stanley was awake.

Lieutenant Marshall snatched the wires from Williams's hands and finished unhooking the first set of wires and hooked up the next set to the detonator box. With the new set of wires hooked up, the Lieutenant dropped the handle.

Nothing happened. He looked back at me. I expected another explosion at any moment. He looked at the wires, then, satisfied that they were hooked up correctly, he raised then lowered the handle again, and again, nothing.

"Shit!" he exclaimed. Two more tries produced the same lack of results.

Williams grabbed the remaining end and set to switching it out.

A moment later, the church bells stopped. A thick gray streak of smoke poured upwards into the sky.

Williams lifted the detonator box and checked it for any signs of damage. Nothing seemed wrong.

"You try it," said Lieutenant Marshall.

Williams obeyed and dropped the handle and again, nothing. Out of pure frustration, he raised and lowered the handle several more times. Exasperated, he looked at the Lieutenant.

"Sir, should I go back and check the explosives and the wires?" I said. *The first detonation might have broken a wire or dislodged it from the charge. Or any number of things. Forget Marines—why didn't we ask for a couple petty officers who'd blown things up before and were good enough at it to still have all their fingers?*

Lieutenant Marshall thought a moment, then shook his head. "No, we don't have the time. We've got to go."

*Well, at least we don't have to worry that the* Denny *won't see our signal,* I thought.

Seaman Allen waved his arms wildly to catch my attention, and his partner lookout facing outward pointed straight at the path from Port

Stanley with a death grip on the back of Allen's coveralls, as if afraid we'd withdraw and leave him behind.

"Boss," I interrupted with an urgent warning: "The militia is coming."

At my signal, all the lookouts hid and Marshall, Williams and I ducked out of sight behind our outcropping.

Almost before we'd gotten behind the rocks, three young boys holding ancient muskets far too big for them came running down the path hollering.

"We're coming for you, Whalers!" This was not going to be a sneak attack, even if our scouts had been blind. They charged straight past us into Petty Officer Wicklow's team. 'The governor's going to—"

The shouts cut off abruptly with some muted grunts. Wicklow's men had them well in hand. *What kind of militia is this?*

Five more armed townsfolk came puffing down the path. The only head not solid gray or near bald with fringes of white was a man in a fine tailored suit with a heavy mustache and expression of fury on his face.

*It's the war,* I realized. *All the able-bodied men not working the whalers have gone for the war.*

"Damn you all!" the well-dressed man yelled. "So help me, I'll triple the price of your coal and impound your next three whales if you've tried to exceed your quotas again! Fifteen per season it is now, you bloody fools, and it'll starve your own children when there's none left to catch, blast you!"

"What the hell?" Lieutenant Marshall said, as he peaked over the hilltop even while I frantically motioned for him to stay under cover. Some of those older fellows might know a thing or two about sharpshooting.

*Keep your fool head down, boss! Just because some folks in Washington would prefer a dead hero was no reason to give them one!*

"What's that you say, sir?" I called back at the man leading the militia, wanting very much for any random shots to come my way rather than a dozen feet further to the left at the lieutenant.

"You heard me!" the leader yelled. "Where the bloody hell is your captain? Gone out to harpoon another whale while you lot try to render one down in secret on my own beaches? Not even bothering to do it on one of the other islands anymore, eh? You tell that puss-rotted fool I'll—"

Lieutenant Marshall stood up, clear in the early morning light. The silver of his collar devices glinted nicely. If the rest of him was rumpled from a night scrambling around with a stained coverall overtop everything, he still stood like an officer.

The man stared.

"I don't believe I've had the honor, sir." Lieutenant Marshall made a short bow, one gentleman to another. "Lieutenant Marshall of the United States Navy. Your islands are under attack."

"Uh, Governor?" One of the four aging militia men with Governor Allardyce leaned in and mumbled in a quavering voice not quiet enough to avoid reaching us. "Shouldn't we be hurrying after the boys?"

Governor Allardyce puffed out his chest again. "We're most certainly not under attack! The sheep girls haven't reported seeing a German ship in nearly a year. After Coronel, of course we were concerned, but then there was Port Doula and von Spee's squadron has been up and down the African coast ever since. There's only been that American flagged vessel lurking about."

"I knew it!" Williams whispered at my side. "There must have been people watching those sheep."

"Hush," I growled out, keeping my voice down. I'd thought we'd be shooting at somebody and then running away by now. I motioned for everyone to keep their heads down while waiting for the lieutenant to give us some kind of order.

Lieutenant Marshall pointed over his shoulder at the smoke still rising from our sabotage.

Governor Allardyce squinted at it. An older man, who seemed to be some sort of advisor, stepped up.

"That's not whale flensing, Gov," he said. "You be able to smell the reek of it from here if'n it was, and besides, the color of the smoke's all wrong, too."

"I believe we've already established that I'm not a whaler captain," Lieutenant Marshall said.

*Or at all likely to make captain of anything if he singlehandedly starts a war with England,* I kept behind my teeth and did not add.

"So." Lieutenant pointed over his shoulder at the still-rising smoke. "A stretch of your coastline is burning. We could sack the town and just leave you with wreckage. Or you could surrender the island."

"But the United States is neutral!" Governor Allardyce protested.

Lieutenant Marshall shrugged. "I have my orders."

"To attack Britain? Here?" The governor's advisor's skeptical expression did not look properly receptive for a man with twenty people pointing rifles at him.

I turned the barrel of mine to get ready to turn him into a leaking former advisor. The man saw my motion and jerked to the side to stand in front of the governor. *Damn brave idiots.*

The other three tried to point their own pistols in all directions, not too sure of where all Lieutenant Marshall's men were. They'd have heard American voices from both sides of the track, and more tellingly, not heard anything from the three youngsters who'd run on ahead.

Governor Allardyce waved his hat from behind the man. "A truce while we talk?" he called out.

"Ah, well, I've got four captives already," Lieutenant Marshall replied. "You might just go ahead and surrender and then we can discuss terms."

Yelps from behind had me jump almost out of my skin.

"Ten!" yelled Petty Officer Wicklow. "Make that an even ten captives now, Lieutenant. The governor had another six of these boys try to sneak up on us."

Another scuffle erupted, and Wicklow's voice dropped to a growl. "Lieutenant, how many of these brats can we shoot?"

The governor paled. "We surrender," he said.

The older gentlemen around him lowered their rifles, and a pack of bruised young boys, with their weapons taken away from them, scurried up over the ridge into the arms of their grandfathers.

"Do you suppose the Americans might lower the whaling quotas back to ten as part of the terms?" one of the older men asked the governor while looking hopefully at Lieutenant Marshall.

Governor Allardyce cocked his eyebrow at my boss.

I expected something like, *"That'll be for Washington and London to discuss,"* but this was the Vice President's nephew. He said, "Of course, gentlemen. The United States must ensure the freedoms and prosperity of its territories."

———

"Lieutenant!" The young local scamp bounced on his toes, eager to make his report. "Sir, the lookouts have spotted H.M.S. *Invincible*!"

"Oh, really?" A broad grin spread across Marshall's face. "What an unfortunate name for a warship."

"Do you think we ought to test the harbor guns, sir?" I suggested. "Just to make sure they are in proper working order, of course."

"But this is ridiculous." Governor Allardyce turned to me to plead, "You don't really want to fire on British vessels. We aren't at war with you!"

"Don't worry." Marshall patted the man on the shoulder. "We'll reimburse the King for the islands. And the ships," he added.

"God help us." Governor Allardyce raised his hands in defeat. "And supposing His Majesty suggests these islands aren't for sale?"

"Funny you should put it that way." Lieutenant Marshall nodded. "Neither were the sixteen American cargos taken in the last month by the Royal Navy in the North Sea, but that seemed to make no difference to anyone. This is only the natural extension." He gave the governor a perfect court bow.

Petty Officer Wicklow looked over at me. "Are the history books going to say the United States entered the Great War today?"

"Could be," I said.

The shore guns boomed a warning shot.

"Do you suppose it'll be called the Battle of the Falkland Islands?" Davis asked me.

"I doubt it," I said. "I don't think anyone much cares what happens down here. How important can one little southern patch of islands be?"

———

# ABOUT JOELLE PRESBY

Joelle Presby is a veteran U.S. Navy nuclear engineer who grew up in West Africa. She hunts cross genre writing opportunities and has snared gigs for everything from urban fantasy and high fantasy to alternate history and humorous science fiction. She wrote THE DABARE SNAKE LAUNCHER and co-writes in the Multiverse series with David Weber.

Where you can find Joelle Presby:

LinkTree:
https://linktr.ee/joellepresby

Author Website
Joellepresby.com

# ABOUT PATRICK DOYLE

Patrick Doyle is a pilot for a major airline and a retired U.S. Naval officer. He has been an airline simulator instructor and check pilot. He graduated college with a degree in history and is an avid sci-fi fan and wargamer who also dabbles in writing projects from time to time.

He co-wrote 2 alternate history short stories in the Phases of Mars series with Joelle Presby. He has worked with BuNine, a group that advised David Weber on his Honor Harrington novel series, and co-hosted Starfleet Tactical on YouTube.

As a gamer, he wrote the "Federation Commander Tactics Manual" (available from the Amarillo Design Bureau) and won several national championships. He is the lead game designer for Mariner Games, focusing on StarForce Commander, a tactical starship combat game. (available at https://www.mariner.games and Wargame Vault).

# AMBUSH AT LINGAYEN GULF

## William Stroock

The meeting room in General MacArthur's Manila headquarters was deceptively normal, as if we were planning a peacetime maneuver. It felt almost like a pregame meeting. Rows of chairs were arrayed before a map board and podium. As assistant to the G-3, I sat in one of the middle rows with the rest of North Luzon Force's staff. A trio of fans turned lazily above. I looked up at the fan closest to me, watched it turn, and wondered why the Japanese hadn't yet bombed the Manila powerhouse. *That's like not advancing a man from first to second,* I thought.

I was only half listening as Colonel Robert Hoffman, North Luzon Force S-3, went over our dispositions preparatory to the Japanese landing at Lingayen Gulf. I knew the TO&E better than anyone.

Colonel Hoffman nodded to me. "Now, Captain Davies did a fine job planning the deployment..."

Those had been my most harrowing staff days since my time on George Marshall's staff in the AEF after St. Mihiel. As a young ROTC lieutenant, fresh off my stint with Patton's tanks, I helped then-Colonel George Marshall manage the transfer of nine divisions from St. Mihiel to the Meuse-Argonne. By the time North Luzon Force was in place, I understood why Marshall had applied for a transfer out of Pershing's PC at Chaumont.

North Luzon Force comprised four underequipped and trained Philippine Army divisions. Those guys didn't march any better than underclassmen of my Yale ROTC unit in 1916. MacArthur had to know the Filipino troops wouldn't stand up the Japanese onslaught for long. Didn't he? North Luzon Force did have the 192nd Tank Battalion, a National Guard outfit, the 45th Infantry Regiment and the 26th Cavalry, plus some batteries of heavy guns on the south Lingayen Gulf shore.

"That's what we have, General Wainwright," Hoffman said to our boss in conclusion.

Wainwright was an old horse soldier, tall and thin, so much so that his friends called him "Skinny," which I'd learned since arriving in the islands in July.

"I'll turn the briefing over to General Brereton," said Hoffman.

General Brereton got up from the first row and turned around. The man was already renowned in Far East Command. On December 8th, as word came over the wires that the Japanese were bombing Pearl Harbor, Brereton had pushed his way past General Sutherland, and convinced MacArthur to drop the idea of hitting Japanese bases on Formosa. Brereton told MacArthur it would be much wiser to disperse the Far East Air Force. As a result, the Japanese bombed mostly empty airfields around Manila that day. The vaunted B-17s were far to the south at Del Monte airfield on Mindanao, kept in reserve for the right time to strike.

The survival of most of the Far East Air Force changed MacArthur's defense plans. War Plan Orange called for the army to hole up in Bataan and await reinforcements, but Brereton talked MacArthur into a more forward defense in north Luzon. "Let the enemy take the airfields at Vigan and Apgari," he said. "We'll meet them at Lingayen Gulf. And you will be the man who saved the Philippines." Brereton's argument appealed to MacArthur's ego. Those of us who'd been in the AEF during the Great War knew how big that was.

Brereton briefed us on the current dispositions of the Far East Air Force and took us through his plan for Lingayen Gulf. The Far East Air Force had a pair of big hitters in its lineup. These were two squadrons of thirty-five Boeing B-17 *Flying Fortresses* and four squadrons of 107 modern P-40 *Warhawks*. We also had several squadrons of aircraft Brereton described as "older but still useful." These included more than fifty P-35 pursuit planes, a squadron of eighteen B-18 *Bolos*, a squadron of a dozen B-10 *Martins*, and a squadron of sixteen P-26 *Peashooters*.

Brereton said, "We were outnumbered and outgunned, until this morning." He smiled and stepped away from the map. "General MacArthur?"

MacArthur stood and slowly walked before the map of northern Luzon. He pointed to a

red pin at Vigan on Luzon's north shore.

"Men…" MacArthur paused dramatically. "This morning, Captain Thomas Trapnell, commanding A Squadron of the 26th Cavalry, launched a daring raid against the Japanese airfield at Vigan. Striking just before dawn, his horse soldiers galloped onto the airstrip and struck a decisive blow against the enemy."

MacArthur took a communique out of his pants pocket and read: "Am pleased to inform Manila that we have destroyed dozens of enemy fighters and retreated back into the jungle. Cannot say more as the Japanese are in hot pursuit and we must now ride. All the best, Trapnell."

The general looked up from the paper. I swear he damn near had tears in his eyes. "General Brereton, tell the staff what this means."

Brereton replied, "We've got a fighting chance to stop the enemy landing in Lingayen Gulf."

One of Sunderland's flunkies replaced the map of North Luzon with a map of the Western Pacific. MacArthur looked out to us, then back at the map and pointed with his cane to Lingayen Gulf on the northwest side of Luzon.

"Disregard the Japanese landing in South Luzon. This campaign is going to come down to the struggle at Lingayen Gulf," began MacArthur with his typical rhetorical flourish. "If we can brace the enemy on Lingayen's shores, that will purchase time for the *Pensacola* Convoy to reach Mindanao."

I looked at my colleague, Commander Happ, the naval liaison to North Luzon Force's G-3 section. He nodded. "Don't worry, Dave," he said. "The navy will get her to the islands."

The *Pensacola* Convoy had been the talk of the Manila headquarters staff for several days now, as if it were a magic talisman whose arrival would save us all. The cruiser USS *Pensacola* escorted seven merchantmen containing dozens of P-40s and A-24 *Banshee* dive-bombers, batteries of 75mm guns, and tons of ammunition. The convoy was even then racing to Mindanao at great risk.

For the move to the North Luzon Force Post Command, I'd packed up a few important things from my office in Manila: gun belt, Colt .45, helmet, and my photograph of Cathy and I. I'd been able to get a letter out to Cathy after the 8th, via PBY to Australia, assuring her I was alive. I knew she'd have been worried, and probably angry. It'd been my idea to join the National Guard after I got my 20 years of regular army service in 1937. Cathy's family's financial firm had never quite recovered from the 1929 crash. My own family firm had survived, but had been stymied for years and finally failed in '37. An army paycheck was good security, even if I was a mere captain after leaving the regular army as major. Cathy's father certainly agreed, so she did, too, eventually.

"What could happen?" I'd asked Cathy. Then the army shipped me out to the Islands in July of '41. Cathy had been devastated, and I promised her I'd keep my head out of the line of fire, no matter what. I knew she'd be languishing back in Connecticut, listening to her friends talk about their kids, and fearing the war would leave her with a big empty house.

I stuffed an envelope of baseball cards into my pocket, too.

The North Luzon Force post command convoy drove out of Manila and up the main highway to Lingayen Gulf in a trio of army trucks and a couple of staff cars. I rode in the second car with Happy and Captain Jim Cloninger, our recently assigned army air corps liaison.

Clon was an old AEF man like me. He'd been in "Spads" during the war, he liked to say. Clon was out of shape, with a big belly. He looked perpetually tired. He said he'd come out to the islands hoping the tropics would "rejuvenate him."

In the back of the staff car, I flipped through the baseball cards one by one.

"What's with the baseball cards, Dave?" Cloninger asked.

"Cathy sends them to me, "I replied.

"Gonna give 'em to the Japanese?" Clon joked.

I gave him a glare. "I give 'em to Filipino kids. I'll burn them before I let the Japanese have them."

I flipped to a Joe DiMaggio card, popular with the Filipino kids, and held it out. "DiMaggio is the Japanese. Great hitter, good at everything."

Happy folded his arms. "And who are we?"

I flipped through the cards and held out Dom DiMaggio. "A slap-hitter. A quick and agile player. We can find a way on base and maybe manufacture a run."

"I'm a boxing man," Happy said. "I'd say we have a puncher's chance."

"Meaning?" Clon asked.

"If we can get a few good shots in, we can stop the Japanese."

"That would be up to us flyboys," Clon said. "We're the puncher."

I shrugged.

Driving up Route-3 leading to Lingayen Gulf, we passed an occasional army truck, but there was very little civilian automobile traffic. Gasoline was precious since December 8th, I knew. I'd spent a long afternoon on the phone making sure North Luzon Force had enough of it. We passed groups of Filipinos traveling south, usually on foot, or in a donkey cart or horsedrawn wagon. As we traversed the flat, open Northern Luzon, I looked at the terrain with the eye of a Great War tank platoon commander. The Japanese could take Route-3 right into Manila. If we didn't stop them up at Lingayen Gulf, we wouldn't stop them at all.

We set up the North Luzon Force PC in a well-appointed plantation house on the beach outside of Daugpan at the bottom of Lingayen Gulf. It still had electricity, and we set up a generator, if needed. From here, the Post Command could observe the Gulf, manage the movement of North Luzan Force, and if necessary, evacuate south toward Bataan. A platoon of Philippine Scouts stood guard. This was supported by a platoon of M3 *Stuarts* from A Company, 192nd Tank Battalion. The rest of the battalion was five miles to the northeast at Mangaldan, waiting for the enemy.

General Wainwright took the dining room with his main staff, including Colonel Hoffman. I ran the operations room out of what had been house's study. I wrote "Bullpen" on a sheet of paper and affixed it above the door. We pinned several maps to the wall. My desk was a folding card table salvaged from a closet. I set my photo of Cathy against the wall, the one I took right after we found out she was pregnant back in 1921. This was before she lost the baby. Our only baby, it turned out. I always liked remembering Cathy that way: sweet, and young and ebullient, her hair still naturally blonde.

In the Bullpen, we had a quartet of phones marked *Army, Air Corps, Navy,* and *Manila.* The last phone went directly to MacArthur. Behind the phone desk was a pair of radios, each manned by a specialist. We had a few other enlisted men. A typist, a phone operator, and we had a local boy for a runner, Aguinaldo. We called him Aggy, and I paid him with baseball cards.

We were ready by the evening. Most of Daugpan had fled and the town was quiet. An eerie calm fell over the area. It almost felt like a night at Cathy's family summer home on Long Island Sound. I pushed those thoughts from my mind.

We heard the waves playing softly on the shore, and occasionally an aircraft above.

"Not ours," Clon told me as we walked along the plantation's north-facing veranda.

We knew a Japanese fleet of more than a hundred ships was heading into Lingayen Gulf. During the night, multiple radio calls came down from Bauteng on the northern end of Gulf, "Trawler spotted..." then, "Ships entering gulf," then, "Many ships steaming south," and then, "Japanese Convoy." Scouts along the Lingayen coast confirmed as the Japanese steamed deeper and deeper into Lingayen Gulf, just as we wanted.

Throughout the night and early morning, gentle rain fell, pelting the roof. Happy was pleased.

"This will make for rough seas," he insisted. "That will hamper amphibious operations, maybe even scatter their landing force. Then..."

The rain helped conceal our own troop movements, though it made things wet and muddy for the 26th Cavalry which had been riding north parallel to the coast ever since we'd spotted the Lingayen invasion force.

Most importantly, the rain ensured Japanese planes would have immense difficulty spotting our own aircraft. At that very moment, twenty-four precious B-17 bombers, flown into Clark Field on Brereton's orders, were arming and fueling. The *Flying Fortresses* were the heavy hitters in our lineup, but not our only hitters. We had the older B-18 *Bolos* and four dozen P-35 pursuit planes. The first few days of the war, we had realized that Japanese *Zeros* badly outclassed the P-35s, but Brereton figured the P-35s could strafe enemy ships and leave the dogfighting to the P-40s.

Just after 0200, we heard Japanese naval guns booming up the gulf.

"The Japanese have begun operations," Happy said.

While the Bullpen took phone and radio calls reporting enemy movement, Happy updated the map of Lingayen Gulf. Reports came in from various units that the Japanese were shelling a trio of areas along the gulf's eastern shore. We could hear them at the PC, a distant banging sound to the north. Happy's red map pins showed the Japanese fleet was arrayed in a long line down the gulf, preparing to land troops in a trio of different places on the east shore. I looked at the map and said, "Let's get some air, Happy."

"Sure thing."

Happy and I walked out of the PC. From there, we had a clear view down to the beach. The light rain pattered upon out helmets. The gulf was misty, but we saw light playing off the fog and heard the Japanese guns in the distance. Aggy, who'd spent the night sitting on a stool in the Bullpen's corner and running messages between naps, came along with us.

Happy took a crumpled pack of lucky Strikes out of his shirt pocket and lit one with his Zippo. "Want one?"

"No thanks." I never smoked. I'd always tried to stay in shape after playing baseball at Yale, though I did like a pipe after Sunday brunch with Cathy's father. "And I thought you'd be rationing cigarettes."

"The *Pensacola* convoy will come through," Happy assured me.

I said nothing.

"What you worried about, Dave?"

"I hope you're right about the Navy," I replied. I looked to the dark, drizzly sky. "And the Army Air Corps. If the Japanese get ashore en masse, we can't stop them. I think MacArthur has an outsized idea about what they can do."

"What about the Scouts?" Happy asked. "And the rest of the Philippine Division? And the National Guard armor?"

I scrunched my nose in thought. "Decent hitters." I held up a finger. "But will the Japanese let them come to bat with anyone on base?"

"What do you mean by that?"

"I mean they may not be enough. I don't care what the papers back home say tanks can do after the what the Krauts did in France." I pointed a thumb at my chest. "I was in tanks in the last war. They're not wonder weapons."

Happy looked out upon the dark Lingayen waters. "You can feel the Japanese out there," he said. "Just a few miles up the gulf. Dozens of ships."

I put my hands in my pockets and took a deep breath and gazed at the gulf sky, eerie in the night fog. "Yeah."

We walked back to the Bullpen and listened as more reports of enemy activity in Lingayen Gulf came in over the radio.

"Many ships at rest opposite Agoo."

"Boats coming alongside transports..."

"Ships at rest and waiting offshore at Arangay..."

"Boats were coming alongside and moving out."

"Patrols saw some smaller Japanese boats cruising close to shore."

"It sounds like the Japanese are loading troops for a landing," I said. "What do you make of all this, Happy?"

We pondered the map, which now showed a long line of red markers running south from San Fernando at the head of Lingayen Gulf thirty miles south to Damortis.

Happy said, "The Japanese landing in several places on a broad front."

"Yes…" I nodded in agreement. "And we have our best hitter right here." I stabbed the blue marking representing the 192nd Tank Battalion.

Happy pointed at the map. "I think there are two or three different task forces," he said. "They could be anywhere along the coast," he added. "You're the army man. You were in tanks!" He smiled. "Where would you land?"

I shrugged. "Anywhere along the road." I ran my finger on Route-3 running along the coast. "I could move south…to right here." I pointed to the floor.

"Excuse me, sirs," Aggy said. "There's something happening out on the water. Some kind of boom and light."

"All right, let's go have a look."

I left Clon in charge of the G-3 section. Outside, the sun wasn't quite ready to come up over the eastern horizon and the night was still dark and misty, but now, on Lingayen Gulf we saw a flame. It looked like a candle from the PC veranda. But Happy took one look and assured me it was some massive conflagration at sea.

"Something exploded," he said.

I put my hands on my hip and looked at Happy and said, "That's good. Right?"

"It could be," he said.

I nodded to the flames. "How far off would you say that is?"

"You army boys can't estimate distance?"

"I was in tanks and later Marshall's G3 section." I shrugged. "I was never in the arty."

"I should have brought my binoculars," Happy said as he considered the conflagration. "Ten miles. A ship of some kind."

"One of our ships?"

Happy shook his head. "We're not supposed to have anything big in the gulf."

'So, it's Japanese."

"Certainly."

Aggy held out his hand. "Oh," I said. I took a baseball card out of my pocket and handed it to him.

"Jimmie Fox! Wow!" Aggy exclaimed.

To the east, the sky was turning just a bit gray.

Happy chewed his bottom lip and then spat in the sand.

Only after the Battle of Lingayen Gulf was over did we learn what happened.

*S-38*, one of our boats patrolling up around San Fernando, followed the Japanese convoy into Lingayen Gulf. When the transports stopped for boarding troops, *S-38* closed to 2,000 yards and fired a spread of four torpedoes. Due to bad aim and the faulty Mark-10 torpedo design, all four torpedoes missed or ran right underneath the target. But this got the Japanese's attention and a pair of destroyers peeled off to search for *S-38*. The Japanese destroyers sailed right past *S-38*, enabling her to get even closer to the transports. She fired off two more torpedoes. One missed, but one exploded underneath its target. This was the explosion and fire we saw at Daugpan.

The navy's second hit came not long after the first. At about 0600 hours, we saw another explosion on the water, this one much closer.

That can't be more than five miles off!" Happy exclaimed as a yellow and orange explosion mushroomed into the sky.

The flaming *Haro Maru* illuminated much of the southern end of Lingayen Gulf. A trio of boats from Motor Torpedo Squadron-3 were hiding out on the east end of Sungyot Island, a mile off the coast of Santo Thomas at the southern end of the gulf. When Commander Bulkeley saw the conflagration *S-38* created, he decided it was time to get into the fight. He led his three boats out from behind Sungyot Island and attacked. In this, Bulkeley's boats were assisted by the dark and the numerous Japanese landing craft and patrol boats then in the water. To the patrolling destroyers, Bulkeley's boats blended right in with the rest of the light traffic.

Bulkeley attacked the first ship he saw, a Japanese transport that must have been carrying tanks and trucks. At an unbelievably close 500 yards, Bulkeley fired two torpedoes into the transport. While the first torpedo failed to detonate, the second hit forward of the transport's superstructure and blew most of the bow off. The transport sank astonishingly quick. We didn't know it at the time, but Bulkeley's boats had just destroyed most of the vehicles of the Japanese 48th Recon Battalion, slated to cover the southern landing.

Chaos followed as Japanese destroyers and patrol boats switched on their search lights to find Bulkeley's torpedo boats. The southern gulf was crisscrossed with light beams, pierced by lines of tracers, and dotted by the flash of machine guns. Most of the Japanese fire hit Japanese ships, especially the light craft and barges. Bulkeley made an attack run on another transport, once again hitting with one torpedo and missing with the other. Unfortunately, it was a dud.

Out of torpedoes and with the IJN rather perturbed, Bulkeley decided he and his boys had done enough. Unfortunately, one PT boat broke north and was never heard from again. Bulkeley's boat and one other boat motored south back to Sungyot Island...and right into a dozen Japanese landing craft coming the other way.

We listened to the PT-Boat driver's excited radio chatter in the Bullpen.

"Give 'em another burst from the 40mm!"

"Pulling up to this boat now—blast 'em..."

"Swim, Tojo!"

Thankfully, these were mostly *Daihatsu* craft, each carrying a few infantry squads. Bulkeley ran his boat up to the side of each *Daihatsu* and had his sailors fire into the hulls. The PT boats sank a couple of landing craft, set a couple more ablaze, and also left several boats dead in the water. Bulkeley and his boys didn't stop till they ran out of ammunition.

Back in the Bullpen, Happy stuffed his hands in his pockets and ground his teeth. "Why so glum?' I asked. "Looks like you navy boys are doing well."

"Yeah, but not well enough," he said. "The Japanese are going to get ashore. And you yourself said most of the Filipino troops are minor leaguers."

I folded my arms. "Yep."

By 0630 hours, we had confirmed reports of two enemy landings, one at the head of the Aringay River, about midway up the coast and another to the south at Agoo. Even though a task force was off Santo Thomas, the Japanese had yet to land there. It seemed Bulkeley's PT boats had ruined their plans. The big guns deployed northeast of our PC went into action. The 155mm howitzers boomed in the morning mist, sending massive shells crashing down upon the Japanese task force. We couldn't tell if they were hitting anything, though the barrage did further hamper the Japanese landing at Santo Tomas.

By 0730 hours, the sun was finally up. For half an hour before, we'd heard aircraft in the air. Soon after, we heard explosions. The 26th Cavalry may have destroyed a couple of dozen aircraft at Vigan, but the Apgari strip on Luzon's north coast was still operational. And the Japanese were flying in bombers from Formosa. Calls were coming in from the landing areas.

"Where's our support?" one asked. "Where are the flyboys?"

I looked at Clon, who shrugged back at me. "Brereton doesn't tell me everything."

"So much for your puncher's chance," I said to Happy.

"Yeah?"

"Feels like the other guys have men on second and third bases with nobody out," I said.

About 0830 hours, Clon got off the line to Nichols Field and said, "Help is on the way."

Brereton finally struck. P-40 fighters of the 21st and 34th Pursuit Squadrons arrived en masse. There began a series of dogfights over Lingayen Gulf. One of the radiomen tuned to the flyboy's frequency and we listened raptly, as if a Yankees-Sox game were on the radio. I couldn't tell the ebb and flow of the battle, but it seemed clear that the P-40 flyers were giving the Japanese a pretty hard time. Our flyboys reported several "splashes."

With Japanese fighter cover engaged, Brereton sent a flight of old P-35s and even older P-26s over Lingayen Gulf. The *Zeros* were superior to the P-40s that were attempting to break up the bomber attacks. They simply outclassed the P-35s and P-26s, bringing down any that they were able to reach. But after losing the *Zeros* at Vigan, Japanese air cover was thin. Brereton apparently sent what the football types called the "all-out blitz" over the gulf. Several fighters broke through and made strafing runs on Japanese ships. We listened intently as two P-35s riddled a destroyer with machine gun fire. Another P-35 managed to shoot up a pair of *Daihatsu* transports. Most importantly, a trio of P-26s emptied their guns into a Japanese transport at the Agoo landing area and hit something important and sparked an internal explosion big enough to lift her out of the water.

The P-35s and P-26s, as obsolete as they were, still required the Japanese to burn fuel and expend ammo to shoot them down. Their sacrifice cleared the way for the Far East Air Force's best punch, as Happy would say. We knew from the radio that the flyboys were coming. When we heard more P-40 engines, we stepped outside of the PC and looked to the sky.

It was about 0930 now. The sun shone down on Lingayen Gulf, and we saw a dozen ships on the water, some obscured by smoke. There were little mosquitos in the air already over the gulf, our own P-40s dogfighting the remaining *Zeros* and some Japanese reinforcements. Guns boomed in the distance.

Flights of P-40s came over the southern Lingayen Gulf in pairs. Then came the Boeing B-17s, each loaded with 500-pound demolition bombs.

"This is it," Clon said. "Here come the big boys."

"The heavy hitters," I said.

The B-17s came in from the southwest, south, and west of the gulf. General Brereton had hoped to get all the groups over the target at the same time. Several B-17s were jumped by freshly arrived Japanese fighters and never managed to unload their bombs, but enemy fighter cover was dispersed now after an hour of fighting the brave, doomed pursuit pilots. Eighteen B-17s arrived on target and caught the transports on the open water. In groups of three, the B-17s set upon the Japanese task force. In truth, the attack was somewhat disjointed, with one trio hitting a Japanese ship, and several minutes later another trio hitting the same ship. The effort was not one mighty grand slam envisioned by General Brereton, or a knockout blow, to use Happy's boxing language. Instead, the B-17 attack was a series of singles and doubles producing four runs all the same.

Though we couldn't see the action in North Luzon Force's PC, we heard plenty, with Boeing B-17 Wright radial engines humming in the sky. The thump of flak and rattle of machine guns. The rumble of bombs hitting water, interspersed with the occasional report of a direct bomb hit. All the while, we listened on the radio, catching bits and pieces of excited pilot chatter from bomber pilots flying their nicknamed ships.

"Forget the destroyers, wax the transports."

"This is *Boxcar.* Follow me in."

"*Zeros* above."

"This is *Klondike*: just landed two hits on that transport."

"Fighters on the left."

"Moving in on that pair of transports. Follow me, *Uptown* and *Breaker.*"

We heard a B-17 named *Slugger* claim a bomb hit on a Japanese cruiser, Happy reported.

"Sounds like things are going well," I said.

Clon bit the inside of his lip and said, "Hard to tell, for sure."

Outside, the nearby battery of 155mm guns boomed.

"Why don't you go see what that's all about, Aggie," I said.

The boy hopped off his stool and ran outside, eager to see what was happening, and also eager to get a baseball card.

I laughed at his sweet exuberance.

A minute later, we heard the drone of several aircraft engines. They grew louder and louder and passed the sky above.

I asked Clon, "Those B-17s?"

He shook his head. "Those are B-10 *Martins*."

"Are the B-17s clearing the way?'

"They probably got the enemies' attention, that's for sure."

"Excuse me, Captain," the radio specialist said. "It sounds like something big is happening, judging by all the navy chatter."

I walked over to the radio.

"It sounds like USS *Stingray* is really letting the Japanese have it up north. The skipper radioed that his torpedo spread missed a Japanese minesweeper, so he surfaced and engaged with the deck gun. You wanna have a listen?" He held out his headphones.

I took the headphones and listened. I heard a lot of excited chatter and gunfire from the crew.

"Watch your aim!"

"Put a round through the bridge! Another one, now another one!"

"Aye, Skipper, but the bridge is already afire."

The steady report of the *Stingray's* deck gun punctuated all the crosstalk.

The skipper said, "Okay, she's afire…let's get down below before the *Zeros* come back."

"Score one for the Navy," I said.

Then we heard a loud *Boom* not too far away on the water.

"What the heck was…?"

Aggie came running back into the Bullpen, shouting in Tagalog and waving his arms.

"What did you see?" I asked him.

Aggie turned his hands into little airplanes and made as if they were dive-bombing something. He made booming and *ack-ack* sounds. The boy beamed and made a big circle with his arms. "Boom!" he exclaimed. Then he made twinkling motions with his fingers and moved his hands in the air. "Smoke, fire. Lots of both."

"It sounds like that flight of *Martins* hit their target," Clon said.

"Good," I said. I took a baseball card out of my pocket and handed it to Aggie. He looked at it and proclaimed, "Wow! Carl Hubbel!"

By about noon, the B-17s were making their way back south over our PC.

Happy and I went out to count the ships. We saw several groups of three, and some groups of two and a cloud of smoke where the *Martins* had sunk a ship. As we watched, a flight of four P-26 *Peashooters* came in low over the gulf from the west and strafed the nearest trio of Japanese landing craft. With my own eyes, I saw one of the landing craft break up. A flight of *Zeros* arrived on scene and chased off our *Peashooters*.

Later, Del Monte reported that we lost four B-17s, but only a pair to *Zeros* thanks to the P-40 flyboys, who claimed eight kills against eleven lost. The B-10 *Martins* suffered badly, and so had the P-35s, with a dozen splashed. But looking out at Lingayen Gulf, we saw several plumes of thick smoke rising over the water. Closer to our position, a ship burned.

"What is that, Happy?" I asked.

Happy put his binoculars to his eyes and said, "I estimate it's about ten miles north of here, off Santo Thomas. It's pretty big, at least a transport."

In fact, a flight of B-17s had hit another transport carrying a company of Japanese infantry, further hampering their landing efforts at Santo Thomas. But the Japanese landings up at Agoo and Buang proceeded, and by noon, they'd put a battalion ashore at each location.

Back at Nichols field, General Brereton was consulting with his squadron leaders. After scoring so many hits, the commanders of both B-17 squadrons wanted to "take another whack at the enemy," as one captain said. Even then, the B-17s were making their way back to Del Monte. It was more than five hundred miles and a two-plus-hour flight, with another hour on the ground to rearm and refuel. The B-17s would be vulnerable the whole time.

I spent the next few hours in the Bullpen taking reports from ground commanders up the coast. "Enemy ashore in strength... Pulling back east... Japanese tanks ashore at Bauang."

Indeed, we could hear the machine gun fire and small arms and artillery. Each time our guys concentrated for an attack, they were broken up by expertly placed Japanese naval fire. The Japanese had control of the air again, too. For the next few hours, we got the worst of things.

At 1500 hours, General Wainwright made a call to General MacArthur in Manila. I was in the room, listening to and watching Skinny. He stood in his khakis and riding boots, steel helmet on his head, hand on his hip as he briefed MacArthur.

"The Japanese are ashore at Agoo, Arangay and Bauang... Yes, sir. The Navy and Air Corps stopped them off Santo Thomas... Yes, I understand completely. Yes, we're fighting hard, but those are mostly Filipino troops up there, General... They just can't... Yes, sir. Yes, sir, right away."

Skinny hung up. "We're waiting for Brereton to get his bombers rearmed and refueled down at Del Monte field. They'll be back by late afternoon, he says," Skinny said. He looked to Colonel Hoffman and said, "I'm to commit the 192nd Tank Battalion right away."

Colonel Hoffman looked at me. "Do we have fuel for it?"

"We do, Colonel," I replied. "I made sure of that."

I sent several tankers to rendezvous with the 192nd Tank Battalion southeast of their Mangaldan staging area. I quickly outlined my supply plan to Hoffman while pointing at the map. The tanks might die, but it wouldn't be because I didn't give them enough fuel or ammo for resupply.

"They'll need infantry support, don't you think, Captain Davies?" Hoffman asked.

"There's a pair of companies from the 45th Scouts up the road at Sison," I said.

Skinny nodded. "Okay," he said. "Get the order out. The 192nd Tank Battalion to link up with those Scout companies near..." He looked to me again.

"Damortis," I said. "Just south of Santo Thomas."

"What about arty?"

"We've got those four 155 heavies," I said.

"Good. Tell them to stop firing on the enemy fleet," Skinny said. "They're not hitting anything, anyway."

Hoffman said, "And get Colonel Wickord on the line. I want to talk to him."

I nodded to the radio specialist. "Right away," he said.

Happy, Clon and me stepped out of the PC.

A haze of smoke still hung over Lingayen Gulf

"So it comes down to you flyboys," I said to Clon.

Clon smiled. "As it should."

"Our heavy hitter," I said.

Happy added, "Our best punch."

Colonel Hoffman walked out and said, "Captain Davies, you were in tanks, right?"

"I was."

"Colonel Wickord says he's down a platoon commander. I want you to go up there and take over."

I looked over at Colonel Hoffman in shock. "Me? Colonel, I haven't been in a tank since the Bonus Army March."

I'd never seen an M3 *Stuart* up close and the only thing I knew about them was what I'd seen in *The Tanks Are Coming*.

"I need someone up there, Captain Davies," he said. "Get going," he said more firmly.

"Yes, sir." I saluted reluctantly.

Colonel Hoffman went back inside the PC. I held up my hands and looked at Happy. "I guess I'm in tanks again."

Happy put a Lucky Strike in his mouth and lit it. "Don't worry, Dave. I'll run the G-3 section for you."

"Great," I replied. "Can I have a jeep?"

"Sure thing."

I went back inside and got my helmet, belt, sidearm and lastly, my photo of Cathy. I looked at Cathy for a moment and realized I was breaking my promise to her.

I saw Aggy in the corner. "I gotta go," I said, and pointed my thumb to the door. I took the envelope of baseball cards off my table and handed them to Aggy.

"Okay?"

"Okay."

I requisitioned one of the PC jeeps and took a driver. As the new assistant S-3, Happy wanted the jeep back. We drove northeast toward the 192nd Tank Battalion. From the road, I saw several plumes of black oily smoke on Lingayen Gulf, and one rectangular shape seemingly dead in the water. Aircraft buzzed above, all Japanese at the moment. We drove past a few ambulances bringing wounded south, and small groups of Filipino civilians getting out of harm's way.

We found the 192nd Tank Battalion just south of Damortis. I whistled when I saw a long line of M3 *Stuarts* parked on the side of the road beneath the trees. I hadn't seen tanks lined up like that since St. Mihiel.

I got out of the jeep and said, "Thanks."

I walked toward the first tank. The crew was lounging on the engine deck. When they saw me, they stood and saluted.

"Anyone know where I can find Colonel Wickord?" I asked.

"Up at the front of the column, Captain," the crew leader said.

I nodded and walked up the road. The *Stuarts* looked ready to go, to my eye. Crews lounged about their tanks, smoking, eating, talking, waiting. Empty fuel drums were off to the side of each tank, I noticed with satisfaction.

Colonel Wickord was with a platoon of halftracks and trucks at the head of the column. He was a slightly stout, round-faced man. *Not a ballplayer*, I thought.

I saluted and said, "Captain Davies, reporting."

"Ah, good," Wickord said, "You'll find D Company over there." He pointed to the other side of the road on the beach. "Report to Captain Rue."

"Right, Colonel."

Wickord looked me over. "Over from the PC, huh? Can you clear up any of the scuttlebutt around here?"

I told Wickord what I knew about the impending aerial attack.

"So we're waiting on the flyboys, huh?" He looked up the road toward Santo Thomas, Agoo and Arangay. "Figures. Okay, get going."

I walked across the road to D company. These were National Guard men from Kentucky with the twang to prove it. I reported to Captain Rue, who looked me over insignia and asked, "You're a tank man?"

I held up a hand. "Captain, my last tank was a M1917 *Renault* on the Anacostia River in 1932. I wouldn't even know where to start with one these things." I nodded to the nearest M3 *Stuart*.

"The crew will see you through it," Rue said.

"What happened to the 2nd Platoon's previous commander?"

"Lt. Jennings was killed by a Japanese anti-tank shell last night," he replied. "Took his head clean off."

"Oh."

"I'll walk you over."

Four tanks were under the trees on the side of the road. "Right over there," Rue said.

"Thanks, Captain." I walked up to the lead tank.

My new crew was sitting in the sand, watching the fire and smoke on Lingayen Gulf. They turned to me, clad in olive drab coveralls and wearing ear-flapped Rawling tanker helmets. It was their turn to look me over.

"Men, I'm Captain Davies."

The tankers stood and introduced themselves.

"I'm Eddie." He nodded to the M3. "I shoot this wreck." He pointed to a small skinny kid who didn't look much over eighteen. "This is Kenny, and that's Det."

Det saluted. "Short for Detlef. I drive."

I pointed to the stenciled name on the turret: *Beatrice.* "That's the tank's name?"

"Yeah," Eddie said. "For Lt. Jenning's wife."

"Okay," I said. I thought of Cathy for a moment.

I climbed onto the engine deck and into the turret. Eddie told me the M3

*Stuart* was cramped, compared to the *Sherman*, but the *Stuart* was much more spacious than an M1917 *Renault.* Eddie laughed when I told him so. Behind me was an M2 .50-caliber machine gun. I had to dismount to man it. Another MG was below me for the driver. On my left was the gunner's hatch.

"Got a helmet?" I asked Eddie.

"Yeah, sure, Captain," Eddie said. He handed me another flap-eared Rawlings tanker helmet.

"That was Lt. Jenning's," he said.

I looked the tanker helmet over and put it on my head. "It's a little loose," I said.

"Jennings had a big head, sir," Eddie joked.

After familiarizing myself as best I could with the *Stuart,* I walked around to the other tanks in the platoon and introduced myself. The tankers looked at me skeptically, though I think I won a measure of respect when I told them I'd been with Patton at St. Mihiel in 1918.

"We got a full tank of gas, racks of 37mm shells, and full belts of .30 and .50-caliber ammo," Eddie told me. "When the call comes, we'll be ready."

The call came a little after 1500 hours. The Philippine 11th Division reported the enemy was coming south toward the Aringay River. The Filipino troops fought bravely, but were outmanned and outgunned. Japanese ships and aircraft hammered them, too. From our position south of Damortis, we could see the dust clouds rising. Over the next few hours, the fire grew louder and more intense.

"Hey, Captain!" Eddie shouted from *Beatrice.* "Captain Rue says saddle up and get ready!"

"Right," I waved. "Okay, saddle up!" I shouted to the platoon.

I climbed into the tank and took my place in the cupola. Captain Rue called D Company. "We'll advance up Route-3 to the Aringay River. We'll find the Japanese on the south bank," Rue said. "Second Platoon, you'll bring up the rear and protect our left flank."

"Roger," I replied.

Det started up the tank. I listened to the hum of the engine and watched as D Company started up the road by platoons.

"Okay, driver advance," I ordered.

Det advanced the tank, sending me lurching at the unexpected power of its Cadillac engine. "Whoa!" I exclaimed. *Renaults* didn't go that fast.

We drove north on Route-3, bringing up D Company's rear, which was just fine with me. I felt like I knew even less about an M3 *Stuart* after Eddie's quick tour. And of course, I was at the head of 2nd Platoon. If we got into it, I'd be the first in the platoon to get it.

Some elements of the 11th Philippine Division retreated past us, but most had pulled back east toward the mountains. The gun and artillery fire lessened, save for the bombardment from the Japanese ships.

*Might be something the B-17s need to take care of when they come back*, I thought. *Otherwise, those cruisers and destroyers are going to murder us after we attack.*

By sixteen hundred hours, we heard firing up ahead, small arms, machine guns and the distinct blast of an M3 *Stuart's* 37mm gun. Captain Rue radioed back, "Contact up ahead. First and 3rd platoons maneuver right. Second Platoon maintain position."

"Roger," I radioed back.

"Contact! Contact!" came the call.

There followed a deluge of machine gun and 37mm fire and a flurry of radio calls, excited tankers shouting, really, proclaiming they'd spotted the enemy. B Company in the center had advanced right into a battalion of Japanese infantry sent to secure a bridgehead on the south back of the Aringay. On the right, two platoons of C company advanced up to the riverbank and blasted Japanese forces on the north side. Wickord ordered D Company to remain on Route-3 on the south bank. Second Platoon was bringing up the left, rear flank, close to the beach.

The time was 1615. We didn't know it, but the first flights of P-40 *Warhawks* and surviving P-35s were back over Lingayen Gulf.

I sat in the cupola, helmet on, chinstrap buckled, listening to the cacophony up ahead. It wasn't quite the barrage at St. Mihiel, but it was still quite a racket. Eddie came up the gunner's hatch and lit a Lucky Strike. I was vaguely aware of aircraft engines in the air above Lingayen Gulf, but assumed they were Japanese.

"Anything new on the radio?" I asked.

Eddie took a drag from his Lucky Strike. "Nah, just lots of fighting and..." He tossed the cigarette over to the left and stopped cold and looked into the brush. Then he nudged me. "Uh, Captain?"

"Yeah?"

"Enemy in the brush." He pointed left.

I looked to where Eddie was pointing. There was a line of bushes, and several figures stirring it.

"Those *are* Japanese," I said. "They wouldn't be acting like that if they weren't. Get down in the turret and traverse left."

"Okay."

As Eddie traversed the turret left, I motioned for the radio. Taking the hand mic, I called to the rest of the platoon. "Second Platoon, this is Davies. Japanese on the left. Traverse left and fire."

"Det, hit them with your machine gun," I said.

"Roger."

"Eddie, fire when ready."

"Right."

Eddie sent a 37mm canister shot into the brush while Det and Kenny fired their .30-caliber MGs. The rest of my platoon did the same. I took the mic and called, "Rue, this is 2nd Platoon. Japanese on my left. Engaging."

Several Japanese had already fallen dead through the brush. A few bullets plinked off my turret. Our MG fire scythed the brush down, exposing the Japanese and forcing them to hit the ground or pull back. I peered forward and saw more Japanese coming up from the beach.

"Aw, hell," I said. "Driver, traverse left and advance." I picked up the mic. "Platoon traverse left and advance."

I pumped my fist in the air and waved it forward.

Second platoon advanced into the brush and under scattered palm trees, firing our guns and driving the Japanese towards the water. We pushed through to the beach, where chaos greeted us.

The beach was packed with hundreds of Japanese. Scattered on the sand were dozens of crates of supplies and ammunition. On the water were half a dozen *Daihatsu* transports, and beyond that a small ship, a mine sweeper, Happy later told me. When they saw us, the Japanese ran in all directions.

"Fire! Fire!" I shouted.

Everyone in my crew fired their MG and 2nd Platoon sent a torrent of bullets into the Japanese. The combined machine guns and 37mm cannons made for a fearful slaughter. The tents and boxes and bodies burned like the Bonus Army encampment. I hadn't seen carnage like that since overrunning a German trench at St. Mihiel. I looked at the beached landing craft and said, "Hey, Eddie, put a 37mm round in the nearest *Daihatsu*."

"Gotcha," Eddie said. "Loader, HE!"

"Up!" Kenny replied.

"On the way!"

The 37mm HE round went right down the beach and exploded in the *Daihatsu's* engine compartment.

"Another," I said.

Kenny reloaded, and Eddie followed up the first 37mm HE round with a second, then a third, till the *Daihatsu* engine compartment and pilot house were aflame. The rest of 2nd Platoon followed my lead and fired on the landing craft till they were twisted and smoldering wreckage. Bodies were everywhere. The scene was actually more gut-wrenching than the German trenches at St. Mihiel.

To the northeast, I saw a half-dozen ships on the water.

"Second Platoon," Captain Rue called. "What's going on down there?"

I picked up the mic and said, "We made contact with the Japanese and found a landing area."

"Landing?"

"Yep, I'd say a company, at least."

Eddie fired the 37mm.

"Hold on," I said to Rue. "What are you firing at, Eddie?"

"That ship is 200 yards offshore. Why not?"

"You're right." I radioed the platoon. "Second Platoon, this is Davies. Fire on that ship."

A volley of four 37mm HE shells shot out from the beach and slammed into the superstructure of the minesweeper. I dismounted from the cupola and got on the engine deck behind the .50-caliber. I pulled back the bolt, aimed at the minesweeper's bridge and let 'er rip. I fired burst after burst. The other tankers in 2nd Platoon followed my lead and fired, too. As we did so, I saw a flight of four P-40s pass low over Lingayen Gulf.

"Ha!" I shook a fist. "Here come the flyboys!"

By then, smoke was pouring out of the minesweeper's bridge. Eddie traversed the turret and brought the 37mm crosshairs onto the minesweeper's forward gun.

"Load AP!" he shouted.

"Round up!" Kenny responded

"On the way!"

I picked up the mic and ordered the other tanks to join in. The platoon sent several rounds into the turret until it exploded in a spectacular pyrotechnic display.

"Whoa..." I whistled.

Up north, the rest of 192nd Tank Battalion had pinned the Japanese on the far bank of the Aringay River. Wickord was getting ready to bring another company across, while P-35s were strafing the Japanese. The big 155mm batteries boomed, hammering the Japanese on the north bank.

I looked again to the transports up the coast. Already, flak shells were bursting above them as P-40s and P-26s made strafing runs. Another wave of P-40s passed our position. Then I heard the distinctive roar of B-17 *Flying Fortresses*. I saw a group of three B-17s pass north, then another, and another. They made straight for the line of transports. Twenty minutes later, half of those transports were beneath the waves, and the other half were afire. The 192nd Tank Battalion was advancing north with the two companies of the 45th Infantry, and Colonel Hoffman was on the horn back at the PC, getting MacArthur to order the 194th Tank Battalion to come north to reinforce the counterattack.

By evening, we had annihilated the Japanese beachhead at Aringay, and they were evacuating the area north around Bauang. *S-36* and USS *Stingray* even got in a couple more hits on the Japanese task force. By dawn, Brereton's Raiders, as the press took to calling them, had chased the Japanese out of Lingayen Gulf entirely.

As the sun rose, I sat on *Beatrice*'s engine deck and wrote a letter to Cathy. It wasn't much a letter, a short note, really, tinged with guilt for being under fire. I just wanted to let her know I was still alive.

I didn't have time to write anything else. MacArthur ordered the 192nd and 194th Tank Battalions on the road to join South Luzon Force "with all dispatch." For two days and nights, we rode south for Lamon Bay, blessedly free from air attack now, thanks to Brereton's Raiders. On New Year's Day, we swept south across the Japanese landing area, supported by Brereton's Raiders once again. We drove the Japanese right back into Lamon Bay.

*Pensacola* brought the letter back to the States after dropping off the A-24 *Banshees*. When Cathy got the letter two weeks later, boy, was she mad.

———

# ABOUT WILLIAM STROOCK

William Stroock is the author of more than 20 novels and two history books. He is a former teacher and adjunct professor of history. Will has published dozens of military history articles with magazines in North America and Europe including *Strategy & Tactics, History Magazine, Military Heritage, Civil War Quarterly, Medieval Warfare, Ancient Warfare, Military History Matters* and many others. Will lives in northern New Jersey with his wife and three daughters.

Will blogs at Stroock's Books (they rhyme) and Substack. His novels are available at Amazon.

# MR. DEWEY'S FIRE BRIGADE

James Young

*For the men of A/2-72 AR. Apaches for life.*

# HEADQUARTERS AND HELLCATS

*TF Kraven HQ*
*1900 Local*
*21 July 1950*

"Sir, you wanted to see me?" Captain Michael Collins said from the door flap of Lieutenant Colonel Leonard Kraven's tent.

Kraven looked up from his map table, fighting the urge to yawn. A single light bulb hung suspended from the tent support, the light slowly swaying as winds buffeted his tent. Two other officers, one Australian and the other his battalion S-3, Major Andy Klein, each flanked him.

*Need to get some sleep tonight*, he thought, looking at the lanky black officer standing in the doorway. *Especially given what is about to unfold in the next twenty-four hours.*

"Yes, pull up a chair," Kraven said, shifting on his own piece of furniture. The issue camp chair creaked ominously under his short, squat frame. Kraven paid it no mind, well aware that the piece of wooden furniture had been bitching at him since he'd acquired it from a German regimental headquarters in North Africa. The Australian officer sitting to his left, Major Anthony Spriggs, was nowhere near as sanguine.

"Sir, no disrespect, but if you fall and break something, Brigadier Esper will somehow blame my presence," Spriggs stated drily, running a hand through his cropped red hair.

"You have my assurances that I'll place proper blame on myself and poor equipment maintenance," Kraven said, then turned to his right. "Andy here will assure your boss he has repeatedly informed me of my resemblance to a damn circus bear sitting on a step stool every time I sit down on this thing. He'll go on to point out I'm lucky I wasn't forcibly sodomized by the thing's collapse."

"Sir, you're going to frighten Captain Collins," Major Klein observed, his tone weary. Like Kraven, he was below average height but resembled a beanpole rather than a cinder block. "Man knows you haven't seen your wife in a year and now you're talking about unlawful carnal knowledge with furniture. Man's about to have enough on his mind without thinking he should have joined the Navy after all."

Collins smiled politely at Klein's joke, the expression coming nowhere near his eyes.

*I don't think "Mike the Mangler" is scared of much*, Kraven thought to himself. *Not after the last month.*

The 72nd Armor Battalion had been the only tank battalion in Japan when President Dewey had ordered the deployment of U.S. troops to South Korea "in order to deter aggression." The North Koreans had swiftly demonstrated that they were not deterred, crossing the 38th Parallel less than 48 hours after the first elements of the 24th Infantry Division had landed at Pusan. To the South Koreans' credit, they had put up a spirited defense north of Seoul. Unfortunately, said defense had seen almost the entire ROK Army annihilated while 24th ID urgently completed its deployment across the Sea of Japan.

*Hard to believe that it's just now thirty days*, Kraven thought, waiting for Collins to get seated. *At least 10,000 KIA and missing for the ROKs, another 1,000 KIA and missing for us.* Seeing the young captain was ready to take notes, Kraven grabbed the woolen blanket that had been covering the table in front of all of them, lifting it to reveal a map with operational graphics.

"Mike, I'll cut to the chase," Kraven began, grabbing a section of old antenna and pointing to the map. "Division thinks our short respite is over and the North Koreans will be attacking within forty-eight hours. As the Australians just got here, they think the hammer's going to fall in the south, near Masan."

Collins nodded his understanding as Kraven continued.

"Unfortunately, X Corps G-2, bless their hearts, has a different opinion. They think the Norks are going to attack right up the gut from Taegu. Again."

Collins's look of understanding became one of confusion.

"I have been specifically told, allegedly at the direction of Lieutenant General Almond himself," Kraven continued, drawing an angry snort from Major Klein, "that I will keep the 72nd Armor here in Miryang as the Corps reserve while we finish reconstituting and refitting."

Kraven gave Collins a small smile.

"Funny thing about unit lineage, but I don't recall the 758th *Anti-Tank Battalion* being part of the 72nd *Armor Battalion*," Kraven emphasized, seeing realization dawn on Collins's face. "Why, it would be sacrilege for such a fine unit to be *limited* by the delusions of some idiot on X Corps staff who fancies himself a regimental or division commander."

Kraven turned to look at Major Spriggs, favoring the Australian with a broad grin. The Australian officer shifted slightly at the expression.

*Whoops, forgot he's not used to the burns yet*, Kraven thought, turning away so Spriggs could gain composure. A Japanese Molotov cocktail had splashed the lower half of his face during a dark, desperate night in Tokyo. The men of his battalion and their attachments were used to the disfiguration and its effect on his expressions.

"Seems to be my recollection also, sir," Collins replied, genuinely smiling for the first time that evening. He turned to Major Spriggs. "Sir, I must confess, I don't know much about your Army."

Spriggs smiled.

"Well, Captain Collins, we've got about an hour's road march for me to get you acquainted," Spriggs replied, standing. "I am not familiar with an American tank destroyer company, so it'll be a chance for both of us to learn about one another."

"We're going to cut you a section of mortars," Klein stated. "Brigadier General Watson has directed Sung's ROKs will fall under your charge when they exfiltrate back through the Australian lines, Captain Collins."

"Sir?" Collins replied, clearly surprised. Kraven watched as Collins struggled with how to ask something without seeming insubordinate.

*Yes, I thought that arrangement quite odd also,* Kraven thought, *but not my place to call someone an idiot to their face.*

"If you're worried about Lieutenant Colonel Sung, he's already stated his men are the division's to do whatever we need," Kraven said gravely. The company commander still looked doubtful, but nodded.

*I think all Lieutenant Colonel Sung cares about is killing Norks, quite frankly,* Kraven thought, briefly turning to look southwest, as if the murderous ROK officer was actually in eyesight. *Brigadier General Watson is just facilitating the man's grief and rage.* When he'd first met Sung, the man had barely a pair of platoon of the ROK infantry with him. In the intervening month, he'd gathered every ROK soldier that he could.

*Then again, he's doing more than President Rhee at this point*, Kraven thought bitterly, then shook his head to stop that train of thought. It was no concern of his that the South Korean president was rumored to have left the peninsula for one of the numerous islands off the coast. Having narrowly escaped one's own capital tended to cause a very pronounced fear response.

"I'm also giving the scout platoon, but with the understanding that they're only going along to learn the route between here and the Australians' positions," Kraven continued. "If the Norks do hit, I'm going to need someone who can drive back here, get us, and then lead the way back."

"There is also a troop, erm, *platoon* of *Achilles* that had arrived just before I came in this direction," Major Spriggs interjected, drawing a surprised look from both Kraven and Klein.

"*Achilles?*" Collins asked, confused.

"The British...well, Commonwealth version of the M-10," Major Klein replied, his visage briefly haunted as he recalled some past battle.

"Sir, we're barely killing T-34s with our gun," Collins said, alarmed.

"*Achilles* don't have *your* gun, mate," Major Spriggs said, his smile almost predatory. "They're packing a 17-pounder."

Collins looked back and forth between Kraven and Spriggs, clearly mystified at the strange nomenclature.

*Damn Brits can't just give something's diameter and be done with it, can they?* Kraven thought, trying to figure out how to explain the weapon.

"It's a heavy gun," Klein stated. "Same diameter as the 76mm on the *Sherman* but hits almost as powerful as the 90mm on the *Pershings*."

"Aye," Spriggs agreed. "However, even better news is the tankies say they've got an improved round for it. I believe it's called the discarding sabot or some similar rubbish."

"Yes, sabot," Kraven said, nodding. "It's French for 'shoe.'"

"With all due respect, sir," Spriggs replied, "I'm just a simple digger who did my time in New Guinea. You'll have to ask *Leftenant* Kane about that bit."

Collins wrote something quickly in his notebook as Spriggs went on.

"In any case, Lieutenant Colonel MacFarlane doesn't have the foggiest idea how to use armor, either."

Spriggs stopped to take as swig of his canteen.

"But I'm the bloke who actually had to plan our defense," he continued. "So even if Kane might not like it, he's going to be working for you because you've actually fought North Korean armor and he was too young for the recent unpleasantness."

Kraven narrowed his eyes at Spriggs's comment.

*The way he says that makes me wonder if Kane's problem has to do with Collins's complexion, not who has actually shot a T-34,* the battalion commander worried. *No matter: Spriggs seems like a good sort. Will probably nip that in the bud.*

"What's your status, Captain Collins?" Kraven asked. "I told Major Spriggs you'd be ready to go by dawn, but I know the port offload in Pusan was chaotic this morning."

"We got 3rd Platoon's new *Jacksons*," Collins replied. "Still waiting on ammunition, but the support platoon says they'll have it to me by 2100. We'll be ready by dawn."

"Very well, meet back here at 0430," Kraven replied. "We won't keep you any longer."

Collins stood at that, nodded, and headed back out of the tent. Kraven turned to look at Spriggs.

"I hope that Sung isn't getting himself into too much trouble," he said grimly.

*Team Bulgae*
*2330 Local*

*I am sure that Brigadier General Watson would tell me it is "quite unusual" for an officer of my rank, much less one who is nominally a deputy regimental commander, to be this far forward of friendly lines,* Lieutenant Colonel Jin-Cho Sung thought as he wiped his knife on the North Korean sentry's corpse.

Glancing about, he saw that the other seven Nork sentries had joined their comrade in death. Waiting for five long minutes, Sung was satisfied that no one had seen or heard the swift, violent and, above all, silent removal of the North Korean guards. It had been a long, arduous road march from the Australian defensive positions around Masan to the hills above what appeared to be the headquarters for a North Korean armored regiment.

*Then again, there is nothing normal about these times,* Sung thought angrily. He pulled off the red lens flashlight, turned so that his body was facing back east, up the hill that he'd slowly crept down over the last two hours. With two quick presses, he sent the signal that the company raid was to proceed. In the bright light of the moon, Sung watched as seventy men rose as one and began rapidly moving down the hill towards him.

*The die is cast,* he thought, turning to regard the hamlet in the small draw beneath him. Forty-five days ago, it would have held maybe one hundred South Koreans. Now it held maybe thirty, all of them people who had been unable to flee before the NKPA's occupation of the town. According to his scout platoon, the hamlet's mayor had unwisely stayed to try and protect his former constituents. The man's corpse still hung from makeshift gallows in the town square, his headquarters occupied by the Nork regimental commander.

*It was unfortunate for Lieutenant Hu to find his home village in such a state,* Sung thought, clenching his fists as he thought about his own family's fate. *But tonight, we shall visit a small bit of vengeance upon the men who would do this.*

"Sir, Bravo company and the mortars are set up in their blocking position," his adjutant, Captain Jeong, reported as Sung's staff stopped by him. "They are ready to fire upon your command."

Sung nodded, pulling out a flare gun while Able Company moved into position. His mortars' target was the resupply point located roughly five hundred yards beyond the headquarters. Normally, the 4.2-inch mortars had been ineffectual against armored units, but Hu's men had been almost giddy as they recounted the Norks' lack of defensive preparations.

*Even a T-34 won't do well when it's parked next to unprotected ammunition and fuel trucks,* Sung thought grimly. *But first, the headquarters.*

Able's troops worked so well together that it was hard believing they'd only been together for a handful of weeks. Sung watched as they quickly moved into position, organizing into demolition and attack parties. Barely ten minutes after the sentries had been dispatched, death waited upon Sung's signal.

"Send the code word," Sung said, then raised the flare gun to the sky. The flare arced into the darkness just as the first *thump! thump! thump!* of the heavy mortars echoed from the hills.

*Good evening, you bastards,* Sung thought angrily as the Able Company's kill teams swiftly set to work. For the next five minutes, the small hamlet was a cacophony of small arms fire, satchel charges, grenades, and screaming men. To Sung's grim satisfaction, Able Company had taken the S-2's suggestion to use white phosphorus grenades in their initial assault on the North Korean sleeping quarters. Resembling something out of Dante, the thirty or so members of the North Korean headquarters company who had been off shift came shrieking out of a large tent right into the waiting guns of Able's 1st platoon.

"That blaze is going to draw some attention," Jeong said, face knitted in worry.

At that precise moment, *something* detonated at the regimental support depot. Whatever it was, it blew up with such force, Sung had a momentary glimpse of a tank turret whipping through the air against the backdrop of the massive fireball.

"I think the burning tent will be the least of our worries," Sung observed grimly, looking at his watch. "Remind me to recommend that mortar platoon leader for a commendation once we return to the Australians' lines."

"Yes, sir," Jeong replied, flinching as a blast from the city hall sent small chunks of stone raining down around them. Sung listened as there were shouts in Korean and, to his shock, *Chinese* from the battered structure. A final fusillade of fire rang out across the town, then silence... then several pistol shots.

*I am sure the Americans will chide me about **that***, Sung thought, looking back towards the now blazing depot. He thought about his family, how he'd found them during that desperate retreat from Seoul. To his shock, they'd been dead for days, their deaths clearly the work of the reported North Korean infiltrators that had wrought so much havoc.

*The first officer who can resurrect my raped daughter or tell me where to find my son's missing...*

"Sir! Sir!" a runner called, running from the village at a rate far too dangerous for either the terrain or available light. The man stopped five yards from Sung, catching his breath as he doubled over.

"Out with it," Jeong barked, moving forward to strike the man before Sung held up his hand to stop him. The soldier, a young corporal, regained his ability to talk.

"Captain Kim wishes guidance on a prisoner," the man rasped. "He said you would understand when he brought the man to you."

Before Sung could answer, there was the distant sound of diesel engines. Whether tanks or trucks, the South Korean officer was well aware his merry band of raiders probably didn't want to be present when they arrived. Looking, he could see Kim, Able Company's commander, heading towards him with a gaggle of soldiers. After a moment, he realized the gaggle was dragging two men between them in the darkness. One of the prisoners, despite being blindfolded, suddenly lashed out and caught one of his captors by surprise. Unfortunately for the would-be escapee, one of Able Company's soldiers swiftly and ruthlessly ended the prison break with a buttstroke to the kidneys, followed by a swift kick to the knees.

*This better be good*, Sung thought, noting that there were other men carrying duffel bags between them. *Or this raid was a lot of risk for no good reason.*

Looking again at his watch, Sung opened the flare gun and removed the still-warm expended pyrotechnic. He stuck another round in the weapon, then pointed the flare gun at the sky and fired once more. The red pyrotechnic arced up, signaling that it was time for the mortar crews to cease fire and break down their weapons. For their part, Able Company flitted back by him and back up towards the route from which they'd come. That is, most of the company besides the headquarters section trudging towards him.

"Sir..." Captain Kim began, coming to attention. Sung stopped him, realizing immediately why the man had taken the two prisoners. It had been a while since Sung had studied the ROK Army's intelligence handbook, but he instantly recognized the field dress of the People's Liberation Army, or PLA.

*This...this is a problem.*

"You will release us, *immediately*," one of the men, an older one, spat. His Korean was heavily accented, but the arrogance and insolence was quite clear. "If you value your..."

Sung kicked the man hard in the stomach. The Chinese officer made a strangled noise, sagging against the two men holding him as he heaved from the blow. Regarding the prisoner, Sung struggled to recall what the officer's equivalent rank was.

*What is a Chinese colonel doing this far south?* Sung thought, concerned. *No matter: we do not have time to question him now.*

"Gag him and the other one," Sung ordered, flinching as another explosion ripped across the supply dump. "If they try to escape again, slit their throats, take their ID, and their uniforms. Let us leave this place, immediately."

"Sir, I have their ID," Kim stated, hand on his knife. "We also have the documents the major was carrying."

Sung nodded at the report, looking back towards the burning depot.

*If only the Americans had some way to bomb at night*, he thought, able to see some additional piles of supplies in the glare from the fires. *There has to be so much more we could destroy.*

If infantry moved on their stomachs, a mechanized force would only move as far as its fuel supply allowed. Sung suspected that the painful lesson his mortars had provided would result in a rapid change of storage methods by the North Koreans.

*Spade work is free*, he thought grimly. *But no matter—we have obtained information and, apparently, proof the Chinese are more involved than everyone has suspected.*

DAGONET
0530 LOCAL
22 JULY 1950

*Only man happier than me to see the sun right now was Van Helsing*, Captain Collins thought, relaxing his death grip on the turret of *Dagonet*, his M-18 *Hellcat*. Like roughly half of D/758th's tracks, *Dagonet* had been dragged out of a depot in the Philippines to replace the unit's losses in the past month. On one hand, it meant the tank destroyer had relatively low mileage and, to Collins's utter surprise, a good maintenance record. On the other, it was taking some time for the vehicle's primary driver, Private First Class Derek Rose, to get used to the new engine and steering controls. With the added danger of a pre-dawn movement that involved far too many trips along hairpin turns while following an insane Aussie jeep driver, Collins was considering pausing the movement just so he could prostrate himself publicly.

*We need some way to see in the dark*, Collins thought.

"Sir, please do not take this the wrong way," his gunner, Sergeant Duncan O'Rourke, said, his voice shaking. "I'm glad I spent all that time doing some lay preaching for those white boys' chaplain, because I thought for certain we were going to meet Jesus today."

*For someone whose name sounds as Irish as a leprechaun, O'Rourke is country as they come*, Collins thought, shaking his head at the Mississippian. Like Collins, the young NCO was Catholic. Unlike the Demons' company commander, O'Rourke didn't usually add "lapsed" as an adjective to his faith.

The sound of distant artillery rumbled over the company, the short barrage yet another reminder that accidents might actually be the least of their worries.

"Day's just started, O'Rourke," Collins replied grimly, then turned to look at the *Hellcat*'s loader/radio operator, Specialist Jerome Carette. The New Orleans native was pressing the headphones to his ear, a perplexed look on his face.

"Hey, sir, the Aussie's stopping," *Dagonet*'s assistant driver, PFC Jason Hase, called from his position behind *Dagonet*'s bow gun. Collins turned forward just in time to catch himself as Rose slammed on the brakes.

"Tarnation, Rose!" O'Rourke snapped, his tone all the scarier due to the lack of profanity.

"Sorry, sergeant!" Rose replied, his tone frustrated. "Still getting used to these dam...erm, dang brakes!"

*I think O'Rourke's no cursing rule is going to have to go by the wayside*, Collins thought, shaking his head with a bemused smile. Collins had brought the NCO with him from 1st Platoon when he'd first become the Demons' XO, then after an unfortunate mortar barrage, the company commander.

*Not bad for some "Negro from Chicago."* Those dismissive words, spoken by a Navy lieutenant, had always stuck with him since he'd disembarked in Yokosuka. The Southerner had not, as a matter of fact, used Negro. Collins had nearly punched the man, but a white lieutenant had stopped him.

*I wonder where Ralls is now?* he thought, then shook himself out of his mental drift.

"Captain Collins!" Major Spriggs was shouting as he ran back towards him, clutching a map. Collins pulled his helmet off so he could hear the man. There were several flashes along a distant ridge line. Collins began to mentally count even as he slid down the front of his M18. He had reached thirty when the distinct *crump!* of landing artillery reached him.

*Hope that's not anyone we know*, Collins thought as Collins reached his track.


*This. This will teach me the danger of wishful thinking*, Collins mused forty-five minutes later as his *Hellcat* began creeping up the back side of a rise.

"Driver stop!" Collins barked, just as the fluttering sound of incoming mortar fire told him it was time to drop down into the *Hellcat*'s turret. To his great relief, the North Korean barrage was not intended for his command, landing four hundred meters to their front among the Australian infantry's fighting positions.

"Sir, I'm not sure I follow what's going on," Sergeant O'Rourke shouted as he turned back from his sights.

"Lieutenant Colonel Sung and his boys apparently kicked a hornet's nest last night," Collins replied, looking at his map. "Whatever they did, it's pissed the North Koreans off and Major Spriggs thinks they're about to attack."

"Demon Six, White One, I am set in position," his 2nd Platoon leader, 2nd Lieutenant Jakob Cohen, reported. A former armor NCO who'd fought in Europe, the Jewish officer had been a banker working to help Japan's reconstruction when the balloon had gone up. Collins wasn't quite certain how that had led to him ending up being brought in as a commissioned officer, but he'd immediately set to getting his fellow replacements whipped into shape in the past week the Demons had been reconstituting.

"Demon Six, Red One, same," 1st Lieutenant Eric Kennings reported. Collins was about to grab the radio hand mike to respond when the hilltop roughly six hundred yards to his left simply *erupted* from a North Korean artillery barrage.

*Those are heavy guns*, Collins thought, closing his mouth as he belatedly realized it was open. *Holy shit, really heavy guns.*

The rip of shells over his head snapped him out of the momentary shock. Thankful to realize that barrage was *outgoing*, Collins was even more happy when the North Korean barrage ceased shortly thereafter. This was immediately followed by several silver jets flashing by overhead, their wings laden with what looked like napalm and bombs.

*About time the Air Force got back into the fight*, he thought grimly. America's junior service had been noticeably absent during the Battle of Taegu. Allegedly, they'd been concentrating on stopping the "second echelon" or something. Collins just knew air supremacy didn't do any good if the side with it was apparently unable to use it.

"Blue One, status?" Collins asked after a long pause.

"Almost in position, Black Six," 2nd Lieutenant Kenny Taylor replied, his speech rapid. "These damn *Jacksons* are so slow."

Collins shook his head, even if he was mostly in agreement with Taylor's assessment. The platoon of five M-36 tank destroyers, like their replacement M-18s, had been wasting away in the Philippines. Fairly slow, compared to the *Hellcats*, the *Jacksons* made up for that lack of speed with firepower and slightly better protection. Their 90mm gun was an earlier model of that on 72nd Armor's *Pershings*. Although they still had no business trying to fight like tanks, they at least gave the Demons some limited ability to kill the heavier IS-2s, should those make an appearance.

"Demon Leader, Demon Leader, this is Apricot Leader, your net," an Australian voice broke in. "I am approaching your position. Where would you like me to plug in?"

"That's Saint George's flag," O'Rourke said, his eyes narrowing as he regarded the approaching vehicles.

"Yep, sure is," Collins replied, voice clipped as he began drumming his fingers on the *Hellcat*'s turret rim. Catching himself, he stopped, but not before O'Rourke noticed it with a grim smile.

*Damn nervous tics*, Collins thought, turning to look up and down the line where the Demons lurked just behind the rise. Ducking down as another mortar barrage savaged the ridge, Collins wished he'd had enough time to actually reconnoiter the narrow valley beneath the Australian positions. Things like target reference points, general range, and avenues of approach would have been good to know before the proverbial hammer fell.

*No use worrying about what we don't have*, Collins thought. *Have to focus on what we can affect.*

"Demon Leader, here comes the enemy infantry!"

Collins didn't recognize the Australian voice on his frequency, but identity was unimportant, given the message contents. North Korean mortars continued to fire intermittently, but it appeared the artillery had either selected other targets or been silenced by the United Nations' various reactions.

"Tanks! Tanks!"

"Demon Six, twelve...no, twenty-four T-34s! Northwest, coming down the valley!"

"Thank you, Red One!" Collins said, looking at his map. The valley feeding down towards the Australian positions from the northwest looked to be about 1700 meters long. Collins was absolutely sure *some* of his more experienced gunners could probably hit a T-34 at that range. Unfortunately, the vast majority of his company, especially the new platoons, would miss an advancing tank at that range.

*Don't have ammo to wa...*

The rippling crack of several North Korean tanks firing was audible even over the mortar fire. Several shells carried high over the ridge, impacting on the hillside several hundred meters behind Collins' position.

"Demon Leader, our positions are taking fire!"

*Wait for it...* Collins thought, mentally counting down the range the hostile T-34s were crossing if they were attacking at top speed, as they usually did. There was another series of shells—most of these actually hitting among the Australian positions.

*Wait for it...*

"Demon Leader! Engage the enemy!"

Collins picked up his hand mike.

"Standby, last station, waiting for them to get into range," Collins stated calmly.

The North Korean mortars abruptly ceased fire. The cessation of explosions allowed Collins to hear friendly mortars dropping shells in front of the Australian positions, the sound still distant. Once more, there were multiple cracks of tank fire, the shells throwing up dirt and rocks.

"They're in bloody range! The bastards are stopped and are shooting into our positions!"

*Goddamn infantry, always panicking the minute some tanks are shooting at them*, Collins thought angrily. He glanced at his map one more time.

"Guidons, Demon Six," he said, hoping that his math was right. "Fire plan Dog, top hat, top hat, engage at will!"

At his command, Demon Company surged forward with the roar of diesels. Fire plan Dog meant that Blue and Red platoon would cross their fires, hopefully getting flank shots. White platoon, in the center with him, would hope to get the closest tanks since they'd be firing at the thicker front slope.

"Try range eight hundred," Collins ordered. "It's longer than I'd like, but folks are getting antsy."

"Roger!" O'Rourke said, bending to his sights. *Dagonet*'s turret crested the hill just as another North Korean volley was impacting, the impacts throwing rocks and debris against the tank destroyer's hull.

*Lucky that, means we're probably going to get off two rounds before they even really see us*, Collins thought. Then *Dagonet* was cresting the ridge line...and he knew true terror as he looked down at over two companies of North Korean tanks charging down the narrow valley towards the Australian positions.

"TANK!" Collins barked, identifying the target even as he charged his commander's machine gun. "HVAP!"

"HVAP up!" Carette sang out, indicating that the round was prepared.

"Right...right...right...ON! Range 800!" he shouted, moving up atop the tank destroyer to stand on the back deck near his machine gun.

"Identified!" O'Rourke shouted.

Red platoon's fire arrived like the righteous fury of the Lord, all four tank destroyers hitting their targets. Unfortunately, two of them hit the same T-34, that being the target Collins had been talking O'Rourke onto. The tank lurched, skidding broadside to the Australian lines either due to the driver's death spasms or some damage to the chassis.

*Goddammit*, Collins thought, sweeping left to look for targets as the T-34's crew began to bail out. Blue's volley, although not nearly as accurate as Red's, accounted for the tank he was trying to align O'Rourke on. Then White opened fire, and it was bedlam down on the valley floor as the North Koreans found themselves down seven tanks in a matter of moments. Clearly not expecting enemy armor, the T-34s began scanning.

"Left! Left! Left! On!" Collins spat out rapidly, seeing what he assumed was a command T-34, judging by the antennas. The fiery demise of several tanks, combined with what appeared to be the friendly mortars starting to shoot white phosphorus, was suddenly starting to obscure things on the battlefield.

"Identified!" O'Rourke stated, just as the enemy T-34 fired at something to Collins's left. The round went just barely over a backing up White platoon *Hellcat*, but Collins had no time to try and identify who.

"Fire!"

*Dagonet* rocked backwards, dirt and debris being thrown up by the blast. Collins didn't have time to wait for the obscuration to clear, as twin gouts of dirt erupting on either side of the *Hellcat* told him North Korean tanks were trying to hit his vehicle.

"Driver back up! Straight back!" he barked, depressing the butterfly triggers to send a short burst of machine gun fire into the advancing North Korean infantry. Turning to look behind their vehicle, Collins felt a sharp impact to his sternum as another *Hellcat* shifted positions. Whatever it was knocked the wind out of him, and he had to take a moment to gather himself as he glanced downward. The offending stone was on *Dagonet*'s back deck, kicked up by the passing *Hellcat*'s treads.

"Sir, you all right?" O'Rourke asked, clearly alarmed. Collins waved at him as he tried to draw a breath, the inhalation exceedingly painful.

The dull *boom!* of a Red *Hellcat* exploding spurred him to action. A distant voice was shouting at him, and he turned to see the St. George-adorned M-10 variant was now only ten yards from him.

"Sir! Sir! Where do you need us?" the Australian officer was shouting. With a rush, Collins was able to focus on the radio as reports were coming in.

"That end of the line!" he wheezed, then reported his command louder while pointing to Blue's position. The Australian officer nodded, turning his *Achilles* just as artillery began to impact around their position. Collins scrambled into the turret, giving orders for *Dagonet* to shift while fragments whirred all around them.

*Thank God the North Koreans have apparently never figured out airburst*, he thought, crouching below the turret lip as the *Hellcat* moved. Poking his head up, he observed another of the Red *Hellcats* was stopped, its crew desperately giving first aid to the vehicle's loader.

*Because if they did figure out airburst, we'd have problems*, Collins thought grimly, quickly figuring out where he wanted *Dagonet* to go. Another series of orders and the *Hellcat* was climbing the ridge, just as the three remaining Red vehicles did. Which, Collins would realize later, was the only thing that saved their lives as a T-34 had apparently found the range, even as two of its companions missed high. The *Hellcat* nearest to them crashed to a stop in a cacophony of steel, igniting rounds, and screaming crew.

"Left! Left! Left!" Collins snapped, seeing the killer T-34 starting to rotate to track their vehicle. The North Korean tank and its companions never got any shots off, having lingered in one spot too long. A combination of 90mm and 17-pounder fire ignited a pair of the Communist tanks, while the third was clearly knocked out. A second Australian volley made sure a few seconds later, the T-34's turret going skyward as the ammunition cooked off.

"Aircraft! Aircraft two o'clock!" Carette shouted, pointing. Collins turned to look and immediately felt relief at the distinctive gull wings of Marine *Corsairs*. There were six of the fighters, with four of the Navy jets in orbit above them. Turning back to the matter at hand, Collins watched as the four remaining T-34s, having turned on their smoke generators, began to back up into their obscuration.

*That's our cue to also leave*, Collins thought, listening and watching as the Australian infantry began to engage their opposite numbers. *No point in staying here and getting pounded by the North Korean artillery.*

"Guidons, guidons, Demon Six," Collins began, looking at his map. "Rally at assembly area Memphis."

As the acknowledgments came in, Collins listened as the aircraft began working the North Korean infantry over.

*Two thousand yards is a long way to move under fire*, he thought, shaking his head. *I wonder what Commissar idiot thought that was a good idea?*

# THE WAGES OF SIN



"Well, mate, you sure do know how to create a royal mess."

The Australian major's words hung in the murk of Team Bulgae's supply tent. The two Chinese officers sat clad only in their underwear, with their arms tied to a steel cross beam over their heads. Neither of them bore any more wounds than they'd collected during Bulgae's forced march back to friendly lines, but it was also clear their current accommodation was anything but comfortable.

"I am not sure I follow, Major Spriggs," Sung said stiffly, looking at the two other officers who'd accompanied the Australian operations officer into Team Bulgae's tent. The brown-skinned American officer, Collins, he recognized. The other officer, a stocky, broad-shouldered officer wearing Commonwealth khaki and a slouch hat, he had never met. The man's piercing blue eyes kept returning to the two Chinese officers even as Spriggs resumed talking.

"You told us you were going to make a slight raid into enemy territory," Spriggs continued, clearly fighting to keep his voice level. "You didn't mention you were going to take almost your entire battalion, to include your mortars, and kick over a hornet's nest."

Sung's nostrils flared as the major continued.

"Nor did you mention that you had bloody prisoners," Spriggs went on, his voice rising. "Much less *Chinese* prisoners. I'm reasonably certain that our American friends would have liked to know *that* little tidbit."

Sung turned his gaze to look at Captain Collins, realizing the American officer was studiously watching his staff as they pored over the documents captured the previous night.

*The disrespect I continue to endure for the sake of my men and nation,* Sung thought. *That a nominally subordinate officer feels that he has the power to lecture me what I do with* my *soldiers in* our *country.*

"I sent a runner to your headquarters as soon as we returned, Major," Sung returned, keeping his voice calm despite his own internal rage. "Lieutenant Kim was informed by your duty lieutenant that both Lieutenant Colonel MacFarlane and yourself were busy preparing for the next North Korean assault."

Sung shrugged.

"Lieutenant Kim remained at your headquarters for two hours, was rebuffed again, then returned here."

Spriggs looked surprised at this news, glancing briefly at the other officer standing next to him before replying.

"It does not excuse it, but you are aware we repelled a sizeable North Korean action," Spriggs replied. "An action that was likely..."

"I am well aware of what kicking a hornet's nest is meant to represent, *Major*," Sung replied icily.

*Calm down,* Sung admonished himself. *You will not teach these men manners any more than you will teach your northern cousins morals.*

"You may not be incorrect," Sung continued, his tone strained even to him. "My intelligence officer was actually quite surprised the North Koreans attacked *your* sector of the line rather than coming for us."

"Terrain isn't really suitable for tanks, sir," Collins observed. "At least, not without proper reconnaissance. Those rice paddies in front of your position would limit them to the causeways coming across. It'd be a turkey shoot if you had any anti-tank weapons."

The two Australian officers turned to look at the American in surprise.

"As opposed to what happened a couple of hours ago?" Spriggs asked, his tone incredulous.

"I don't think they were expecting us to be there," Collins replied. "Plus, that was a hasty attack, even with all the artillery they used."

*Kraven was correct to promote Collins*, Sung thought, keeping his face impassive. *He is young, but he clearly has studied his craft.*

"What makes you so sure?" the other Australian officer asked. Sung was surprised to hear genuine curiosity in the man's voice.

"Sir, the North Koreans are fanatical, but most of the stupid ones are dead," Collins replied. "This is the first time since our initial fight that I've seen them just charge down a valley over open ground. No attempt to build a base of fire, no bounding overwatch. Just a Charge of the Light Brigade."

Collins caught himself.

"No offense, of course," he quickly stammered.

"None taken, Captain," the other officer replied. "We diggers prefer to do our suicidal cavalry charges in Mesopotamia, not on the Black Sea."

*What in the hells are they talking about?* Sung wondered, but pushed his curiosity away as the officer turned to him.

"Lieutenant Colonel Sung, I am Brigadier Esper of the Australian Army," the man said, extending his hand. Sung took it, noting the man's firm grip and calloused hands.

"Let me first give my condolences for what these bastards have done to your country," Esper continued, clenching his fists. "I can only hope that we manage to hold them here so that the troops following us can begin pushing them back."

*I think he genuinely means that*, Sung thought, surprised at the Australian's fierceness.

"I sincerely hope that we do also, sir," Sung said, choking back a wave of emotion. "Communism is a scourge upon humanity."

"On that, we can heartily agree," Esper replied. "Now, what else can you tell us about your guests..."

The two men were interrupted by the tent flap flying open. Turning as one, with both Sung and Collins reaching for their sidearms, the group of officers came face to face with an excited Korean first lieutenant. The young man's eyes narrowed as he saw three foreigners, but the expression quickly faded as he found Sung.

*Lieutenant Yoon never gets that excited unless it's bad news*, Sung thought grimly, his mind going back to a different time when the young officer had burst into his office. Yoon gave a slight bow towards his commander.

"Sir, pardon me for interrupting," he stated in rapid-fire Korean. "But we have finished sifting through the documents and have found proof the enemy will be attacking here, in our sector. They have two infantry regiments reinforced with an armored battalion slated to strike here!"

Sung took a deep breath as he felt the tension rise among his soldiers in the command tent, with several of the men looking worriedly at one another.

"First, calm yourself," Sung replied evenly, also in Korean. He switched to English for the next part. "Now explain, *in English*, what exactly you found."

It took Yoon approximately ten minutes to lay out just how bad things might be for the United Nations forces. The North Korean plan was to wait for the weather system expected in the upcoming week to negate much of the United Nations' airpower. The cloud cover would both prevent reconnaissance and allow the Norks to shift their forces by truck rather than road march. Once in place, the infantry was expected to infiltrate close to UN lines in the hour of darkness, then launch a dawn attack supported by heavy armor units.

*If they get through us, there's nothing between those tanks and Pusan,* Sung thought, seeing the same realization on Esper and Spriggs's faces.

"How confident are you in this information, Lieutenant Colonel Sung?" Brigadier Esper asked after a long, tense pause.

"Quite confident, sir," Sung replied without hesitation. "Lieutenant Yoon is one of the officers who accurately predicted the time, place, and direction of the initial North Korean assault on our nation."

*If those idiots at higher headquarters had listened to us,* Sung thought, *many of them and my family might still be alive.* Forcing himself not to think of the past, Sung watched as the Australian brigadier considered the information he'd been given.

"Major Spriggs, I'm going to need you to come with me to X Corps headquarters," Esper said, turning to the Australian field grade. "We'll stop and fill in Lieutenant Colonel MacFarlane on our way."

The Australian officer turned to look at Yoon, then Sung.

"Can we borrow the good lieutenant?" he asked, then gestured at the two Chinese. "As well as these two gentlemen?"

Sung thought about the last request.

*We had plans for them after you gentlemen left,* he thought, briefly glancing over at the two bound men. *Namely trying to figure out what their purpose was in being this far south.* Sung sincerely doubted the men would have just blurted out their mission. He was just as certain they would have told the

S-2 shop everything they wanted to know within 96 hours. Looking at the Australian brigadier, Sung suspected the man was quite aware what was going to happen if he left the two Chinese officers under ROK care.

"Of course, sir," Sung replied with a slight nod. "When will your men be by to collect them?"

"Might as well grab them now," Esper replied with a smile. "I'm sure the Americans will want to have a word with them as soon as possible."

Sung smiled even as he wanted to scream at the other man.

*What right do you have to take these men to a place of relative comfort?* he seethed. *After what they've done to spur the North Koreans into this war?*

"Of course," Sung replied aloud.


*TF Kraven HQ*
*1555 Local*


"With full understanding of our cultural differences," Brigadier Esper said, "I am certain if I had not grabbed those two men, the South Koreans would have done all sorts of untoward things to them."

*I'm failing to see where that's a problem*, Kraven thought, keeping his face impassive. The Australians had sent a runner to his location indicating they would be en route. They had failed to mention they were bringing additional guests.

"You did the right thing, Brigadier Esper," Lieutenant General Ned Almond, commander of X Corps, United States Army, stated. The senior officer stood just in front of his personal jeep, a rigid three-star insignia affixed to the radiator behind him. Kraven had been completely surprised when Almond's vehicle, accompanied by its familiar khaki-painted Australian counterpart and a 5-ton truck, had both rolled up to his command post. Brigadier General Watson and his aide had arrived shortly thereafter.

"We have to remember that these people are only one step removed from the Japanese," Almond stated, glancing over the group. "I don't think any of you have to be reminded of their usual barbarity until we beat it out of them."

*The only thing worse than a goddamn Pointer from the South is one of these fuckers from VMI*, Kraven thought angrily, taking a sip from his canteen lest his face show contempt. He'd never served under Almond, as the man had made his reputation in Italy rather than northern Europe. Still, the postwar Army had been small, and Almond had established a reputation while serving as General Eichelberger's chief of staff during the occupation of Japan. Whether that reputation was good or bad depended on who you asked and when.

Kraven glanced behind Esper to see Brigadier General Watson fighting hard to keep an exasperated look off his face.

*Nice that people who show up a month after this war started want to start lecturing those of us here from the beginning about proper manners*, Kraven thought. He'd seen what North Korean special forces had done to United Nations and South Koreans soldiers they'd caught unawares, never mind civilians. While he would not have condoned his own soldiers partaking in some aggressive interrogation, Kraven also wouldn't have blinked at Sung's doing so.

As if Kraven's thoughts had been on an external loudspeaker, Almond turned to look at the armored battalion commander.

"Lieutenant Colonel Kraven, *you*, on the other hand, allegedly have not done the right thing, according to my G-3," Almond stated. He held up his hand as Watson started to speak. "However, it would appear that your actions may have prevented disaster."

"Yes, sir," Kraven replied.

*I'll be goddamned if I'm going to leave it at that*, he thought.

"However, as I reiterated your staff this morning, the Demons were *not* part of my battalion," Kraven continued.

"Yes, I am quite aware that your abilities to parse hairs apparently rivals your skill at armored combat," Almond responded drily. "Thankfully, your gambit with a company of colored troops did not go awry, or I fear we'd be having a much different discussion."

*I could go the rest of my life without hearing one more Southerner talk about people's complexion*, Kraven thought angrily, even as he saw Watson giving him a warning look. *But I'm not any good to Collins or his men if I get fired here.*

"Understood, sir," he said aloud. Almond took a long pause, as if reminding everyone present just who was in charge.

"Now, my staff seems to be evenly split on just where the main North Korean blow is going to land," Almond continued, gesturing for his aide. Kraven noted the captain's almost immaculate uniform and lack of dirt as the junior officer pulled out a round case. Moving quickly, the man unfurled a map that showed the X Corps' sector, friendly icons, and suspected enemy locations on an overlay. Once he had it arranged, the captain pulled out four round steel ingots and placed them with great exactitude on the map's four corners.

*That would have been real fun to watch you use about two weeks ago when we were fighting for Taegu*, Kraven seethed. *Rear echelon showmanship at its finest.*

"If that ROK lieutenant was correct," Almond began, "we'd be seeing indications of armored movement here, here, and here."

Kraven watched as the general's fingers moved over the map. He was pointing at various intersections north and west of Waegwan along the main north-south artery.

"None of the reconnaissance photos we've seen indicate any such thing," the corps commander continued. "Instead, there have been several dozen tanks located here, just south of Yongdok. Unfortunately, the Air Force informs me, after a couple of losses, that they cannot risk any more of their available aircraft flying reconnaissance missions that far north due to the presence of North Korean jets flying south from the airports around Seoul."

Krevan noted that statement caused everyone around the jeep to stir, looking at one another with various emotions.

*I'd sure like to be able to opt out of my damn job due to a few losses*, he thought angrily. *Why, it must be downright frightening having to sleep in warm beds and take actual showers every night.*

"It still boggles my mind that the North Koreans have jets, sir," Esper said. "Is there no way to have your Navy attack them?"

"That is being planned, from what I understand," Almond replied, grimacing. "Thankfully, much like our own aircraft, they're very short-legged and need a larger runway."

*Problem with us having to give up Taegu is the North Koreans can move east to west fairly quickly*, Kraven thought as he looked at the map. *The 1st Cavalry Division is getting here, just not quickly enough, and the Marines are fought out like the rest of us. If not for the Navy, we'd all be dead or in cages.*

"Our sister services' relative abilities aside, I have no intention to remain on the defensive," Almond continued. "We are provided with a unique opportunity, if either my staff or the ROKs are correct."

Almond paused to scan the group.

"If the enemy armor is attacking in either the southwest or the northeast of this perimeter, *we* can counterattack to take Taegu," the X Corps commander stated.

*Wait,* what? Kraven thought, trying to remain calm as he looked across at General Watson. The one-star briefly looked as dumbstruck as Kraven felt before he regained his demeanor.

*He can't be serious. That is madness. Utter madness.*

"Sir, the North Koreans have us outnumbered at least three divisions to two," Watson said after a moment. "While the 1st Cavalry is fresh, the 24th plus the Marines are..."

"I'm well aware of our current force disposition, Brigadier General Watson," Almond snapped, fixing Watson with a glare. "The staff briefed me on it this morning, as a matter of fact."

Almond turned and fixed each man in turn as he continued.

"There is a lot of discussion among those who have been here for weeks on the prowess of the North Koreans. How we are outnumbered, they have the initiative, and similar sentiments."

Almond turned and pointed to the north, in the direction of Taegu.

"That way lies a force that you have battered for the last three weeks," the Corps commander stated. "Your tanks and the infantry, despite giving ground, have rendered it a shell of itself."

Kraven heard the distant hum of propellers as Almond continued. Looking up, he realized an intermittent cloud cover had started to form over their position.

"Lieutenant Colonel Kraven, am I boring you?" Almond asked sharply, jerking Kraven's attention back to the proceedings. "I am sure, by this point, you are more than familiar with airplanes."

"That's the thing, sir," Kraven said, worriedly glancing as the droning got louder. "Those aircraft don't sound right to be ours."

Kraven turned and was about to scream to sound the alarm when the warbling sound started up down the line. Men sprang into action as six twin-engine aircraft burst out of the scattered clouds roughly two miles away, heading directly for the battalion's laager.

*Guess our folks aren't the only side that can take pictures!* Kraven thought, turning to run for his tank, *Crusader 66.* He had taken only a dozen or so steps before the North Korean aircraft were on them.

The half dozen North Korean People's Air Force aircraft were IL-10 *Beast* attack aircraft. Descended from the ubiquitous IL-2, the *Beast* was fundamentally a *Sturmovik* that had been through a summer weightlifting program. Heavily armed with rockets complemented by four 23mm cannon, the *Beasts* were strafing nightmares well suited to their assigned task of disabling the lone American tank battalion identified south of Taegu. As their two dozen Yak-9 escorts engaged the surprised and almost out of full United Nations combat air patrol (CAP), the *Beasts* set enthusiastically about their task.

As if in slow motion, Kraven watched the lead IL-10, flanked by two wingmen, zero in on the supply trucks located near the center of the battalion laager. Rockets flashed from underneath the big aircraft's wings even as the four cannons lit up like camera strobes.

*Oh, shit*, Kraven thought, diving towards a cluster of rocks just in front of him. With a *whoompf!* two of the four fuel trucks in the center of the laager exploded, the fireballs consuming their crews and the hasty revetments they'd been parked in. The strafing runs continued across the support area to hit a pair of Dog company tanks that the mechanics had been working on. Kraven held his breath, waiting for one or both of the tanks to catch alight from the hail of cannon fire. He had just enough time to process that the cannons had apparently not done fatal damage before the second trio of IL-10s were attacking.

If the Soviet lieutenant colonel flying at the head of the formation had had experience with ground attack from the Great Patriotic War, he might have recognized that the two remaining fuel trucks were the highest priority target available. Unfortunately, before his semi-exile to train the nascent NKPAF, the lieutenant colonel had been a relatively successful P-39 *Airacobra* pilot. Gunning down over forty German fighters had done absolutely nothing to prepare him for this moment, and at the critical moment, the man made the first of two bad decisions that day. Kicking his rudder, he swept down on the 5-ton truck and pair of jeeps near the center of the American tanks.

Seeing the two black objects falling from each attack, Kraven threw himself completely flat. To his horror, the bombs were not the high explosive weapons he was expecting. Instead, with a loud *crack!* half of them split open in midair, while the other half exploded in bright, long gouts of flame upon hitting the ground. In a moment, the two Australian jeeps, the 5-ton, and the cluster of visitors to the Crusader laager were engulfed in a whirlwind of explosions.

*Fucking napalm*, Kraven thought, horrified as the heat washed over him. *They have fucking napalm.* The flames were hot enough to singe his skin, terror rising in him as his mind flashed back to that night. Rolling quickly away, he heard horrific screams behind him. Coming to his knees, he was just in time to see a flaming body he recognized as Lieutenant General Almond stumble out of the inferno. The man took two jilted, stuttering steps, then fell to the ground.

Glancing behind his IL-10 at his handiwork, the Soviet pilot proceeded to make his second bad decision. Signaling his wingmen, he put his aircraft into a left bank, turning further south to line up a second strafing run. Had he turned right and ran, there was a slight chance the three IL-10s might have been able to duck into the clouds and flee north. Unfortunately, his greed was immediately fatal, as a flight of F9F *Panther* fighters, rushing north in response to the CAP's frantic cries, arrived on scene. Pouncing like their namesakes, the quartet of USN fighters swiftly and lethally ended the North Korean airstrike.

"Sir!" Kraven dimly heard a voice shouting. He was sitting on his haunches, trying to take a breath in his shock. The roar of jets and sounds of aircraft cannon above him was dim, as if on the far end of a tunnel. He looked up from Lieutenant General Almond's still-burning corpse as several of the surrounding men broke out in cheers and cries of joy.

*What are they so...oh*, he thought, watching a burning IL-10 cartwheel into a rice paddy a couple of miles away.

"Sir!"

This time, the shout was accompanied by a firm shake. He looked up to see the worried face of his gunner, Sergeant Scarborough, looking down at him. The short, squat man had clearly run all the way from *Crusader 66*. Turning to look at the command tank, Kraven was startled to see several new marks and gouges in the turret.

"They got a piece of us, sir, but everything's fine," Scarborough said, glancing briefly back at the tank.

"Get Major Klein on the horn," Kraven bit out, shaking his head to clear the mental cobwebs. "We have to let division know the corps commander is dead. Pass the word the Aussies are out their brigadier, also."

It was only then that Kraven heard the sound of artillery fire from the battalion's rear. It was echoed by additional fire to the north and west. Turning to where he knew the infantry was located forward of his position, he saw impacts erupting on the ridge where the 24th ID's front-line units were dug in.

"Then tell Able and Baker Company to get ready to move," he continued, his voice growing in strength. "Looks like we're back to saving the infantry's ass."

"Yes, sir!" Scarborough said, pulling out a notepad.

"I need the Hussars," Kraven continued, referring to the HHC Company as he stood, "to get me a detail of twelve men. We've got to confirm that everyone is dead."

Kraven felt sick as he realized who else had been standing in the circle.

*Thank God they dropped the Chinese prisoners off,* he thought, running a shaking hand through his hair. Brigadier General Watson, with his knowledge of the peninsula, was going to be a critical loss, and it was highly unlikely the Aussies were going to be happy about losing a general that had just arrived.

*Almond may have been guilty of underestimating the Norks,* Kraven thought, once more turning towards the burnt body on the ground, *but no one deserves to burn like that for the sin of pride.* The wind once again shifted, and he nearly wretched at the smell.

"Sir, what about Charlie Company?" Scarborough almost groaned, clearly fighting down his own vomit.

"One platoon goes south to reinforce the Demons," Kraven bit out. "The rest of Charlie and Dog needs to get ready to head east, quickly."

"Yes, sir," Scarborough said, closing his notebook.

*I only hope this is the main assault,* Kraven thought. *If it isn't, we're going to have problems.*

He unconsciously reached up towards his face, then jerked his hand back as both it and the skin he touched hurt. Looking down, he was startled to see his hands were a bright red, as if he'd been out in the sun a tad too long.

*Goddammit.*

The stinging pain that was starting to register was unfortunately familiar, and he tried to avoid screaming in frustration.

*Adrenaline is a terrible thing.*

"Sir, I think you're gonna need a medic," Scarborough observed.

"I think you might be right at that," Kraven replied, just as more artillery hit the far ridge once more. "We've got work to do right now."

Scarborough's expression conveyed just what he thought of *that* idea.


*DAGONET*
*2030 LOCAL*


"So the old man has first-degree burns on his face and hands," First Lieutenant Alex Shea said, recounting the horrors of what he'd seen before his platoon of M26s had been sent south. "Able and Baker had to launch a counterattack to restore the line. Charlie and Dog were getting ready to do the same when we ended up out of radio range."

Collins shook his head at the news. It had been eerily quiet in the Australians' sector, so much so that Lieutenant Colonel Sung had been making noises about pushing forward across the valley that night. Collins had politely but firmly suggested that they should probably see to additional defensive measures instead.

*Glad that 5-ton of mines arrived right about the time Sung was about to pull rank on me*, Collins thought, looking up as lightning flashed across the clouds above them. That the Norks hadn't even reacted to the United Nations' forces starting to surface-lay the mines in front of their positions was a troubling sign.

*Did Sung's boy get it wrong?* Collins wondered as the wind began to pick up. The rumble of artillery was once again audible to the east.

"Allegedly, the Navy moved a battlewagon to help," Shea continued, running a hand through his blonde hair. "That's just insane."

*I thought we were done with war back in 1945*, Collins thought, shaking his head. *You'd have thought the world would have had a bellyful of it after six years.*

"Can't even imagine what it's like having a battleship shell someone," he remarked. "Had a cousin who served on the *Tennessee* during the war, right at the end when they were shooting up the Japanese coast. Said they fired the broadside into some village and it was like a giant kicked the place."

Shea was about to respond when a huge bolt of lightning struck the ground several miles to their northwest.

"Good thing this weather didn't happen earlier," Shea said, then paused. "Then again, the North Koreans wouldn't be able to fly in it, either."

"Is the rumor true about Lieutenant General Almond?" Collins asked, concerned. "And Brigadier General Watson?"

"Yes," Shea said shortly. "I mean, I didn't see the bodies, but I saw where those damn airplanes killed them."

"Holy sh...shoot," Collins said, catching himself. There was a soft chuckle, followed by a hushed correction in *Dagonet*'s turret.

"I don't think anyone here is gonna care if you swear, sir," Shea said with a smile.

"Trying to cut back on it," Collins replied. "With the way things are going, might be talking to the Lord soon enough. One less thing to explain."

"If the damn Koreans get another breakthrough, you're probably right," Shea said grimly. Another bolt of lightning arced down, so close the thunder made both men jump.

*Did that hit in front of the Australians?* he thought, concerned.

"Guess I better go get back to the platoon, sir," Shea said, starting to get off the turret. He stopped, clearly remembering something.

"Oh, SFC Barnes said to tell you or 1SG Frazier that we've only got about four of five hours' worth of fuel left," Shea said, gesturing back towards where his *Pershings* were. "Major Klein said he'd get us fuel by tomorrow noon if he has to hijack it himself."

*That's a platoon sergeant trying to train his lieutenant to consider these things himself*, Collins thought appreciatively. He was pretty sure Barnes wasn't exactly happy about being cross-attached to the Demons, but at least the man was trying to be semi-professional about it.

"The Australians are working on that, also," Collins replied. "There's going to be a bit of a problem if the Norks are putting pressure on the east side of the perimeter, though. Allegedly, there's also a company of their *Centurion* tanks that will be here in about three days."

*That is, if we have three days*, Collins thought grimly. *It's feeling a little like we're about to have to shoot the horses, hide behind them for cover, and then pray Fort Apache's reinforcements get here in time.*

"Best get some sleep if you can, Shea," Collins said. "The Aussies are sending an infantry platoon to help set up a perimeter, but I want each vehicle to have one crew member up at all times."

Shea nodded, clearly making a mental note while Collins finished up his orders.

"I doubt the Norks will come at night, but if they do, you're to stay here in reserve until we figure out if the main punch is landing on Sung or the Aussies. Sung's mortars have limited illumination, so we better light some bonfires early."

Shea smirked at Collins's impromptu nickname for burning enemy tanks.

"Good thing about those T-34s," Shea noted as he began climbing off the back of *Dagonet*, "they sure do burn real…"

The sound of incoming artillery cut Shea off. Diving off *Dagonet*'s rear, the platoon leader hit the ground with a cry as he twisted his ankle. He reached to grab it just as the first sheaf of heavy shells walked right through the Demons' area. Fragments sang around Collins's body as he finished his own dive into *Dagonet*'s turret.

*I swear to God, I'm going to weld a top onto this turret myself…*

His thought was interrupted as first one, then a second M18 *Hellcat* erupted in flames, bright lights illuminating the inside of *Dagonet*'s turret in the dusk.

*We've gotta move, we've gotta move*, he thought, reaching for the radio hand mike as *Dagonet* pitched like a ship in a tumultuous swell. He noted with alarm the new motion, well aware that had never happened before with North Korean artillery fire.

*They're using heavier guns*, Collins thought, the blasts and fear making his actions slow and clumsy. O'Rourke looked back at him from the gunner's seat, his eyes wide and crazy as the *Hellcat*'s turret rang with an impact.

"All Demon elements," Collins began, then took a deep breath as he realized his tone sounded unhinged. "Move to rally point Lincoln. I say again, Lincoln! Execute!"

*Dagonet*'s engine roared as Rose got the tank destroyer underway.

*Shea…* Collins thought belatedly, starting to put his head above the turret ring. O'Rourke's grasp stopped him, the NCO yanking him backwards by his belt. He was about to turn and berate the NCO when a still-glowing hot fragment whirled right where his head would have been if he poked it upwards. Rocks arced into the turret and off his head, as if to further reinforce O'Rourke's point.

"Sir, you can't do anything for him!" O'Rourke shouted as *Dagonet* began lurching forward. "He'll either make it back to his tank or he won't."

Collins hated to admit that the NCO was right, but got ahold of his emotions as *Dagonet* pushed down the road to the company rally point. It only took a few moments for them to move out of the primary radius of the artillery barrage. The company rally point was an abandoned structure that one of the ROK officers had informed him was a former Shinto church left by the Japanese. It amazed him that the structure still stood, but it was a landmark that was easily visible in the dark.

*Just hope the Norks didn't register it as an artillery target*, Collins thought, realizing that easy recognition could be a double-edged sword. He was mulling whether to shift position once again when the first raindrops began to fall. In what seemed like moments, the night went from heavy and oppressive humidity to sheets of pouring rain inundating everything in sight. For 20 long, wet minutes, *Dagonet* and the rest of the Demons were cloaked in wet, thunderous darkness interspersed by brilliant flashes of lightning.

*They must have had observers somewhere*, Collins thought, realizing that the North Koreans had stopped shooting artillery. *That or they ran out of ammunition.*

"Carette! Open the escape hatch!" O'Rourke shouted, barely audible over the pouring rain. *Dagonet's* loader sloshed across the turret, Collins surprised at how high the water had already gotten in their enclosed space. As if the act of opening up the *Hellcat's* belly hatch calmed the rain gods, the monsoon ended almost as suddenly as it had begun. Cool winds swept in behind the swiftly scuttling rain, causing Collins to shudder.

*At least I can say I've been through a mon...*

The first explosion was relatively slight in comparison to the auditory assault of the North Korean artillery. It was the second, much larger secondary that followed immediately that caused Collins to whip his head around towards the ROK positions just a few hundred yards away and below his perch. There, at most a thousand yards away from him and barely five hundred yards of where he knew the South Korean positions to be, was a tank blazing in the middle of the formerly dry rice paddies. The shadows thrown by the dancing flames revealed that the vehicle had a mine roller attached to its front.

*Looks similar to ours*, Collins mused, then shook his head as he realized that shock and surprise were starting to send his thoughts astray. Realizing that their advance had been betrayed, the field suddenly became alive with scores of North Korean infantry coming to their feet with an almost collective yell. To Collins's horror, he saw the closest forms were barely two hundred yards in front of the South Koreans. As several more tanks snapped on searchlights and began opening fire, he realized that this was the dreaded main assault.

# DEATH BY STARLIGHT



*Team Bulgae*
*2055 Local*
*Battle Position (BP) Wombat*
*22 July*

The first thing to hit Sung was the stench. As he clawed from the collapsed foxhole like some berserker revenant, the first intake of breath hit him with a massive olfactory assault. A mix of blood, stinking fuel, burning flesh, and the churned paddies' soil, the smell would have made him gag if he had not been filled with utter rage.

The first thing he saw, barely two feet in front of him, was one of his men's broken carcass. The corpse's face, or at least the top half of it that was still recognizable as such, stared at him almost accusingly.

*You did this to us,* it seemed to silently scream. *You did this when you told us we were done running.*

Shaking himself from the stupor, Sung was next hit by the cacophony of the North Korean assault. Men screamed all around him, the Hangul curses indistinguishable from one another. Light flickered from burning vehicles, the North Korean tanks' searchlights, and main gun muzzle flashes. Before his eyes, a North Korean IS-2 turned its turret towards him, seemingly for a moment to point right at him.

*Oh, fuck,* he thought, covering his ears as the 122mm roared. The concussion smashed the breath from him, loosening his tenuous grasp on consciousness. He was fighting to breathe when first one *crack!* then several others, followed by at least two high-pitched *klang!* impacts rang off the tank. His eyes briefly tracked one of the armor piercing tracers arcing up into the darkness as the tank's engine clattered to a stop. There was a moment of calm before frightened screams from inside the tank drew his attention.

*At least one of the damn Americans managed to do some good*, he thought, the screams being interrupted by frantic yelling. The reason for consternation became clear as he rolled onto his side and looked at the tank. The dark hole that was large enough to stick his hand through indicated at least one United Nations tank destroyer had achieved a through-and-through with its penetrator. Sung had the feeling that part of the turret had flaked off at high velocity inside the tank.

*Well, this is an opportunity*, he thought, reaching down to his belt. With a start, he realized that he had no weapons other than his flare gun and two hand grenades. Although the exit hole was large, it was unlikely that he'd be able to get a grenade into it. Although firing a flare into the hole would probably have some...interesting effects, Sung doubted it would be immediately fatal. As he was pondering what to do, another IS-2 began maneuvering towards the damaged tank he was near.

*Not again*, he thought as the approaching tank rotated its turret towards the northeast. Once more, he covered his ears, screaming in anticipation as the vehicle's searchlight snapped on. Rather than the massive blast of the main gun, the night was once again split by the sound of rounds rushing over Sung's head as at least three and possibly five vehicles engaged the onrushing tank. Sung's brain process at least two penetrations before the IS-2's onboard ammo detonated in a massive secondary explosion, the blast throwing Sung flat on his back as the turret popped off the tank then landed right side up just behind the flaming hull. Something that had once been human but was now just a screaming, blazing ball of meat attempted to claw itself out of the commander's hatch. The burning figure expired halfway through the process, sliding down the turret's side into the paddy in a hiss of hot flesh hitting water.

*Ancestors save us all*, Sung thought, feeling his hands shaking in terror. His sojourn into insanity was interrupted by the thud of someone landing behind him. Sung whirled just in time to see a North Korean tanker, his left arm broken, struggling to his feet.

"We have to..." the man started to say, then stopped as he realized the soldier standing in front of him was *not* Communist. His right hand had started for the sidearm on his hip when Sung kicked him in the groin. The blow landed with a satisfying thud that elicited a sharp cry of pain from the man as he doubled over, clutching his genitals. Sung grabbed he back of the man's helmet, twisting the tanker's face to the side as he slammed him into the side of the tank. The crunch of bone told Sung he had shattered nose, teeth, or both, but the North Korean feebly lifted his one to try and block the next drive into the tank. Sung took the opportunity to slide his arm around the man's neck in a chokehold, dragging him down into the paddy as the North Korean cried out again.

*For my family,* Sung thought angrily, squeezing as he simultaneously pushed the man's head down into the mud. The North Korean was at least twenty pounds lighter than him and only had one good arm. Even so, the man fought mightily for his life once he realized that Sung intended to both choke and drown him. After several long minutes of struggle, the majority of which was lost in the chaos and noise of the battle raging around him, and Sung was finally satisfied the Nork was dead. Taking a deep, shuddering breath, Sung released his grip and fell back on his haunches, fatigue suddenly washing over him.

"Sergeant..." a voice called from inside the turret. It was barely audible, as if its owner was straining at the top of his lungs. Sung turned as yet another round of ammunition went off in the destroyed IS-2. The majority of the gunfire seemed to have drifted off to the east, towards Pusan.

*They have penetrated our defenses,* Sung thought resignedly, jumping as a mired North Korean tank fired at something in the darkness. *There's nothing between them and Pusan but cooks, wounded, and perhaps some American or Royal Marines.*

Tears of frustration ran down his face as he considered the situation.

*We have lost the war tonight,* he thought, nausea roiling over him. *They will close the port. The Americans and Europeans will go home. It is all for nothing.*

"Sergeant! Please!" the voice cried again. "Help me!"

Sung turned towards the turret, his frustration turning to rage.

*Still, I can do one more thing,* he thought, reaching over to the Nork tanker's corpse to pull the man's pistol out of its holster. *I can make sure at least one more Communist dines with Marx tonight.*

Tucking the weapon in his belt, Sung dragged himself to his feet. Walking down the disabled tank's side, he found the footholds to climb up the hull. Striding to the turret, he reached down to his belt and unclipped a grenade. Looking down as he realized the shape was oblong, not round,

Sung realized his extraordinary luck continued to hold. It was a white phosphorus grenade, almost useless against troops but perfect for the task at hand.

*Here goes nothing*, he thought, leaning over the turret and just above the hatch.

The world turned brilliant white as several small explosions occurred over his head. The battlefield was so bright Sung was almost blinded, turning his head away and looking into the tank's turret. Blinking, his gaze met that of a young man, surely not much older than sixteen, sitting on the turret floor. The tanker's right leg ended in a bloody ruin, a hasty tourniquet tied off above. The bewildered man looked up into the brilliant illumination that ringed Sung like an avenging angel.

*Heavy artillery*, Sung thought as he pulled the pin. The spoon flew off the device and Sung counted to two.

"Sergeant?" the tanker asked, clearly not able to see.

"No, cousin, your doom," Sung replied, tossing the grenade down into the tanker's lap, then falling away from the hatch. The brilliant illumination continued to cast strange shadows as he fell to the ground, machine gun fire whipping across clumps of North Koreans caught in the white light. The *pop* of the white phosphorus grenade igniting was drowned out by the horrified screams of the tanker that caught the majority of the device's contents. Sung was twenty yards away when the first of the tank's ammunition propellant, stored separately from the shells, caught with a low order deflagration. Twenty more yards and the ammunition began to explode, ripping the IS-2 apart in a series of blasts rather than one large one. As machine gun fire continued to rip across the North Koreans, he laid flat on the ground, looking up towards the hill where he knew an abandoned church lay.

"Pilsung!" a familiar voice cried out, maybe fifteen yards away. Sung rolled slowly to look at the person calling to him.

"Jugeullae!" he replied, just as another series of illumination shells burst over the battlefield.

*Those are too bright even for heavy artillery*, Sung thought, hearing the distant rumble of guns firing from the south. He crawled over to where Captain Jeong and three soldiers, all wounded, crouched behind the remnants of a stone dike.

"Sir, what are we going to do?" Jeong asked, looking frightened in the dancing light. Several more cannons cracked, resulting in a pair of North Korean tanks exploding into flame.

"Hide here until morning when we can actually tell who is who," Sung said grimly, flinching as yet another Nork tank exploded. "There's too much light to try and retreat now."


DAGONET
*2230 LOCAL*


*Don't look...don't look...don't look*, Collins thought to himself. He kept his eyes on the trail in front of him and *not* the 600-foot rocky slope descending towards a gully that was to his left. *Dagonet's* engine strained as they labored up the back side of the ridge, gravel and mud spraying backwards as the *Hellcat* fought to keep up with the Australian jeep in front of them. Gloom had descended upon the road once more, and only the blackout shaded tail lights of the jeep in front of them any illumination.

"Sir, when are those Aussie shells going to..." O'Rourke asked nervously, glancing skyward.

Before O'Rourke could finish his question, six brilliant orbs burst well above their head. Just like that, the path that had heretofore been dark before them lit up...and Collins almost wished things had stayed dark.

*There's no way we're making it over that switchback at this speed*, he thought, gripping hard onto the side of *Dagonet's* turret. The distant sound of tank main guns and small arms told him they'd have to figure it out. Good men were dying to try and help Collin get in front of a mixed company of North Korean armor and infantry.

*At least they can kill the bastards riding on the tanks*, Collins thought grimly, taking a swig from his canteen. It would be a very near run thing, but if his ragtag group successfully traversed the various back roads in time, they'd come out on the North Koreans' flank.

"Sir..." Rose said nervously, *Dagonet's* engine lowering in volume as the man took his foot off the gas a little bit.

"Keep going, Rose!" Collins barked. "We gotta beat the Norks to Pusan."

The timely intervention of the cruiser H.M.S. *Jamaica* had allowed the Australians to just barely hold the northern half of their sector. The British cruiser's guns had disrupted the Norks' second echelon, while her star shells had allowed the reinforced Demons to bring accurate, rapid fire to bear against the heavy IS-2s trapped in the rapidly sodden rice paddies.

The cost, however, was steep. Collins had left the four surviving *Pershings* and two *Hellcats* back with the Australians. The single *Hellcat* and brace of *Achilles* that followed him were all that remained of the reinforced company he'd started with the night with.

*Now I'm off trying to beat an enemy tank company to the docks of Pusan,* he thought grimly. *All while a cruiser has almost grounded herself to give us long-range illumination to drive by, a bunch of rear echelon troops are preparing to make a last stand, and some Australian is trying to drive us off a cliff.*

Collins held on as Rose made the final pivot steer back from the cliff's edge. With an audible sigh of relief, the young driver pressed down hard on the gas again to try and catch up with the jeep that was flying off into the distance.

"That had to be the..." O'Rourke began.

There was a sound like thunder behind them as the mountainside erupted in shell fire. Before Collins' horrified eyes, a North Korean barrage that seemed to have initially missed two hundred yards up the ridge caused a slide of loose dirt that carried the rearmost *Achilles* off the side. Collins saw the vehicle commander, realizing that the tank destroyer was doomed, attempting to leap from the open turret to safety. The man almost made it, but had the main gun's muzzle brake catch his right foot like the end of a cricket bat. Thankfully, the noise of 29 tons of steel going for a tumble combined with impacting artillery drowned out the crews' screams as their vehicle rolled down the hill.

*Goddammit,* Collins thought. It had only been a matter of time until the traveling star shells would draw some unwanted attention. Now they had to flee before whomever had called in the initial barrage adjusted fire.

*Not that anyone probably survived that,* he thought, forcing himself to discount the forlorn hope his conscience tried to serve up. The North Koreans hammered the switch back for a good ten minutes after Collins and his men had already moved on.

"Sir, I'm gonna make a prayer real quick," O'Rourke said, glancing at his watch. If the Australians were correct in their estimate, the Demons would be in contact in about five minutes.

"Make it quick," Collins said, his voice thick with emotion. O'Rourke's lips moved as there was the sudden sound of heavy artillery landing somewhere to their southeast.

*Someone is calling naval bombardment on the advancing North Koreans,* Collins thought, seeing the flashes on the southern horizon. *They almost have that cruiser ashore, seems like.* As he had the thought, the horizon suddenly started flashing more rapidly, followed by a sound like freight cars rustling over their heads. Moments later, there were many, many flashes in the far distance, somewhere behind North Korean lines.

*I don't have time to wonder about who is shooting artillery at whom*, he thought, as *Dagonet* finished its descent from the ridge. The jeep turned hard right, and with a start, Collins realized they were starting to move through a small village. The jeep came to a screeching stop, Major Spriggs jumping out and running back towards Collins.

"Kill your engine! Kill your engine!" the Australian officer shouted. Before Collins could say anything, Rose followed the order. Spriggs finished running down the line, the short officer moving like a man possessed as each vehicle followed suit.

The sound of approaching diesels was just barely audible as Spriggs ran back to Collins's *Hellcat*.

"What happened to the last bloody tank destroyer?" Spriggs asked, his eyes wild. With a start, Collins realized the officer was wounded, his right arm cinched to his side even as he clutched an M-1 carbine in his left.

"Artillery, sir!" Collins said.

"Blimey," Spriggs cursed, his voice thick. Regaining his composure, he turned and pointed to the south east where the sounds of diesels was getting louder.

"The bastards are going to come from right to left, about seven hundred meters away," Spriggs said quickly. "You'll have flank shots, but I'm not sure how many of them there are. The *Jamaica* is waiting to fire star shells on my trigger. I'm going to take the jeep and move a half-mile that way."

Collins looked where the Australian field grade was pointing.

"If any of them get past you, I'll try to adjust fire from the *Jamaica* onto them."

Collins clenched his fists.

"They're not getting past us, sir," he said. "I don't care if we have to ram the bastards."

Spriggs nodded at that.

"Godspeed, Captain Collins," the shorter man said. "It's been an honor fighting with you tonight. You can serve with us diggers anytime."

"Thank you, sir," Collins replied, realizing the deeper meaning in the man's words. As the major moved off towards his jeep, Collins turned back towards the vehicles to find the tank destroyer commanders all standing behind him.

"All right, here's what we're going to do..."

Ten minutes later, as *Dagonet*'s engine shut off for the second time, Collins turned to look at O'Rourke.

"I'm going to fire my first burst with the sights at eight hundred meters," he said, shimmying back to this machine gun. "Judge the range from where you see my tracers."

"Yes, sir," O'Rourke said, then looked as if he had an epiphany. "That's if those darn shells don't make it too bright to see your aim."

"They are pretty incandescent," Collins mused, seeing his gunner's concern. "Must be because they're supposed to be used to seeing ships at far greater distance."

"No matter, we'll figure it out," O'Rourke said, the sound of North Korean tanks growing larger. "Rose, as soon as I fire, you get us started back up and then reverse us. I'll probably get a second shot off in the time it takes you to do that, but do *not* wait for me or the CO to tell you to back up."

"Roger, Sergeant," Rose replied.

*Here they come*, Collins thought as the Nork engines grew louder. Checking for the umpteenth time that he had charged his .50-caliber machine gun, Collins fought to steady his shaking hands.

*Hope that Aussie crew can shoot*, he thought, glancing down the line towards where the last *Achilles* sat. In all the preparation and chaos of the day, Collins hadn't had time to meet each of the Australian tank destroyer commanders. He wasn't even sure of the man's rank, just that he was now the sole survivor of *Leftenant* Kane's small command.

*For all I know, he's the worst shot in the platoon and survived because they ran and hid during that fight*, Collins thought, then shook off the paranoia. *Doesn't matter now. They just better get that last tank in line.*

Once again, there was a sharp procession of flashes in the southern distance.

"Get ready!" Collins hissed.

The Australian cruiser's star shells once again lit the night in brilliant relief. Before him, Collins saw a dozen of the Nork T-34s, their hulls black with infantry, rushing down the road towards Pusan. Leading the first vehicle by two lengths, Collins let loose with his machine gun. The tracers seemed off-color in the harsh star shell light, but were clearly visible as they passed just barely over the lead T-34. The turret whirred as O'Rourke adjusted his aim, tracking for a moment as Collins fired another longer burst that began knocking infantry off the vehicle like ten pins.

Then it was all madness, as the main gun roared. To Collins's initial astonishment, then pride, O'Rourke's first shot was bang-on in the T-34's flank, hitting just below the starting to rotate turret. With a brilliant flash, the tracer ignited something in the tank's turret, flames starting to spurt as the vehicle careened to the side. Collins continued to fire his machine gun as the diesel came to life, walking his fire over the infantry spilling from the tilting tank. O'Rourke's next shot went out just before *Dagonet* lurched backwards, hitting the edge of the now-exposed back deck and penetrating into the engine compartment. Another burst of flame erupted from the tank, this one immediately becoming larger as it was fed by fuel.

"Next tank!" Collins shouted, letting off the butterfly trigger as *Dagonet* lurched backwards. Looking down the line, he could see the other tank destroyers also backing up...except for the *Achilles*, its crew searching for another target as the engine remained off.

*You need to move! You can't stay...*

The four T-34s that fired towards the dimly discernible vehicle all missed, their surprise and movement combining to throw the gunners' aim off. They did not get another chance, as with the sound of ripping canvas, the ground simply erupted all along the roadway. Before Collins's shocked eyes, a massive artillery barrage, its fragments spewing uncomfortably close to his own position, walked in a ladder pattern across the roadway. It was only two, maybe three minutes, but in that unholy time, almost thirty large caliber shells turned their target area into a charnel house. *Whatever* it was, Collins had never seen the like of it in the short conflict, and the sight of what it did to the North Korean formation made his stomach drop even as the concussions battered him atop *Dagonet*.

"My God, sir," O'Rourke said as the night went dark once more. Several of the T-34s burned, their destruction lending a Stygian air to the area in front of Collins's force.

"Captain Collins, you want me to move forward?" Rose asked.

"No, Rose," Collins said, swallowing. "I don't think those bastards will be bothering anyone else tonight."

# EPILOGUE



"It never occurred to me that you Yanks would build a cruiser with machine guns," Major Spriggs said, his voice slightly shaken as he regarded the churned earth in front of the 72nd Armored TOC.

Kraven took a deep breath and regretted it. Graves and Registration was supposed to be along any time, but it was not taking long for the stench of several dozen bodies to start moving with the breeze. Mixing with the smell of spilled fuel, still-lingering explosives fumes, and the aroma of singed foliage, it was a potent brew that Kraven hoped he *never* "got used to."

*Hovering on the edge of vomiting is annoying*, he thought, swallowing hard, *but the point where shattered lives and scattered remains is as normal as freshly mowed grass is not a place I want to be.*

"I don't recall the Navy mentioning that to me, either," Kraven replied, glancing out to where the heavy cruiser U.S.S. *Des Moines* lurked just on the edge of sight. "Of course, I never would have thought they'd come so close to shore that they'd be able to answer your call for fire."

Spriggs nodded at that.

"I'm sure there will be some staff paper written about the cooperation between the *Jamaica* and that beast," the Australian major noted. "I just hope I'm alive to read it, as I'd like to know how they were so bloody accurate."

"You and me both," Kraven replied. "I think another tank battalion or two needs to hurry up and arrive here in Korea. I'm tired of being Mr. Dewey's Fire Brigade here on Freedom's front line."

Spriggs watched as another group of field ambulances moved through the small town where Collins had made his stand. Kraven could see the Australian wrestling with those vehicles' probable contents, given the at least a dozen times that they had made the trip from BP WOMBAT back towards central Pusan.

"I don't think I have more than two companies left," Spriggs stated, glancing over at his American counterpart. "I'm glad that the X Corps staff shifted your battalion here permanently."

"I don't think it matters where we're at," Kraven said. "If the North Koreans have enough starch to launch another attack after what happened yesterday, we're all going to be speaking Hangul by dawn tomorrow."

"If they don't shoot us out of hand," Spriggs replied, running a hand over his bald head.

"We're not ROK troops," Kraven countered, his tone gallows. "They'll want hostages."

"Oh joy, sir," Spriggs said, giving Kraven a look of mock horror. "I'm sure they'll be as well-behaved as our own allies have been."

Kraven shrugged.

"I'm sure you can take that up with Lieutenant Colonel Sung once he gets out of the hospital," Kraven replied.

"Did you hear what he did?"

"About destroying that tank?"

Spriggs nodded.

"Yes," Kraven replied. "Made me resolve to never jump off the tank if *Crusader 66* gets knocked out."

"I thought you lot were always all *death before dismount*," Spriggs chided. "I'm surprised you even jump when the option is burning to death."

"Yes, well, getting my brains bashed then drowned in a rice paddy is making that seem like less of a horrible fate," Kraven replied with a shudder.

"I am told the ROKs don't even have a form for writing up their version of the Victoria Cross yet," Spriggs noted. "I think, once they do, I'll be sure to provide the necessary witness statement."

Kraven smiled.

"Funny you should mention that," he said. "I'm putting Collins in for the Medal of Honor, and I'd like to get testimony from you in front of witnesses tonight if I can."

Spriggs laughed.

"Thinking I won't be around much longer?" he asked grimly.

"Want to make sure Collins's award has the best chance of making it," Kraven said. "I...I had a bit of difficulty with his predecessor's. Of course, I think one obstacle has been removed."

Spriggs shuddered at that as Kraven continued.

"In any case, just easier to have all the paperwork done in case you, I, or both of us are 'unlucky' in the coming days."

"I'd be honored," Spriggs replied, his tone utterly serious. "I know he's pretty much a spent force, but he and his company are probably the only reason there aren't tanks shooting at that cruiser right now."

Kraven laughed at that mental image.

"I think that would be a very short fight," he stated. "Then again, everyone thought that this would be a very short one when we landed back in June."

The sound of several aircraft caused both of them to look up and out towards the ocean.

"What in God's name is that?" Spriggs asked, his voice genuinely shocked as they regarded the two extremely large aircraft approaching their position. With the light of the setting sun reflecting off its nose, the airplanes resembled massive birds of prey covered in jewelry. Eight fighter jets circled the large aircraft, the Navy *Panther*s giving some indication to just how large their charges were.

"That, I believe, is that new *Peacemaker* bomber the Air Force had been going on about earlier this year," Kraven said, surprised at the hope he felt as he recognized the aircraft.

"It's so damn loud," Spriggs almost shouted as the two craft began a slow, lazy circle over Pusan. The two bombers waggled their ponderous wings, their passage bringing cheers from the men below, even as the ground shook from the noise. Pointing their noses back out to sea after a pair of passes, the massive bombers began climbing back into the sky.

"What the Hell was all that about?" Spriggs asked once the noise had subsided enough for them to talk normally once again.

"Oh, I think Hell is *exactly* what that was about," Kraven replied. "With the rumors of the Chinese sending soldiers to Pyongyang being verified by those two officers Sung captured, Satan's about to open up an office in North Korea."

*I just hope the bombs work in action as well as they allegedly finally did in testing*, he thought. *We don't need another fizzle.*

# AUTHOR'S NOTE

This story is a continuation of the "Lightnings and the Cactus" and "Mr. Dewey's Tank Corps" timeline (both of which can be found in my short story collection *Dispatches from Valhalla*). This POD for this timeline is the USN actually fighting to a bloody draw at the Battle of Savo Island, with the resultant knock-on of a much stronger USMC initial lodgment at Henderson Field. This in turn leads to several events that facilitate an earlier invasion of the Japanese Home Islands.

What happens when you couple this with a misfiring atomic test at Trinity? Well, you get Harry "The Butcher of Honshu" Truman run out of office on a rail in 1948 and President Thomas E. Dewey "winning" a chance to unscrew the start of the Cold War. As you can tell, it's not going well.

Will there be more in this universe? *(Camera cuts to glowering* Usurper's War *and* Vergassy Universe *fans plotting my eventual kidnapping)* Likely, but not anytime soon until other obligations are met. But thanks for coming along on another jaunt to the "Land of the Morning Calm," and we'll see what the alternate past and current present shakes loose. After all, to crib on an internet meme, if there's a large bunch of cash just lying on the side of the highway, I'm smart enough to "lift with my knees."

# ABOUT JAMES YOUNG

James Young is an American author of science fiction, alternative history, and post-apocalyptic fiction. His primary series is the *Usurper's War*, which is set in an alternate history where Adolf Hitler is killed by an RAF bomb in November 1940. He is also the author of *The Vergassy Chronicles*, a military sci-fi universe set in the 3050s. In addition to his own work, James has edited anthologies including bestselling authors Sarah Hoyt, S.M. Stirling, and David Weber. His non-fiction writing credits include *Eagles, Ravens, and Other Birds of Prey*, winning the United States Naval Institute's (USNI's) 2016 Cyberwarfare Essay Contest, and various articles in *Armor, The Journal of Military History*, and *Proceedings*.

## LINKTREE (I.E., ONE STOP FOR EVERYTHING): HTTPS://LINKTR.EE/JAMESYOUNGAUTHOR

## BLOG (I.E., THE THING I WISH I UPDATED MORE OFTEN):

Jamesyoungauthor.com

## SOLDIERS OF THE REPUBLIC

### Justin Watson

Jack struggled to appear calm and unfatigued even as the altitude, heat and humidity of central Vietnam at midday conspired to steal the air from his lungs and drain life out through his pores. From his position traveling between second and third squads, he could see ten to twelve guys of the forty-man platoon of the Viet Minh— *Free Vietnamese Army,* Jack corrected himself mentally. They marched single-file along a narrow footpath on a hillside winding between thick stands of bamboo and growths of dagger-edged elephant grass.

A soft *thunk* drew Jack's eyes away from scanning the verdant landscape for threats to the rear of the column. One of the Vietnamese troops, a short rifleman carrying an M1 carbine, bent to pick something up from the ground; a curved magazine. A sheepish expression was apparent on the Vietnamese soldier's face, and he kept his almond-shaped eyes downcast as Jack stormed towards him. Jack's interpreter, Corporal Dong, followed close on his heels. Slinging his own Garand rifle on his shoulder as he walked, Jack snatched the lighter weapon and magazine away from the shamefaced young trooper.

It was the third time on this patrol that one of the Vietnamese had dropped a magazine from their weapon unintentionally. Instead of tearing into the hapless private, Jack snapped in French, "Who is this man's squad leader?" Dong repeated the question in the singsong Vietnamese language.

An older man turned from his place in the column in response. Unlike the soldier who had dropped his magazine to the ground, the FVA sergeant approaching Jack looked more annoyed than intimidated. This man was tall, for a Vietnamese, only surrendering two inches to Jack, and the ease with which he crossed the jungle floor and the faint burn scars on his right cheek bespoke experience.

"Sergeant," Jack said in French. "I know we talked about this when we got the new thirty-round magazines. They do not fit in the old $M_1$ Carbines, only the $M_2$ Carbines, the ones that can fire fully automatic. I know they look the same, but they are different."

As Dong translated, Beasley held up the curved thirty-round magazine in one hand and shook the $M_1$ in the other, then shook his head vigorously side to side.

The FVA sergeant's nostrils flared, and he exhaled sharply before he turned to Dong and started chittering away. Jack, who had drawn this assignment in part due to his knack for picking up languages, hated the sound of Vietnamese. It pitched up and down too fast and too sharply. Much as he tried, Jack couldn't get a grounding in it like he had Tagalog, Korean, Japanese, French and Spanish.

"Sergeant," Dong said in French to Jack. "He says that his men are trading them out because they don't want to run out of ammunition before their friends do. He says they think you're playing favorites with who gets them."

"Jesus H. Donovan Christ," Jack said, English profanity slipping into his French. "I'm not playing fucking favorites. You see here—"

Jack flipped the carbine in his hand upside down so the magazine well was facing up.

"It doesn't have the right latch," Jack said. "The $M_2$ does, but if you use a thirty-round mag instead of the fifteen-round mag in an $M_1$, the fucking magazine falls out of the fucking gun, and some Franco-Fascist sonofabitch turns you into swiss cheese while you're fumbling for it. I don't know how to explain it any goddamn simpler than that."

Dong struggled to keep up with the rapid-fire, profanity-laced rant.

"Sergeant Beasley, a word," a calm voice from behind Jack said.

Jack took a deep breath before turning around, knowing who wanted a word. The words were English, but the man's accent made his name and rank sound like, "Sar-zhaun Beez-lee." Jack thrust the carbine back at the soldier and the magazine at the NCO, then turned to face his commanding officer.

Captain Rapicault was shorter than Jack, with dark eyes that never seemed surprised at anything. He wore the same uniform as Beasley and the Vietnamese, save the captain's bars on his collar and the black stenciled USMC and Eagle, Globe and Anchor insignia on his breast. He carried a radio in his rucksack and a Thompson submachine gun held at the low ready in his hands. Rapicault's posture was relaxed and his perpetually amused expression pissed Jack off every time he looked at him.

"Yes, Captain," Jack said. "How can I help you?"

Instead of annoyance, Rapicault smirked at Jack's avoidance of the word "sir." The Gallic nonchalance only pissed Jack off worse.

*Bad enough I'm humping a ruck through a goddamn jungle...again...but I had to pull a CO who is a frog* and *a fucking jarhead on top of that.*

Military Assistance Command-Vietnam wasn't run by the War Department, but by the OSS. Jack, Captain Rapicault, and all the other American ground personnel were on detached duty from their parent units to serve as advisors to the Viet Minh. Their detachments were mixed, Marines and Army, willy-nilly.

In Jack's case, a short, bespectacled man named Feldman had shown up with orders pulling him away from his platoon in the 10th Mountain Division. He'd been on year one of an accompanied tour with his wife and kids in the comfort of Pyongyang. Six years after the end of the Japanese War, Korea was booming economically. Better yet, an American sergeant's paycheck was more than enough for a family of five to live very comfortably.

*Instead, I'm here, in the crotch of the Orient, where the country smells like shit, half our "friends" are goddamned Reds and the other half are cavemen who haven't learned to wipe their asses.*

"Sergeant, you have some experience working with foreign troops, no?" Rapicault said.

"Yes, Captain," Jack said.

It was true, he had worked with both Filipino and Korean troops in war and peace, respectively. But he *liked* Filipinos, brave little brown bastards, and he *liked* Koreans, who were open, friendly and industrious to a fault.

"Then you know," Rapicault said. "Or you should know that how you communicate information is easily as important as the information itself."

Jack paused, passing a sleeve over his sweat-drenched face before answering. If he did not like Vietnam, or the Vietnamese, he liked turncoat French officers telling him how to do his job even less.

"That's true," Jack said, keeping his voice even. "But given how aggressive your countrymen have been lately, I think by now these troops should understand how to put the right magazine in the right weapon, Captain."

Rapicault's brow furrowed in irritation for a moment, gratifying Jack.

Their team was responsible for advising the 1st Battalion of the 112th Regiment of the FVA. Unfortunately, the 1st of the 112th had been rushed to the contested Central Highlands of Vietnam a mere week after receiving its basic loadout of American equipment and their advisors. Other FVA units had spent a month to six weeks with their American advisor teams training in relative security near Hanoi or Saigon.

"My *former* countrymen, Sergeant," Rapicault corrected, sardonic half-smile back in place. "Despite my mellifluous accent, I have been a US Marine since 1943, and an American citizen since 1944. Regardless, if my *former* countrymen decide to take Vietnam back by overt force, and if you were to be wounded in the ensuing battles, how likely are our little yellow friends to haul your overfed American ass up and down these mountains when you've been treating them like dogshit for weeks?"

Jack frowned, but didn't respond. Rapicault nodded at his silence.

"And while you're pondering that question, Sergeant, you might also ask yourself how long you're going to sulk before you start discharging your duties like a professional," Rapicault continued sharply. "Perhaps it is different in the Army, but Marine sergeants don't generally pick and choose which missions they will accomplish and which they won't."

His fatigue forgotten, Jack's spine stiffened, and he opened his mouth to respond furiously, but Rapicault had already turned away to address the column.

"*Không sao đâu, trung úy,*" Rapicault said, issuing the Vietnamese song-speech without apparent effort. "*Chúng ta có thể tiếp tục di chuyển.*"

No more magazines fell on the return march, nor did the platoon make contact with the enemy. All Jack had to take his mind off the oppressive climate was the knowledge that, whatever he thought of Rapicault, he'd earned that ass-chewing.

———

From his hide position in the tall, sharp elephant grass, Adjutant Jean-Baptiste Vanderburgh of the Groupement de Commandos Mixtes Aéroportés saw and heard the entire altercation between the Americans. He'd followed the French and Vietnamese conversation easily, but then the American sergeant and captain had switched to English, of which he didn't speak a word. He could tell they were not happy with one another, though.

Though he laid mere meters away from dozens of the enemy with only one comrade beside him, Vanderburgh was unafraid. He was renowned for his ability to blend with the countryside. He had spent his boyhood stalking game in the Alsatian countryside, then the subsequent decades stalking men everywhere from the woods of the Low Countries to the burning deserts of Algeria, all the way here, to the sweltering jungles of Indochina.

The American officer turned more towards Vanderburgh, giving him a straight-on view of his face for a moment. Vanderburgh's breath caught in his throat, and his eyes grew wide.

*Lieutenant Rapicault? No, it can't be...*

It was. It was Pierre Rapicault, a comrade he'd thought long dead in a Japanese prison camp.

*Obviously he escaped and linked up with the Americans. Jesus Christ, has he been here in Indochina the whole time?*

Rapicault finished his conversation with the American sergeant abruptly, then switched back to Vietnamese and ordered the platoon to move out. Foom and Vanderburgh waited long minutes after the soft tread of the FVA rear guard was no longer audible before they moved, each rising like a strange jungle denizen, cloaked in layers of vegetation and dirt to obscure their bipedal forms.

"Something troubles you, sir?" Foom asked in a low voice as they made their way west, toward the rest of Foom's company. Although Foom was a captain and technically outranked Vanderburgh, a warrant officer, it was understood the Vanderburgh retained command over not just this GCMA company, but also their parent battalion.

"I know their officer," Vanderburgh said. "He was my platoon commander before the Japanese occupied Indochina."

"A Frenchman fights for the Viet Minh?" Foom said, aghast.

"Many of my countrymen still resent France's position in the Greater Reich," Vandeburgh said. "I knew some of them had defected to America. I didn't know they were being used here."

Foom shook his head. In the Hmong captain's devout Catholic mind, the Viet Minh forces were comprised of nothing but godless, communist butchers and their brainwashed slave soldiers. Rebranding themselves the "Free Vietnamese Army" meant nothing. The idea that any Christian, much less a Frenchman, fought alongside the Viet Minh was anathema to him.

For his part, Vanderburgh understood why de Gaulle's fanatics fought. He, too, hated German hegemony over France. But siding with the Viet Minh to rob France of one of her rightful colonies? How would that hurt the Germans? France's economy would falter as money from Indochinese rubber, rice and opiate exports lined foreign pockets instead of French ones. It would degrade France's already diminished status as a power in the world without thwarting Hitler one whit. The so-called Free French were cutting of their nose to spite their face.

"So, Foom," Vanderburgh said, putting the thought out of mind. "What did you think of our erstwhile opponents?"

"Definitely a new regiment. City boys, most of them," Foom said, his tone clinical. "But they are trained well enough, and they seemed alert and motivated despite their shoddy treatment by the big white sergeant. They will not be easily defeated in the defense."

Vanderburgh nodded.

"The 3rd Foreign Legion regiment will attack the base camp," Vanderburgh said. "Our part will be to cut up any outlying patrols, then delay any relief force from the main base at Plei Mrong."

"Yes, sir," Foom said. "How long before we begin?"

"Not long. Most of the light forces are in their assembly areas," Vanderburgh said. "They haven't moved de Castries's armor into place yet. Once they do, we'll have to move fast or lose the element of surprise. I think our friends back there have about a week to live, at the most."

———

Jack squeezed the trigger on an M1 carbine. The recoil drove the butt of the weapon into his shoulder and, as he'd intended, his magazine hit the ground for the third time. He carefully safed the weapon and placed it on a plywood stand pointed down range. Then, with comically exaggerated movements, he scratched his head underneath his helmet, then bent over, looking back at his audience between his knees, allowing his helmet to fall off. The Vietnamese troops sitting in a half-circle on the ground watching him howled with laughter. Seeing the wayward magazine, Jack snatched it up and stared at it, eyebrows quirked quizzically to more laughter.

"Corporal Dong," Jack said, his French pronunciation artificially deep and gruff. "What is wrong with my magazine?"

Dong trotted up to him with an M2 carbine in his hands. The weapon was physically identical to the M1 in outward appearance. He didn't bother translating Beasley's French for the non-Francophones in the audience, but he spoke in Vietnamese himself. Having rehearsed this, Jack knew he was saying, essentially, "Sergeant, the magazine isn't the problem, you're just using the wrong weapon, here—"

Jack took the proffered weapon while Dong delivered a string of Vietnamese narrative on the features of the M2 and in particular how the 30 round magazine only worked with it. Jack waited for him to finish then, nodding appreciatively, he rocked the magazine into the M2's well, pulled the bolt back and let it fly forward to chamber a round, flipped the selector switch near the trigger assembly from SAFE past SEMI straight to AUTO, and pulled the carbine's stock into his shoulder.

*BRADADA...BRADADA...BRADADA.*

Aligning the sights at the right hip of the silhouette, Jack methodically treated each target in turn to a short, staccato burst of automatic fire. Then, still careful to keep the muzzle pointed away from his audience, he held the carbine so that the audience could see the thirty-round magazine was still firmly in the M2's magazine well.

"So, you can see," Jack said in French as he ejected the magazine and cleared the carbine's chamber. "The thirty-round magazine is very useful *if* your weapon has the automatic function. Otherwise, it's just going to end up on the ground."

As Dong took up a running translation, Jack saw Captain Rapicault step around one of the sandbag embankments at the rear of the range complex. Rapicault gestured with his chin for Jack to join him. Turning the class over to Dong, Jack followed Rapicault to the other side of the sandbags, and up wooden steps to the platform of the observation tower. Rapicault told the sentry on duty there to take a break.

This firebase encompassed a lakeside fishing village of no name and was just large enough to accommodate one rifle company from the 112th on a rotational basis. This week, it was 2nd Company of 1st Battalion. The range where Jack had been training the men on the M2 was on the southern side oriented toward the lake to the south, southwest and southeast. To the north, northeast and northwest, the battalion had cleared the vegetation away from the perimeter for five hundred meters. The camp's defensive engagement area was defined by the treeline on the far side, and by multiple rows of triple-strand razor wire on the near side, punctuated by anti-personnel minefields.

The perimeter fighting positions themselves were well dug in and carefully laid out to create interlocking fields of fire and eliminate dead space. But Jack frowned at their overhead cover. They'd done the best they could with bamboo, earth and those cypress trunks they'd been able to harvest from lower altitudes. Jack wasn't confident they'd withstand concentrated mortar fire. He *knew* a well-placed artillery barrage would collapse most of them, even the heftier machine gun nests and command dugouts.

Jack knew that Rapicault sent weekly requests for engineer support to further harden their defenses, but thus far those requests had gone unanswered. Even the company command post and the advisors' own operations centers were just Quonset huts surrounded by sandbag walls.

"The classes seem to be going well," Rapicault said, tapping a cigarette out of a pack and holding it out to Jack.

Jack took the proffered cigarette, his brow furrowed. Rapicault's tone betrayed no hint of I-told-you-so, but maybe the Frog sonofabitch was just being subtle. Jack decided to take the observation at face value.

"Yes, Captain," Jack said. "They seem to be dropping fewer magazines lately."

Rapicault lit his cigarette, then passed his Zippo to Jack. After he got the cherry on his cig glowing, Jack heard the crack and rattle of small-arms fire as the range went hot. He glanced over his shoulder and saw that the platoon he'd left in Dong's care was going about the range in good order, firers standing at the line engaging targets, their mates queued up nicely a safe distance behind them.

"The balloon is going up, Sergeant. We have reconnaissance photographs of 1st and 3rd Moroccan Spahis staging near Xayden and the 1st Foreign Cavalry at Pak Nhai," Rapicault said without further preamble. "What's more, Colonel Huu tells me that his intelligence people may have underestimated the number of infiltrated French units. There may be as many as a regiment of French Colonial Regulars in the Plei Mrong area already."

The Spahis were units of armored cavalry comprised of Panzer IIIN light tanks and Stug self-propelled assault guns. The 1st Foreign Cavalry was a lighter force comprised mainly of Sonderkraftfahrzeug 234 Armored Cars. Each unit, fully manned, amounted to roughly two-thirds the strength of an American regiment of similar function.

The French armored forces were indeed formidable. Taken together, they were unquestionably the most powerful ground combat force in Southeast Asia, but Jack wasn't worried about them.

Plei Mrong, their area of operations, was several kilometers of dense jungle away from Colonial Routes 9 and 14, the only paved roadways in the area. It was possible that the French, through determined effort, might bring their armor to bear on Plei Mrong by moving it cross-country. It would take them days, perhaps weeks, to do so due to the combination of dense vegetation, steep elevations and water obstacles. Thus, Jack's *immediate* problem was the possibility of a couple thousand regular infantry already within striking distance.

"What the fuck?" Jack said, cigarette dangling from his lip. "How the hell did we miss a regiment of fucking Frenchmen?"

Rapicault shook his head.

"Very little about the French Army is French nowadays, Sergeant. German weapons, colonial troops," Rapicault said. "Can you tell the difference between a Thai or a Laotian and a Vietnamese? I grew up here, and I can't until they start talking. The locals could, but the Viet Minh have never been popular here in the Highlands, nor is the 'new' FVA. Not that the locals love the French, either, but until they figure out who is more likely to win, most of them aren't going to go out of their way to help either side. Safer for them to keep their mouths shut, no?"

"Shit."

"Indeed." Rapicault extinguished his cigarette. "*Merde.* They will move soon. They cannot keep that many soldiers concealed and supplied for long."

The two men stood in uncomfortable silence, looking out at the camp and the mostly green troops who defended it. Jack had found, once he stopped feeling sorry for himself and started acting like a sergeant again, that they weren't bad soldiers at all. Some of the NCOs were hardcore bastards, as their senior guys had fought the Japs during the war and the French off and on ever since. But he didn't know if they were enough to stop a regiment of professionals, equipped and trained by the most successful Army in human history: Hitler's Wehrmacht.

Jack *did* know that he didn't want to die here. Fighting the Japanese had been one thing. They had started a war with the United States. The reason they had to be stopped, had to be forced into *abject surrender*, was abundantly clear. Breaking Japan down so they never threatened America again was imperative.

The French, on the other hand, had never done anything to him. Even the Nazis who pulled France's strings had done nothing to him, personally, or to his country. He'd heard they were evil, murderous bastards, but the world was full of evil, murderous bastards. Was it America's responsibility to fight every last one of them?

Jack stole a glance at Rapicault's impassive face.

*If I don't like this situation, what is he thinking?*

"Captain, I'm going to ask a rude question," Jack said.

Rapicault chuckled.

"I am shocked," he said. "You've been the soul of tact thus far."

Jack smiled sheepishly.

"Right, well," Jack said. "Look, you were right: I needed to get my shit together and do the job."

"Yes," Rapicault said, still smiling. "I'm glad we agree on that. Now ask your rude question."

Jack exhaled sharply before he spoke, trying to phrase the question in a way that wasn't a flat-out challenge to Rapicault.

*Oh, fuck it.*

"Captain, if I don't want to be here," Jack said. "And, frankly, I don't, doesn't it bother you to be here? I know you renounced your French citizenship, but doesn't it bother you to fight your old countrymen?"

Rapicault didn't answer for long moments, staring out at the treeline of the jungle, his perpetually amused expression having given way to something more pensive.

"Sergeant, if a man broke into your house, killed your father, raped your mother at gunpoint and declared himself your father, would you go along with the fiction?" Rapicault said. "Would the fact that your siblings accepted the tragic, murderous farce as reality change your mind?"

Jack's eyes widened.

"That's a hell of a way to think about it, Captain," Jack said.

"It's the way I see it, Sergeant," Rapicault said. "My great-great-great grandfather fell at Valmy in 1792. My great-great grandfather manned the barricades to restore the Republic in 1832. He lived, but was imprisoned. His *son*, however, fell in the revolt of 1848. His son, my grandfather, lost an arm and an eye to Prussian shells at Sedan. My father...he's buried, for certain values of buried, somewhere near Verdun. Every man of my line for more than a century has served the republic. For me, there is only one credible republic left on Earth, and if it is not the republic of my birth, it is at least more worthy of my service than a cabal of Nazi puppets."

The silence lingered as heavily as the midday humidity between them.

Jack chewed on Rapicault's pronouncement until his concentration was broken by the staccato cracks of distant small-arms fire—too distant to be on the range behind them. Jack made eye contact with Rapicault. Wordlessly, both men snatched up binoculars from a shelf and began scanning the jungle.

*There*—Jack saw three dull gray clouds rising above the treetops. *Fuck. Someone is pitching grenades.*

"Captain, one o'clock, three thousand yards." Jack gave the distance and direction to the explosions.

"I see them," Rapicault said, turning and taking the stairs down the tower two at a time. Jack followed close behind.

———

The American advisory team maintained their own operations center in a Quonset hut right next to 2nd Company's command post. It was to this semi-cylindrical structure that Jack and Captain Rapicault sprinted. Corporal McClung, their radio operator, already had the advisor with the platoon in contact on the horn by the time they barreled through the door. Over the speaker, audible even among explosions and the consistent roar and rattle of concentrated small-arms fire, Jack could hear Sergeant Carabastas's Puerto Rican accent.

"Negative, Ajax-One," Carabastas said. "We are under intense fire, I can't get a good count. We've had visual contact with at least two battalions, we are currently engaged with two or more company's worth."

Rapicault gestured for McClung to give him the hand microphone for the radio.

"Ajax-One-Red, this is Ajax One-Six," Rapicault said. "We're spinning up a reaction force to come get you. What else can you tell me about the enemy and your situation?"

"Sir, they've got a ton of automatic weapons," Carabastas said. "Machine guns and automatic rifles. No mortars or artillery yet. These aren't raggedy-ass locals, sir. They're regulars in camo-pattern and fritz helmets."

"Roger, Red," Rapicault said. "Hold out, we're coming for you."

"One-Six, I don't think we're going to last," Carabastas said. His voice shook slightly, but he maintained his composure. "We're down to one squad of effectives. They're pressing hard. We'll kill as many as we can, but you should get ready—"

The transmission ended abruptly. From outside, the sounds of battle began to fade.

"Red, this is Six," Rapicault said, not shouting, but with unmistakable urgency. "Red, Six, acknowledge... Red, this is Six, do you copy? Damn it."

Rapicault stood up, handing the mic back to McClung.

"I'm going to head next door," he said. "Sergeant Beasley, you and McClung report to Ajax Main, relay our situation and request air support—"

A high-pitched, whistling shriek filled Jack's ears.

"DOWN!" Jack and Rapicault screamed in unison, each grabbing one of McClung's arms and flattening themselves to the floor. A brief flash of heat rolled over him, and Jack felt his guts undulate from a wave of concussive force. Sheets of fragmentation penetrated the thin, tin walls of the operations center hut, shredding equipment but, miraculously, missing Jack's vulnerable skin.

*Well, now we know what they were saving their mortars for...*

Lifting his head, Jack saw the room was well and truly shredded from frag. His ears were ringing as he staggered to his feet, and it sounded as if all the noises around him were coming from the far end of a metal funnel. Rapicault was shouting something.

"Grab weapons and radios, we have to move!"

Jack lurched to comply, still punch-drunk from the nearby blast. Stumbling through the smoke-filled hut to the weapons rack, he grabbed McClung's carbine and tossed it to him, followed by a rucksack with a radio. Then he secured his own Garand and another ruck with a radio in it. Rapicault already held his own Thompson and was slinging another radio onto his back, headed out. Jack followed, pushing McClung ahead of him through the door, now swinging wildly ajar.

The first sight that greeted Jack as he stepped outside was the smoking ruin of 2nd Company's CP. Looking around, he saw dozens of FVA troops milling about, unsure of what to do. Another whistling shriek split the air.

Rapicault was screaming in Vietnamese. Jack himself screamed, "*Descendre!*" as he dove for the muddy ground of the camp.

Once again, he was rocked to his innards from the detonation, and he felt mud, dirt, and harder particulate matter clatter against his steel helmet before he looked back up. He saw a boot, somehow still upright, with the bloody, jagged remains of a human foot in it, but no sign of the victim. A few feet away, one of the FVA troops lay clutching his stomach, dark, almost black blood pouring through his fingers as he screamed his agony to the heavens. The rest of the soldiers he saw stood, crouched or laid where they were, unmoving, clearly in shock.

"New plan," Rapicault said, slightly more rapid speech the only crack in his characteristic aplomb. "You two get to a fighting position and check in with Ajax Main. I'll organize the defense."

Without waiting for an answer, Rapicault sprang to his feet and began issuing orders to the Vietnamese troops, gesturing emphatically toward the camp's defensive line to the north, then to the wounded and to the sandbagged dugout that was the Camp's aid station. In short order, Vietnamese NCOs and officers began herding their men per Rapicault's direction. Most ran toward the line; a few carried or dragged the wounded to the aid station.

A sound like a half-dozen buzzsaws roaring into operation drew Jack's eyes north just in time to see several streams of tracers emerging from the treeline, across the engagement area and toward the battalion's fighting positions.

"Come on, McClung," Jack said, grabbing the kid by the arm and running toward one of the platoon command dugouts. "You heard the man."

———

Spotting a radio antenna sprouting from behind a rock in the middle of the kill zone, Foom settled his elbows into the soft jungle floor and pressed the select-fire toggle on his STG-46 to E for *Eisenfeurer*, "Single Shot." He lined up the hooded front sight post on the dome of the green enemy helmet just below the antenna. Even as grenades detonated nearby and rifle and machine-gun fire cracked, stuttered and buzzed around him like a cavalcade of malicious, deadly insects, Foom took a deep breath and then exhaled, squeezing the trigger steadily so that the rifle recoiled into his should with a sharp, sonic crack at the bottom of his natural pause.

Foom was rewarded with an audible metallic CLINK and a puff of pink as the helmet flew several feet away from his victim. Foom allowed himself a grunt of satisfaction.

The FVA platoon was dying with a whimper. They'd fought bravely, but Foom's ambush had caught them completely unaware. Rather than having to assault through their position, Foom and his men walked through the kill zone, treating every corpse in the wrong uniform to a burst of fire.

Foom found the corpse of the radio operator he had killed slumped against the rock. The upper left quadrant of the man's face was a grisly ruin, the exit wound of Foom's shot having blown out the man's eye socket, cheekbone and half his nose. Foom noted the chevrons and rockers on the dead man's fatigues: an American sergeant, despite his darker skin. And in his rucksack—

*His radio!*

Foom stripped the pack off the corpse's back and put the radio hand mic to his ear. His pulse jumped; the Americans were still talking on this frequency. He couldn't understand a word of it, but they were definitely still sending traffic over the net. Foom motioned for his own radio operator.

"Adjutant, this is Foom," he said when he got Vanderburgh on the net. "We have an intact American radio, and they are still transmitting on its frequency."

———

Jack's Garand barked twice in quick succession, and a camouflage-clad enemy fell to his knees and then face first into a razor wire obstacle. One of the dead man's comrades stepped on the corpse and hurtled the wire, a long tube, at least fifteen feet in length, in his hands. Jack acquired the new target and fired, but his enemy had dropped to the prone, out of Jack's sight picture. Jack tried to reacquire and fire again, but his empty clip ejected from the rifle's chamber with a quiet *ping!*

As Jack thumbed another eight-round clip into the Garand, the *THROOM* of an explosion split the humid jungle air, followed by several smaller blasts as the enemy's Bangalore set off a dozen sympathetic detonations. A linear fountain of dirt twenty feet high erupted straight through the minefield.

Jack's hand slipped, and the bolt of the Garand kept a tiny scrap of Jack's thumb as it rammed forward, chambering another round.

"Damn it," Jack hissed. In moments, the two nearest .30-caliber machine gun positions altered their sectors of fire to rake the newly opened lane through their minefield with bursts of automatic fire. Four enemy soldiers jerked and fell in the breach, but more hurtled past them, rising and falling, crawling, then sprinting inexorably toward 2nd Company's main position. From the mixture of black, white and brown faces advancing toward them, Jack assumed that it was a Foreign Legion unit they faced.

*We're slowing them, but we're not stopping them.*

Rapicault did a credible baseball slide into the company command dugout. He was speaking Vietnamese into his radio. As he finished speaking, a volley of artillery shells impacted in the treeline five hundred meters in front of them. Three orange-black detonations shredded tree and man alike, and the flow of enemy infantry out of the jungle slowed just a bit.

"Just three tubes?" Jack shouted over the din of battle.

"Every one of the outposts is getting hit," Rapicault said. "And at least three regiments are converging on the main base at Plei Mrong. I was lucky to get an arty platoon in direct support."

"Three regiments? They missed a fucking *division?*" Jack shouted as a burst of enemy machine-gun fire kicked up a row of mud fountains right in front of his sandbags. "What the hell have the intel assholes been doing? Diddling each other over their typewriters?"

"What did MAC-V-Air say about air support?" Rapicault said, ignoring Jack's outburst.

"Major Jordan told me they would scramble what they could," Jack said, gesturing to his pack on the floor of the dugout. "I couldn't reach Pleiku, so the regimental advisory team is relaying to MAC-V-Air. Maybe your railroad tracks will get them moving faster."

Rapicault nodded, taking Jack's hand mic and keying it.

"Ajax Main, Ajax Main, this is Ajax One-Six," Rapicault said. "We are under attack by a reinforced regiment. We will be overrun in less than one hour without support. What's the status of our air, over?"

"Ajax Main, this is Tiger Four checking in." Before Ajax-Main could answer, a deep, smoothly modulated southern voice announced its presence on the net.

"Glad to hear it Tiger Four." Major Jordan's voice from Plei Mrong sounded as relieved as Jack felt. "Stand by for the advisor on the scene. Ajax One-Six, we have air, over."

"Roger, Ajax Main," Rapicault said. "Tiger Four, this is Ajax One-Six: recommend you make your run northeast to southwest, parallel to our position, initial point on or north of Zebra-Baker Zero-One-Zero, One-Five-Two. That pattern should keep you clear of the gun-target line from the artillery at Ajax Main."

"Ajax One-Six, roger," the southern gentleman in the plane answered. "You have sixteen P-8os with two thousand-pound bombs each. We can't see shit through the canopy. Can you mark your forward position and the enemy's approximate center of mass?"

Rapicault smiled and Jack grinned, too. Sixteen jets—maybe MAC-V cared if they lived or died, after all.

"Roger, Tiger," Rapicault said, motioning for Jack to throw a smoke grenade. "Marking our forward position first."

Jack found the first smoke grenade on his gear, a green one, pulled the pin and threw it in between the command dugout and the nearest fighting position so as not to obscure 2nd Company's field of fire.

"One-Six, I see green smoke," Tiger Four drawled. "Confirm green smoke, over."

Rapicault was on the other radio, speaking rapidly in Vietnamese for a few seconds before he took the hand mic back to talk to the jets. Even over the constant cacophony of artillery, mortars and gunfire, Jack could hear the big American jet engines now.

"Roger, Tiger," Rapicault said. "Green smoke. Stand by for enemy center of mass."

Another volley of artillery landed: two orange-black detonations sent frag raining upon the enemy, but the third round, in the center of the sheaf, plumed into a white cloud.

"Ajax One-Six, I tally white smoke," Tiger Four said. "I say again, white smoke. Be advised target mark is well within danger close of your position."

"Roger, Tiger Four," Rapicault said. "I confirm white smoke on the target, acknowledge danger close."

"I have visual on friendly markings, I tally target marking," Tiger Four said, and Jack could hear the eagerness in his voice. "I am at the IP now. Four-ship in the initial pass."

"Roger, Tiger Four, you are cleared hot," Rapicault said.

"Get small, Ajax," Tiger Four said. "This is going to be close."

There—Jack saw four silvery winged shapes diving out of the sky like avenging angels, their engines drowning out the rifles and machine guns below. They were low enough that Jack could make out the shark's teeth on the nose jet intake and bright red tail paint.

As they slowed and leveled, a finned cylinder dropped from each of the planes' bellies, falling gracefully until they hit the jungle floor and detonated. Each bomb contained the explosive force of ten artillery rounds. Jack was rocked back in the dugout by a wave of heat and concussion, his ears popping with the sudden, violent pressure change.

Pulling himself back up, Jack returned to the dugout's firing position and scanned the battlefield. He saw dozens more broken bodies and four great craters in the soft, muddy ground. Seeing a cluster of the enemy staggering as if punch-drunk, Jack had the presence of mind to bring his Garand up and engage them. His shots seemed to wake the rest of 2nd Company from some sort of trance, and those FVA soldiers still standing raked the dazed Legionnaires with rifle and machine-gun fire.

"Good drop," Rapicault said, shaking his own head to clear it. "Keep laying it on."

"All right, Benny, you head to thirty-thousand feet and keep an eye out," a new voice, this one a Texan drawl, said over the radio. "Robin, head for the IP."

Another flight of jet-propelled birds of prey swept down upon the enemy, incinerating dozens more with their bombs and sending the remainder to their bellies to avoid obliterating death. Finally, it seemed, they had stalled the enemy's advance.

"We have to be ready to move," Rapicault said. "We have one chance to break out. According to the 112th staff, the enemy's main axis of advance is east of the lake. We will end-run round the lake to the west, keeping the water obstacle between us and them, and force-march south to link up with the rest of the regiment."

Jack thought about the plan. There were a lot of things that could go wrong. They would have to carry their wounded on litters for at least ten kilometers. Even with the enemy suppressed by bombs and artillery, their chances of outrunning them were small. Still, their minefields were breached and their wire obstacles were largely shredded. This outpost was no longer a tenable position.

"All right, sir," Jack said. "We'll be ready."

The last four jets finished their run. After the thunder of their bombs and the roar of their engines had receded, the staccato cacophony of rifles and machine guns resumed, but at a much slower tempo.

"Much obliged, Tigers," Rapicault said. "We're still taking fire, but we've got some breathing room."

"Can you make it back to friendly lines, One-Six?" the Texan pilot asked.

"We're certainly going to try, Tiger," Rapicault said. "We've got a lot of wounded, though."

"Stand by," a feminine voice interjected. "This is Angel Three-Five. We are a flight of three Ravens. Meet me at the clearing on the riverbank one hundred meters south by southeast of your green smoke. My rotor cone will fit there. I can take your wounded first, then drop my litters and ferry the rest of your men on the skids."

"Helicopters?" Jack asked.

"That's right," Rapicault said. "We're about to get a lift from the famous flying lady doctor of Vietnam."

Jack had heard of her, of course; everyone in MAC-V had heard of the beautiful French doctor who flew helicopters, plucking men from the battlefield like an angel of mercy. He'd never thought he'd meet her, though, much less get his ass pulled out of the fire by her.

"Roger, Angel Three-Five," Rapicault said into the hand mic, his smile much broader, and far less ironic than usual. "Thanks a lot, both of you. I take back every unkind word I've ever said about flyboys."

———

Vanderburgh recognized the voice coming out of the radio even though he couldn't understand the language. He'd never seen a need to learn English. He'd enlisted at sixteen expecting to fight the Germans, the Algerians, or perhaps the Thais and Vietnamese, but not Americans.

*And certainly not other Frenchmen. God damn you, Rapicault.*

Vanderburgh and Captain Foom were standing in the operations center of the *3rd Regiment Etranger Infantrie*. The regimental commander, a big burly colonel named Faucher, and his operations officer stood on the other side of a folding table, a young lieutenant sat between them at the captured American radio, listening intently. When the radio went silent for a moment, the lieutenant looked up.

"Sir, they're going to try to use helicopters to evacuate across the lake," the lieutenant said.

Faucher looked at the map.

*"Merde,"* he said in a gravelly voice. "We don't have anything that can reach in time. Major, can we finish this business before they escape?"

Major Grenault, the operations chief for 3rd REI, shook his head.

"No, sir," he said. "Second Battalion was mauled by those jets. We're moving 3rd Battalion forward, but it will take time to complete the forward passage of lines since we're still taking artillery and mortars."

At that moment, an American jet dove on the treeline, fire spewing from six fifty-caliber machine guns in its nose. The pilot had to be firing blind through the thick green jungle canopy, but it still sent men running for cover.

"And strafing runs," the intelligence lieutenant added lamely.

Vanderburgh studied the map for a moment, then exchanged a look with Foom, who nodded agreement.

"Sir," Vanderburgh said. "We can make it to their LZ in time. Captain Foom's men travel light, and we know the terrain."

Faucher considered that for a moment.

"You'll be on your own, too far for us to reinforce or even to support with mortars if something goes wrong," he said.

"With all respect, *mon Colonel,*" Vanderburgh said. "What else is new?"

A harried-looking captain pushed a tent flap aside and jogged up to Colonel Faucher.

"Sir, from General Cogny regarding the air situation," the captain said, then saluted and left the tent as rapidly as he'd come.

Faucher's eyes scanned the paper for several seconds, then he grinned.

"Our friends in the Air Force have a surprise for the American mercenary pilots," he said. He scratched his chin for a moment, then nodded. "All right, Vanderburgh. You're clear. Get moving."

———

The late afternoon sun cast the nameless fishing village in dappled gold as the last lift of 2nd Company boarded their helicopters. Several dozen stone-faced civilians stood, watching them embark. Jack felt a twinge of conscience, but quickly dismissed it.

*The French probably won't fuck with them. Besides, the enemy had pretty accurate targeting data on the command post and ops center. Likely a lot of these fuckers are working for them.*

The *thwapthwapthwapthwapthwap* of the Hiller H-23's rotor blades drowned out Jack's thoughts, and hot rotor wash threatened to blow away anything not tied down. Jack looked dubiously at the insectile metal airframe of the unnatural aircraft as it settled on its skids. He leaned over, putting his lips practically to the captain's ear and screaming to be heard.

"Sir, are you sure about this?" he shouted.

Rapicault shouted his answer in Jack's ear.

"You may swim if you'd rather, Sergeant!"

Jack shot the Marine a baleful look, but Rapicault only grinned at him. Without another word, he slung his Thompson, and ran forward at a crouch under the rotors. Rapicault grabbed a hold of the skids and the side of the cockpit. McClung joined him on the other side. Growling under his breath, Jack followed suit, running at a crouch to the next helicopter, a Vietnamese squad leader, the highest-ranking NCO left in 2nd Company, took the opposite skid.

*I'd rather fucking swim.*

A set of dazzling white teeth and full lips smiled up at him from under a flight helmet when Jack looked in the cockpit. Despite his terror, Jack tightened his grip on the helicopters and smiled back, giving the famous flying lady doctor a thumbs up.

Jack's stomach lurched as the bird gained a few feet of altitude and started to fly slowly southward over the green water of the lake. They were so close to the water, closer than the high dive board of the pool back at the YMCA. The urge to jump off and swim the rest of the trip was strong, but he resisted. Duty aside, there wasn't a body of water in Vietnam that didn't have leeches and other parasites floating about in it.

Without warning, the leftmost helicopter disintegrated, its skeletal metallic frame crumpling like a crushed beer can. The helicopter burst into flame as its fuel stores ignited, and then the ruined bird crashed into the muddy water with a *SPLOOSH*. Jack's heart hammered as a stream of tracers passed in front of his face, missing him and tearing into the mud and vegetation of their intended landing zone.

Jack's eyes snapped left, to the helicopter's six o'clock. He saw a swept wing jet closing on them fast. Instead of speeding up, the helicopter slowed. Jack looked incredulously at the pilot, only to see her jerk her head to the side, motioning for him to jump.

*Don't have to tell me twice!*

Jack took a deep breath, let go of the helicopter and fell into the water with a splash. He fought instinctive panic and let himself sink to the bottom, knowing they'd been near the shore when he'd bailed. Sure enough, his feet hit the muck long before he ran out of breath. Squatting down, Jack dumped his ruck, knowing his radio wouldn't have survived the submersion, anyway, then kicked back up to the surface, and took another deep breath before re-immersing himself in the lake, not wanting to stay a target for longer than necessary.

The murky seconds it took to reach shore seemed like an eternity; his muscles and lungs burned as he kicked his way through the lake. Finally, his boots hit mud and Jack dragged himself onto shore, rifle at the ready.

Looking up, he saw the swept wing jets and the American P-80s turning and diving on one another.

*Godspeed, Tigers.*

Jack had no idea where the rest of 2nd Company was other than that they were somewhere on this side of the lake. A few meters to his right, he spotted the FVA NCO wading out of the lake, as well. He realized it was the scar-faced sergeant he'd yelled at over the M2 magazines six days and a lifetime ago. Looking back south, he saw, to his surprise and relief, that their helicopter had managed to land more or less intact among sharp blades of the elephant grass.

Jack turned back to Scar-face, pointed a thumb into his own chest, then pointed to the helicopter. Then he pointed at Scar-face and scanned the horizon with his rifle to indicate the FVA sergeant should cover him. Scar-face nodded, running out of the water to a bamboo copse, where he knelt and scanned the area with his rifle shouldered.

Cover set, Jack sprinted forward to the H-23's cockpit.

He was greeted with the muzzle of a Colt 1911 pistol in his face.

"Whoa, Doc!" Jack shouted. "Friendly!"

The lady doctor looked at him for a second, nodded and put down her weapon.

"Sorry, can't be too careful," she said. "Help me out of here, would you? My buckles are bent."

"Are you hurt?" Jack asked as he took out his bayonet and began sawing on her restraints.

"Bumps and bruises," she said, and Jack noted her French accent. Another expat like Rapicault. "My name is Durand."

"Jack Beasley, ma'am," Jack said.

Just as he severed the last restraint, Jack heard voices in French, followed by two gunshots.

"Into the grass," Jack hissed as he pulled Durand out of the cockpit. Smart woman, Durand did not question or complain, but followed him down into the dagger-sharp elephant grass. As he dove, a bright green grass blade ripped a gash across Jack's left forearm, leaving a bright trail of blood on his fatigues.

As he laid in the grass, barely daring to breath, the French voices became more distinct. Jack could make out one in particular:

*"Abandonnez-vous, Lieutenant Rapicault! Ne me force pas à te tuer, Pierre."*

———

Vanderburgh saw the man stumbling away from the burning wreckage of a helicopter and he knew. He *knew*. The man started to reach for an American Thompson sub-machine gun lying on the ground. Vanderburgh fired two shots into a bamboo tree a few feet away from the man.

"Surrender, Lieutenant Rapicault!" Vanderburgh shouted. When the man paused, he continued. "Don't make me kill you, Pierre."

Rapicault straightened, spared a glance for the three other men with Vanderburgh, then looked Vanderburgh in the eye.

"It's actually Captain, now, Jean-Baptiste," Rapicault said. "And congratulations on your promotion as well, Adjutant."

"Forgive me, sir," Vanderburgh said, suddenly furious with his old friend, a lieutenant he'd mentored from a teenager into an outstanding young officer. A friend who'd betrayed his country. "I had difficulty discerning your rank since you seem to be in the wrong uniform."

Rapicault snorted.

"Indeed," Rapicault said, glancing meaningfully at Vanderburgh's camouflage fatigues. "It was very reasonable of the Nazis to allow you to keep French rank insignia when they put you in their uniform. Then again, the Americans don't make me hand over children for them to gas or vivisect."

"Is that how you justify betraying your country to the Viet Minh?" Vanderburgh said, stepping closer to Rapicault, STG-46 trained on his chest. "American propaganda about the Jews?"

"It's not propaganda, Jean-Baptiste, and you know it. I would've happily died for France," Rapicault said, uncowed despite the automatic rifle leveled at him. "But I will kill every last one of you before I let the Reich have the world."

Vanderburgh's jaws clamped shut on his next words.

*There is no point to this. He is a prisoner of war, and we have fucked around long enough.*

"You won't be killing anyone, *Captain*," Vanderburgh said. "The war is over for you, Pierre. For what it's worth, I hope they treat you like an American POW, and don't hang you."

———

Jack risked whispering his plan in Durand's ear.

"I'm going to throw this grenade, pin still in it, and shout 'grenade,'" he said, voice barely a breath. "When they scatter, I will shoot any of them I see, you grab the captain, and start heading that way. Once you're back in the grass, low crawl. I'll cover you. Move out quick, because after the bluff, I'll be throwing the real thing."

She rolled slightly away from him, met his eyes and nodded. Her expression was stern, her gaze steady. He didn't know what had happened to make this woman born again hard, but he had no doubt he was dealing with someone just as accustomed to killing as himself.

He didn't have time to communicate with Scar-face, but he hoped the FVA sergeant would have the initiative to provide covering fire from the bamboo copse once the ruckus started and the marksmanship not to kill any friendlies while he was at it.

Jack risked another peek at the spot where Captain Rapicault stood, hands in the air, surrounded by a Frenchman and three native troops with weapons trained on him. From the prone, Jack tossed the grenade into their midst.

"GRENADE!" he screamed.

As he'd predicted, all five men scattered, diving for cover in different directions. He cranked off a shot at the Frenchman and missed as the big man circled behind a cypress tree trunk with surprising agility. He shifted fire and put a round through one of the native troop's neck, sending a spray of bright arterial blood into the air.

Durand closed the distance in two seconds. One commando was getting back to his feet, his STG-46 coming up to his shoulder. Durand, one hand on Rapicault's arm, leveled her .45 in her other hand and put a round right through that man's eye socket with a loud *CRACK*, emptying his cranial cavity onto the elephant grass behind him.

Rapicault quickly snatched the dead enemy's weapon and fired a few quick bursts, splintering bark off cypress trunks and kicking up great clods of dirt before turning and running alongside Durand south toward Jack's position.

Jack cranked off a few more shots to keep the enemy's heads down. From across the clearing, Scar-face's M2 joined the hail of gunfire, allowing Jack the chance to move south himself.

Regrouping in the grass, they systemized their retreat. Durand and one man at a time peeled back, with the other two men firing north to keep their pursuers honest. Durand argued that she should provide covering fire, too, but Rapicault quickly tore that argument apart.

"Doctor Durand, your courage is already beyond doubt," he said. "But given that you have only a pistol, and that a helicopter-flying surgeon is unquestionably more valuable to the war than three mere grunts, kindly do as I order you."

They ran and traded fire with their pursuers for agonizing minutes as elephant grass cut them, vines pulled at their feet and the persistent heat pulled life-sustaining water from their bodies at a frightening rate. Finally, as they cleared a rise, several blasts of machine-gun fire flew over their heads toward their pursuers.

Jack and his companions hit the ground.

*"Kết bạn sắp ra! Kết bạn sắp ra!"* Scar-face and Rapicault both shouted at the top of their lungs. The fire slackened long enough for the four of them to sprint into the midst of 2nd Company's defensive lines, and then the jungle erupted with carbine, rifle and machine-gun fire.

Despite its ordeal, 2nd Company still stood at more than three quarters its original strength combat-effective. Faced with such a force in good order on terrain of its choosing, the pursuing GCMA commandos chose the better part of valor and retired from the field. The sound of gunfire faded as the setting sun bathed the jungle in pink and orange light.

Rapicault's radio crackled to life. Jack was surprised to hear the same modulated southern voice that had coordinated the bombing runs with them. But he sounded worried, almost frightened rather than the calm, collected fighter ace.

"Angel Three-Five, Angel Three-Five, do you read? Margot? Do you read?"

Durand stood from where she'd been resting, stumbling over in her haste to reach the radio. Rapicault handed her the mic without comment.

"Benny, I'm all right," Margot said. "I'm walking out with the boys. I'll see you back home."

"Roger," Tiger Four, *Benny*, croaked. "Be safe."

"Whoever this Benny is," Rapicault said, grinning as he accepted the hand mic back. "He is a most fortunate man. I have never met anyone quite like you."

"Second that, Doc," Jack added.

"You are both too kind," she said, favoring them with a dazzling smile. "It has been quite the experience, but if you would be kind enough to escort me to the nearest airfield, I believe I have had enough of this infantry bullshit for one war."

Jack and Rapicault both laughed.

"Of course, *mademoiselle*," Rapicault said. "If you'll follow me, your airliner is just a few kilometers down this mountain."

The FVA base at Plei Mrong fell a week behind schedule, and only after the Americans airlifted most of the materiel out and the 112th Regiment escaped into the hinterlands with approximately seventy-five percent of its personnel strength. Already the armored force under de Castries was being slowed by anti-armor ambushes along Colonial Routes 14 and 19.

Thus, Adjutant Vanderburgh stepped into the Central Command headquarters with trepidation. As a warrant officer, he was normally far too junior to be the whipping boy for such a military setback. Protocol demanded a general, or at least a senior colonel take the fall for such a catastrophe. Given the importance of the GCMA's part in this operation, though, perhaps he was the sacrificial lamb this time.

The main operations center was a bustle of activity. Vanderburgh saw not just French and colonial officers and NCOs, but two Wehrmacht and one Luftwaffe officer meandering through the operations center, offering comment on occasion, but mostly radiating smug superiority to their French "allies."

Asking one of the French staff NCOs for directions, Vanderburgh was gestured to a quiet corner of the operations center. Vanderburgh was surprised to see General Trinquier, the commander of all GCMA forces in Indochina, waiting for him there. Trinquier was a tall man with close-cropped gray hair, overly prominent and pointed ears, and a hard-edged face.

Young for his rank at forty-two, Trinquier's theories on how to deal with guerilla and terrorist forces were in vogue, not just in the French Army but in the upper echelons of the Greater Reich itself. Additionally, unlike many of France's effective combat commanders, Roger Trinquier was unsullied by any association with de Gaulle whatsoever. Vanderburgh had served under Trinquier in some capacity for a large chunk of his career, first in Algeria, then in Indochina both before and after World War II.

"Sir," Vanderburgh saluted crisply. "Adjutant Vanderburgh, reporting as ordered."

Trinquier returned the salute casually.

"Hello, Jean-Baptiste," Trinquier said. "I've heard from the regular Army. Now I want your thoughts on the operation."

Vanderburgh spent the next hour recounting his part in the mission. Trinquier interrupted rarely, only asking a few questions for the sake of clarity. When Vanderburgh finished, Trinquier stood quiet and still for a full minute.

"I am convinced you did as well as anyone in your position could have done, Adjutant," Trinquier said. "You will retain command of your GCMA battalion."

"Thank you, sir."

Trinquier nodded. Another silence ensued for several seconds, then Trinquier shook his head sadly.

"He really was such a promising young officer," Trinquier said. "If it were not you reporting it, I could not bring myself to believe he had turned coat."

There was no need to clarify who "he" was. Vanderburgh's glance flicked to the three Germans taking up space in a French Army operations center. Days of prolonged battle and exhaustion loosened his tongue.

"Who hasn't these days?"

Trinquier's eyes snapped over to Vanderburgh, then to the Germans, then back to Vanderburgh.

"Ours isn't to set policy, Adjutant," Trinquier said, his voice low and furious. "We are sworn to obedience. Dislike of our allies is no excuse for treason."

Vanderburgh stiffened to attention.

"Of course not, sir," Vanderburgh said.

Trinquier glared at him for another long moment, then turned and walked away.

"Return to your command, Vanderburgh," Trinquier said without looking back.

Vanderburgh exhaled and made his retreat from the operations center with all possible haste, his mind churning.

*No excuse at all, sir. Then again, if there's an excuse for any of us, it's lost on me.*

## THE END

# LEGATE GUDERIAN STANDS ON THE CREST OF THE HILL

## Philip Wohlrab

*SARMATIAN PLAINS*

*JUNE 1, 1330 HOURS*

Legate Guderian didn't actually stand on the crest of the hill; such action would have invited a Sarmatian, or possibly Abbasid, sniper to take a shot at him. Either was a real possibility, given what he was looking at. On the plain below was the better part of an Abbasid armor regiment moving slowly across the open country.

"Do you see that, Erich? They aren't ready for us," Guderian snorted.

"*Ja*, boss, they are in for a surprise today!" replied a rather young-looking Optio Erich Kuhn. He was Legate Guderian's aide, and while young for the rank, he showed the makings of being a good officer.

"Where is their air support, I wonder, and why haven't they deployed it here? Are they that overconfident? Perhaps they are relying on those fucking pagans down there to tell them where we are? Fucking Sarmatians devils."

The comments was somewhat heated from Legate Guderian, for he hated the Sarmatians, and with good cause, too. As a young Optio, or company commander in the Equites, he had been blooded in the guerilla skirmishes with the Sarmatian pagan tribes that acted as a buffer between Roman Magna Germania and Abbasid-controlled Scythia. Now, as a field commander with an entire combined arms Legion at his command, he had more than enough to do something about that hatred.

Guderian looked back down the hillside at his tanks, a cataphract each of *Chariot IIIs* and the much larger *Chariot VIs*. He also had a Triari of mechanized infantry, which amounted to three companies with around 30 vehicles. The rest of his legion was further back on the other side of the ridges that separated this small valley and the plains below. Wheels turned in his head as he considered the odds. The *Chariot IIIs* he had with him only had a 90mm gun, but they had the ability to fire the new *Pilum* anti-tank missile as well. The *Chariot VIs* had 125mm guns and were armored to boot, an assault tank designed to be thrown into the breach of an armored breakthrough the Abbasid had yet to develop a counterpart for. At first unofficially, it had been called *Aurelian* by its crews, after one of Rome's greatest Emperors, but the name stuck and was now officially recognized.

Below in the valley, though, was the better part of six companies of tanks and another six to eight of infantry. He counted 60 tanks and what looked like 70 light APCs.

"This is too much for what we have here, Erich. Cornicen Engel, call up our artillery and air support—we are going to fire up that column."

"*Ja*, sir," replied Cornicen Engel. "Ballistae 6, Felix 6, prepare fire mission, how copy?"

Guderian tuned out the radio chatter from his cornicen behind him and turned his attention back to the armor column. *Where is their air support? Their scouts? It isn't like the damn Sids to be this incompetent.*


*SARMATIAN PLAINS*
*JUNE 1, 1335 HOURS*


Moqaddam Abdul ibn al-Walid was not a happy camper. The battalion commander kept nervously glancing at the ridge line to his west and then back up towards the front of the column, at that idiot Aqeed Mujahid ibn Faisal al-Saud. Bad enough that he got saddled with a political commander, but this guy was as dumb as a box of rocks. How Liwa Wassel tolerated the man, Walid had no idea, let alone gave him a brigade command.

"Moqaddam, this damn *ibn il-wisxa* has no idea what he is doing, does he?" asked a rather plaintive Areef Hammad.

"I don't care if Aqeed Saud is the son of a filthy woman, Areef. You will not use that language about our illustrious commander again."

The sarcasm of the reply was not lost on the areef.

"Seriously, though, sir, I am watching that ridge line through the sights and I am pretty damn sure we are being watched."

"I know, but there isn't a whole lot I can do while the aqeed is in charge. Keep an eye out, though. I don't trust these *hayawanaat* Sarmatians. That bastard leader of theirs was just a little too complacent about whether or not a Roman force was nearby."

At about that moment, things started going truly bad. Moqaddam Walid's tank was halfway down the column, and at first, he didn't hear the screaming of the incoming shells. However, he did see the great gouts of earth that signified large shell impacts. He didn't wait for the sounds to hit: he dropped down into his seat and slammed his commander's hatch. His tank lurched to the side from a nearby impact.

"Jundi Rahman, hard right and get us out of here!"

Jundi Rahman, the driver, cranked his steering column to the right and pushed his acceleration for all the *Saladin* was worth. Through his driver's periscope, he saw the *Saladin* in front of his explode from a direct hit. Rahman's friend Jundi Ayub was the driver of that track, and they had both just finisher tanker school together before joining the unit. He said a quick prayer to Allah for Ayub and one for himself, as well. Whatever the Romans were dropping on them, it was heavy stuff. He continued to scan out of his periscope, looking for terrain that he could put between his tank and the ridgeline above.

*Where there is artillery, there are almost certainly* Roman *bastards with something that can capitalize on the confusion it is causing*, he thought, *and I don't feel like stopping a tank round today.*

The gunner, Areef Hammad, traversed the turret so that it was facing the ridgeline. Shouting a warning, the noncom fired the HE shell that was in the *Saladin*'s 105mm breech. The shot was more in frustration than in any hope of hitting a useful target, but it would hopefully start to suppress what was calling for the indirect fire. The moqaddam was busy at the moment, passing orders to the column. Aqeed Saud wasn't saying anything over the radio. Jundi Rahman hoped that the son of a whore was dead, but he wasn't giving all that much thought to that particular problem at the moment. Another HE round went out as Hammad continued to fire up the ridgeline, his example being followed by other *Saladins*.

Moqaddam Walid knew that the chances any of his tanks hitting anything was about zilch, but it gave his gunners and loaders something to do other than concentrate on being shelled silly. That bastard Saud's tank wasn't hit; he could see it with its jaunty guidon whipping furiously as his tank maneuvered. But Saud wasn't doing anything to direct his Muaqddimah, either, and that wasn't good. Was the man dead and his tank still alive? Walid finally saw what he was looking for: observers on the hillside must have got careless because he could see something manmade sticking up over that ridgeline.

"Gunner, HE, vehicle, left 40 degrees," Walid said quickly.

As Hammad traversed the turret, the gunner peered through his sights to look at what Walid had seen. To their horror, they spotted a flash of flame and smoke spout from the ridgeline, followed by others. What he was seeing was the *Chariot IIIs'* box launchers firing their *Pilum* missiles down into the broken column of tanks and APCs. More flashes followed, and Hammad identified a target.

"TANK! RANGE 1100, FIRE! FUCK LOAD SABOT!" Hammad shouted, his voice panicked.

Hammad's first round had impacted below the *Chariot III* on the ridge itself, and he began to elevate his gun as the loader placed a sharp-tipped sabot in the breech. Before the gunner could squeeze his trigger, there was a tremendous crashing sound and impact that threw him forward into his gunner's console. Hammad's world went black for a moment...and when he came back around, he could smell smoke, hear screaming, and see nothing thanks to a steadily pulsing scalp wound.

*Oh Allah, I am hit*, he thought woozily. *We are burning.*

Hammad wiped his face trying to clear the blood out of his eyes. He could feel heat now coming from behind him, and turned to see Moqaddam Walid scrambling through the commander's hatch. To his left, the loader, Jundi Baten, was going nowhere due to the jagged piece of steel embedded into his back. Hammad kicked free of his station, turned to grab the commander's seat, and began to climb up towards the hatch when there was another violent lurch and everything went black.

*Sarmatian Plains*
*1 June, 1346 hours*

The *Chariot VI* was a monster of a tank. It was designed to be thrown into the most violent of conflicts, with its thick armored hide and 125mm main gun. It was also cutting-edge technology for the Roman military and something that the Abbasids had yet to encounter on the battlefield. That Guderian's Limitanei Legion had been issued *Aurelians* spoke to the high confidence Rome had in him as a legion commander. Most Limitanei used older equipment, as the most advanced stuff was usually reserved for the Roman Legions proper: those recruited from Rome, Italia, Gaul, and Iberia. The legions recruited from Britannia, Lesser Germania, Magna Germania, and the Roman colonies across the Atlantic formed the Limitanei, or frontier legions, and were seen by many as second-rate troops, while in reality they tended to be far better than most troops they would likely be asked to fight.

Optio Fritz Lang was in his element. Looking down his sights, he had just plugged a command *Saladin*, obvious with their extra radio antenna and striped paint jobs. As he scanned down the column of tracked vehicles, he could see many burning from hits from the artillery—mainly the light-skinned APCs, as they were really not much more than battle taxis and had no business being in an engagement with enemy tanks.

Lang spotted another command tank, this one with a silly guidon with a lion on it. He lased the target with his range finder, then arranged the *Aurelian's* sights. Again, the big 125mm gun spoke and another command *Saladin* blew apart. Unlike the last one, where at least the track commander appeared to make it out, this one blew apart with no survivors.

"Good job, Lang, keep hunting the command tracks." This came from the track commander, Centurion Wulf. "Heydrich, move to the left 10 meters. Keep those Sids guessing where we are."

"*Ja*, sir."

Centurion Wulf had his head up out of the commander's hatch so that he could get a better look at the battle that was unfolding before him. His *Aurelian* was shooting and moving from a reverse slope onto an enemy that couldn't easily get back at his or the other tanks in Guderian's forward element. Even though it wasn't easy, that didn't mean it wasn't impossible, as two burning *Chariot IIIs* were showing. They had to expose more of themselves to fire their missiles. Their 90mm guns were also having a harder time getting through the *Saladin's* armor.

In the valley below, fires were burning from multiple destroyed vehicles. A pair of Roman *Tiger* fighter bombers screamed through the valley, strafing the enemy tanks and APCs. As they flew over the column, they began to disgorge bomblets from their bomb dispensers while also dropping a couple of canisters of napalm. The jellied gasoline didn't do much to the *Saladin*s or even the APCs, but the men that had poured from the broken vehicles were caught in the open by it. Their shrieks of horror were thankfully masked by the noise of battle. The bomblets, on the other hand, exploded over the column, shredding thin topside armor and blowing off tracks.

*SARMATIAN PLAINS*
*JUNE 1, 1428 HOURS*

Moqaddam Walid had no idea how he'd managed to survive that bombing run by those damned Roman fighters. Surely Allah was with him. He had managed to scramble up on top of one of the few command *Gamals* still left. The *Gamal* being the standard APC for the Abbasid army, this version had a higher rear deck to allow for the extra command and control equipment needed for a mobile HQ. The most important thing from Walid's perspective was radios.

"Call back to the Qalb, inform them that we have engaged the enemy, give them our coordinates, tell them I am attempting to break contact and retreat back to the main column," ordered Walid.

The radioman on the *Gamal* immediately complied with Walid's command and radioed back to the Qalb. Walid ordered the second one on the tactical net to issue the command to the surviving members of the Muqaddimah to withdraw. He didn't know what the butcher's bill was yet, but he knew it was going to be bad. At least that idiot al-Saud had managed to get himself killed; too bad about his crew, but *inshallah*. He also took comfort in that his command, now that al-Saud was dead, hadn't gone to death alone.

Looking back at the ridgeline, he could see fires from at least a half dozen or so enemy machines rising to the sky, flickering their souls to the wind.

*SCYTHIAN BORDER*
*JUNE 2, 0106 HOURS*

Liwa Dawud ibn Adnan al Wassel watched dispassionately as the battered remnants of the Muqaddimah, or lead element, returned to the staging areas of the Qalb. A tall man, he was the scion of an Egyptian military family and his features marked him as coming from nobility of a sort. His uniform wasn't immaculate, but instead denoted that he was a general officer who valued comfortable utility over impractical finery.

He sighed and considered his options. Clearly, the Muqaddimah had done its job in one respect and that was to confirm that there was indeed a Roman force nearby, but just as clearly, it was a powerful one based on what had happened to al-Saud's command. The Muqaddimah had left the staging ground with 130 vehicles and nearly 900 men; what limped back in was barely 75 vehicles, many showing battle damage, and Allah knew how many men. Wassel reflected that it was a poor showing for his force to be badly bloodied so early in the battle. There was a silver lining, though: based on reports, he knew that al-Saud was dead and that Moqaddam Walid was now commander of his Muqaddimah. *Allah's ways are mysterious indeed.*

The wind was blowing a steady 20 knots over the area as Moqaddam Walid strode over to Liwa Wassel. Even though it was the middle of the night, the staging area was alight with activity as the entire Qalb appeared to be readying itself to move. Walid knew that the poor showing of the Muqaddimah was not his fault, but he still felt shame that it had been caught so flat-footed. He was prepared for the epic tongue-lashing that he was sure was in his future as he walked up to his commander.

The liwa had very cold grey eyes, and Walid was sure the man was looking straight into his soul. Then something changed. The coldness left the liwa's eyes, and Wassel smiled at Walid.

"Moqaddam Walid, I don't know how you managed to make it back with so many of your troops alive," said Wassel, "but I am glad that Allah has seen fit to end the miserable existence of that *wisix* Saud."

"Thank you, liwa," replied an exhausted Walid.

"Reorganize your men and units. We will be pushing out to strike back, and your units will make up the al-Khalf for now. Once we get replacements for your losses, I will push them back up to their rightful place in the vanguard of the Qalb."

"Liwa, I feel that we were betrayed by our Sarmatian *tali'ah*. I want their leader, and his troops, heads on pikes."

"Moqaddam, it is already done." The coldness had returned to the liwa's eyes as he said this.

*Sarmatian Plains*
*June 2, 0745 hours*

Legate Guderian removed his crush cap and ran his fingers through his thinning hair. The greasy feeling reminded him that it had been some time since he had had a proper shower. He chuckled ruefully to himself.

*What was that bastard Wassel up to?*

Guderian's intelligence had managed to identify the enemy commander and provide him with his opponent's dossier.

*This next phase of the battle will not be the walkover as the last one*, he thought.

Liwa Wassel's record was impressive, and it showed that he had a degree of competence that far too many of the Caliphate's officers were known for. Unlike Guderian, Wassel had attended the premier schools for the Caliphate; he was a graduate of their military academy in Cairo. Guderian had been trained in the best schools of Magna Germania and attended the military school of Heidelberg. Even though it was considered a second-class school compared to the military academy at Arretium in Italia proper...

To punctuate Guderian's musings, a score of enemy fighters screamed towards his command. He had moved his entire force into prepared positions so that he could cover the plains below. Missiles lifted off from Guderian's rear, streaking out to strike at the enemy fighters, their vapor trails billowing out on this warm morning. The enemy fighters reacted by jinking into evasive maneuvers and dropping flares. They were low to the ground and went from being mere specks on the horizon to distinct silhouettes as they came closer. One was smashed from the sky by a missile while the others unleashed a barrage of rockets towards Guderian's tank positions.

"GOTT IN HIMMEL," shouted Guderian as three of his tanks blew apart from direct hits.

The aircraft were not done, though; they closed even further to open up with their guns. That proved to be more of their undoing. A score of shoulder-launched SAMs rose up from the ranks of the infantry, and a pair of Scorpio anti-aircraft tanks opened up with their quad 40mm guns. Five more of the Abbasid aircraft joined their companion in death as SAMs and AA fire plucked them from the sky. The surviving fighters wheeled away, streaking back toward Abbasid territory.

Guderian knew that what had just transpired was likely not the best of things to happen. The enemy knew his position now, while he could only guess where their main force was. He had sent out scouting formations, but none of the light vehicles had reported back in. Turning to his cornicen, he ordered up his frontal aviation commander to get not only some air cover, but also to throw some aircraft forward to find the enemy main body.

*Sarmatian Plains*
*June 2, 1137 hours*

The Qalb had been moving in lines all morning. They knew where their enemy was, and their aviation units had been hitting it nearly continuously since 0900. But that was proving to be an expensive proposition, as many of the aircraft were failing to return.

*Who knew that shoulder-launched SAMs would be that effective on low-flying aircraft?* mused the Liwa.

Worse were that the Romans had managed to get up a combat air patrol, which meant that more of the Abbasid aircraft had to be outfitted for air-to-air rather than air-to-ground. Liwa Wassel made a mental note to himself that next time they needed to bring up more of their dedicated strike aircraft like the *Saqr*. Given the depth of the air defense, he was considering whether or not to send the helicopters forward. The advantage would be to get his air mobile troops on the ground and engaging the enemy. While not an armor force, the infantry had antitank weapons and could be used to pin the enemy in place. It would also provide him with forward air controllers and artillery spotters. While his fighters were giving him a solid idea of where the enemy was, they couldn't loiter to call for fire, as any that had tried were shot from the sky or had been cleared away by enemy fighters.

But if he could throw all of his aviation units forward at once, it may provide cover for the air mobile troops to get in and on the ground. It was an untried concept and the Mosheer's general staff were curious to see the capabilities of air mobile troops in a conventional war. The last time Rome and the Caliphate had seriously clashed, airplanes had been at the level of canvas and wood, firing antique machine guns at each other. Helicopters had proven themselves tremendously useful, though, in running down Mongol and Hindu insurgents.

*No foot or vehicle traffic can move as fast as their rotors*, he thought. *Chase with one force, drop the other in front, and suddenly the problems are permanently solved. But how well will they do in an air environment like the one developing up ahead?*

He took a swig of water from his canteen as he regarded his ground columns.

*Well, nothing ventured, nothing gained.*

"Order the *Tulay'a mutaharikkah* forward and Allah go with them."

*ABOVE SARMATIAN PLAINS*
*JUNE 2, 1214 HOURS*

Titus Suetonius couldn't believe his eyes. He and his formation of fighters were tasked with watching for strike aircraft while the rest of their air cohort was busy mixing it up in the largest furball since the Great War nearly 60 years earlier.

On the one hand, Titus was pissed that he wasn't in the middle of that fight; on the other, though, he realized that his *Tiger* was no match for the Abbasid *Nasrs* that were out there. Instead, air-to-air combat was left to the *Ospreys*, which were designed for it. But the target below him was a new one: dozens of helicopters were advancing toward Guderian's lines, but were still some distance off. They were flying low to the ground, as well, to avoid SAMs and AAA fire.

*What are they doing?* They didn't appear to be armed with anything significant: door guns and a couple that mounted guns and rocket pods on stubby wings.

*Well, whatever, time to kill them*, thought Suetonius.

"Felix 6 to all Felix elements: target those things and shoot them down."

It was a slaughter in the first pass. The ten Roman fighter bombers streaked over the helicopters, engaging them with cannon that shredded the bulbous fragile machines. Men screamed in terror as they were torn apart or flung burning from crashing machines.

*We don't have enough planes to kill them all*, he thought. The glint of sunlight on canopies caused him to glance upwards. Several descending dots foretold nothing good.

*The ground boys will have to deal with the helicopters*, he thought, bringing his nose around to face the oncoming *Nasrs*. *We've now got our own problems.*

As the helicopters came into their landing zones, or LZs, they didn't bother to touch the ground fully. Instead, the troops jumped from the aircraft, and as the aircraft finished disgorging its troops and supplies, it wheeled away from the LZ and headed away from the main fighting. None of the gunships that were sent in with the troop helicopters managed to survive, though, for as soon as they revealed themselves for what they were, they were brought down in a hail of fire from the enemy lines.

Neither the commander nor the second-in-command of the *Tulay'a mutaharikkah* had survived the initial landing. Instead, command had devolved down to his senior Rijal company commander. None of the five companies of the *Tulay'a mutaharikkah* were fully intact; yet, enough of a force had made it onto the ground to still remain coherent. Naqeeb Karim could see his raqeebs and areefs gathering up and organizing troops into fire teams, squads, and platoons, while his molazims began to direct fire at enemy positions. Light though that fire might have been, his forward observers that had survived were also on their radios and calling for artillery support on specific locations. They were far enough back that the only Roman weapons they had to fear were artillery, but close enough to reach out with their antitank missiles to try and strike at targets with them.

*We should advance*, Karim thought briefly. A sudden barrage of Roman mortars and some disturbingly accurate tank fire convinced him this would be suicide.

*We need armor support*, Karim thought. *I can't attack advance against tanks, even with the missiles in support.* The whole plan had been suicidal, he realized.

*If we survive, we are going to have to rewrite the doctrine for air assault*, Karim thought, wincing as a nearby missile team was savaged by a bursting tank shell. *A new chapter on* advancing *into a set piece battle.* The naqeeb ruefully chuckled to himself at the realization his name would probably be in the history books.

*I will have to try and unfuck this cluster*, he thought, ducking as more Roman mortars exploded around him. *By Allah, it will be an* honorable *mention.*

Many kilometers away, Liwa Wassel realized that he had made a mistake in sending his air mobile forces that far forward. As the reports came in, the division commander nodded at Karim's attempts to salvage *something* from the chaos.

*I am going to put Naqeeb Karim in for the Order of the Star of Abbasid*, Wassel thought. *And a promotion, whether he survives or not.*

Looking at the map and his available assets, Wassel nodded.

*Allah willing the man* will *survive*, Wassel thought. *The* Tulay'a mutaharikkah *is serving its purpose of disrupting the Romans and giving us eyes forward.* Already, his artillery's launchers were busy sending scores of rockets at the enemy's rear and reserves while his mobile guns were getting the range of the Roman lines.

*Time for those bastards to bleed,* thought Wassel.


*Sarmatian Plains*
*June 2, 1245 hours*


Gouts of flame and earth sprang up all along Guderian's lines. He saw dozens of fires from burning vehicles, and the hostile troops that were forward of his lines were sniping his tanks with shoulder-launched antitank missiles with varying degrees of success.

*This is untenable,* Guderian thought.

"Cornicen, call for counterbattery fire on those rocket positions and get some additional mortars on that infantry forward," Guderian barked. "We need to keep their heads down."

"*Jawohl,* sir."

"Erich, head over to 6th cohort and have them roust out that infantry."

"*Ja,* sir," replied Kuhn, grabbing his weapon and jogging off down a communications trench towards the 6th cohort. Bringing up his binoculars, Guderian rapidly barked commands for his tanks to prepare to meet the enemy. Even now, he could see the dust clouds marking the enemy column. Overhead, a fierce air battle still raged between Roman and Abbasid air forces. Mixed in with those sounds, a new sound emerged from behind Guderian as large guns and rocket batteries from behind the ridgeline to the west of him opened up their own fire. Nearby, the *crump* of mortars let him know that the infantry to the front of him was about to have a hot time of it.


Naqeeb Karim knew they were done for. He was picked up and thrown to the ground by another mortar blast, and now his troops were being engaged by light and medium machine gun fire from advancing Roman infantry His men were fighting back as best they could, but there were not enough of the *Tulay'a mutaharikkah* left to fight off an entire cohort of Roman infantry. Wassel's armor column was still miles away from him and, based on the overhead noise from Roman artillery, it was about to slow down even further. He picked himself up and turned to give an order to his radioman, only to find the poor man facedown, radio smoking, and in a pool of his own blood. The mortar round that had thrown Karim to the ground had blown splinters of metal through the poor enlisted man. Karim looked around and found a young rifleman nearby him, the man's eyes wide as he took in the surrounding battle. Reaching over, Karim shook the young man.

"Go find me Raqeeb Awal Latif. Do you understand me jundi?"

"Yes, sir, right away, sir." The young jundi ran off in the direction that the raqeeb awal had last been seen in.

Naqeeb Karim issued orders to the soldiers around him to begin a bounding retreat back. Word quickly spread down the lines of the air mobile force that it was time to pull back. Karim's heart swelled with pride to see his men maintain their discipline. Despite their losses, they didn't break and run. Instead, they maintained fire on the approaching infantry as they bounded back. The raqeeb awal found Naqeeb Karim with a squad of soldiers, who were manning a medium machine gun.

"Sir, you sent for me?"

"Yes, Latif. We have begun to fall back, but I want to lay some surprises for the Romans. Have our engineers scatter mines on our back trail. That should slow them down long enough for us to get away," replied Karim.

"Yes, sir, I will see to it," replied Raqeeb Awal Latif. The raqeeb awal was the senior noncommissioned officer of the battalion; a fearsome man in his mid-forties, he had a meticulously groomed mustache and an upright bearing. His very presence was a steadying influence and he used it to good advantage. He scrounged up the *Tulay'a mutaharikkah's* engineers, and they began their business of scattering mines as the rest of the force laid down covering fire. They knew that the Romans could see what they were doing and many of the engineers were killed as the Romans engaged them with heavy fire, but the Roman troops also slowed to a snail's pace for fear of running headlong into a minefield.

The artillery duel was in full swing now, with both sides' mobile guns and launchers firing, then moving to avoid counterbattery fire. This slackened the pace at which they could fire, as moving took time. It was the mobile rocket launchers which proved to be the greatest killers of artillery, as both sides' weapons possessed the range to strike near and deep targets. Everything from mobile forces to opposing artillery parks felt the sudden, violent lash of multiple rocket launcher volleys. For their part, mobile guns, desperately trying to avoid succumbing to these hammer blows, concentrated their fire on decimating the opposing side's maneuver forces. Despite superior Abbasid numbers, it was a near-run thing, and it quickly became apparent to both commanders that the matter would be decided by direct fire.

Liwa Wassel gave the order to move from tactical columns to lines by units. They were getting close to the enemy lines and he knew that the real battle was about to begin. He rode in the commander's hatch of a *Saladin II*, the newest tank model of the Abbasid Caliphate. It was an improved *Saladin* with better armor, better optics, and a more advanced 120mm main gun. Around him, he saw his Qalb shake out into an armor wedge with which to break the Roman forces ahead. He had hoped they would have been flushed from their prepared positions by his artillery, but that hadn't happened. However, he did see dozens of smoke piles that indicated destroyed enemy vehicles.

*Our losses, while not pleasant, were definitely lighter in comparison to theirs*, Wassel thought. *Time to finish this.*

As the guns of his Qalb opened up on the Roman lines, Wassel squatted down in the hatch to make himself a smaller target. Briefly, he considered fully buttoning up the tank, then gritted his teeth and decided against it. The extra protection was not worth losing an unobstructed view of the battle.

*If Allah wills me dead, so be it.*

The Qalb was in its element; the field was about as near-perfect for armored warfare as any armor unit could ask for. The APCs carrying their infantry had slammed to a stop once they started taking hits from tank fire and disgorged their infantry squads. Those men then began to bound forward from pieces of cover to other pieces of cover or concealment. The infantry wasn't as close as they wanted to be. However, it was far better to take their chances on foot rather than be caught in an APC and torched by the squad. Some men carried rocket-propelled grenades (RPGs), and they would lift their tubes to their shoulders and squeeze off a rocket at an enemy vehicle as they closed. This often as not invited back a storm of fire from heavy machineguns or tank fire. All around there was fire, smoke, the sounds of rapid fire, and the screams of dying men.

Liwa Wassel could smell burning vehicles, and worse, burning men. It was a distinctive scent of burning metal, plastics, oil, diesel, and overdone pork. It was the stench of a modern battlefield, almost as disturbing as the constant racket. The latter was only slightly abated by the noise-cancelling headset he wore over his ears so that he could communicate. He felt the overpressure ripple through him as his gunner fired the main gun of his *Saladin II*. Giving a moment to see where the shot went, he saw a Roman tank turret lift into the air as the vehicle blew up.

"Good shooting, Raqeeb Mohamed!"

"Thank you, sir."

Liwa Wassel was now participating in the largest armor action since the Great War. Truth to tell, he realized he had more tanks in this one place than they had ever had in all the units of the Great War. The machines fighting today bore only superficial resemblance to those vehicles, with almost as broad a technological gap as muskets and modern rifles. Great War AFVs had been slow, with weapons so inaccurate the crew had to be damn near on top of their targets in order to hit them. By comparison, his *Saladins* were fast, nimble, and could reach out and hit a target at a distance of over a mile while on the move.

Again, Raqeeb Mohamad found a target with his gun and another Roman machine brewed up into flame and smoke. Wassel stood a little higher in his hatch, straining to see over the *Saladin* to his left. He had just brought up his binoculars when the accompanying vehicle blew apart. The concussion bounced Wassel off his hatch coaming, and he fell limply down into the turret, bleeding from his ears and nose. Wassel had not time to realize what had happened before losing consciousness.

"THE LIWA HAS BEEN HIT!" Raqeeb Mohamad yelled into the tank's radio set, and the driver, Areef Rahman, moved the tank into a patch of ground where it was hull down and brought the tank to a halt. The crew in the turret began to tend to the liwa, trying to get him to come around. Meanwhile, the Qalb continued on into battle, unaware that its leader was out of the fight for the moment.


*SARMATIAN PLAINS*
*JUNE 2, 1638 HOURS*


Legate Guderian was in the commander's hatch of his *Aureilian* now. All around him, his Legion, Limitanei though they were, fought like demons. The Romans proper may not think much of them, but here on the frontier of their empire, his Germans were doing their level best to turn back an Abbasid assault. He barked out orders to his legion as the battle was fully involved now. Each side's forces were now so close to each other that their respective artilleries had ceased firing at them and were instead concentrating on killing each other or tearing up their lines of supply.

Guderian issued orders for the 11th and 14th cohorts to slide to the right side of the Abbasid formation. Something was up over there, and Guderian couldn't exactly put his finger on it. Looking at the formations of the enemy Qalb, he could see there was still command and control of the various units, but it seemed to be lacking control between the units, as if each one was fighting on its own rather than as a unified effort. The 11th and 14th cohorts were outfitted with *Chariot III*s, and while their guns were having some trouble getting through the front armor of the *Saladin*s, they would penetrate the side armor. Their *Pilum* missiles could also prove to be decisive, given broadside shots on enemy tanks.

The two cohorts managed to disengage themselves from the front, but it was slow going. It took a long five minutes before they began to work their way around to the right flank of the enemy formation. Several Abbasid units opposite the two shifting cohorts noticed what they were doing and began to shift in a haphazard manner.

*What is wrong with them?* Guderian thought, noticing that the units nearest to the emerging Roman threat actually weren't responding.

*Are they so concentrated on his cohorts of Aurelians that they couldn't see the threat coming around on their flank?* Guderian wondered, watching as a volley of 125mm fire killed or damaged several *Saladin*s. *Well, their loss...*

The two cohorts of *Chariot III*s were no longer at full strength. From their original strength of 100 vehicles between them, they only had 73 vehicles left. Still, they managed to hit the Qalb from its right flank and, in at least some cases, the rear. Dozens of *Saladin*s blew up as *Pilum* missiles struck their vulnerable sides or rear decks. The battalion of armor that made up the Qalb's right flank was effectively destroyed under the combined weight of fire from the two cohorts. It died hard in that five minutes, taking a score of Roman machines with it, but it still ceased to exist under the Roman charge The *Rijal* companies of the Qalb on that flank wheeled to meet the threat of the twin cohorts, but found itself in an untenable position of being flanked on three sides by armor and infantry.

*That went better than expected,* Guderian thought, glancing in astonishment at his watch. It had been less than an hour since the main engagement started, and now he had a chance to drive the Qalb back out of the Sarmatian border region, if not destroy it altogether. He ordered his legion to charge into the broken Qalb and destroy it. *Aurelians* took the lead in this, exploiting the gaps made in the Qalb by the disintegration of its right flank. The heavy tanks shrugged off the 105mm shells of the *Saladins* while punching them out with their 125mm guns. Occasionally, one would meet a *Saladin* II and would lose the bout, but those losses were negligible. *Chariot IVs* followed in their wake, and the battle between tanks was on more equal terms there.

The *Chariot IV* was in every way comparable to a *Saladin*, to include using the same caliber main guns. The *Chariot IIIs* used their advantage of speed to get through the broken enemy formation to fall on the infantry carriers and support tracks. The battle turned from a massacre to a rout, as individual units of the Qalb fell out of formation and turned for the border.

*Only to the border*, thought Guderian. *I have no orders to go over the border in this situation, and perhaps our governments will turn off this madness before it becomes another Great War.*

*SARMATIAN PLAINS*
*JUNE 2, 1831 HOURS*

Liwa Wassel hurt all over. He was coming out of the blackness of unconsciousness and into the full awareness of the horror that had taken hold. He could feel his tank bouncing along at full speed.

"What happened?" croaked Wassel.

"You were knocked unconscious when Naqeeb Qasim's track blew up, sir," replied Raqeed Mohamad. "I don't know what happened in the larger fight, sir. One minute, we were blowing up those *xawalaat* Romans, and then the right flank just disintegrated. The Romans hit us hard when the right flank came apart, and now we are running for the border."

"Who is in command?" asked Wassel.

"No one, sir," answered Mohamad.

"Right, well...we need to get this sorted out. I will be damned for an *ibn il'ahba* before I see my command destroyed!"

Wassel lifted his head and torso up out of the commander's hatch to look around as his tank bounced along. He could see the remnants of the Qalb were in full retreat. Every now and again, one of the *Saladins* would fire to the rear, but most just drove on towards the border.

He picked up his radio handset, and looking around, he spotted one of his battalion commanders' tanks. He called to that man and issued instructions for him to get his unit back under control. Wassel repeated the process for the other battalion commanders or senior surviving officers. His calm orders, issued in a stern but reassuring voice, began to take effect as he saw the individual units begin to shake down in what looked like organized formations as opposed to disjointed rabble. Next, he got on the Qalb command net and called up Moqaddam Walid, who now commanded his rear guard.

"Walid, I need you to form a line across our axis of retreat. Punch the Romans in the nose so that I can once again shake us down into a battle formation," ordered Wassel.

"Roger, sir," replied Walid.

Walid's unit was some miles to the rear of Wassel's force as a blocking element to keep the back door open, should a disaster occur. Wassel had thought ahead and arranged for this, a "just in case." Now he was thanking Allah for granting him the foresight to do so. Fortunately, it appeared that the Romans had used up all of their air support for now, because none of it was falling on his forces at the moment. Nor was their artillery, but that was probably because of the fluidity of the situation, and again he thanked Allah for small mercies.

Raqeeb Mohamad had the turret traversed to the rear and was taking shots at the enemy as he could, but the range was extremely long, over a mile at this point. The shots were either falling short or going wide as the ballistic computer couldn't keep up with the rapid movement and the extreme range. Wassel watched as gouts of flame and earth erupted around the Roman formations. Apparently Walid had ordered an artillery strike on Wassel's back trail to slow the Roman forces even more.

*Thank Allah for good subordinate commanders...*

*SARMATIAN/SCYTHIAN BORDER*
*JUNE 2, 1927 HOURS*

Guderian knew that the battle was over. The two forces had mauled each other badly in that final exchange a few miles back. The Sids had a rear guard that was waiting for him and had given their Qalb enough time to turn back around into a fighting formation. This, in turn, had allowed them to retreat back across the border in good order. The Sarmatian plains were littered with the detritus of war: burned-out tanks, helicopters, jets, and dead bodies laid where they fell. The enemy commander had arranged a flag of truce, and the two men got a chance to look each other over in the flesh.

Before Legate Guderian was a tall lean man, his olive complexion turned somewhat darker from years of exposure to the sun. In contrast, to this tall Arab, Guderian was of average height; his thinning hair had turned grey, as had his bushy mustache. The two men eyed each other with frank curiosity.

"I would like to arrange for the burial of my dead, as I do not wish to see them left on the plains to be eaten by vultures," said Wassel in a smooth cultured baritone. "It would be unseemly."

Guderian cleared his throat before replying, mainly to give himself a moment to think. While there was an enmity between the two forces, it was a professional one. it wasn't seen as personal by either side. They were soldiers doing their duties to their respective governments, nothing more than that.

"Permission is granted for your graves registration people to come collect your bodies, and I propose a 72-hour truce," replied Guderian.

Wassel considered that. He knew that he had another Qalb here in Scythia, plus several independent border battalions, but he also knew that the better part of two legions of Roman troops, one an actual Roman legion as opposed to a Limitanei legion, were within two days' march of their positions.

"I believe 72 hours may be too much. I will agree to no more than 48 hours. After that, the truce will expire and any forces approaching the border will be fired upon. I propose that both forces return to their position of the previous day. We shall see whether our governments will further this conflict."

"I agree," replied Guderian.

Legate Guderian extended a hand to Liwa Wassel, and the liwa took it.

*"As-salaam alaykum,"* said Guderian with a twinkle in his eye.

Surprised, Wassel replied, *"Wa-Aaikum-Salaam."*

———

I wrote this story several years ago, and it has gone through a few various iterations. Yes, the title is a play on a line from Al Stewart's "Roads to Moscow." In the air anthology that precedes this one, I wrote about the Great War between the Roman Empire and the Abbasid Caliphate. I gave a bit more backstory as to how we get to Rome and the Abbasid Caliphate fighting over the area that would today be known as Ukraine and Moldova. I would highly encourage the reader to go and read that story if they haven't already done so.

The Abbasid ranks used in the story correspond to the Jordanian and Egyptian military ranks of today, but with some variance. If I have made any errors in Arabic, I apologize, for my Arabic is not much and I have had to rely on translation software. The tanks used in the story roughly correspond to the *Centurion* on the Abbasid side and the M-48, M-60, and M-103 on the Roman side. I hope the reader has enjoyed this story as much as I did writing it, and I do intend to write more in the Abbasid/Rome setting in the future.

# ABOUT PHILIP WOHLRAB

Philip Wohlrab has spent time in the United State Coast Guard and has served for more than 18 years in the Virginia Army National Guard. Serving as a medic attached to an infantry company, he earned the title "Doc" the hard way while serving across two tours in Iraq. He came home and continued his education, earning a Master of Public Health degree in 2016. He has written short stories in Mil-SF, Hard SF, fantasy, and alternate history. He currently works as a wargame designer for the United States Marine Corps and has also designed and executed wargames for the USAF, USN, USSF, and the Intelligence Community. He also does game design work for the civilian market. When not crafting new stories or new games he can be found hiking in Appalachia or attending Sci-Fi Cons.

https://www.amazon.com/stores/author/B01HTBZ57A

# UNINTENDED CONSEQUENCES

## Peter Grant



The four-man Reconnaissance Regiment stick moved slowly and carefully along the half-overgrown footpath through the African bush. Few people still used it after several years of warfare between the Angolan government's FAPLA forces and their Cuban supporters on the one hand, and UNITA guerrillas and their South African allies on the other. Most of the villagers in or near the fluid, ever-shifting combat zone, with its unpredictable troop movements that could transform an area from tranquil to terrifying without warning, had long since fled.

The point man brushed sweat from his eyebrows yet again, waving away the flies that buzzed around his head trying to drink it. He began to repeat the gesture, then stopped dead in his tracks and sank to his haunches, making a sign that the others understood. *Enemy ahead.*

First Lieutenant Viljoen moved up beside him, eyes flickering to left and right. The brush ended abruptly ahead of them at the edge of an open area, probably a former cornfield, now covered with low vegetation as the African bush reclaimed it. On the far side were a few broken-down mud huts, between which at least a dozen dark olive Soviet military trucks could be seen. A bulldozer was parked at the edge of an eighty-by-two-hundred-foot patch it had cleared and leveled in the field. Well over half of it was already covered with a layer of concrete, two to four inches thick.

"What the hell is FAPLA doing here, Hannes?" the officer murmured to the scout. "This is just a transit route for troops and supplies. They've never had a base here—there's no need for one."

"*Ja,* sir, but maybe they've changed their minds. There's a waterhole nearby, and that looks like a foundation slab."

"It's not thick enough for that, and there's no rebar or wire frame— although both might be because it's a slipshod, half-done job of work, which would be nothing new for Angolans. Whatever it is, the brass will want to know more."

The patrol took up observation positions along the edge of the field, staying hidden in the thick brush as they observed the Angolan troops. Several of them were unloading cement sacks from the back of a truck, while others worked on the engine of a portable cement-mixer. Idlers lounged around, not making any real effort to maintain security over the area. The smell of cooking rose from a line of fires over to one side, where the evening meal was being prepared.

As the sun dipped towards the horizon, the engine of the cement-mixer finally spluttered to life, and its drum began to revolve. The troops standing around it gave a cheer, then looked towards an officer for instructions. He began to shout orders. Some of the troops began to mix more concrete, while others lined up with wheelbarrows to take it to the next section of the slab to be laid. The officer hurried over to ensure that the planks placed around it were still in position, to hold the concrete until it had dried enough to remain in place without support. He summoned a soldier with a can of paint, and had him mark a big black X equidistant from the three concrete edges on the finished portion of the pad.

"It's already late afternoon, but they're still working. Whatever this is, they're in a hurry," a Recce corporal muttered.

"You're right, Boeta," the patrol commander agreed. "They don't usually work this hard or this late." He thought for a moment. "Remember that intel we got last month about the helicopters?"

The other nodded thoughtfully. Another Recce patrol had spent a week infiltrating the port of Namibe, watching Soviet cargo vessels unloading materials to be ferried to the battlefront hundreds of miles to the east. They'd noted a major transport bottleneck, with warehouses overflowing into immense stacks of supplies exposed to wind and weather. Some ships were forced to wait at anchor in the bay because there was no room to unload their cargoes.

Shortly before they left Namibe, the patrol had reported the arrival of a squadron of Mil Mi-8 transport helicopters, flown by Angolan and Cuban pilots. It had established its base at the rundown airport south of Namibe, and had begun flying covering missions for road convoys. However, the Mi-8s carried no weapons. The Angolans had Mi-24 gunships, so why were they misusing unarmed transports for a job that might well lead to combat?

"Those choppers don't have the range to ferry supplies all the way from Namibe to the battlefront," the lieutenant pointed out, "but if they built a refueling point, they could. That cleared area's the right size, and we're halfway between Namibe and Cuito Cuanavale—just the right place for it. That big X is a giveaway. A second, on the other side of the pad, will make this a two-helicopter landing pad, with plenty of space between them for their rotors to turn."

"And there's two fuel tankers in that convoy," Sergeant Bothma commented, pointing at the vehicles in question. "Thing is, why use concrete? Why not just bare earth?"

"Could be so the rotors will throw up less dust and dirt. That'll make visibility very poor during landing and takeoff. Also, during the rainy season, the ground gets so muddy it's like a swamp. I think we should discourage them. I'm going to call this in."

His encrypted message, sent on a frequency-hopping tropospheric-scatter radio system, caused a flurry of activity in an Operations Center in northern South West Africa. Approval for the patrol's proposed course of action was transmitted within the hour, along with instructions for a nearby UNITA patrol to rendezvous with the Recces the following day.

—————

The same evening, an Antonov An-24 twin-engined transport aircraft of the Angolan Air Force landed at the airport south of Namibe. It taxied to the terminal building in the last of the sunlight, where a guard of honor had been hastily assembled. Its members—local levies unfamiliar with drill of any sort, let alone an honor guard—shambled to a ragged semblance of attention, and falteringly presented arms as a man disembarked, wearing a major-general's uniform of the Soviet Union. Tabs identified him as an officer of the Strategic Rocket Forces.

An East German major stood to one side. He came forward, snapped to attention, and saluted stiffly. "Welcome to Namibe, General Shpagin! It is an honor for us to receive a visit from so senior an officer."

The new arrival peered at his nametag. "Not that much of an honor, Major Brinkerhoff. I was at loose ends between postings. That's why Moscow sent me to investigate this logistics mess—I just happened to be the most senior officer available. I wasn't impressed to see stacks of supplies all over the place as we came in to land. Lobito looked no better as we overflew it on the way down here from Luanda. Why haven't both ports been better organized? Why is it taking so long to clear this bottleneck?"

"I can't speak with any authority, sir, as I'm not involved in port operations or military logistics. Local officers will brief you in the morning." He lowered his voice to a confidential murmur. "If you ask me, sir, it's largely because they're incompetent and bone idle. In the Warsaw Pact, we'd be shot if we worked this way!"

The general eyed him carefully. Brinkerhoff was a professional like himself. As such, his judgment was probably as accurate as it was damning. "*Hmpfh!* We'll see about that. Take me to the visiting officers' quarters, Major. I need a bath, a good meal, and a night's sleep."

His aide followed with the general's suitcase as his boss strode to a waiting utility vehicle.

The next morning, General Shpagin's invective blistered the hides of the staff as they tried to make excuses for the logistics bottleneck. He pointed out acidly, "The Soviet Union has generously provided thousands of trucks to Angola, free of charge, yet you claim you don't have enough vehicles to move these supplies. *Where are they, then?*"

As to claims that the roads weren't good enough, he noted bluntly that South Africa appeared to have few difficulties supplying UNITA rebels with material support over a much greater distance, through terrain that often had no roads at all. "If they can do it, why can't you? Your inefficiency is causing weeks of delay to valuable ships that are needed elsewhere. This must stop!"

Nor would he give credence to claims of the mass destruction of transport vehicles by South African forces. "We know beyond doubt, through satellite reconnaissance and other intelligence sources, that South Africa currently has only a few hundred troops north of the South West African border. You have thousands of Cuban troops, fighting alongside tens of thousands of Angolan soldiers—far more than enough to defend against such a small number, no matter how skilled or well-equipped they may be."

A timid Angolan Air Force officer offered what he hoped would be good news. "S-sir, our new helicopter route will open within a day or two. We're building a refueling pad halfway between here and Cuito Cuanavale so that Mi-8s can fly there with a full four-ton cargo of urgently needed materials. If Moscow gives us the heavy-lift Mi-26s we have asked for, we will be able to lift twenty tons on every flight!"

Shpagin's eyebrows rose. "That will help, although it'll be much more expensive than road transport. When's the first mission?"

"In three days' time, sir."

"Book seats on it for myself and my aide. I want to see this refueling pad for myself, and inspect the cargo handling facilities at Cuito Cuanavale, too."

That evening over supper, his aide tried to remonstrate. "Sir, the Defense Ministry's instructions were clear. You were not to enter the combat zone or expose yourself to danger."

"*Pshaw!* They sent me here to investigate a problem and solve it. The only way I can do that properly is to see everything for myself. UNITA and the South Africans don't know I'm here, and they can't possibly be aware of the new helicopter route. It hasn't even been used yet! As for the combat zone, there's no major fighting going on right now. All anyone's doing is local patrolling. I don't think there'll be any risk."

———

While the two Soviet officers were finishing their meal, Lieutenant Viljoen welcomed a UNITA officer to the camp the patrol had set up half a mile from the Angolan work site. The two shook hands, and got down to business without preamble.

"The signal said to deliver to you all our explosives," the UNITA man began. "We have four TM-46 anti-vehicle landmines."

"That's great! Just what we need. Here, let me show you what's going on." The South African officer drew a quick map in the dirt using a stick. "The enemy is here. On a circle surrounding their positions, we're here. I'd like you to place your patrol in an arc behind their positions a third of the way around the circle from where we are. That way, we won't shoot at each other through them. I'm guessing the helicopter pad will be ready in the next two days—the first half is already dry. As soon as it's complete, I reckon they'll send out a proving mission, to make sure everything's as it should be. I want to hit them when they come in."

"How can you be sure they'll land on the mines? The pressure plates won't work unless they have enough weight on them."

"We'll make sure they go off. I want your people to stay quiet until they blow, then shoot the hell out of the Angolan vehicles and positions for two minutes, no more. As soon as two minutes are up, get out of here. The main convoy route isn't far away, so the Angolans may be able to get a reaction force here quickly. We aren't strong enough to take them on."

"All right. You head south and we'll head east to divide any enemy attempt to follow us."

"Agreed. Use anti-tracking, too, to make it as difficult as possible for them."

The twenty-man UNITA patrol headed into the bush to work their way around the enemy's position. The lieutenant laid out the four big steel landmines in a row, and started removing their pressure plates.

"What's the idea, sir?" Sergeant Piet Bothma asked as he knelt to help.

"We have to make sure these blow, even if the chopper doesn't land right on top of them," the officer explained. "We're going to replace their pressure plates with plastic explosive and a command detonator. We'll connect them all to a firing position at the edge of the bush, and let the enemy lay concrete over them."

"Will they have enough blast to take out a chopper through concrete, sir?" another asked.

"Four TM-46s have as much explosive between them as a couple of 155mm artillery shells. I think that'll be more than enough."

The questioner winced. "That's headache city, all right!"

After midnight, when all the Angolan soldiers were asleep—including the sentries, because what possible threat could there be so deep in the bush, and so far from the battlefront?—the South Africans crept out into the cleared area. The lieutenant estimated where the second X marker for a landing helicopter would most likely be painted, then dug holes for the four mines close together around that point. The others covered them, then led the detonator wire to and beyond the edge of the cleared area, burying it. They patted down and smoothed the disturbed earth, then brushed it with leafy branches as they withdrew, removing all signs that they'd been there.

As the sun rose and the Angolans began to pour more concrete, covering the mines, the Recces settled down to wait.

———

Antennae all over the operational area, and up and down the coast, fed their intercepted harvest to the South African electronic warfare station at Rooikop, near Walvis Bay in South West Africa, eight hundred miles to the south. In the underground operations center, the signals were analyzed, decrypted, if possible, then forwarded to interested parties for further action.

Late the following night, an operator called the Officer of the Watch to come to his station. "Sir, a visiting general is making life difficult at Namibe. The Angolans are complaining to their HQ in Luanda that he's 'insensitive to the difficulties of operating in a war zone.'"

"Awww, my heart bleeds for them," the OOW joked as he began to read the signal. "Hey, that's not a Cuban or East German name. 'Shpagin'—that sounds Russian. Have we seen it before?"

"Nothing in the database, sir."

"Then let's get this off to the Ops Room at Defense HQ in Pretoria. They may know who he is."

They didn't, but the Operations Room knew who would. By early the following morning, the CIA in Langley, Virginia confirmed to their representative in the United States Embassy in Pretoria that a major-general in the Soviet Union's Strategic Rocket Forces bore the same name. What would a man of that rank and importance be doing in an out-of-the-way place like Angola? Questions flashed from Langley to the U.S. Embassy in Moscow, but the answers didn't satisfy anyone.

"Why the hell would they send a senior strategic missile commander to untangle logistics snarl-ups in the third world?" an American analyst demanded. "That makes no sense. They've got to be up to something!"

South African Defense HQ duly ordered Rooikop and other facilities to be on the lookout for any further mention of Shpagin's name and mission, while interested eyes in America sharpened their focus on southern Africa. Cuba was the main Soviet surrogate in the region, after all, and Angola's ally. Could the general's visit be the first move in a new Cuban missile crisis more than two decades after the last one?

———

The day of the first helicopter resupply mission dawned fine and clear. General Shpagin dressed carefully, the rows of award ribbons on his chest making a colorful display. He inspected his boots with displeasure, and insisted that his Angolan servant polish them again.

"Wouldn't it be better to wear battledress, like the Cuban officers do, sir?" his aide asked.

Shpagin shook his head disapprovingly. "They're playing at being fighting soldiers. They aren't even in the combat zone, yet they all look casual and sloppy. Let's show them what it means to be proud of one's uniform!"

"As you say, sir."

Sighing inwardly, the aide resigned himself to another day of tugging at his tight collar while sweating buckets beneath his heavy jacket. *Why is it,* he wondered, *that generals can go through the whole day looking as fresh as a daisy while their underlings wilt? Must go with the rank.*

A utility vehicle took them to two Mi-8 helicopters parked on the airport hardstand. They were already loaded with urgently needed supplies, strapped down in their cabins. An officer motioned the general and his aide towards the first helicopter, but Shpagin held up a hand.

"Captain, you go in the second helicopter. Nothing's likely to happen, but let's travel separately, just in case. If anything goes wrong, one of us must survive to submit a report to Moscow, and you already know what I plan to say to them."

"Yes, sir."

The crew chief pulled down a folding chair against the bulkhead. General Shpagin strapped himself into it, frowning at the memory of many uncomfortable hours spent in similar transports. At least, here in the southern African heat, he wouldn't freeze his ass off.

"What's our flight time?" he asked the crew chief.

"Two hours, ten minutes to the refueling point, sir, then another two hours, twenty minutes to Cuito Cuanavale."

The general grimaced, already regretting his second cup of coffee over breakfast. "I'll need a pee break very badly by the time we land to refuel."

The Cuban NCO guffawed as he handed him a set of headphones with a boom microphone.

"Just don't piss out the open door as we fly, sir," the man stated, his tone turning morose as he continued. "The rotor wash will blow it back all over you, and everyone else in here. Ask me how I know that."

Shpagin had to laugh as he nodded in response.

The helicopters lifted off with a snarling clatter of rotors, and turned west, staying low over the trees and bushes. A few minutes later, the An-24 transport also took off to fly high overhead and serve as a communications relay, if required. A routine signal was dispatched to the Angolan air defense network at Cuito Cuanavale to confirm that the flights had departed. The identity of the VIP passenger was emphasized, to ensure that no missiles were launched at him in error. Their Soviet benefactors would not be amused by such a mistake.

The routine signal was duly intercepted at Rooikop, and General Shpagin's name noted. Within minutes, a message was on its way to Pretoria.

———

The concrete had dried quickly under the hot African sun, and the Angolans clearly weren't going to waste any time putting the landing pad into service. The fuel tankers had been driven closer to the edge of the pad, and the encampment had been tidied up. The construction crew were dressing in clean uniforms, while their NCOs marked out parade positions for them.

Lieutenant Viljoen ordered everyone to pack their gear and be ready to move out on the run.

"If they come this morning and we blow them up, they're not going to be very pleased with us," he pointed out with a grin. "We'll have to get away before they can get organized. I'll be on the detonator. Hannes, we don't have anyone else to spare, so the two of us will have to be a quick-and-dirty snatch party. If we see an opportunity to take a prisoner, let's grab him during the confusion when UNITA joins in. He can answer questions later. Boeta, you're on the missile." He nodded to the team's sole SA-14 shoulder-launched ground-to-air missile, captured from the Angolans like all their weapons and equipment.

"Give them a chance to land," Viljoen emphasized. "If one doesn't, and you get a clear shot, take it down. Piet, you provide covering fire for the snatch team if we need it, then take point when we leave. Head back down the footpath we used to get here. As soon as we've broken contact, we'll change direction and start using anti-tracking to stop them from following us."

They waited in the thick brush as the sun rose higher and the heat began to grow oppressive. At last, shortly after ten, the distant sound of helicopter rotors intruded on the silence and began to grow louder. "They're coming!" the lieutenant exclaimed, his face lighting up. "Packs on, weapons ready, and stand by!"

Two familiar silhouettes appeared over the bushes and trees. The leading helicopter slanted down towards the pad in a curving approach, while the second circled above the clearing, obviously looking for any signs of danger. They ignored it. By now, camouflaging their positions against aerial observation was second nature to them. Boeta picked up the SA-14 launch tube, trying to get a clear view of the second helicopter.

The lead helicopter settled almost exactly where Lieutenant Viljoen had anticipated it would. His finger trembled on the detonator switch as he waited, hoping for the second aircraft to land so that blast and fragments from the mines might damage it, as well. Instead, as the engines of the first helicopter began to shut down, a smartly uniformed figure jumped down from it and hurried directly towards them, ducking beneath the rotor blades, one hand holding his cap on, the other fumbling with the fly of his trousers.

"Holy shit, boss, he's coming right for us!" Hannes whispered urgently.

"Stand by to grab him!"

Viljoen waited until the new arrival had almost reached the bush behind which he was concealed, then hit the switch. With a colossal blast, the four landmines blew up beneath the concrete, sending fragments flying in all directions, including into the fuselage and fuel tanks of the helicopter above them. It came apart, erupting in flames as its undercarriage collapsed.

Chaos broke out. The UNITA patrol opened up with AK-47s, RPK light machine guns, RPG-7 rockets and hand grenades. Both tanker trucks exploded, one after the other, in massive orange-red fireballs and billowing smoke, spraying burning fuel and debris in every direction. Many of the Angolan soldiers, who'd been drawn up in formation to honor the new arrivals, were mown down as if by a scythe. The survivors scattered in panic.

In the confusion, Hannes leapt to his feet and tackled the man who'd run towards them, clouting him with a mighty blow on the jaw that knocked him out. His cap came off. Hannes picked it up, staring at it, then at his victim.

"Lieutenant! This guy isn't Angolan or Cuban! It's a white man, and he's wearing a shitload of medal ribbons and what look like general's stars. Who *is* this fucker?"

"I don't know, but he's got to be important. Come on! Let's grab him and get out of here!"

———

In the second Mi-8, the pilot was screaming into his microphone. *"Emergency! Emergency!* The refueling pad is under attack! The lead helicopter has crashed and blown up! General Shpagin has been captured by the enemy—I saw them tackle him and bring him down! For God's sake, somebody help us!"

Looking out of the open side door, Shpagin's aide saw a trail of smoke erupt from a clump of bushes and head straight towards the helicopter. There was a loud explosion over his head, and pieces of the rotor blades flew in all directions. The aircraft dropped like a stone. The last thing he saw was the whirling ground coming up very fast before his eyes as the helicopter spun in.

High in the sky, the An-24 radio relay plane saw and heard it all. Even as its pilots hauled the plane around and clawed for more altitude to put as much distance as possible between themselves and any other ground-to-air missiles, its radio operator passed the news to Namibe. From there, a message was broadcast at full power across southern Angola, in clear, to all FAPLA and Cuban forces. "General Shpagin has been captured in an enemy ambush at the new refueling pad! All available forces are to converge on that location and rescue him!" Map coordinates were provided. MiG fighters and Sukhoi strike aircraft scrambled, and helicopters launched to carry responding forces to the scene at top speed.

Almost as fast as the message spread through the Angolan armed forces, it reached South African Defense Force HQ in Pretoria via the Rooikop listening station. The initial reaction was one of shocked incredulity. Who could have launched such an attack against such a high-value target? It didn't take long for the Special Forces liaison officer to inform the Operations Room about Lieutenant Viljoen's patrol and his intention to take out the first helicopter to use the landing pad they had discovered. Was that what the Angolans were talking about?

"Send a signal to Viljoen at once!"

"We can't, sir. He won't be listening—in fact, if that was him, he'll be running like hell to get clear before reaction forces arrive. His next scheduled communications window is tonight."

"And until then, we'll have the top brass jumping down our throats demanding to know what's going on. What are we going to tell them?"

———

The patrol had covered only a few hundred yards, dragging their unconscious prisoner with them, when they heard the roar of an overstressed engine drawing nearer from behind them. They scattered to either side of the narrow footpath as a Soviet ZIL-131 six-by-six military truck appeared, gears whining in low ratio, wheels churning in the thick soft sand, bashing through the bushes on either side of the track, its fear-crazed driver intent only on escape from the carnage behind him.

Sergeant Bothma spun in his tracks, shouldered his AK-47, and squeezed off a pair of snap shots that went through the door and killed the driver instantly. His foot came off the accelerator and the truck slowed to a standstill, jerking as its engine cut out. Bothma ran after it, pulling open the door to check on the driver.

"Well done, Piet!" Viljoen called breathlessly. "Throw him in the back so he won't be found, and take his place. I'll join you. The rest of you, get in the back with the prisoner."

Within moments, the truck was bouncing down the track again. Viljoen consulted his map. "This footpath comes out at the main east-west trail in about two clicks. When we get there, turn west towards the coast."

"*West,* sir? But that's closer to the enemy!"

"Yes, it is, but if our prisoner's as important as he looks, they're going to be after us with everything they've got. They'll expect us to head east and south, towards our own forces. Let's throw them off the scent by doing what they won't expect. The truck's wheels will leave ruts in the sandy soil, but you can't tell from the rut which direction it was moving. Once we hit the main trail, they won't know which way we went. We'll abandon this truck somewhere convenient, and head south from there."

"Okay, sir. That guy's uniform and insignia looked different from anything we've seen before. He may be Soviet. If he is, they'll be flying in search parties from all directions. Moscow will be baying for our blood."

"If you're right, we've got less than an hour before aircraft will be overhead looking for us. A truck moving alone will stick out like a sore thumb. Remember that convoy the Air Force hit two months ago just east of here?"

"Yessir! The Angolans dragged all the wrecked trucks off to the side of the road and abandoned them." He sniggered. "The Air Force uses them as a navigational landmark now."

"That's right. It's about thirty clicks from here. Let's park this truck with them. I reckon no one will bother to count, to see if there's one more vehicle than there was before. That'll buy us time to get away clean."

"Great idea, sir!"

It took them thirty-seven agonizing minutes to reach the trucks, peering out of the windows all the while to spot any other vehicles or a fast-moving aircraft coming towards them. At last, they reached the place. The lieutenant pointed. "Take us around the back there, into the bush, on the far side of the wrecks. That'll put this one furthest away from passing traffic, so they're less likely to notice it's not damaged like the others."

They parked the truck, then Viljoen hurried around to the rear while the sergeant started to knock the valve stems out of every tire. The prisoner had regained consciousness, and was sitting nursing his jaw, looking around balefully.

The lieutenant tried his meager, halting Spanish, learned in case he needed to interrogate Cuban prisoners. *"¿Quién eres tú? ¿Cuál es su nombre?"* No response. He switched to English. "Who are you? What is your name?"

"I am Major-General Shpagin of the Soviet armed forces. That is all I shall tell you."

"What the hell are you doing out here in the middle of bloody Africa?" Silence. "Are you attached to the Angolan armed forces?" Silence. "What is your mission?" Silence.

"We can't waste time making him talk, sir," Boeta warned. "Listen!" They cocked their heads. Faintly, but growing louder, they heard the sound of jet engines at high altitude.

"Those will be MiGs looking for us," Lieutenant Viljoen agreed. He looked back at the general. "Sir, you're a prisoner of war of the Republic of South Africa's armed forces. We're going to take to the bush and head south until we can arrange to be picked up. If you don't make trouble, we'll allow you to walk unrestrained. If you make trouble or try to escape, we'll tie your hands, put a tether round your neck, and bring you with us the hard way. Understand me?"

"I understand." Another baleful glare.

"Right. Everyone, fill your canteens." Viljoen gestured to the drum of water tied down in the load bed. "When you've done that, drink as much as you can, then we'll drain the rest of the water. Take what you need from that box of ration packs. They're Angolan, so they won't be very tasty, but they're better than nothing. We'll carry seven days' food per man. Empty that backpack." He pointed to what had presumably been the personal gear of the late driver. "Fill it with ration packs and the driver's canteens. General, you'll carry it. If you refuse, you'll have nothing to eat or drink, so don't argue. Hannes, make sure he's unarmed—no dinky little officer's pistol concealed anywhere. The rest of you, take the canvas cover off the truck, fold it a few times, and lay it in the load bed over the driver's body. From the road or a low-flying chopper, this truck's got to look like just another abandoned wreck."

"Not going to booby-trap it, sir?" the sergeant asked as he straightened from removing a valve stem.

"No. If it explodes or burns, the Angolans will wonder why."

Within ten minutes, the patrol moved out in single file, heading south, sticking to the cover of the trees and bushes, moving slowly and carefully, covering or disguising their tracks whenever possible.

Their prisoner walked in the center of the formation. General Shpagin seethed inwardly, but made no trouble. South African troops had a well-earned reputation for violence towards anyone who resisted them. He had no doubt that any attempt at obstruction or escape would have extremely painful consequences.

———

The atmosphere in the meeting room at Soviet military headquarters in Moscow seethed and roiled with barely suppressed tension. The Defense Minister glared at the assembled senior officers. "How do you know it was the South Africans who got him? It could have been UNITA!"

"Minister, the reaction forces captured two UNITA guerrillas, part of a larger force trying to escape after the ambush. Under separate interrogation, both said their unit was ordered to join a South African Reconnaissance Regiment patrol to help them attack the refueling pad. UNITA took no prisoners during the attack, so General Shpagin must be in South African hands."

"And who the hell thought it was a good idea to send a Strategic Rocket Forces general to Angola in the first place? He knows our nuclear target lists for every NATO country! If the South Africans get him back to their base, the Americans will give their eyeteeth and sell their own mothers to interrogate him!"

"H-he was just...available, Minister," a hapless official stammered. "The Foreign Ministry said they wanted someone senior enough to impress the Angolans. General Shpagin had just returned from a period of leave. He said he was tired of sitting around, waiting for his predecessor to depart so he could take up his new post, and volunteered for the Angolan inspection mission in the interim. No one even thought about his branch of service."

A wordless glare from the Minister promised retribution for so grievous an error of judgment. "What do you propose, Marshal?" he demanded, turning to the Commanding Officer of the Strategic Rocket Forces.

"Three things, Minister. First, I want the Air Force to send a couple of dozen of their best pilots to Angola at once, by the fastest available means. Some good maintenance technicians would also be useful. They can take over some of the Angolan Air Force's MiG-23s to fly top cover, and some Mi-8 and Mi-24 helicopters. They'll assume primary responsibility for stopping the South Africans from interfering; and, if we locate Shpagin, they can land troops to rescue him. Second, I want a Spetsnaz air assault unit sent to Angola, also by the fastest available means. They'll mount the rescue mission if we find Shpagin. Finally, we need to send a very strong signal to South Africa that they've gone too far. I suggest ordering a Guards Air Assault Division to prepare for immediate deployment to Angola."

"You're crazy!" the Minister exclaimed. "The Politburo would never permit that! The Americans would regard it as an intolerable provocation!"

"We don't have to send them, Minister—just order them to get ready to go, and let it slip that they're preparing. The South Africans will get the message. If we don't get Shpagin back quickly, their war in Angola is going to turn a lot hotter than they bargained for."

"And if they respond by calling up their own reinforcements?"

"Then let's send the division. The South Africans can see how they like facing a real enemy, not third-rate Africans or second-rate Cubans. They won't enjoy it."

The Minister shook his head. "I doubt that'll be approved. Remember, Secretary Gorbachev is putting a lot of emphasis on *glasnost,* reconciliation with the West. He won't want to jeopardize that."

"That's a political consideration, Minister. We're military men. We deal with military solutions."

The Minister managed, not without some difficulty, to restrain himself from pointing out that those same military men had caused the problem in the first place by sending General Shpagin where he should never have gone.

"Very well, Marshal. On my authority, get the aircrew and Spetsnaz unit moving. Tell the Air Force I want them to assign sufficient jet transports to get them to Angola as fast as possible, along with any equipment they need. They can arrange to refuel in Libya, if necessary. Have the Foreign Ministry clear that with Gaddafi, and tell them not to take 'no' for an answer. Hold off on the Air Assault division for now. That'll have to be discussed by the Politburo. Have the relevant agencies see to it—discreetly, of course—that the Americans and South Africans learn of these steps, but try to avoid the news spreading more widely."

———

General Shpagin nibbled at a ration pack cracker, nursing his still-painful jaw, washing down the crumbs with water from a canteen as he watched Lieutenant Viljoen, forehead creased in concentration, compose and encrypt a message. At last, the officer sighed, pressed a button, and sat back. "There. That's saved for transmission later." He reached for his ration pack.

"Are you telling them you've captured me?" the prisoner asked.

Viljoen laughed. "I reckon they already know, General. You saw and heard all those aircraft flying around today. They were looking for you. I'm sure there's signals all over the place about you, and I reckon our people will have intercepted some of them. We've thrown the searchers off the trail for a while, but sooner or later, they'll realize they're looking in the wrong place. I hope we'll have you across the border by then."

"How will you do that?"

"I don't suppose I'm betraying any secrets when I tell you I'm going to ask for a helicopter pickup. That's far and away the fastest method. Otherwise, it'll be a three- to four-week walk through the bush. That'll be no fun for any of us."

"But you have only enough rations for a week."

"We'll live off the land, general. We're used to that."

"So you are like our Spetsnaz, then? Special Forces?"

"Yes. We're Reconnaissance Commandos." The pride in Viljoen's voice was evident.

"I have heard something about you, yes." The general hesitated a moment. "How can you fight for a government that denies the humanity of so many of its people because of the color of their skin?"

"You mean the policy of *apartheid?*" Shpagin nodded, and Viljoen sighed. "I'm not saying South Africa's perfect, General. We've got at least as many problems as any other nation, maybe more than most. What we're doing, the four of us and others like us, is buying time for our country to sort out its own problems in peace. Have you ever seen what happens when a terrorist landmine goes off underneath a trailer full of kids on their way to school?"

"I... No, I never have."

"I have. I still wake up screaming sometimes when I remember picking up the pieces of those kids... Feet... Hands... Fingers... Half a head that had come right off a little girl. She must have been pretty, once."

The younger man's eyes were far away, filled with remembered pain.

"That's what we're fighting to keep out of our land, General, for long enough that those bastards won't dictate the solution to our problems out of the barrels of their guns." He looked up. "I might as well ask why you serve a government that arms the terrorists who do such things, and that starved millions to death, and sent millions more to the gulag, and invaded Afghanistan. Doesn't that make you just as bad as I am, General?"

Shpagin grunted. "A point to you, Lieutenant. I, too, want to make my country a better place. Perhaps we are not so different, you and I."

"I don't think military professionals are all that different, sir. I've met soldiers from Britain, the United States and Israel. They're all a lot like us, under the skin."

"Yet, despite those similarities, you would shoot me without hesitation if I tried to escape."

"Uh-huh, just like you'd shoot me if that was the only way you *could* escape."

———

VIPs crowded a conference room in Defense HQ in Pretoria. When Lieutenant Viljoen's signal reached them shortly after midnight, mingled jubilation and concern swept through the gathering. The Chief of the Defense Force swiftly called them to order.

"They've moved beyond our normal operational area. Can the Air Force get a Puma helicopter up there to collect them?"

The Chief of the Air Force frowned. "We have long-range tanks we can install in the cabin, sir. Trouble is, they're all down here, for use during maritime rescue missions. We'll have to take one—no, two, in case one goes wrong—out of choppers at the coast, fly them up to Grootfontein, and install them in helicopters there. That'll take a full day, longer if there are technical issues. Meanwhile, you can bet the Angolans will be looking for our patrol with everything they've got."

"Not just the Angolans. We heard from the Americans a short while ago. The Soviets are sending in their own pilots to take over some Angolan planes, and bringing a Spetsnaz air assault unit with them. If they can find and fix our people, they'll lead the attack."

"When will they get there, sir?"

"They left Moscow aboard Ilyushin-76 transports a few hours ago. They'll have to refuel somewhere, but you can assume they'll be in the operational area within thirty-six hours from now."

"We'll only just have finished installing the tanks by then and test-flown the helicopters, sir. I can't guarantee success if we have to infiltrate defenses manned by front-line Soviet pilots and technicians, particularly if they bring more advanced weapons with them—better air-to-air missiles, electronic warfare pods, that sort of thing."

"We may have no choice but to try. What fighters do we have up there?"

"Half a dozen Mirage F1s, sir, but they're 'A' models configured for ground attack rather than air-to-air."

"Get some of the 'C' models up there right away, armed with the new Python-3 air-to-air missiles we bought from Israel. If our helicopters have to go in, the fighters will have to keep the MiGs off their backs while they pick up our people. Fortunately, the Angolans and Cubans don't yet know we have Pythons. They'll be a nice surprise for them, and the Soviets, too."

"Yes, sir. Will the Cabinet authorize us to engage Soviet forces?"

"Let me worry about that." The Chief of the Defense Force turned to the Special Forces representative. "Danie, send a big 'Well done!' to Lieutenant Viljoen and his team from me personally; then tell them to crawl into a hole and pull the top in after them until we can sort out this mess. We've got their backs, and we won't abandon them, but we have to avoid this thing getting any hotter than it is already. Right now, it's like we're all sitting around an open gunpowder keg tossing lighted matches at it. If we're not bloody careful, things are going to take on a momentum of their own—and then where will we be?"

"Won't the United States back us against the Soviets, sir? They'll have to, won't they?"

"Why don't you ask South Vietnam how well relying on America worked out for them?"

"Ah... I take your point, sir."

———

Major Brinkerhoff was at Namibe airport to welcome the Spetsnaz assault team when it landed. He saluted the colonel in command. "Sir, I've put up tented accommodation for your unit behind that hangar. A field kitchen is ready to serve you a meal right away. It's good food—I tasted it myself. When you've eaten, I'm ready to give you a briefing on local conditions, including video of the scene of the action, and provide a current situation report."

Colonel Voronezh looked at him with approval. "Major, you're the most professional soldier I've run into since we landed in Angola! Thank you for making those arrangements. We'll look forward to your briefing in half an hour."

Some still chewing, the Spetsnaz officers and senior NCOs assembled in a tent used as a briefing room, and listened closely as the East German officer walked them through the events of the past few days. He showed them on a large-scale map of Southern Angola where various units were searching, and the patrol patterns they were using.

"What have the South Africans been doing?" Voronezh asked.

"They've brought up more Mirage fighters, but they haven't flown across the border into Angola yet. Moscow signaled a short while ago that satellite imagery shows the newly arrived Mirages are carrying Israeli Python-3 air-to-air missiles. That's a type our forces hadn't seen on South African aircraft before. They're extremely effective heat-seekers."

"That's not good news," the colonel grunted. "What about their helicopters?"

"Satellite reconnaissance showed two Puma helicopters being worked on outside a hangar, sir. It looked like they were installing long-range tanks in the cabins. They may be going to try for a pickup."

"But they didn't have them already fitted with the tanks, ready to go? That means they were surprised by General Shpagin's presence. They can't have expected to capture him."

"I suppose not, sir."

"Hmmm... As a military professional with local knowledge, Major, what's your opinion of the South African special forces—these Reconnaissance Regiments, as they call them?"

"They're as good as you can get, sir, within their scope. Let me explain. You Spetsnaz and the American SEALs and Green Berets and the British SAS train to operate anywhere. You can jump into the Arctic, or into the Amazon jungle, and be equally at home. The Reconnaissance Regiments are different. Their selection standards are as rigorous as any other Special

Forces unit anywhere in the world, but they train to operate in an African environment. You may spend three months training in Arctic warfare, then three months in the jungle, then three months mountaineering, and so on. They'll spend all those months training just as hard, but focused solely on sub-Saharan African operations. That concentration of effort means that man for man, on their home turf, they're the best there is."

The Spetsnaz officers looked thoughtfully at one another. They understood the professional evaluation for what it was: a sober reflection of reality. This was not going to be easy.

"So," Voronezh said slowly, "if it comes to a fight, you're saying we'll have our work cut out for us, even though we'll probably outnumber their small ambush team many times over."

"Sir, if it comes to a fight, some of you won't be coming back. Guaranteed. Even if you kill them all, they'll bleed you first."

"And the general?"

"I don't know what their orders are, sir. If they've been instructed not to let him get away, you won't recover him alive. They'll make sure of that."

"Thank you, Major. I'm going to make that point to Moscow when I speak to them in half an hour. They need to take that into account."

————

When the recording of the Colonel's conversation with his superiors was played back to the Politburo, the shock on the faces of some of its members showed that they hadn't considered that possibility.

"How can we ensure General Shpagin is not killed out of hand?" one demanded.

"If this comes down to a combat operation, we can't," the Defense Minister replied bluntly.

"Then we must make sure it doesn't come down to a combat operation," Secretary Gorbachev said quietly. "I think we'll try extreme diplomatic pressure, and see what that can achieve."

"But we don't have diplomatic relations with South Africa," another member objected.

"True—but the United States does."

————

As the moon rose over the African bush, the Recce patrol settled down in a dense clump of trees and bushes. Two sentries kept watch at all times, one over the surrounding area, the other over their prisoner. The general hadn't given any trouble, but that didn't mean he might not do so if he got the chance. They were too professional to take that risk.

"May I ask a question?" the general asked as he ate his meager rations next to Lieutenant Viljoen.

"Sure, go ahead, sir."

"Why have the Angolans not found us yet?"

"They're probably still convinced we're heading east and south to get closer to our own forces or the border, sir. That would be our logical direction of movement, after all. We haven't seen or heard many aircraft or helicopters over the past couple of days. They're all searching over there trying to stop us getting through while we're sitting over here, not even trying to reach the border."

"Why aren't you trying?"

"Orders, sir. I reckon the brass have something in mind. They've been clear that we're to take no chances, just sit tight and remain undiscovered until they get back to us. It grates, but they're in charge."

"I suppose so. It must be as frustrating for you as it is for me, just sitting here in the bush."

"Yes, sir, but that's what they pay us for." Viljoen cocked his head, listening. "There's a jet up there, very high. I reckon it'll be carrying a reconnaissance pod. It'll be looking for fires, heat signatures, things like that."

"Is that why you don't have fires at night?"

"Yes, sir. The glow is visible from a long way off, and their heat signature shows up on infrared like a flashlight in a dark room. So do vehicle engines. That's why we dumped the truck rather than use it to move at night."

General Shpagin snorted. "And I suppose that's why you took my lighter and cigars."

"Yes, sir. We couldn't risk you starting a fire. It wasn't because we wanted them as souvenirs!"

"Why don't the Angolans look at lower altitude with infrared sensors on helicopters?"

"Because they lose aircraft when they do that, sir. We shot down your second helicopter using a captured SA-14 missile. We don't have any more with us, but the Angolans don't know that. UNITA has American Stinger missiles. We've captured dozens of your old SA-7s, a couple of SA-9 vehicle-mounted systems, a few SA-14s, and recently, we've started to come across your new SA-16s." He snickered. "You copied or stole so much American technology for it that we call it the 'Stingerski.' It's a good missile—better than the Stinger, in some ways, according to our comparative tests. Anyway, thanks to all those missiles, Cuban and Angolan aircraft generally don't fly below fifteen thousand feet in the operational area unless they're flying nap-of-the-earth."

"So, to put it bluntly, my country is one of your arms suppliers whether we like it or not?"

Viljoen laughed.

"I'm not giving away any secrets by saying this, sir, because it's either been publicized in South Africa, or the Angolans and Cubans know all about it from fighting us. We've captured literally tens of thousands of your infantry weapons over the years—SKS rifles, AK-47 assault rifles, grenades, land mines and so on. We Recces carry them almost all the time."

"Why?" Shpagin demanded. "Why not use your own weapons?"

"Oh, come on, General! If we left South African cartridge cases and other evidence lying around, it'd be obvious we'd been there. This way, the Angolans can't tell that, since our debris looks the same as theirs or UNITA's. South Africa has some of your T-34, T-55, T-62 and PT-76 tanks, against which we test and assess our own vehicles and tactics."

Shpagin seethed as the South African officer continued.

"Our Army's standard-issue rocket-propelled grenade launcher is your RPG-7, and we make better rockets for it. We have plenty of captured Soviet equipment in storage: heavy machine guns, mortars, anti-aircraft guns, cannon and rocket artillery, armored personnel carriers and trucks. We gave a lot of our captured stocks to UNITA, and they've taken a lot themselves. Every time we beat FAPLA or the Cubans, we hand over more to UNITA, unless it's something advanced like missiles that we want for ourselves. In reality, the Soviet Union is arming both sides in this war, and has been for years."

The general's mouth twisted bitterly.

*When I return, certain people are going to hear about this in no uncertain terms,* he thought angrily. *That my aide died as the target of a Soviet missile is a disgrace! I cannot shoot the men responsible, but I* can *try to see to it that we stop arming the very people acting against our interests!*

———

A gathering in Washington D.C. the following afternoon was, if anything, even more tense than the South African cabinet meeting under way at the same time. A CIA representative was ebullient. "We've lined up an interrogation team to head for South Africa the instant we're notified that General Shpagin is there. He must know every Soviet nuclear target in NATO, and what weapons are aimed at it. That'll reveal just how much they know about us. It'll be the biggest intelligence coup of the decade!"

"But will South Africa let us have access to him?" a State Department advisor wondered.

"They'd better, if they want us to continue with constructive engagement in any form at all! We can throw them a bone or two—sell them some spares for their old C-130 Hercules transports, or turn a blind eye while they buy more missiles from Israel or West German fire control system components for their new armored vehicles, or something like that."

The State Department man was about to reply when the telephone on the sideboard rang. An aide answered, listened briefly, and turned to him. "It's for you, sir—the Secretary."

The advisor walked over to the sideboard, took the phone, and listened for a long moment. "Yes, sir...but are they serious?... I see...yes, sir. I'll tell them. Thank you, sir." He replaced the phone in its cradle, took a deep breath, and turned back to the conference table.

"There's been a new development. Secretary Gorbachev has just spoken with President Reagan on the hot line." A rustle of surprise ran around the room. "He's made it clear that unless General Shpagin is returned at once, unharmed, the Soviet Union will withdraw from further negotiations on the Intermediate-Range Nuclear Forces Treaty."

There was a stunned silence. At last, the CIA man said, clearly astonished, "They can't be serious! They've been working on that with us for years. Why would their diplomats call it off over a simple general?"

The State Department observer shook his head. "It's not only the diplomats who have a say. Their military knows we'd love to learn all he can tell us, and they're bound and determined to make sure that doesn't happen. Gorbachev's still settling into power after Chernenko's death. He's not yet secure in his position, and he can't afford to ignore them. If he has to, he'll strengthen his domestic position by going along with them, even at the expense of his most cherished diplomatic project."

"What did the President say?"

"He's called in the Secretary of State, and they've summoned the South African Ambassador. We're to stand by until further notice."

———

The Commanding Officer, Special Forces of the South African Defense Force, put down the phone and breathed a long, slow sigh of relief. He consulted a map, scribbled some notes, then picked up the phone again and dialed a number.

"Signal to Lieutenant Viljoen, flash priority. He's to take his prisoner and his patrol to map reference..."

———

That evening, Lieutenant Viljoen decoded the latest message, read it three times, and swore loudly.

"What is it, sir?" Sergeant Bothma asked.

"Pack up, everybody. We've got to be at a rendezvous by dawn."

They marched through the night, taking all the usual precautions against being spotted, but they saw no sign of enemy movement. Even the usual faint sound of high-altitude jet engines was absent. By shortly before dawn, they were concealed in a clump of bushes on the north side of a large grassy clearing in the brush, almost a quarter of a mile across.

"What now, sir?" Bothma asked.

"We wait."

It didn't take long before they heard two aircraft approaching from the south. As they came into view in the early half-light, the South Africans recognized the familiar silhouettes of Puma helicopters, but they didn't land. Instead, they circled just south of the clearing, as if waiting for others to arrive.

Sure enough, within minutes more engines were heard, this time approaching from the north-west. Two Angolan Mi-8 helicopters appeared, circling to the north of the clearing. After a few minutes, probably consumed in establishing radio communication, one Puma and one Mi-8 landed in the center of the clearing next to each other, facing north. Their pilots kept the engines running and the rotors turning as two figures disembarked from each chopper. They came together, exchanged salutes and handshakes, and moved out ahead of the aircraft. One of them, a South African officer, raised his hand and made a pumping gesture with his fist.

"That's our cue," Lieutenant Viljoen said, standing up. His team stared in shock as their officer abandoned any attempt at cover or concealment, then slowly, reluctantly followed his example. "General, you're going home in that Mi-8 over there. We're taking the Puma back to our base."

"But... How? Why?"

"I've no idea, sir. I guess we may never be told all the details. Put it this way. We didn't expect to find you aboard that chopper we blew up, and we didn't know what to do with you once we'd captured you. I suppose the situation caused so many complications for so many people that they decided to cut their losses like this. I can't say I'm sorry about that, sir. It'll be good to get a shower and a cold beer instead of a dust bath and sun-heated water from a canteen."

"On that, we agree." General Shpagin hesitated, then held out his hand. "I won't say it's been a pleasure, but this has been an experience I'll never forget."

Viljoen shook his hand. "We won't, either, sir. Here, you'd better take these." He held out the general's cigar case and lighter. "You can enjoy one when you land."

Shpagin laughed. "Please keep them as a souvenir, Lieutenant. There are four cigars, one for each of you, and you can have the lighter and cigar case. I shall drink a toast to you and your men in some good Russian vodka as soon as I'm back in Moscow."

"And we'll do the same for you in South African brandy, sir, as we smoke your cigars."

The two groups climbed aboard their respective aircraft, which took off and headed back to their bases. Within minutes, the only evidence that they'd ever been there was the drifting haze of dust thrown up by the helicopters' rotors.

Soon, even that was gone.

———

# NEMO ME IMPUNE LACESSIT

## Carabiniers and Greys

## Jan Niemczyk

*"The Royal Scots Dragoon Guards and its antecedents have served the Crown faithfully for over three hundred years. In that time, they have ridden with Marlborough, charged Napoleon at Waterloo and the Russians at Balaclava. They fought the armies of the Kaiser and Hitler, and more recently those of Saddam Hussein.*

*"However, after 1945 the main preoccupation of the regiment was preparing for The War – World War Three. Spending much of its time based in West Germany. That war was to come in April 2005 and was to prove to be one of the toughest tests the regiment had faced."*

— EXTRACT FROM *SECOND TO NONE – THE ROYAL SCOTS DRAGOON GUARDS IN PEACE AND WAR* BY MAJOR GENERAL RICHARD STEVENSON, MC (EDINBURGH 2018).

*15TH MAY 2005.*
*OUTSIDE ELZE, WEST GERMANY*

"How many rounds do we have left, Angus?" Lieutenant Tom "Sherman" Potter asked his loader. –

"We're down to three sabot and a couple of HESH, Boss," Trooper Angus Malcolm replied.

"Christ," Potter muttered under his breath. The sabot rounds were their most effective rounds against tanks. The high explosive squash head (HESH) might work in a pinch, but Potter was loathe to try them.

There should have been a resupply well before now, but it seemed that the vehicles carrying fresh ammunition had gotten delayed somewhere in the chaos of 1 (British) Corps' rear area. Or perhaps there was no resupply?

*"Here they come again; time for us to earn our pay again,"* the voice of the Officer Commanding A Squadron said over the radio. Oddly, the voice was not the one Potter was expecting, but it was familiar somehow.

*Too tired to care, not sure it matters*, he thought.

Putting his doubts aside, Potter scanned the ground ahead of his Challenger 2 – there they were! Dozens of Soviet T-80s and BMPs were rapidly advancing on his position. He selected a tank with additional aerials, which marked it out as a command tank.

"Sabot! One eight hundred! Tank! On!"

"Loaded!" Trooper Malcolm reported, confirming that a discarding sabot round and separate charge were loaded and that he was clear of the breech.

"On!" Lance-Corporal Gregor Blamey, the tank's gunner, said, confirming that he could see the target.

"Fire!" Potter ordered.

"Firing now!"

*KABOOM.*

The Challenger's big 120mm gun spoke, throwing the sabot round at the T-80. The depleted uranium dart struck the Soviet tank on the turret ring, burrowing through to the crew compartment. Less than a second later, the T-80's ammunition exploded, sending its turret into the air.

"Target!" Potter barked. "Next target right!"

The next few minutes were a blur as Potter and his crew fired off their remaining sabot rounds before switching to HESH to try and kill the lightly armoured BMPs.

"Last round, Boss... Oh, Jesus! It's not a HESH...it's canister!" Malcolm said in horror.

"What!" Potter exclaimed.

"Oh, shite, we're *goanna* to die!" Blamey said, with an uncharacteristic hint of panic in his voice.

"We need to get out of here! Driver, reverse!"

"What, Sir?" Trooper IIivia "Mac" Macawai, the driver, asked. "I don't understand."

"Back! We need to go back!" Potter yelled, panicking now as he could see a T-80 bearing down on them.

"Reverse, Mac, you fucking fanny, or we're all dead!" Blamey yelled.

"What? I don't understand?" Macawi repeated.

Potter saw the flash of the T-80's 125mm gun. This was it.

*WHANG!*

———

"Oh, sorry to wake you, Boss," Trooper Malcolm said as he closed the loader's hatch behind him.

"What?" Potter said, sitting bolt upright with surprise. "I wasn't asleep, was I?"

"Aye, you've been out for a while," Malcolm confirmed. "Gregor said we should leave you be."

"Yeah, thanks, I think, Angus," Potter replied, rubbing his forehead before pinching the top of his nose, thankful that it had all been a nightmare.

"Boss!" Blamey called down from outside the tank. "The OC is on the prowl!"

"Okay, thanks, I'll get myself cleaned up."

Potter grabbed his crewman's helmet and ran his right hand over his face. There was a day's growth of stubble, but it was too late to shave before his superior arrived.

———

"Morning, Boss," Sergeant Stephen Miller, the Troop Sergeant of 1 Troop, A Squadron, Royal Scots Dragoon Guards (Carabiners and Greys) said in greeting as the Officer Commanding A Squadron arrived. "How are you?"

"I'm fine, thanks, Sergeant," Captain Alison Currie replied. "Mr. Potter about?"

"Think he was having a kip, Boss; he really needed it," Miller replied.

Currie nodded. She understood all too well. She, too, could feel the fatigue that no amount of sleep could get rid of. It came with command, and even if she technically should not have been in charge of an armoured squadron group, that particular perk had come with the job.

*Oh, if all those chauvinists could see me now*, Currie thought. One of the first women qualified for combatant positions, Currie had initially only been allowed to serve with a Home Defence Yeomanry regiment, and she'd commanded a company before transferring to the Scots as a Media Operations Officer. The opening of the war had seen her supervising a group of journalists visiting the regiment; initial attrition had led to Scots' commanding officer effectively conscripting her to replace A Squadron's second-in-command. Forty-eight hours later, a T-80's main gun had simultaneously disabled the squadron commander's tank and given her a battlefield promotion.

*I guess it's unlikely the Queen's going to insist a woman can't properly be in charge of forces in combat, regardless of what her regulations might say,* Currie thought wryly. *Indeed, if rumours are true, she's already gently prodded the PM to amend those documents.* Currie was one of a number of women who had, by chance, either found themselves leading a combat unit or fighting on the frontline regardless of the alleged illegality of such events.

"I think we all need a kip, Sergeant," Currie said with a weak smile.

Currie especially wanted to check up on 1 Troop because it had recently taken on the one remaining tank from 3 Troop, making it four vehicles strong rather than three. There had been promises that at least one replacement tank and crew would arrive soon to reconstitute the Troop, but it had yet to appear, and Currie had begun to doubt that it ever would.

———

"Good morning, Mr. Potter, I trust you've had a good rest?" Currie said by way of greeting when she reached Potter's tank.

"Ah, yes, thank you, Ma'am," he answered, slightly sheepish.

Currie smiled inside at the subaltern's apparent guilt. "Don't feel guilty, Lieutenant. Commanders need to be properly rested if they are to remain effective."

*God, do I feel like a fake, giving advice to a junior officer with more combat experience than me!*

"Anyway, how are things? Corporal Campbell and his crew settled in okay?"

Potter nodded. "Yes, Ma'am. They're a good crew, but I'm keeping my eye, or rather, Sergeant Miller is keeping *his* eye on them."

"Good, they may well need a bit of extra TLC. Any other news?"

Potter shook his head, deciding not to share the nightmare.

"Any news on when we'll be getting back into action, or if we'll get any new tanks, Ma'am?" he asked instead.

Currie shook her head.

"Nothing yet, but as soon as I know, you'll know."

Captain Currie spent half an hour inspecting on Potter's troop, speaking to the men and checking on the tanks before heading off back to Squadron HQ. As he watched her leave, Potter realised who the voice had been in his dream – it had been his father. He wondered what Freud would have made of that.

———

*16*<sup>TH</sup> *MAY.*
*OUTSIDE ELZE, WEST GERMANY.*

"Good morning, gentlemen…and lady," Lieutenant Colonel Richard Stevenson, the regiment's Commanding Officer, said to the assembled "O" Group. "I think I may have some good news for you. Brigade have told me that we are to expect some replacements in the next few hours, so, Alison, you'll be able to reconstitute 3 Troop, and Roger, you'll be able to bring your 3 Platoon back up to strength."

Major Roger Carter, the Officer Commanding, A Company, 1st Battalion, The Black Watch, nodded and looked pleased. The attached infantry had taken quite a few casualties.

"I'm assuming, Colonel, that there's a catch?" Major Ian Anderson, the regiment's Second-in-Command, asked.

Stevenson nodded. "You've got it in one, Ian. Corps has not decided to release men and vehicles from what reserve it has left to us, and the other battle groups, from the goodness of its heart. We are going to be crossing the Leine…again."

The SCOTS DG Battle Group, and indeed, the rest of 1st Armoured Division, had already made two crossings of the Leine River. The first had been a withdrawal, as part of wrong-footing the Soviet 3rd Shock Army. The second had been a follow-up to that – an assault crossing to relieve the airborne troops of the Parachute Regiment Group, who had been defending the city of Hildesheim. The operation had given the 3rd Shock Army a bloody nose and allowed 1 (Br) Corps to pull back to a strong defensive line unmolested. It had also given the British breathing space to rest and refit.

"This time, however, I think that we will be going for good," Stevenson continued. "As you know, the fighting going on as part of efforts to relieve Hamburg has been pretty heavy. The Soviets have been shifting their reserves up there to try and blunt our attacks. As a consequence, 3rd Shock Army has not been significantly reinforced. The only new troops reported were what the Paras thought looked like penal battalions."

There was a low murmur at that, and Stevenson gave a feral smile as he continued.

"There is one bit of real good news before I move on: since we've once again given the 3rd Shock a good kicking, they have apparently been stripped of their honorifics and are now just the plain old 3rd Combined Arms Army."

That brought a round of hearty laughter from the gathered group.

"Couldn't happen to a nice bunch, Colonel," Major Carter commented.

"Quite," Stevenson agreed. "And we are going to be the ones who make sure that they don't get them back."

Stevenson turned to a map board. The fingers of his right hand rested on the Leine.

"The operation we will be taking part in has been codenamed CONDOR, your guess is as good as mine why. At least the *Septics* are not getting to choose the names, or we'd have something like Operation OBVIOUS NAME.

"We will cross the Leine here before swinging south of Hildesheim. The Soviets are still clearing a route through the city – the PRG and the West German engineers left one hell of a mess for them. Their armour is on this side of the city, but they can't get their supporting vehicles through, which is why they have not attacked us yet."

Stevenson looked to make sure his officers were understanding what he was saying.

"Our initial objective will be Schellerten," he continued, indicating the West German village with his right index finger. "Depending on how things go, we will then push on to Braunschweig."

"Do we have a final objective, Colonel?" Captain Currie asked.

"Helmstedt," Stevenson said simply.

There was silence for a moment.

"That's ambitious, Colonel," Major Anderson commented, breaking the silence.

Stevenson nodded. "I know," he agreed. "Now, this is for your ears only – the Brigadier let me know that American reinforcements from their I

Corps started landing in French ports during the night. That's at least four big, armoured and mechanised divisions, plus an armoured cavalry regiment and a great deal of artillery. It's still going to be at least 72 hours before any of those units arrive in-theatre, but SACEUR is willing to take a risk and mount a major counteroffensive all along the line. Quite what form that will take, outside of our part, I don't know, but I would not be surprised if there will be a major push for the border."

*That's got their attention*, Stevenson thought, seeing several apprehensive looks.

"The Soviets still have a lot of troops heading our way; the Byelorussian Tank Army Group, for example, is still transiting across Poland; and this will be a good chance for us to spoil any potential new Soviet offensive."

"Any chance we'll be allowed to cross the border?" Major Carter wondered.

"That's supposed to be a political decision, but the informal order is not to stop pursuit of the enemy just because you reach the inter-German border," Stevenson said. "If it was up to me, I'd not stop until we reach Poland. But it's not up to me."

He waited a long ten count, scanning the group.

"Well, if there are no further questions, get back to your troops and brief your own command teams. We've got 24 hours before the kick-off, so make the best of the time you've got."

———

*17TH MAY.*

Lieutenant Potter watched from the turret of his Challenger 2 as Royal Engineers finished off the bridge. In the early hours of the morning, the "Toms" of 4th (Volunteer) Battalion, Parachute Regiment, had been inserted by helicopter to secure the eastern bank of the Leine River. The plan was for the paratroopers to clear space for 7th Armoured Brigade, the spearhead of 1st Armoured Division, to cross unmolested.

*So far, so good*, Haig thought. M3 amphibious rigs had been used to carry the 9th/12th Royal Lancers, the division's reconnaissance regiment, across. They'd been closely followed by a squadron of The Queen's Royal Irish Hussars and the Royal Scots Dragoon Guard's Recce Troop. However, the engineers were now finishing off a pair of more permanent general support bridges to allow the rest of the brigade to cross more smoothly.

With the engineers apparently finished, a Royal Military Police "Redcap" motioned to Potter that his troop should cross.

"Keep it down to twenty kays while you're crossing, Sir," the RMP Sergeant said, as Potter's Challenger drew level with him. "Otherwise, the Wedgeheads get upset that you might break their bridge."

"Right-o, Sergeant. Don't want to upset the Engineers."

"Good luck, Sir, and give 'em one from the Monkeys."

"Don't worry, Sergeant, we certainly will," Potter replied before ordering his driver to proceed.

———

*PARP!*

The sound of someone in the troop compartment of the Warrior Infantry Fighting Vehicle was clearly audible in the turret. The smell of the noxious emission arrived a few seconds later.

"God allmighty, what have you lot been eating? *Stinkin'* up my track like that, ah think I'll put on *ma* respirator!" Corporal Andrew Lonnie, the section and vehicle commander, complained.

"You think it's bad up there? Try sitting down here!" Lance Corporal Paul MacConachie, the second in command of the section, and commander of the second fire team, replied. "I blame those '*Boxhead*' rations Deeky 'obtained' for us."

"You never complained when I got them at the time," Private Derek 'Deeky' Wilson said defensively. "Anyway, it *wisnae* me; smelt it dealt it!"

"Well, don't look at me," Private David "Jock" Stein, one of the section Light Machine Gun gunners, said. "I think it was *defo* Deeky!"

"Man, that smell is *boggin'*," Private Robert "Robbie" Robertson complained. "Can we no' open a hatch? If the Russians get a whiff of that, they'll think we're trying to gas them!"

The other three men of the section and the Warrior's gunner also vociferously denied that they had been responsible for polluting the air inside the vehicle.

"*Awwwfirfucksake*, we're a couple of minutes away from assaulting a Ruskie position and all you lot can argue about is who's farted," Lonnie said finally, putting an end to the argument. "Anyway, those of you who have got them, fix bayonets."

Private Wilson, the guilty party, despite his protestations, reached down, drew his bayonet and fixed it to the barrel of his rifle.

*Well, this is about to get serious,* he thought. *To think that we've paid tons of money for a fighting vehicle and it's still going to come down to "stick them with the steel" like we're fighting the Zulus or something.* Each member of the section went through a ritual of checking that he could reach his spare magazines and grenades easily enough, that his helmet and body armour were properly fitted and the straps secured, and that their comms were working. Wilson watched as Stein double-checked the LMG's ammunition belt again, the nervous action clearly a comfort. On the other side, Robertson loaded his grenade launcher and then affixed his own bayonet.

*Even worse that there's only two of us with the pigstickers, even if the LMG and underslung grenade launchers add to our firepower,* Wilson thought. Before the war, he'd remembered his section sergeant complaining loudly about the new section and squad organization's "deficient in cold steel."

*I guess there's a point to all—*

The Warrior halting interrupted his thoughts. The rear door opened as the IFV's 30mm RARDEN cannon engaged some unseen target.

"Troops out!" Corporal Lonnie ordered.

Wilson, Stein, Robertson, McConachie and the other three men of the infantry section sans Corporal Lonnie spilled out of the vehicle's back. Lonnie remained aboard the Warrior for the moment, the vehicle's optics and radio allowing him to better control the action and coordinate their fire support. The reason for this decision became readily apparent as Wilson sprinted forward, as the wood A Company had been assigned to assault was still dark. Smoke from phosphorous rounds was drifting through the trees, further reducing visibility.

Private Wilson saw a few shadowy figures ahead of him through the swirling smoke, and their helmets looked "wrong."

*Soviets!* He charged forward, screaming to release the tension, firing a few shots as he did. The rest of the section was similarly engaged, and a few of the figures dropped. The shock caused the majority of the others to turn and run. One Soviet stood still, either planning to stand his ground, or rooted to the spot by fear. Wilson did not care either way, as he was upon the man before the Soviet could really make any decisions. The British soldier plunged his bayonet into the man's gut, then twisted his rifle to the right as his victim screamed. Operating purely on muscle memory, Wilson withdrew the weapon as his section and squad continued after the fleeing enemy. Looking down as the Soviet soldier twitched then went still, Private Wilson wiped off some of the blood that had spattered onto his face.

*Well, guess we're in it*, he thought, striding to keep up with the rest of his squad. To his shock, Private Wilson was not scared any more.

Lieutenant Potter watched the infantry assault progress against the Soviet anti-tank gun battery. The battery, equipped with the 125mm towed 2A45M Sprut-B, had hoped to ambush the SCOTS DG battle group as it crossed at the expected ford site to the north.

*Good thing these idiots didn't understand thermal camouflage*, Potter thought. The guns had stuck out like a sore thumb to the reconnaissance vehicles, and the battle group's fire support officer had brought down a mortar barrage on the battery and its supporting infantry company. That had allowed the Black Watch to get on top of the position before the Soviets had a chance to dust themselves off.

*Oh no, that won't do*, Potter thought, watching as one of the guns attempted to reposition so that it could engage the friendly infantry. *He's probably got flechette or HE loaded...*

"HESH! One six hundred! Anti-tank gun! On!" Potter barked.

"Loaded!" Trooper Malcom reported a few seconds later.

"On!" Lance-Corporal Blamey confirmed.

"Fire!"

"Firing now!"

*BOOM!* The L30 120mm gun fired, kicking up a huge dust cloud as it sent the HESH round downrange. The shell slammed into the anti-tank gun and exploded, almost obliterating it and bowling over all of its crew.

"Target stop!" Potter ordered.

The rest of the assault was over in minutes. With the anti-tank battery and infantry company eliminated, there was now no significant Soviet formation between the SCOTS DG battle group and Schellerten. Soviet forces in Holdesheim were now horribly vulnerable to being cut off.


*Hildesheim.*

Acting Major Pavel Krylov held a cloth over the lower part of his face as he surveyed the rubble that was once a city. A platoon commander at the start of the war, Krylov was now a veteran soldier who had seen his unit rebuilt several times. Each time, he'd taken great pains to properly incorporate the survivors of other shattered units. Now, for the first time, as the new commander of the 243rd Motor Rifle Regiment's new 4th Battalion, Krylov wondered if his task was beyond him.

*At least No. 1 Company is solid*, he thought. No. I Company was formed from the survivors of his old unit, reinforced by some newly arrived reservists. Numbers II to V Companies, however, were formed from a mix of soldiers who were regarded as having "failed," mainly political prisoners and common criminals. No. VI Company was made up of MVD personnel, all experienced prison guards, along with a platoon from a KGB "Security Battalion."

*Allegedly the last is to keep the prisoners "honest," but it fills me with dread,* Krylov thought. The appearance of the KGB unit, combined with penal soldiers, was a sign of the Kremlin's increasing impatience with the Soviet Army. No longer would discipline be the sole province of the Commandant's Service (the military police) and the GRU. The KGB had been given near *carte blanche* to do whatever it felt was necessary.

*Which means this stench will surely get worse before long.* Although Krylov had smelled death a great deal since the start of the war, he had never grown used to it, hence the cloth. The stench was especially bad as his battalion, or at least the "penal" portions of it, had been assigned the task of clearing a route for vehicles through part of Hildesheim. That had resulted in uncovering decomposing bodies that had been buried by rubble. Krylov had been saddened to see that by far the majority of the bodies wore Soviet uniforms.

*BOOM!*

Krylov ducked reflexively as a boobytrap left by West German *Wallmeister* pioneers exploded. Small pieces of rubble and "other" material spattered the Soviet major, fortunately not causing him any injury.

*Why do those idiots not listen to the warnings?* Krylov brushed himself down, noticing to his disgust that there was a piece of intestine on his left boot. He shook it off and tried not to think about the fact that some carrion creature would probably soon be eating it.

"Comrade Major! Comrade Major! Are you all right?"

Krylov turned, seeing his orderly jogging over. The man was a reservist old enough to be the major's father. Like all the other replacements, Krylov had not bothered to learn his full name, just knowing that he was called Boris.

"I am fine, Boris," he replied. "Which is not something I can say for those clots over there."

"I am glad you are well, Comrade Major. As for those men..." Boris shrugged, evidently indifferent to his fellow soldiers' fate. Krylov regarded the man coolly. "I have a message from headquarters," Boris added, remembering the reason he had been looking for his commander. The older man handed over a message slip.

*"British forces have cut Autobahn 7 southeast of Hildesheim and Bundesstraße 1 at Schellerten. Enemy forces also reported to south of Sarstedt near Bundesstraße 6. You are to prepare your battalion for road movement and counterattack."*

Krylov could see that the message had been signed by the Regimental Commander, Colonel Ivanov. Evidently the message had been regarded as too sensitive to risk passing by radio, even though the Major was accompanied by a radioman wherever he went.

The Major opened a case containing a rare and secret item in the Soviet Army: a map. It showed Hildesheim and the surrounding area as he unfolded it. Casting about for a flat surface, Krylov finally beckoned Boris across so that he could use the orderly's back to support it.

"Damn," he muttered on seeing where the locations on the map were. Enemy forces were now to the rear of Hildesheim and would not have to make much more of an advance to surround the city.

*They have effectively done to us what we have done to their paratroopers, like a python eating a barn snake that is swallowing a rat.*

"Come on, Boris, time to get back to HQ. I have some proper work to do."

Boris enthusiastically hurried off ahead of Krylov, who marvelled at the energy a man of his age had. The orderly opened up quite a gap between himself and the Major. This proved fortuitous for Krylov, as after a short distance, Boris unwittingly caught his foot in a trip wire connected to the pin of a grenade. The resulting explosion, while not as impressive as the most recent one Krylov had experienced, was still sufficient to strike him with organic debris.

*Well, looks like I am going to need a new orderly,* Krylov thought with equal parts annoyance and apathy.

———

*Schellerten.*

The Royal Scots Dragoon Guards Battle Group had halted just to the east of the village to allow its vehicle to refuel and replenish ammunition. Its men would also take the opportunity to rush a quick meal.

Lt. Colonel Stevenson was finishing up eating in the turret of his Challenger 2 when he was interrupted by the Regiment's Adjutant, Captain Thomas Young.

"Got the Brigadier on the line for you, Colonel," Young informed him.

"Damnation," Stevenson muttered, putting the plate of curry aside and climbing out onto the roof of the turret, before following Young across to the Sultan Armoured Command Vehicle.

————

"Stevenson here," he said once he had put the radio headset on.

*"Hello, Dick, got a bit of a change of mission for you,"* the voice of Brigadier Harris said. His voice sounded a bit like a Dalek over the scrambled radio link, and the comparison was an apt description of the short, powerfully built officer. From the tone of voice, Stevenson could tell that the impending mission was going to be a tough one.

*"The Soviets are beginning to react, a little faster than we'd hoped, in fact,"* Harris said, the distortion forcing Stevenson to pay much more attention. *"While the bulk of their forces to the west of Hildesheim have been pinned in place, a Motor Rifle Regiment in the city itself is moving towards where you are. Division needs you to re-orientate to the west and halt that regiment before they threaten the bridgehead. While you hold them, the Queen's Dragoon Guards Battle Group will hit them from the left flank."*

"I'll need as much support as you can give me, sir," Stevenson replied. A MRR wasn't far off from a British brigade. Stopping one of those would have been a tough task for his unit at full strength, never mind its current state.

*"You'll get it. Corps is going to give your battle group priority for artillery and air support. When your Forward Observer and Forward Air Controller ask for support, they will be at the front of the queue."*

Stevenson grew worried at that.

*That assumes there's anything in the queue to answer the call*, he thought.

*"Dick, I can't emphasis how important it is that you stop this Soviet regiment. If they get past you, they'll be in a position to disrupt our advance on Helmstedt. The Black Watch and the Queen's Royal Irish are practically at Braunschweig. I'd have to turn them around, never mind what other units would have to stop. I imagine that General O'Connor would be seriously displeased if CONDOR is messed up,"* Harris said.

*The corps commander can be as upset as he wants*, Stevenson thought. *Facts is, that's a lot of combat power I've got to stonewall for this to work.* While a gulag or business end of a Makarov were unlikely for a British officer, O'Connor had developed a reputation for being fond of "sacking" people.

*Of course, have to be alive to get sacked.*

"Don't worry, sir," Stevenson replied. "If that regiment gets past us, it will be because none of us are left standing."

———

*651 Squadron, Army Air Corps.*
*Forward Arming and Refuelling Point.*

Captain Rachel "Firekitten" White carried out a "walk-around" check of her Apache AH.1 attack helicopter before climbing up into the rear cockpit. She took a moment to reflect on the irony that the current FARP was only a few miles away from the squadron's peacetime home: Tofrek Barracks in Hildesheim.

*I hope the Paras or the Soviets haven't wrecked grandma's china*, she thought unhappily. *Mum will never let me hear the end of it.*

White shook her head at the memory of her mother fussing at her about "a bloody war likely breaking out" as she finished pre-flight.

"Ready to rock and roll, Dav?" White asked her Gunner, Staff Sergeant David "Dav" Jones.

While White's nickname was a slight mystery – it had come with her to the squadron – Jones's was quite the opposite. It had originated from an army form that had left off the "id" of his first name, and from then on he had been known as "Dav."

"Certainly am, Rach," Jones replied.

White glanced to her right to check on the other Apache that would be flying tonight's mission, flown by Warrant Officer Cliff "Spooky" Budden, Canadian exchange pilot, and Sergeant John "Jack" Newton. Budden gave her a thumbs-up from the other aircraft's pilot's seat.

"Okay, I'm firing up No. 1," White said, pressing the button to start one of the Apache's RTM322 engines.

———

Half an hour later, the pair of helicopters were over the battlefield heading towards their first target. The airspace at low level had proven to be almost totally lethal for helicopters and fast jets during the day, so both now preferred to operate at night. Even so, it was still a very dangerous environment. Other than the standard 30mm cannon, each Apache was armed with eight Brimstone missiles and two CRV7 rocket pods under their stubby wings, while four Starstreak missiles adorned the wingtips.

Both Apaches slowed to the hover behind a small wood, and White slowly climbed until the Longbow on top of the rotor hub was exposed. She briefly illuminated the radar, which scanned the ground ahead of them.

"Looks like we've got some customers ahead," White remarked as she studied the CRT display showing the Longbow data.

————

The 243rd Motor Rifle Regiment's sole tank battalion had started the war with forty T-90A tanks. In twenty-three days of conflict, it had already gone through that complement one and a half times. It had recently been brought back up to strength, but the replacement tanks were older T-72Bs from reserve stocks.

While a single platoon of four tanks had been detached to the Regiment's Advance Guard, the remainder were following the BMP-2s of No.2 Battalion. Unfortunately, none of the regiment's four 2K22 Tunguska (SA-19 "Grisson") anti-aircraft vehicles were in a position to protect the tanks from what was about to happen. For that matter, no one had even passed a warning so that the tanks might attempt to protect themselves.

————

"One away! Two away!" White announced as she fired two Brimstones.

Both helicopters ducked down behind the woods after firing a pair of missiles and rapidly relocated to a new firing point. Not staying in one position too long was a lesson hard learned by both NATO and Warsaw Pact attack helicopter crews. Even when an enemy formation had no dedicated anti-aircraft systems, tanks had proven quite capable of shooting helicopters with their main guns.

In an engagement that lasted only around five minutes White and Budden fired sixteen Brimstone missiles at the tank battalion, destroying ten tanks outright and disabling two more. They finished off their attack by subjecting the surviving tanks to several salvos of rockets, a mix of Semi-Armoured-Piercing High-Explosive Incendiary and Flechette Anti-Tank, from their CRV-7 pods.

As the two Apaches departed, they left a scene of total chaos. The tank battalion had been reduced to eighteen operational tanks and found that its route of advance was blocked by burning vehicles. As a parting gift, White requested a fire mission from a Royal Artillery battery equipped with GMLRS, which would drop AT-2 anti-tank mines ahead of the battalion and further slow it down.

———

*18TH MAY.*
*EAST OF SCHELLERTEN.*

Captain Currie lowered her binoculars and then herself down into the commander's seat, shutting the hatch above her head. Despite the best efforts of the Army Air Corps, the Royal Artillery and the RAF, just under two-thirds of the 243rd Motor Rifle Regiment had made it through. While the enemy might now be short of tanks, they still had approximately sixty to seventy BMP-2s and a dozen 2S1 *Gvozdika* 122mm howitzers in support. It was still going to be a close-run thing.

"Who are those poor bastards riding in what look like trucks ahead of the main Sov force?" Currie's gunner, Corporal David "Gearbox" Brown, wondered.

Currie, too, had noticed the rather odd-looking formation following close behind the Soviet Advanced Guard. There were a few BTRs mixed in, but that group was otherwise made up of URAL trucks.

"Could be they want to use light infantry to take and hold the village," Currie replied. "Or..." She left the thought hanging for a moment.

"It's one of those Penal battalions we've heard about?" Brown wondered. "Poor sods will get shot to pieces when the '*Dropshorts*' open up."

"Well, I guess that's their problem and not ours, David," Currie replied. Part of her recoiled in horror at how casually she dismissed the suffering that was about to be inflicted on men being forced to advance against their will.

*When did I start to lose my humanity?*

———

Private Wilson peeped out of the downstairs window of the West German home his section had occupied. While the majority of the battle group had been positioned to the east of Schellerten, a single infantry platoon had been sent to contest control of the village. It was not expected to hold, but to simply delay the enemy. The platoon had been joined by a party of four Royal Engineers who had been busy preparing demolitions and other "surprises" for the approaching Soviets. The unit's Warriors and engineers' single Spartan APC were hidden a short distance away, engines running in preparation for evacuation.

*Well, there the poor sods are*, he thought, spotting the approaching URALs and BTRs.

"Here they come!" he called out as the approaching enemy column halted and its troops started to debus.

"Hold your fire until the boss gives the word." Corporal Lonnie told his section. "I'll shoot *yous* myself if someone opens up too early!"

Being a well-trained and experienced infantryman, Wilson was not impressed with their attackers' tactics. *Like drunks coming home on a Friday night*, he thought as the Soviets milled in his general direction.

"Who are these stupid pricks, Robbie?" he asked his "Oppo." "*Dae* they *aw hiv* a death wish, or something?"

"Fuck knows, Deeky." Private Robertson replied with a shrug. "Makes the pricks easier to shoot if they *dinnae* take cover."

The scream of incoming artillery made the men of the section flinch. It was only when the first 155mm shells exploded amongst the Soviet troops that they realised it was "friendly."

"Makes a change from shelling us, I suppose. So nice one, '*Dropshorts*,'" Private Stein remarked with a wide grin.

"Now! Now! Now! Open fire!" Corporal Lonnie ordered. "Shoot the stupid fuckers!"

Wilson pulled the trigger on his L85A2 rifle in quick succession, aiming at shadowy targets, not really seeing how many of them he hit, if any. To his left, Private Robertson alternated between firing his rifle and launching grenades from the UGL fitted to it. To his right, Private Stein fired short bursts from his LMG

The artillery fire lifted as the AS90 howitzers relocated to avoid any counter-battery fire. Barely had the barrage ceased when the air was again rent by the sound of shell fire. This time, it was not friendly.

"Incoming!" Stein yelled, dropping to the floor of the house.

122mm shells from the Soviet regiment's *Gvozdika* howitzers began to methodically smash up the village. The house that Lonnie's section was sheltering in shook as the shells crept ever closer.

*This is it*, Wilson had a moment to think.

————

Unbeknownst to any of the artillerymen, the Soviet artillery battalion had thrown the proverbial "one shell too many." British counterbattery radars, their lobes queued to provide coverage over the village's position, quickly determined the *Gvozdikas'* locations. Mid-salvo, the counterfire from the GMLRs of 39th Heavy Regiment, Royal Artillery, arrived with their typical precision and savagery. Two of the dozen *Gvozdika* survived the steel rain unleashed on them, their crews shaken by the cluster munitions and secondary explosions signifying their comrades' deaths.

————

"Well that was short." Stein said, picking himself back up. "Looks like we were pretty lucky...*aww naw*, shite. Paul's *deid*."

While the house had not been hit directly, a near miss had caused a roof beam to collapse. Unfortunately for him, Lance-Corporal Paul MacConachie had been directly underneath it.

"*Aww*, shite!" Lonnie exclaimed. "Get his ammo, gat, grenades and tags. Robby, you're acting assistant section commander until I hear different."

"Well, here's to bloody wars and..." Wilson began to say, quoting a well-known saying.

"Shut the fuck up, *Private Wilson*!" Lonnie snapped. "Paul's not even cold and you're making jokes. Show some fucking respect!"

"Sorry, Corporal," a contrite Wilson said, as he searched through the late MacConachie's ammunition pouches, taking any spare magazines he found, along with some ration bars.

"It's no' me you should be apologising to, *ya bam*!" Lonnie growled.

"I hate to interrupt, lads," Stein remarked from the window. "But we've got infantry at the edge of the village."

"Well, shoot the silly bastards, then!" Lonnie replied, crossing to one of the other windows.

————

Acting Major Krylov had watched with horror as the British artillery barrage cut the leading two companies of his battalion to pieces. Thankfully, as far as he was concerned, at least, they had been Penal companies and not his old unit. He cursed the British gunners for not managing to hit the Guard Company; he would have settled for the KGB platoon.

*I cannot depend on anyone these days*, he thought angrily. *Not even the enemy.*

The survivors of II and III Companies, piteously few though they were, had simply dropped into cover until IV and V Companies had reached them. The survivors had been incorporated into these units and the advance continued. No. I Company was now close enough to the village to begin to use its BMP-2s as direct fire support. Annoyingly, the British were not using tracer fire, making it difficult to locate them.

The snarl of machine gun fire from the Guard Company caused him to look to his right. A few small groups from the Penal Companies had started to drift back from the murderous British defensive fire, and the Guards had provided a sharp reminder which way they should be moving.

*Well, at least they put that first burst over their heads*, Krylov thought. *It would have been a double waste if they'd actually shot some of them.* His battalion wasn't short of machine gun ammunition yet, but he knew how quickly that could change in the offense.

"Comrade Major, the IV and V companies have reached the village," his new orderly stated. Krylov smiled as he heard the sounds of the initial assault.

*The British might be better trained, but we certainly have many, many more troops*, he thought.

———

*"Hello, all call-signs, this is Sunray, time to go, repeat, time to go. Off,"* Lieutenant Gary Beaumont, the platoon leader, said over every member of the platoon's Personal Role Radio.

The platoon's four Warriors and the engineers' Spartan roared into the village, taking cover and then opening their rear hatches. The survivors of the platoon broke out of their buildings and sprinted towards the vehicles as the Warriors laid down suppressive fire. As he ran, Wilson saw one "Jock" from another section get hit and go down, wounded.

*That poor bastard*, Wilson thought, ducking behind some rubble in preparation of laying down covering fire. To his shock, a RAMC medic dashed out of one of the Warriors and grabbed the man.

*Bloody hell, Private Norris is stronger than I thought she was*, he thought, watching the slight woman drag the man towards safety.

"Come on, Wilson, shift your arse!" someone shouted. Wilson shook himself and started dashing for his own Warrior just as a BMP-2 rounded the far intersection corner. There was a short, intense exchange of 30mm fire between the platoon's Warriors and the oncoming Soviet vehicles. Wilson's Warrior was untouched, while another Warrior in the platoon was damaged but not penetrated due to its heavy armour. Unfortunately for the engineer section and their Soviet counterparts, neither the Spartan nor the three BMP-2s were nearly as lucky, their burning wrecks contributing to the general pall starting to surround the area.

———

*Battle Group HQ (Main).*

The Sultan ACV from which Lt. Colonel Stevenson was controlling the battle shook as an artillery shell exploded nearby. Waiting to see if it was the start of a barrage, Stevenson was pleasantly surprised to see it was just a stray. Turning, he regarded his staff as they all came back to their feet.

"D Squadron is getting hit pretty hard," he noted. "They're down to seven operational tanks and three Warriors; it looks like my counterpart has concentrated all of his tanks and now his reserve on our left flank. How bad are things there now?"

"Pretty bad, Colonel," Captain Young reported, his face pale as he listened to a radio report. "Their squadron HQ just got hit by artillery." The man paused. "Sir, Major Mollison and Captain Baxter are out of action," Young said quickly. "Major Mollison is dead, I'm afraid."

Stevenson swallowed.

*I've known Brian since Sandhurst*, he thought. *My God, will there be any of us left when this is over?* Getting a mental grip on his emotions, Stevenson put those thoughts aside. *Not if you don't save that for later, you idiot.*

"Who is in charge down there now?" Stevenson asked, his voice harsher than he wished.

"Lieutenant Patel; he commands the attached Black Watch platoon."

With the pressure D Squadron was under, he needed an experienced officer in charge, not an infantry subaltern.

"Right, I'm going to head down the myself," Stevenson declared, deciding that he needed to resolve the crisis himself. "Captain Young, get onto Major Anderson at Forward HQ and tell him he's in charge for the moment. You take command here."

———

As Lieutenant Colonel Stevenson's Challenger 2 crested a small rise, he could see why D Squadron had been badly mauled. At least a company of Soviet T-72s were only a few hundred meters away from the British positions, and at that range even the Challenger's heavy armour was vulnerable to penetration from their 125mm guns.

"Right, time to make ourselves look like a whole tank squadron," Stevenson told his crew. "Heyman, find your targets while I get a hold of this situation."

As his gunner, Sergeant Charlie Heyman, followed orders, Stevenson got onto the D Squadron command net, informed the unit he was taking command, and what his instructions were. Heyman, like all good command tank gunners, was able to control the Challenger 2 effectively from his position. By the time Stevenson was done, his tank had fired four times, all from separate positions. As the second T-72's turret flew into the air, the Soviets quickly became convinced that another armoured squadron was falling upon their left flank.

"Uh, oh, Boss," Heyman remarked. "Looks like we've pissed them off!"

"And we're a *wee* bit short of ammo now," the loader, Lance-Corporal Nick White, commented.

*So this is how it ends*, Stevenson thought, the first volley of 125mm shells going over his head. Anderson tried to think of something inspiring to say, but a text message on his Bowman radio terminal saved him.

"The Queen's Dancing Girls are hitting the enemy's right flank!" he said exultantly, referring to the 1st Queen's Dragoon Guards Battle Group. "I'd say we've done it!"

Stevenson was right: starting with the attack on D Squadron, the enemy found themselves caught between the hammer of the QDG battle group advancing from the south, and the anvil of the SCOTS DG.

The 243rd Motor Rifle Regiment's attack broke down, and shortly after that, the regiment itself began to fall apart. Both British battle groups now pursued a beaten enemy, which was also subjected to near constant attack by attack helicopters and fast-jets, now that its air defence vehicles had either been destroyed or were out of ammunition.

Flying a rare daytime mission, Captain White and her wingman, Staff Sergeant Jones, joined the chase in their Apaches, picking off fleeing enemy vehicles with relative ease. She was only brought up short when she realised that she had started to target individual soldiers on foot.

———

*19TH MAY.*
*SCOTS DG BATTLE GROUP.*

"That was a great bit of work, Colonel," Brigadier Harris told Stevenson. "Well done to you and your men. But I don't want to see you playing at squadron commander next time."

"Thank you, sir, and I certainly don't want to have to do that again," Stevenson replied. He was happy that Harris had taken the time to come down and see the battle group personally.

*Shows he's not just a mad sacker*, Stevenson observed.

"The divisional commander and General O'Connor also pass along their own congratulations," Harris continued happily. "If that Soviet regiment had gotten past you, there's no end of trouble it could have caused. As things are, the Black Watch reached Helmstedt in the early hours of this morning. Other battle groups from our division and the other divisions, from what I hear, have reached the border in several places."

The man paused for a moment, and a shadow of doubt crossed his face.

"The only fly in the ointment is Braunschweig – there are still Soviets troops in the city," Harris said grimly. "They're mainly rear area types, but they'll need dealing with. I'm told that one of the infantry brigades from 2 Division is being brought up to handle that particular problem."

*Glad I'm not the poor bastard who gets to go with them*, Stevenson thought, then looked worriedly at Harris.

"And the rest of 3rd Shock...I mean the 3rd Combined thingy. Well, you know who I mean, Sir."

"We've started to have surrenders from the units pocketed to the west of Hildesheim," Harris said. "They have run out of fuel, are low on ammo and are now running out of food."

Captain Young stuck his head into the Sultan. He was holding a copy of the previous day's *Guardian* newspaper.

*Enterprising lad to get a hold of a daily that quickly*, Stevenson thought. *No end to the surprises with that one, as usually they're days late.*

"Got some news that I thought you would be interested in seeing, gentlemen," the officer said.

"Holy hell, they've passed the National Service Bill," Harris stated, reading the banner headline.

"Looks like we're planning on the long-term, Sir," Stevenson remarked.

"Not that story, Sir, the one below." Young replied, jabbing his finger at the paper.

*"Revolts break out in Poland and Czechoslovakia."*

Stevenson and the Brigadier smiled.

"To paraphrase Churchill, I think this could be the end of the beginning," Harris remarked.

————

*20TH MAY.*

*NEAR SCHELLERTEN.*

Acting Major Krylov was tired, dirty and hungry. He had been on the run for nearly two days now. He had been very lucky to escape the destruction of his BMP-2K command vehicle when British tanks had overrun his headquarters. It had been sheer luck that he'd stepped out to relieve himself shortly before a 120mm HESH round had knocked on the vehicle's flank with explosive results. Krylov had been able to escape into the night, but without rations and armed with nothing more than a pistol. He had decided to start to head east, hoping to run into friendly forces.

For the last two hours, he had been hidden in a ditch beside a road as convoy after convoy of British vehicles rumbled past. On seeing a gap, he got up and began to sprint across.

"Halt!" a female voice yelled. "Halt, or I shoot!"

Krylov started running as fast as he could, his legs burning and his chest feeling like it was going to burst.

*I will never surrender*, he thought. *How could I—*

Krylov was suddenly surprised to find himself facedown on the ground, with two sharp *crack*s seeming to come an eternity later.

*I've been shot*, he thought stupidly. Strangely, he could not get any of his limbs to move, and breathing seemed to be a struggle. There was the crunch of gravel behind him, but he just couldn't make himself roll over.

"Stupid sod just wouldn't stop," the same female voice observed.

"Well, he won't make that mistake again," a second woman observed just before it all went black.


*21ST MAY.*
*THE INNER GERMAN BORDER, EAST OF HELMSTEDT.*


"WELCOME TO EAST GERMANY – COURTESY OF 21 ENGINEER REGIMENT, ROYAL ENGINEERS."

The sign, marking the point at which West became East, was in large scarlet letters. Captain – no *Acting Major* – Currie (she had to remember that) smiled as her Challenger 2 rumbled over a Medium Girder Bridge that the engineers had laid across a crater in the autobahn. It reminded her of pictures of similar signs she had seen from the Korean War.

*Well, time to finish putting a stake in this beast*, she thought.

British troops had captured the Helmstedt-Marienborn border crossing and pushed on for four kilometres into East Germany before halting and digging in. Going any further was considered both militarily and politically unwise – for the moment. The Scots were far from the only NATO troops to have crossed into the East – American, Dutch and Belgian, but not West German troops had all crossed the IGB. To their south, French and Canadian forces had crossed into Czechoslovakia.

*We'll see what the Pact gets up to now*, she thought. The enemy had initially retreated in good order. However, NATO forces had started to advance quicker than the Warsaw Pact could retreat. The well-ordered retreat had unravelled very quickly, becoming a rout in many places. Now only a relatively small area of West Germany, bordered by the Elbe to the southeast of Hamburg and by *Bundesstraße 207* to Lübeck, was still under enemy occupation. Hamburg itself had also been relieved, although it was now very much on the frontline. Someone on the other side had finally stopped the operational bleeding, but Currie couldn't shake the sense that there was only a matter of time and reinforcements before NATO got the next lick in.

*Of course, that's if the politicians let us get on with it*, she thought grimly. *In any case, not my problem for a couple of days.*

What NATO should do next was something that was currently being discussed in Brussels and in capital cities across the alliance. Some countries wanted to continue to push east, liberate the nations of Eastern Europe, and finish the job. Others counselled caution and pointed out that there was still friendly territory, including the Danish capital, Copenhagen, under Soviet occupation. The latter members' logic ran that friendly territory should be liberated first before other nations were freed from the Soviet yoke.

"Okay, lads," she said into her intercom, seeing the Squadron assembly area up ahead, "let's get this old girl into position so we can get some rest and refit done."

"It'll be about time," the gunner muttered. "At least we don't have as much work to do as those poor bastards in D squadron."

Currie winced. After the action at Schelerton, the battle group's casualties had been fairly low thanks to the Challengers' and Warriors' protective capabilities. Still, around fifty men had been killed or wounded. While four of seven of D Squadron's knocked out Challengers and its damaged Warrior had already been returned to service, the crews had suffered roughly half casualties. The three remaining Challengers had taken major damage, with one a total loss and the other two a return to the factory. None of the twelve men inside had survived.

"No, that we don't," Currie said. She saw that the refuelling tankers were busy with C Squadron, and realized it was going to be another fifteen minutes, at least.

"I'm going to get a quick catnap," she said as they pulled into their hasty hide. "Wake me up only if the Queen or Kremlin calls."

———

"Captain! Cap...I mean, Major! Have you heard?" Lieutenant Potter called out as he saw Major Currie's tank halt by the refuelling tanker.

*Why are you not on your vehicle?* Currie almost screamed, but figured it would be better to deliver that sentiment in relative private.

"I'm hopping off," she called down to her gunner. She quickly swung down and began hurrying over to Potter.

"What is it?" Currie asked as she approached. The tone did nothing to diminish Potter's smile, and for a moment she wondered if the man had finally cracked.

"It's the Soviets, Ma'am. They've declared a ceasefire! It's over! It's over!"

"Calm down a minute, Mr. Potter. What are our orders regarding them?" she asked, ever cautious.

"Um...orders from SHAPE to all NATO forces are to not engage Warsaw Pact forces, unless they approach within one kilometre," Potter said, holding up a message flimsy. "If they do that, they are first to be warned before being fired on."

"Thank you, Lieutenant," Currie said, taking the flimsy and reading it. "I hate to burst your bubble, but I'm not sure that it's over quite yet," she stated, handing back the paper. Potter looked exactly like a puppy whose master had strong-footed it like a soccer ball.

"But perhaps now it is out of our hands, and in the hands of the politicians," she observed, then smiled. "Ask the Sergeant-Major if he still has any of that whisky that he thinks has remained hidden from me. I think this may call for a small celebration."

Potter's infectious grin returned, and she found her own expression broadening.

"But remind everybody we are in hostile territory, so keep alert. No one wants to be the answer to a future trivia question."

———

Despite Major Currie's pessimism, the ceasefire stuck. All across Europe and eastern Turkey, wherever NATO and Warsaw Pact forces met, fighting sputtered to a halt. NATO forces dug in, while those of the Warsaw Pact pulled back a few kilometres before doing the same. Within two days, the Warsaw Pact opened negotiations in Geneva with their NATO counterparts. With revolution spreading, the former were understandably far more motivated to strike a deal than the latter.

———

# AUTHOR'S NOTE

Readers who have read my web novel, *The Last War*, will notice that this story shares the general scenario and some characters from that work. However, as I said in relation to my last story, "Per Ardua ad Astra" (in *To Slip the Surly Bonds*), it is not a TLW story, but from a very close parallel universe.

Again, I want to thank all of those who have helped to make my work better. And I want to thank all those who have read my stories in the past. You make it all worthwhile.

I also have special thanks to my German *kamerad*, Henrik Löhr, who drew the maps using the www.map.army website. He is, as he has put it, a "former German Navy officer" (a fish-head doing grunt work, go figure) and occasional contributor to "Mr. Niemczyk's online magnum opus."

# ABOUT JAN NIEMCZYK

Jan Niemczyk was born and brought up in Scotland, where he currently lives. He has long had an interest in military history, aviation, naval warfare, cats and horses. He also has an interest in the Cold War.

Mr Niemczyk is the author of the web novel The Last War, an alternative history where the USSR has survived into the early 21st Century. He is currently employed in the public sector.

# EXCERPT FROM MR. DEWEY'S TANK CORPS

James Young

*To the men of Task Force Smith. Outgunned, outnumbered, and undeservedly forced
into being a cautionary tale.*

## WORD HAVE MEANING

TF McPeak
0830 Local
1 July 1950

"If you use that word to describe *any* of my men again, you best either make sure your deputy can perform your duties or learn how to give orders in sign language," Lieutenant Colonel Leonard Kraven, commander of the 72nd Armored Battalion, spat out.

Unsurprisingly, given his martial profession, Kraven was a short, squat block of man hailing from upstate New York. As he looked at the commander of the Lieutenant Colonel Ramsey McPeak, commander of the 24<sup>th</sup> Infantry Battalion, Kraven could feel the bottom half of his face, horribly marked by a pattern of burn scars, starting to throb.

*I couldn't give less of a fuck that I look like a freak show right now*, he thought angrily, well aware that the flesh tended to glow stark white against his flushed face. It seemed to have a salutary effect on the three officers standing on the other side of the terrain model, as the trio of company commanders took an involuntary step back.

Their commander, on the other hand, simply raised an eyebrow, his face serene and unconcerned. A tall, slender man, McPeak had seen combat during the Second World War as an infantry platoon leader and company commander. However, unlike Kraven, this service had been in

Europe, a fact which seemed to have given him a much different perspective on "colored" troops. Which must have been why the commander of the 24th Infantry Battalion felt so comfortable using a racial slur in reference to his imminent reinforcements.

*Freakin' cake walks make it easy to be a bigot*, Kraven thought. *Russians did most of the killing for you idiots once that bomb saw off Hitler. Hell, when **we** killed Hirohito it made things **worse**.*

"My point remains," McPeak said, his Southern accent growing thicker as he began to drum his fingers on the map board. "Ni... *Negro* troops are unreliable, and I respectfully request that you reconsider your order of movement."

*Unreliable?* Kraven thought, his mind's eye turning back to a night of absolute madness. Screaming waves of Japanese soldiers, their faces contorted with rage as they swarmed towards his tank. Women and children bearing improvised Molotov cocktails, spears, and even rocks as they ran with their men. The flames of Tokyo burning all around his platoon and the company of armored infantrymen desperately holding onto a crossroads...

"Sir," his S-3, Major Andy Klein, grabbed Kraven's shoulder. The familiar voice brought Kraven out of the fugue state, and he realized he'd taken another step forward. McPeak's slightly shaking hand had drifted down to the bayonet on his belt during, and Kraven mentally smirked.

*I think my S-3 just saved your life, asshole*, Kraven thought angrily. *Too bad **your** S-3 decided it was a good idea to try and reconnoiter north in an unarmed liaison plane. Having met you in person now, I can see why such idiocy would be acceptable in your unit.* The North Koreans had been demonstrating their anti-aircraft prowess against aircraft far superior to a Piper *Grasshopper*.

*I'd sooner have Demon company at my back than your whole battalion.* Dog Company, 758th Anti-Tank battalion, was not technically part of Kraven's unit. However, the "Demons," as the last Japanese holdouts had nicknamed the M18 *Hellcat* company, had been assigned to 72nd Armored when the latter had shipped to Korea to "deter aggression." Which it seemed had now morphed into "stopping" the same.

"Lieutenant Colonel McPeak," a third voice interjected from the tent entrance, "it would be extremely entertaining to watch "Mad Dog" Kraven forcibly sodomize you with that bayonet you're foolishly thinking of using. However, may I remind *both* of you that the North Koreans are a more pressing issue."

The gathered officers all came to attention as Brigadier General Jeffrey

Watson, Military Advisory Command-Korea (MAC-K) stepped into the tent. Like McPeak, Brigadier General Watson looked the part of a stereotypical Southern gentleman, with a patrician face, blue eyes, and graying cropped hair.

"If you don't want Lieutenant Colonel Kraven's men supporting you, Lieutenant Colonel McPeak, then I strongly suggest you do *your* men a favor and go stick a .45 in your mouth," Watson spat, completely erasing any thoughts the gathered men might have about 'Southern solidarity.' Whipping the walking stick he carried up in one savage motion, Watson speared the map that was between the two men.

"Major General Paek informs me that his men, quite possibly the last one thousand good men the ROKs have, are giving way as you are here, busy complaining about having to work with colored troops," Watson continued angrily, his voice savage. "If you cannot bring yourself to close with the enemy regardless of who is beside you, take off that damn rank and tell me which one of your company commanders has fighting spirit."

*Well, at least he acknowledges the losses the ROKs are taking*, Kraven thought. The United States had not provided many heavy weapons to the Republic of Korea (ROK) Army. ROK soldiers, or 'ROKs' as most Americans called them, had been heavily mauled by their northern neighbors as a result.

McPeak drew himself up to his full height.

"I will..."

"You will *what?*" Watson cut the man off angrily.

*I'd choose your next words carefully*, Kraven thought, feeling bemused as he looked over at Klein. There was a pause as McPeak's Adam's apple moved several times before he looked down at the map.

"Sir, I will integrate Lieutenant Colonel Kraven's men into my defenses," McPeak said, his voice just above a whisper.

The brigadier general turned to Kraven. The sound of distant artillery made the senior officer's lips purse. The explosions were carried by the strong wind out of the north, but Kraven could tell the North Korean People's Army (NKPA) forces would likely be through Suwon by that afternoon.

"Lieutenant Colonel Kraven, how soon until your company of *Hellcats* can be here?"

"Captain Gibson's M18s can get here in two hours," Kraven replied. "The rest of my battalion will likely take another hour beyond that."

Watson scowled at the report.

"Well, hopefully the North Koreans will have to take a pause when they get through clearing Suwon," Watson said, his eyes darting towards the tent door. "Lieutenant Colonel McPeak's men will have lanes marked for the M18s when they arrive."

The brigadier general gave the infantry commander a hard look.

"Let me know if they're not, Lieutenant Colonel Kraven," he finished. "I'm sure Major Klein would like a chance to get promoted."

"Sir, are my orders to defend or delay?" Lieutenant Colonel McPeak asked stiffly. "*Major* General Dean..."

"Major General Dean has placed me in command of all American forces north of Taegu," Watson replied, well aware of what McPeak had been trying to infer. "Your orders are to punch the North Koreans in the face until you can't punch anymore. Do you need any additional guidance?"

"Sir, words have meaning," Lieutenant Colonel McPeak replied angrily. "I do not want to be accused of cowardice if I judge it prudent to leave my position..."

It was not Lieutenant Colonel McPeak's day to finish a sentence.

"Lieutenant Colonel Kraven?" Watson asked.

"Yes, sir?" Kraven asked.

"You may order the general retreat when you feel that the position has become untenable here north of Osan," Watson replied. "Lieutenant Colonel McPeak's surviving forces will ride on your tanks if you are forced to retreat, and he has no remaining transportation."

*Holy shit*, Kraven thought.

"Understood, sir," Kraven replied, watching as McPeak's jaw moved in frustration.

"And *where*, pray tell, will you be, sir?" Lieutenant Colonel McPeak asked. The implication and belligerency in his question were clear.

"In Osan with my damn .45 to the head of the ROK engineer lieutenant," Watson snapped. "His charges are currently on the bridge over the river," Watson replied.

Kraven winced at that.

*If that bridge drops, we'll have a long way to go to find another.*

"I'll be damned if the only armored battalion for at least a thousand miles is going to end up on the wrong side of a dropped bridge," Watson snapped. "Happened to those poor ROK bastards in Seoul a couple days ago when the Han River bridges got blown. Fat lot of good giving Rhee an armored regiment last year did at that point."

Watson looked at the map, then at Kraven and McPeak. Just as he was about to speak, he was interrupted by the snarl of several piston engines flying close overhead.

*Sounds like Navy birds*, Kraven thought. The Marines had just finished establishing airfields around Pusan when the North Koreans had struck.

"Too bad we can't get lucky and have one of those guys carrying Oppenheimer's Firecracker, can we?" one of the captains joked nervously, referring to the name the newspapers had given to the bomb tested the previous June. The redheaded officer's comment drew a hard look from Lieutenant Colonel McPeak.

"Captain, I'm pretty sure those will be going to Moscow whenever they've got one ready," Kraven replied. "But it would have been nice if a couple of those had been available in '45 when we could have used them."

"If wishes were horses, we'd all ride," Brigadier General Watson said. Once more, the general met the eyes of every man around the room.

"We can hope for wonder weapons all we want, gentlemen," he stated. "The fact of the matter is, with China gone red, you are standing on the last piece of free ground between the Sea of Japan and Siam. If you don't want our children and their children to curse our names, we have to stop the damn Reds here in Korea."

*If we can stop them*, Kraven thought, sharing a look with Klein.

"Your role in this is to slow them down long enough for more help to get here and for defenses to be prepared," Watson continued. "You have your orders. Godspeed."

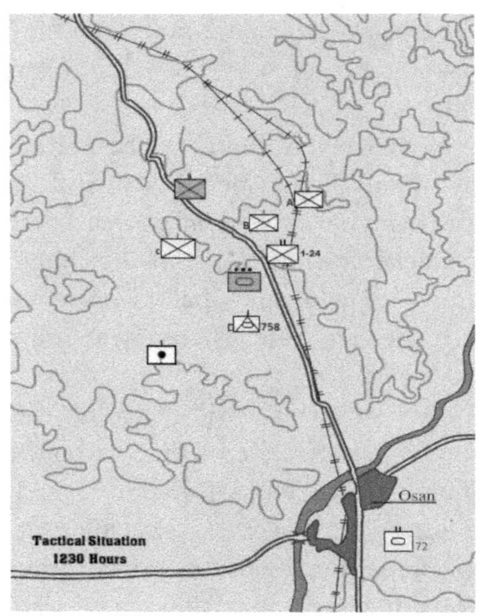


## Dotty III
### 1230 Local

*Sweet mercy, what the hell do they have in these fields?* Captain Jeremiah Gibson thought, holding onto the ring mount that enclosed the commander's position on his M18 *Hellcat*. The tank destroyer was going north from Osan as fast as its driver, Private First Class Schiller, could force it. Unfortunately, the vehicle's open turret and the wind coming from the north was pushing the rice paddies' stench directly into the destroyer.

*I feel like I'm in the middle of a manure tornado*, Jeremiah thought glumly, looking to his left over the M18's side. Unlike American tanks, the *Hellcat*'s commander and gunner sat to the left of the vehicle's 76mm gun, while its loader sat on the right. Although it made feeding the main gun difficult, Jeremiah had to admit he liked sitting on the same side of the vehicle's turret as he had when driving his father's fruit truck back home.

*Although I'm pretty sure if I drove this into town back home people would be... upset.* Before he could continue that thought, the sound of piston engines brought his eyes up, and he saw four dots rushing down from the north.

*Oh my word*, he thought for a brief second, his hand tightening on the butterfly grips of the *Hellcat*'s .50-caliber machine gun. As the shapes grew closer, he relaxed at their familiar gull-shaped wings, shaking his head grimly as he noted the trail fighter was streaming thin smoke behind it.

"Oh shit!" the loader, Specialist Washington, shouted as he grabbed Jeremiah's arm. Jeremiah looked down just in time to see an ox cart enter the road from a hidden entrance to his left.

"Schiller, right!" he shouted into the intercom, gripping the turret edge as the poor farmer, farmer's wife, and five children riding on the cart's back all looked at their onrushing doom. Schiller and his assistant, Private Downs, both worked the controls to throw the nimble M18 into a hard right turn. Unfortunately, the road they were on was not accustomed to that sort of abuse from pivoting tracks, and Jeremiah felt it start to crumble under the tank destroyer's weight. Washington, lacking a platform, tumbled down onto the turret's floor with a surprised cry.

*Hold on, dammit, hold on!* Jeremiah thought, hearing the right track threaten to slip off its sprockets. With several audible pops the tread remained where it was, and Jackson turned around to make sure the next *Hellcat* in line saw the farmer. To his relief, D32's commander was on the ball, his evasion far less violent than that of his company commander's.

*Those poor bastards,* Jeremiah thought, turning to give the man a wave. Compared to even a few short days ago, the ROKs had managed to start gaining control of their refugees, but the clog of humanity streaming out of Osan had still considerably slowed the Americans' movement north. Jeremiah couldn't help but be sympathetic and understanding of the people's fear and anguish as the Communists struck south.

*Like a damn Klan convention rolling down the road towards a town of Freedmen,* he thought. As the son of dirt poor Alabama sharecroppers, Jeremiah knew exactly what his fellow man was capable of. Burying his lynched uncle in a closed casket, the sickly sweet smell of burned flesh filling the church, had been his first introduction to man's inhumanity to man. Being a platoon leader during the final weeks of the Battle of Tokyo had just further cemented it.

"Sir!" Washington, shouted, slapping his arm. He looked to where the man was pointing, squinted his eyes, and saw nothing.

"I saw a tank!" Washington said, his eyes wide. "Just crossing that ridge over yonder."

Jeremiah checked his map. The sound of artillery opening off somewhere to his right, followed by an eruption of small arms, bazookas, and the crack of several tank main guns told him more than his loader's warning did.

*Looks like the North Koreans got out of Suwon quicker than Lieutenant Colonel Kraven thought they would,* Jeremiah thought grimly.

"Schiller, there's a railroad cut fifty yards in front of us! Take it and find us a hull down, now!"

"Yes sir!"

As *Dotty III* made the turn, Jeremiah quickly whipped his binoculars up. With the diesel suddenly quieted, the sounds of warfare were much louder. He estimated that the fighting was just on the other side of the low rise, roughly five hundred yards in front of him. Jeremiah watched as mortar rounds began impacting on the ridge, and instinctively knew that's where the friendly infantry they were supposed to be linking up with had been.

"Demons, we have armor to our front," he said, switching the microphone to radio. There was nothing but static.

*Of all the times to have problems,* he thought angrily, looking over at the device. It was half out of its mount, clearly thrown off in the hard turn.

"Washington, fix the radio!" he snapped. Looking over *Dotty III*'s rear, he saw that his 3rd Platoon was already deploying towards a nearby hill, the lighter M18s fighting their way up towards the top. His 2nd Platoon was just starting to round the ox cart, the farmer having managed to overturn the vehicle while cutting across to a paddy trail. Inexplicably, D24 had stopped, its crew starting to dismount to help the South Korean family.

*Should have let 1st Platoon lead!* he chastised himself. *Ignorant officers or not!* Major Klein's hurried briefing as the Demons left Osan hadn't given Jeremiah much confidence in 1/24 IN's leadership. Which was why the Demons had changed their usual march order from 1-2-3 to 3-2-1. His 1st Platoon Leader, 2nd Lieutenant Collins, was a mouthy college kid from Chicago. It hadn't struck Jeremiah as a good idea to bring him into contact with some racist wearing oak leaves.

"Wash, what's in the breech?!" his gunner, Sergeant Mullock, asked.

"HVAP!" Washington replied, referring to the High Velocity, Armor Piercing rounds that were the M18s primary tank killer. Jeremiah looked at the five ready rounds next to the gun.

*Here's hoping we can shoot straight,* he thought. *Also, that the intelligence idiots are right about them working against the North Korean tanks.* One advantage the M18s had over their armored brethren had been their ability to cross most of Japan's remaining bridges and thus find areas to train in. The 758th's former battalion commander had been a stickler about gunnery, even in the resource-strapped Truman years. Jeremiah had taken the man's teachings about training to heart, even as his men had grown dismayed at their fellows slowly rotating home.

*All that time away from the whorehouses is about to pay off, I hope,* Jeremiah thought. *Even if the men thought I was just making sure that if I wasn't getting laid, neither were they.* His eyes briefly turned towards the picture taped on the front of his ring mount.

*Dorothy, I'll see you soon.*

"Sir, I don't see a thing!" Sergeant Mullock stated, scanning to their front.

"Four tanks came over a hill and then down into a valley," Jeremiah responded. "They're going to be coming at our eleven..."

Jeremiah was interrupted by an artillery piece opening fire to his left front. Whatever it was shooting at fell just behind a slight rise roughly six hundred yards to their front, just below the ridgeline. The shot was a hit, however, as the artillery shell ricocheted up towards the heavy clouds that seemed to be getting ever lower in the sky.

*Clearly that wasn't effective,* Jeremiah had time to think before a dark green tank, red star prominent on its prow, was hauling over the hill. The vehicle's turret was traversing right towards the offending artillery piece, and the tank stopped suddenly.

"Tank!" Jeremiah barked.

"Identified!" Mullock replied.

The North Korean vehicle's 85mm gun belched fire towards the artillery position.

*At least that confirms he's hostile!*

"Fire!"

"On the way!"

The 76mm gun had originally been designed to equip the ubiquitous M4 *Sherman*s fighting across Europe. The M18, bastard child of the tank destroyer corps, was half the *Sherman*'s weight at best, and *Dotty III* rocked backwards like a toy truck nudged by a clumsy St. Bernard. Jeremiah held onto the ring mount as the muzzle blast washed back over the vehicle's open turret in an unpleasant stench of gunpowder, fertilizer, and singed dust.

———

The HVAP round would have had more than enough power to punch through the T-34/85's front turret at 500 yards. Hitting the much thinner side armor, the tungsten penetrator hardly slowed down before passing first through the ready ammunition, then the loader and commander, and out the structure's other side before the 85mm rounds began exploding. The eruption of flames from the North Korean tank's turret hatches signaled the transition from fighting vehicle to crematorium, but not quickly enough to prevent 3rd platoon from putting two more HVAP rounds into its front hull.

———

*Oh man, that rain needs to just start falling*, Jeremiah thought, his eyes burning. Reaching upwards, he dropped his goggles as 3rd then 2nd platoon engaged the next four North Korean tanks to come over the rise.

"Driver back up, seek alternate," he managed to croak out as Washington slammed another HVAP into the 76mm gun's breech.

*Now I see why they said the company commander riding his own **Hellcat** might be a bad idea*, Jeremiah thought. The muzzle blast had completely obscured things to his front, and he was no more coordinating the company's fire than the man on the moon.

A round impacting in front of the reversing *Dotty III* highlighted another danger, the spray of dirt clods washing over the M18's front. The offending T-34/85 did not live long enough to try and correct, two rounds knocking it out. Its three surviving crewmen attempted to bail out, only to die in a hail of .50-caliber fire.

*At least we seem to have justified our reorganization*, he thought. Originally Delta company had had only two four-vehicle platoons, rather than its current 13-vehicle organization. In less than two minutes, it appeared the Demons had killed five T-34/85s, and no more North Korean tanks were trying to rush down the road. A single T-34/85 was attempting to turn away from the Demons, misses throwing up dirt as smoke poured from the tank's diesel.

"...get that bastard trying to pass east of the road!"

The radio traffic in his headphones told him Washington had worked magic with the electronics. The Demons' net was a bedlam of crosstalk as 1st platoon joined the fray with three solid hits to the lone remaining tank. The Russian-made vehicle burst into flames.

"Clear the damn net!" he shouted into the microphone, then waited for the chaos to simmer down.

The sound of machine gun fire and mortars to the north told Jeremiah that some sort of fight was still going on, and as he tried to get his bearings he saw men running south roughly five hundred yards to his right front. Bringing up his binoculars, Jeremiah focused in on the group even as he heard 2nd Lieutenant Collins call out a warning about infantry sneaking around the Demons' right flank. The distinctive rhythm from at least two M2 machine guns told Jeremiah others had sighted the dismounts.

*Holy shit, has 1/24 been overrun?* Jeremiah thought, focusing. What he saw through the lenses caused a wash of nausea. The men diving into the muck wore olive green uniforms and steel pot helmets.

"Cease fire! Cease fire! The infantry are friendly!" Jeremiah shouted into his radio. Even as he received acknowledgments, he saw one of group of men bowled over by an accurate burst.

"Schiller, get us over this railroad and follow the paddy trail," Jeremiah said, hoping his voice wasn't as shaken as he felt. Third platoon, with its elevated vantage point, was continuing to lob desultory rounds at some distant target.

"Third platoon, what are you shooting at?" Jeremiah asked over the radio as Schiller pulled them onto the narrow dirt roads leading towards the infantry positions. There was a long pause, then 2LT Hamm's belated answer.

"There's some infantry huddling under an enemy tank, Demon Six," Hamm replied, his voice apprehensive. In his mind's eye, Jeremiah could see the skinny, bookish lieutenant standing in his M18 turret. The sole white officer in the Demons, Hamm had never given Jeremiah an ounce of trouble despite being from Birmingham, Alabama.

"Let the mortars and artillery take care of them," Jeremiah said. "We need to save that ammo for the next bunch. Cover Red and White while we all get moved up."

Fifteen minutes later, Jeremiah was grabbing his Thompson submachine gun from its makeshift scabbard within the turret and preparing to dismount. 1/24 IN had dug in on a low ridgeline through which the Osan-Suwon road passed. From Jeremiah's quick glance as he'd directed Schiller into position, he'd seen the North Korean probing force had apparently come hell for leather down the road towards the American infantry positions.

*Infantry riding tanks always seems like a good idea... and then the artillery arrives*, Jeremiah thought, gazing over the clumps of mustard brown bodies lining the road. *Of course, artillery doesn't do a damn thing to actual tanks.*

A lone T-34/85 sat off the side of the Osan-Suwon road, looking like it had thrown a track. The vehicle's crew had bailed out and, along with some of their infantry brethren, taken shelter near their vehicle. 1/24's mortars had made Jeremiah a prophet, a quick barrage quickly killing most of the hiding North Koreans.

"Captain Gibson!" a man shouted from roughly 50 yards away. "Captain Gibson, you need to get over here *right now*."

Looking over at the tall, Caucasian officer, Jeremiah had a feeling he knew who the man was. That guess was reinforced by the numerous NCOs and enlisted nearby trying to be inconspicuous in paying attention to the two men's interaction.

"Sir, I have to see to the platoons' sector," Jeremiah called back, gesturing to where 1st and 2nd platoons were arranging their vehicles then holding up his radio microphone.

"Goddammit, boy, I didn't *ask* you, I said *come here*," Lieutenant Colonel McPeak shouted, starting to come out of his foxhole.

Jeremiah set his microphone down and looked at 1/24's battalion commander.

*I will **not** be summoned like some cur*, he thought.

"Don't get yourself shot, sir," SPC Washington muttered from beside him.

"If anyone's going to get shot, it's going to be that asshole," Sergeant Mullock muttered.

*Then again, I can't expect my men to have discipline if I ignore a superior officer*, Jeremiah thought angrily.

"Both of you, hush," Jeremiah snapped. He pulled his Thompson submachine gun out of its traveling scabbard just below the ring mount. Moving just the right side of glacial, he started clambering down the M18's front.

*Stupid son-of-a...*

Jeremiah did not hear the initial shells of the artillery barrage. One moment he was getting ready to jump down off the M18. The next he was face down in the Korean dirt, struggling to breath from the blast that had knocked the wind out of him.

*CRUMP! CRUMP! CRUMP!*

As the world heaved beneath him, he finally began to hear the tearing canvas sound that signified incoming artillery. That was almost as much a relief as the dull, throbbing pain in his left shoulder, as experience told him both meant he was not in shock from a severe injury. Rolling over, he slithered underneath *Dotty III* as the bombardment shook the ridge.

*Dammit, dammit, dammit*, Jeremiah thought, dragging in a shuddering breath. He looked down and was unsurprised to see he'd literally had the piss knocked out of him. The front of his body felt like a giant bruise, and even as the M18 rocked above him Jeremiah did a quick check to make sure he actually hadn't caught some shrapnel.

*Thank God*, he thought. The bombardment stopped almost as suddenly as it began, the explosions stilling causing Jeremiah's ears to ring. As his hearing gradually returned, he realized two things. First, as if the shells had pierced the clouds and opened them, a hard rain was starting to fall. Second, a high-pitched, terrible screaming told him that someone close by had been hit.

*Oh damn, please not one of the crew*, he thought, adrenaline suddenly giving him a snake's alacrity as he slithered out from under *Dotty III*.

"...get out and check the damn track!" Sergeant Mullock said.

"Someone shut that fucker up!" an infantryman was yelling, hopping out of the foxholes to *Dotty III*'s front. Jeremiah saw the chevrons and rockers of a platoon sergeant, the NCO's eyes wild and darting. From the way the man was holding his pistol in the deluge, Jeremiah had a feeling the sergeant didn't intend to render first aid.

*This is profoundly not good*, he thought, slowly sliding the Thompson off his shoulder as he also moved towards the screams. Men were running around in the chaos, attempting to treat the wounded and prepare weapons for an assault that could be right behind the artillery barrage. Looking to either side, Jeremiah felt bile rise in his throat as he spotted at least two of his M18s ablaze.

*Damn open turrets*, he thought. *That had to be heavy guns.*

"Holy Christ..." the NCO muttered in front of Jeremiah. The man was stopped stock still at the edge of an impact crater, looking down at what was within. The man who had been screaming slumped at the bottom. Jeremiah, upon stepping up to the crater, realized why the NCO had stopped dead in his tracks. While the ruin that had been a healthy human being not two minutes before was startling in and of itself, it was not the half severed right arm or savaged lower abdomen and groin that had stopped the sergeant and made him fall to his knees.

*Well, looks like we get to find out how the senior captain in 1/24 is*, Jeremiah thought, seeing the decapitated body just beyond Lieutenant Colonel McPeak's mortal remains. It was hard to tell in the rain, but given that McPeak's lieutenant colonel's rank was visible on his helmet, Jeremiah could only assume the headless body's oak leaves were gold, not silver. Which meant that 1/24 had, ironically, also been decapitated.

"Sergeant, you need to go grab your company commander," Jeremiah stated. The man turned to look at Jeremiah, and the black officer could see the moment of hesitation.

*No time for that shit.*

"Now, Sergeant!" Jeremiah shouted.

The man shook himself out of his moment of near insubordination and hurried off. Jeremiah looked south, then north.

"Lieutenant Colonel Kraven, you need to hurry the hell up."

———

*If you liked this excerpt, the rest of "Mr. Dewey's Tank Corps" can be found in* Dispatches From Valhalla, *available from booksellers everywhere.*

# OTHER BOOKS BY JAMES

## First in Series or Standalone Books

Usurper's War

Has Audiobook

Alternate History Collection

Available in ebook and print

Available in ebook, paperback and hardback

Cavalry Stories

Raconteur Press

Mecha Stories

Raconteur Press

Standalone

(Vergassy Universe)

Has Audiobook

The Spartan Trilogy

(Vergassy Universe)

Has Audiobook

9 781963 830095